G000113264

HOLY
AND THE
FALLEN

Amanda Strong

CLEAN TEEN PUBLISHING

THIS book is a work of fiction. Names, characters, places and incidents are the product of the authors' imagination or are used factiously. Any resemblance to actual persons, living or dead, business establishments, events or locales is entirely coincidental.

NO part of this book may be reproduced, scanned, or distributed in any printed or electronic form without permission. Please do not participate in or encourage piracy of copyrighted materials in violation of the author's rights. Purchase only authorized editions.

Holy and the Fallen
Copyright ©2015 Amanda Strong
All rights reserved.

Cover Design by: Marya Heiman
Typography by: Courtney Nuckels
Editing by: Cynthia Shepp

For more information about our content disclosure,
please utilize the QR code above with your smart phone or visit us at
www.CleanTeenPublishing.com.

For my daughter, Lillian.
Never stop loving life.
Your smile is contagious!

Chapter One

"Eden, hurry, Micah's on the news!" Eden's mom, Beth McCarthy, exclaimed from the living room. Her voice carried into the kitchen where Eden was finishing lunch. Sandwich forgotten, she bolted from her seat, ran to the adjoining room, and skidded to a halt next to her mom.

Her mom glanced over. "They're interviewing him about something that happened at that farm you all went to."

Eden could only nod, her eyes remaining glued to the TV. It felt like weeks ago that Micah had left with his cousins, Trent and Damon. When in reality, it had only been three days. *This is probably the perfect time to tell Mom what really happened at Vern's farm*, Eden thought, but Micah's blue eyes danced back at her through the screen, captivating her attention.

A news reporter held a microphone out to Micah, her voice taking a professional tone as she spoke. "This spot of land has attracted a lot of attention lately. Just days ago, this particular farm here in DeKalb County, Illinois experienced rare seismic activity. Which, as I understand, you actually witnessed?"

"Yeah, my friends and I saw it happen. Hard to believe, but pretty cool," he answered.

He sounds so confident. I'd be a nervous wreck! Eden shifted her weight, feeling her mom's eyes bearing down on her. *No escaping the talk this time.*

The reporter glanced at the screen, her bright red lipstick contrasting with her powdered face. "For those of you who haven't been following the story, on July 14th, an unprecedented earthquake shifted the plates enough to cause the land to suddenly rise, forming this mountain in the otherwise flat cornfields. We've already told our viewers how they are still trying to determine the magnitude of the quake, since it didn't leave the usual aftershock waves."

Memories of sprinting through sheets of rain, sliding down a steep hill that had suddenly appeared, flashed through Eden's mind. She could still feel Gabriel's arms pulling her along. Thinking of him, a pang of sadness hit her. Since Micah left, she hadn't actually seen Gabriel again, though she felt him near. She wondered if he had spoken to the angel counsel and somehow fixed her 'seeing' problem. At least, *he* saw it as a problem.

"We're following up today because there have been reports in about some more strange activity going on here of a different nature." The reporter's clipped phrases brought Eden back to the present. "Vern Brown, the owner of this property, has begun construction on his new mountain and… can you get a shot of this?" she asked, sweeping her hand out to the side.

The cameraman swung away from the reporter and Micah, giving Eden a clear view of what she was gesturing to.

Eden gasped. The mountain still stood erect where Damon's words had planted it while desperately trying to save Micah's life. Eden shuddered, remembering Micah lying in his own pool of blood, and Sage, his guardian, clinging to his lifeless form, pulling the barbed whip from his flesh. That part of the story she did not want to relive while telling her parents. If it hadn't been for Andrew's ability to heal, Micah would've died that day.

Now the mountain was under excavation. Eden knew they'd gone back to clear some land, but she'd figured even with Damon's 'magical' words, it would take longer. The ground had not only been cleared, but the foundation had also been laid—a seemingly endless labyrinth of concrete. *Just how big is this city going to be anyway?*

Micah's voice brought her attention back to the news story. The reporter must have asked him a question because he said, "It's going to be a city."

"A city?" the reporter repeated, her brows furrowed.

"Yeah, well, a city of sorts," Micah continued. "It'll be a gathering place."

It was as if Micah's words were in a foreign language she didn't understand. "Gathering place?" she repeated.

He grinned and faced the camera. Eden's heart twisted and her stomach summersaulted. *Still can't believe he likes me...*

Micah's words were firm. "Yeah, a golden city on the hill. Those with ears to hear—let them hear."

Eden's mom gasped at the same time the reporter stuttered, "Uh, oh... a city of gold? How interesting. Well, we will have to follow up with this once it's done." Her tone didn't sound too confident anymore.

Eden knew why too. Micah sounded just like some kind of religious nut job. She felt her mom's eyes bear down on her. *Guess I better explain things.*

Eden had dreaded this conversation since the moment Micah encouraged them to tell their parents everything. How did she explain without her parents throwing her into therapy?

She cleared her throat and dove in. "Mom, Micah's special now." *Oh, that sounded terrible!* She bit her lip and tried again, her mom's face looking less and less delighted about Micah being on the news.

"What I mean to say is Micah is the Seer. I know it sounds crazy, but it's true. He sees things, like what's going to happen in the future. He saw that city in a vision, and that's why they're building it."

Her mom's brows knit together. *Maybe she still thinks Micah's just crazy.* "What? Does Lacey know about all this?"

"Yeah, you can call her if you don't believe me."

"It's not that I don't believe you, Eden. It's just this is..." She hesitated.

"Crazy, freaky, weird," she offered her mom.

"Well, yes. You talking about Micah predicting the future... It sounds completely insane."

"I know, but it's true. Micah's not lying."

Her mom frowned. "How do you know he's not? Don't get me wrong—I love Micah and his family, but this is all so," she shook her head and sighed, "bizarre."

Eden felt her face heat. *Here goes nothing.* "I know he's telling the truth, Mom, because I've seen things too."

Her eyes widened. "You have?"

"Yeah, I've seen my guardian angel. He keeps me safe."

"You've seen angels?" There was a flicker of something in her mom's face, and then she asked, "Wait, safe from *what?*"

Darn, shouldn't have said that. This wasn't going to pleasant. "Um…demons."

"*Demons?*" she practically shouted. "Eden, what's going on?"

"Mom, you don't need to worry. Everything's fine. Like I said, my guardian watches over me." Hearing her mom's worry made Eden realize something; her mom believed her. "Maybe we should get Dad. I've got a lot to tell you both," she admitted.

Her mom swiped her forehead with her fingers. "I think I need to sit down. I'm feeling a bit lightheaded."

Eden linked arms with her mom and led her toward the living room saying, "Good idea. Let's go sit." But her mom stopped abruptly, and her hand flew to her mouth. Perhaps the reality of everything had finally sunk in because panic was written all over her face.

"Wait a minute, demons, *real demons*, are trying to hurt you? What on earth for? You're just a girl! Does this have to do with Micah being that Seer thing?"

"Well partly, but that's not the only reason." Eden met her mom's hazel eyes. "Micah's not the only one *different* now. You see, I'm the Awakener."

Eden waited for the onslaught of questions. Instead, her mom turned her head to the side and yelled, "*David!* You better come in here for this!"

Chapter Two

Her dad shoved his hand through his sandy blond hair, disheveling it one more time. Eden had basically regurgitated the last few months for them. Demon attacks, angel battles, teenagers with hidden powers, and a buried ancient temple... It would be a lot for anyone to take in.

"Guess your little vacation was a lot more than riding rollercoasters," her dad said.

Eden sighed. "Yeah, you could say that."

He ran his palm along his jawline and then peered up at her. "So, you're saying that by simply hugging someone, you awaken gifts or powers in them? Like you did with Micah?"

"Pretty much. I didn't even know I was doing it, really. I changed Micah first, and then Trent."

"And you said Trent's his interpreter, right? Helps him figure out what all his visions mean?" her dad asked. During the whole conversation, her mom remained quiet, sitting on the couch, eyes fixed on the carpet.

"Yes, exactly. I hugged other friends too, like Andrew, who can heal people now."

Her dad nodded. "Good thing too. Sounds like Andrew saved your life and Micah's."

Her mom glanced up, finally making eye contact. Eden was dying to know what she was thinking.

"I know he did," Eden admitted softly, her face warming. She still harbored guilt over the fact she'd chosen Micah over Andrew, despite Micah's vision of her marrying Andrew. She wasn't sure what the future held for any of them; even Micah's dreams couldn't always predict how things unfolded. Regardless, she owed Andrew everything. It was a debt she wasn't sure she could ever repay.

"Do you see him now?" her mom asked, breaking her silence.

Eden forced herself to make eye contact with her mom, worried she'd say it had been a mistake to break up with the person who'd saved her. Logically, she was free to love whom she wanted, but Micah's vision had a way of haunting her.

She swallowed and asked, "Who? Andrew?"

"No, your guardian angel. Can you see him all the time?"

"Oh," Eden said, relief flooding her at the same time her heart throbbed. She knew Gabriel was still there, but she longed to see him face to face. "No, I rarely get to see him. Usually only when I'm in trouble. I started seeing him more often, but that seems to have stopped."

Her mom said nothing as her dad chuckled softly.

Eden glanced up. "What?" she asked.

Her dad rubbed his forehead with his hand and then shook his head, smiling. "Just trying to wrap my head around the fact our daughter sees angels. That angels are even real."

Eden grinned. *Maybe if I focus on the angel part, they'll forget about the demons.*

"You have a guardian angel too, Mom." Her mom looked up, and Eden continued. "I didn't see who it was, but Gabriel told me your guardian was there with you in the kitchen one day."

"Gabriel?" her dad asked, when all color drained from her mom's face.

Eden turned to her dad, unsure how to handle her mom's reaction. "Yeah, that's my guardian's name."

"Gabriel?" her mom asked quietly. "Like *the* Gabriel from the Bible?"

Eden nodded, the absurdity of such a powerful, high-ranking angel being her guardian still shocking her too.

Her mom sighed. "Well, if that's true, I feel a little bit better about things."

"You do?" Eden asked.

"Well, at least if he's with you, he'll keep you safe," her mom said, trying to smile.

"Mom, don't worry. Gabriel is always with me. He never leaves me alone."

"Gabriel?" Eden called softly. It was late, she knew she should be sleeping, but talking about him today with her parents had left a void in her heart. Her once again, one-sided conversations were not as comforting as they use to be.

"I guess I got a bit spoiled seeing you so much," she admitted, staring off into the distance. "You probably ran straight to the angel council and told them to fix it so I couldn't. Was it *that* bad? Me seeing you?"

She felt nothing and sighed. "I know you said it made things complicated."

Again nothing.

"Gabriel? Hey, are you there still?" She tried to push the panic down and gripped her blankets tighter.

Nothing.

Now her eyes roamed her room, darting to her floor just to make sure there were no claws coming out from under her bed. She knew she was being ridiculous. He was always there. Maybe she wasn't focusing on the good feeling. Maybe if she just held still and stopped freaking out, she'd feel the calmness and know he was there.

Maybe...

She felt something else. A cold, draining sensation in her back.

Chapter Three

It spread down her limbs, leaving her wrist searing in pain. Eden doubled over, gripping her arm to her chest.

"Gabriel!" she gasped. She peeked down just to make sure no blood oozed out. Her flesh remained intact, pink and healthy, but her insides screamed, like her bones were being snapped in two. Pain rocketed her whole frame, shooting from two points of origin—where the demon had nearly bitten her hand off and where Oeillet's staff had punctured her back.

She curled into a fetal position, hugging her knees, pinching her eyes shut, trying to manage the agony. When her lungs refused to fill with air, she panicked. *Oh my gosh! I'm suffocating!* She tried to scream for help, but nothing came out except mangled sounds. Hot pain coursed through her chest, wrapping around her heart like fingers made of fire. *What's happening?* She saw no demon, no staff protruding from her heart, but it felt like one was there.

Gabriel, where are you?

"Eden!" a voice bellowed at the same time white light shot through her room. Arms wrapped around her and pulled her from her bed. A hand brushed hair from her face, clearing her vision. Bright blue eyes gazed back at her, practically buried under the furrowed brow line.

"Gabriel," she gasped through gritted teeth.

"Eden, what's wrong?" While holding her, his eyes scanned her body. "What's happened to you? Where are you hurt?"

She clutched at her chest and tried to speak, but nothing came out.

His eyes widened. With one swift motion, he laid her down and placed both hands on her head. Shutting his eyes, he moved his hands down her frame, lightly touching her shoulders, arms, wrist, back, and torso. He stopped where the staff had punctured her months ago. A stream of fluid words came from his mouth, none of which she understood.

"Curses," he muttered in English. "I should've known."

With his hand still on her lower back, air seeped into her lungs again. She inhaled, the pain ebbing, becoming less ragged, and turning from fire to a dull ache. When she'd taken three or four deep breaths, she found her voice again.

"What's happening to me?" she asked, placing her hand on his arm, not wanting him to move an inch. Whatever his touch provided, it took the pain away, and the thought of it returning terrified her.

"I'm sorry, Eden. I was…" He stopped.

"Where were you? You were gone, weren't you?" She tightened her grip on his arm.

"No, I wasn't *gone*. I was fighting."

For the first time, she noticed his hair was wet. *That's why it looks so curly.* His face was smudged, his arms scraped, and his flaming sword hissed from its sheath.

"Fighting?" she asked, afraid of his answer.

"You've attracted a lot of attention since the temple was reclaimed. Don't worry. It's nothing we can't handle."

"We?"

His mouth twisted into a half smile. "I recruited a few other Cherubim. Seems you're a high-maintenance girl."

She knew he was trying to lighten the mood. She tried to smile back at him, but her fears finally won out. "What just happened, Gabriel? I felt like it was prom night all over again. I thought Andrew healed me."

Instantly, his blue eyes clouded over. "He did, but we are dealing with more than just demons here. I should've known when Oeillet bragged about his staff. He all but told me it was special, but I wasn't thinking about what that could mean."

"I don't understand. What does it mean?"

"Means his staff had, for lack of a better word, been dipped in magic. Remember asking me about angel and demon hierarchy, how they each have their own order and powers?"

Eden nodded, hoping he didn't expect her to remember the details.

"Oeillet wasn't much of an opponent for me—I far outranked him. His staff, however, was a different story. I should've known when he made a point of telling me that it was a cherub staff, and then it took a minute to break the thing."

Eden remembered that all too well; Gabriel's sword had been temporarily derailed by that staff, long enough for Oeillet to attack her.

"Is that why I'm still not healed all the way, because of the staff?" she asked, trying to understand.

"Sort of. It was obviously a gift to him since it didn't belong to him by rank. Just makes me wonder who gave it to him."

Gabriel remained quiet, and Eden began to put the pieces together.

"Oh, you think it was that Watcher who's after me and Micah." She licked her lips and forced herself to say his name, "Semjaza. You think he gave Oeillet the staff?"

He removed his hand and leaned back. In all their urgent talking, she had sort of forgotten he'd been leaning over her.

"I need to find out more before I can say for certain, Eden. But Semjaza's known for his enchantments. I felt your wounds just now... There's something familiar about them."

She sat up and wrapped her arms around herself. "You've been around Semjaza before?"

He glanced away. "Another time, another life," he mumbled.

"Gabriel? What happened?"

"Nothing that will help us now."

Eden leaned forward and placed her hand on his arm. "Did he hurt someone you knew... loved?"

His brows lowered. "Why do you think that?"

"I know you were one of the holy angels who got rid of The Watchers." That part, Eden remembered quite clearly. Micah had been unfolding the tale of the angels, who'd destroyed the Watchers' offspring and banished them to be buried in the earth, then he'd rattled off the main four angels who'd done it—Michael, Raphael, Uriel, and Gabriel.

"It makes sense you had to face Semjaza, and you said my injuries are familiar to you. Who was it?"

"Who was what?" he asked.

"The one he hurt—who was it?"

He shook his head. "None of that matters now, Eden."

She gazed back at him. It felt like his mood seeped into her soul. Sadness overwhelmed her. "I'm sorry," she whispered, tears welling in her eyes. "I didn't mean to bring up something painful, and I'm sorry Semjaza hurt someone you cared about."

Gabriel met her gaze. "Semjaza will pay for his crimes, then and now. We may not have as much time as we'd like. He seems to be gaining more power from his bindings. Soon, he will have to face justice for all his deeds."

"What do you mean by face justice and we don't have time?"

Gabriel went silent, his face suddenly a blank slate. Eden knew that expression all too well; it was the one she got from Gabriel and Micah when they'd said too much.

"Oh, come on, Gabriel, you have to tell me! What's about to happen?" Eden begged, gripping his arm.

"Nothing you need to worry about," he paused, "tonight. Now get some sleep. I won't leave your side. You have my word." His jaw was set.

Eden sighed and settled back into her bed. The one highlight of the excruciating pain she'd just experienced was Gabriel was here again. Visible and beside her. It almost made it all worth it. *Almost.*

Chapter Four

Micah felt the gawking eyes. It wasn't a big town to begin with and having been just featured on the news making a bold statement, gazes shifted to and away from him in rapid succession. He pretended not to notice as they perused the market's aisles.

"Sheesh, you'd think we're the most excitement this place has had since sliced cheese," Trent mumbled.

"I think you mean sliced bread," Micah countered.

"No, my friend, that's where you're wrong. Sliced cheese is the bomb. Comes out all easy. You've got provolone, Swiss, maybe a little pepper jack, and why not lay some cheddar right on me? No wonky chunks, just sweet bliss."

Micah gaped at him. "What *are* you talking about?"

"The sandwich I was supposed to get an hour ago."

"Food beat out girls. You must really be hungry."

They had waited for the camera crews to clear before resuming their work. Damon hadn't seemed to care what the reporters thought of Micah's statement. He'd kept right on working, commanding the elements to do his bidding while Trent began complaining about needing lunch. Having spent the last few days eating up Vern's food supplies, Micah and Trent had offered to head into DeKalb for lunch and to restock the shelves. Micah had voted to hit the grocery store first, then find some fast food to take back to Vern, his dad, and Damon. Huge mistake.

"Seriously, Micah?" Trent griped when Micah piled more cookies into their shopping cart as they passed the bakery.

"What?" Micah asked. "I'm hungry too."

"We need meat. Not cookies." Trent took hold of the shopping cart, shoving Micah out of the way. "Give me this. You are shopping like a friggin' girl, man. Now where's the deli?"

"Lead the way. I'll eat anything at this point," Micah agreed just as he felt someone tug on his arm from behind. He turned to find a young girl with red braids and olive-green eyes gazing up at him.

"Hey, I saw you on the news today," she announced unabashedly.

Micah grinned. "Oh, really? Cool."

She returned the grin, dimples lighting up all her features. "I can't wait to go in the city you're building. My mom said we wouldn't be able to, that it was all just crazy, plus it's private property, but I told her I would."

"Oh, uh... that's great," Micah said, unsure what to say. When Trent pushed the shopping cart forward, Micah followed after, adding over his shoulder, "Maybe one day you can."

To his dismay, the girl followed. Micah glanced around, hoping to see someone who might claim her. Last thing he needed right now was for the locals to think he was some kind of pedophile.

"Hey, where's your mom?" Micah asked.

The girl shrugged and flipped a braid over her shoulder. "Don't know."

"Maybe you should go find her," Trent said. Micah could tell by his tone that he wasn't comfortable with the girl following them either.

"I told my mom I've seen the city," the girl continued, following close on Micah's heels. "I've been dreaming about it for a long time."

Micah halted and stared at the girl. "Wait. You have?"

The girl nodded just as a woman's voice rang out. "Olivia Anne Barlow, you get over here this minute." The guys glanced up to see a redheaded woman marching their way, with a look of both relief and horror written all over her face.

"Oh, that's my mom. Guess I better go. See you, Micah and Trent," Olivia called as she dashed toward her mother.

Micah just gaped after her.

Olivia's mom wasted no time and even her hushed tones carried over. "Just what do you think you're doing? You can't wander off like that! I was worried sick. And why were you with *those* two?"

"Sorry," Micah called out to her, wanting to explain. "She just came up to us and started talking. We were trying to find you."

The woman's eyes narrowed, but then she gave a curt nod.

Olivia piped up, "Mom, they *are* building that city! I'm so excited!"

"Think that's our cue to exit," Trent murmured.

"Hardly touched your food. Is everything okay?" Jared Hawkins asked Micah. They were the only ones left at the table. Vern and Trent had gone into the den to commence with the translations. For all his complaining, Trent came alive when it came to getting his hands on the ancient tablets. Having been called by Micah to be the Architect of the city, as well as owner of the farmland the city was being built on, Vern wanted to absorb everything he could from Enoch's blueprints too.

Micah glanced out the window behind them and spied Damon crossing the lawn, heading back to the construction zone. *The guy's hardly stopped to take a break. Don't want him collapsing on me.*

Micah's dad cleared his throat, bringing him back to the present.

"Oh yeah, no. I mean, everything's fine. It's just…" Micah stopped.

"What is it?" his dad asked.

Micah met his gaze, glad he was not only going along with all this, but believed him. *Of course, it didn't hurt to have Damon uproot a tree or two to prove it to him.*

He decided he could tell him what was on his mind. "We met this girl at the store today—Olivia. She couldn't have been more than seven or eight. She said some things that got me thinking. And then there was the way her mom reacted to us, like we were bringing back the plague for the heck of it."

His dad smiled. "I'm sorry about that part. I know after the news and you making that bold—"

"Crazy, you mean."

"No, bold, brave statement, some people will take it differently. Religion is a funny business. You only said what Sage told you to say."

Micah nodded. "Thanks, Dad. I know. Still, I'm glad it was just a local channel."

His dad glanced down at his plate, breaking eye contact. His reaction made Micah uneasy.

"Dad, what is it?" Micah asked.

"Your interview was a little more than local. That was national news."

"What? Why on earth would constructing a huge... *building* make national news?"

"Apparently, that particular station has been covering all the seismic activity in the area, or just Damon." His dad chuckled. "Still hard to believe what that kid can do. Anyway, this spot keeps attracting attention. If you ask me, your guardian angel had more to do with that than anyone. Seems she wanted more than just DeKalb, Illinois to hear you."

"Oh, great." Micah wasn't sure why the thought of everyone at home watching the broadcast filled him with dread. *Maybe I'm not ready for this.* He pushed his self-doubt aside. He knew what he was doing was important and needed to be done. Still, it didn't make the gawking any easier.

His dad cleared his throat and asked, "So what was it about this Olivia girl you mentioned? Did she make fun too?"

"No, actually, she was excited to go in the city." Micah glanced at his dad, feeling new resolve fill him. The visions strengthened him mentally, even if they still left him feeling physically exhausted. He grinned. "Seems she's been having dreams about it for a while."

"Really? Do you think she has?"

"Yeah, I do. Don't know if her mom will ever let her go near it though."

"Oh, I don't know. You convinced your mom and me. Might not be that hard."

"I'm not sure it'll be so easy. And it's not just Olivia's mom I'm worried about."

His dad glanced over at him. "I'm sure your friends' parents will be on board. I can talk to them if you think it'd help. I already know Eden's folks are good with it all."

"They are?" he asked, a little surprised. He'd been planning on Damon doing another 'show and tell' when they got back, just in case they weren't.

His dad grinned. "Well, I think your mom helped smooth things over with Beth. She's not too thrilled with any of it. No one wants to hear demons are after their kids."

Micah nodded, glad to know Eden had her family's support. Just hearing her name made his heart ache. *Has it only been a few days?*

"Well, that's good," Micah said. "Let's just hope everyone else's folks are as believing as Eden's."

Chapter Five

*D*amon stretched out his hands and closed his eyes. He found it was the easiest way to block out all distractions. The stream was there, ever-present, incessant, and thrumming with life. The moment Micah had shown him what he was, he'd stopped fighting it. He let it take over him. The thousands of small voices welcomed him with open arms, swallowing him up. He belonged here. It was the first time in his life he belonged anywhere.

He knew Micah worried he was doing too much, but he didn't understand. Being here, tuning into Nature's fluid language, changed who he was. The power coursing through his veins didn't feel foreign anymore; it felt like it was the real him. The person he was intended to be.

He gathered what he needed to know the soil. The earth was ready to excavate. A new underground tunnel was to be dug just east of the property. Even with the foundation laid, Vern had informed him during lunch that Trent had seen something else in the blueprint—a tunnel. He thought at first it was an afterthought, but the more Damon communicated, the more he realized this was meant to be. It was a secret compartment, one that wouldn't be visible to the average person. And looking at the lay of the land now, Damon knew exactly where the tunnel led. *Right to the last chamber of* Fr *underground temple.* A place he longed to go to again, but since the stone tablets, Micah informed him the last chamber was *Just need to get Caitlyn here. She can open it back up.* st with himself, it was more than curiosity calling him he'd taken into that temple that day had felt like he'd been peeling back a layer of time. Each level had pricked his memories, whispering its familiarity. Damon shook his head. The strangest part was he had the uncanny feeling Gabriel had watched him the entire time—as if waiting for him to say something. *And Willow. She sees something she's not telling me.*

"Pretty impressive," Micah said from behind him.

Damon's eyes popped open. He hadn't realized he'd still been conversing with the soil. Coming back to the present jarred him. Micah stepped up next to him and peered down into the deep hole in front of them.

Micah whistled. "Wow, Trent sure about this? Thought we already did all the underground stuff. This thing's massive."

"The ground didn't protest, so yeah, I think he's right about it. Besides, I think you know more about this than you're letting on."

Micah chuckled. "Who? Me? I learned long ago not to keep things from you."

Damon grunted. "If only that were true."

Micah kicked a bit of dirt and sent it cascading down the drop-off. "Okay, I give. I know where this goes."

"Chamber nine," Damon confirmed. "But why?"

"We'll need it one day. I don't know everything yet, but whatever those plans say to build, we build."

Damon nodded and when Micah remained silent, glanced over. "Something else on your mind?" he asked.

Micah met his gaze. "I think we don't have as much time as we thought before. You and I might need to start doing something *different* sooner rather than later."

"I speak many languages, but riddles are not one of them. Do I need Trent to translate?"

Micah grinned. "Damon, Damon. You're one in a million. *Literally*."

Damon grunted. "Just tell me what you need me to do."

Micah sobered. "Remember The Watchers? The Fallen angels buried in the earth?"

"How can I forget?"

"Seems it's time for them to start facing their Judgment Day."

Damon squinted back at Micah. "You mean, we go find them? Unbury them?"

Micah nodded. "We give them their choice... and if they choose wrong, *you* destroy them."

"*Me?*" Damon asked, his pulse pounding in his ears. His fingers twitched. A rush spread over his body. The elements around him whispered, "*Yes, yes, you. You are the one to undo the binding. You are more, Damon. Stop fighting who you really are.*"

Damon met Micah's gaze. He seemed to be waiting for him to speak so Damon asked, "Why me?"

Micah grinned and clapped his shoulder with his hand. "Why any of us? Because the Captain knows you can do it."

Damon nodded. He knew there was more to it than that. *Micah knows it too.*

"*Damon,*" a soft voice whispered.

Damon stirred, rolled over, and mumbled for the voice to go away.

"*Damon,*" it whispered again.

He figured it was something in his room trying to communicate, but he was tired. Hadn't he put in a full day already? Hadn't he given everything he could physically? He opened his eyes. Recognizing which language he needed to use, he murmured back, "Can it wait 'till morning? I'm still mortal you know."

"*Yes, we know. Mortal for now. But do not forget who you really are.*"

There was that phrase again. It was like everything around him kept telling him to remember who he was.

He bolted up, determined to know why. "I'm Damon. I know the pure language of Adam, the language Enoch spoke. I can command the earth, the elements. I know who I am now. Why do you keep telling me this?"

"You will need to know. You will need to know," the voice chanted back at him. He'd identified with who he was conversing—the large elm tree outside his bedroom window. The elm had been his silent friend. He'd felt its welcome when he'd arrived, and he'd felt its approval of him being there. Now, its words pressed into the room. Urgency laced them.

Damon knew this would be the last night at Vern's farm. With the city underway, Micah had informed them at dinner it was time to head back. He'd said it was time to regroup with friends.

"Why, dear friend, why must I know?" Damon asked, remembering it would be best if he showed the Elm respect. There was a certain kind of brotherhood in nature. Elements of the earth loved to be spoken to in kindness.

"You are more. Feel it within you. You will remember. Discover your untapped power. You must. The Watchers know you. They have not forgotten. In their cruelness, they have made the earth weep."

"I know," Damon responded. "They're evil. Micah told me I'm the one to destroy them, but I don't know how."

"You will not be alone. You will see what needs to be done. Now sleep."

The voice was gone, but Damon didn't lie down. One phrase chased all thoughts of sleep away. *The Watchers know you.* How would they know him? Had they heard of him? Seen some kind of vision of him moving the earth? Had some of the demons told them about him?

The Elm said they not only know me, they haven't forgotten. Damon's eyes widened. *What does that mean? Forgotten what?*

Chapter Six

Caitlyn ignored her phone. *It's Andrew again.* She threw the brush she'd been using on her hair down on her bed and frowned. The bigger question wasn't why Andrew kept calling and texting. *It's why am I ignoring him?*

She sighed and sat at the edge of her bed. Her eyes traveled to her nightstand where her phone finally fell silent. She peered around her room, debating. She knew Alaina, her guardian, was probably near. *Do I dare talk to her? Would that just be crazy?* She needed someone to talk to and as much as she loved and trusted Eden, this was one thing that she could *not* discuss with her.

She cleared her throat. "So, um, I'm not sure you are here or are even listening, but—"

"Caitlyn," her mom's voice called from down the hall. "Time for dinner."

Caitlyn jumped to her feet. *Alaina probably doesn't want to hear about this stuff anyway. Better to keep it to myself.*

She opened her door and met her mom in the hall. "What's for dinner?"

"Meatloaf and potatoes," her mom answered before spinning on her heel and marching back down the stairs.

Caitlyn sighed heavily. Living with her mom had never been easy. *But after what I told her today, it just got impossible.* She heard her phone chime from within her bedroom. *Another message from Andrew. Maybe I should just check to see. . .*

"Caitlyn, come along now," her mom commanded, like she sensed her hesitation.

She glanced down to see her mom gazing back up at her from the base of the stairs. "And don't be thinking you are leaving after to meet up with those friends of yours."

"I know, Mom. I'm not."

As of today, I officially have no friends if my mom has her way. Caitlyn's heart sank with each step she took down. Entering the dining room, she saw her brothers were already piling their plates up with food. She took her seat and waited her turn to dish up.

Her mom sat down and cast a glance at her brothers. "Slow down, you two." Then she proceeded to load peas on to her own plate. "Saw your friend Micah on the news today."

Caitlyn glanced over at her but said nothing. She had no idea why Micah had been on the news, but she waited to see what her mom thought about it.

"He sounded like a complete crazy," her eleven-year-old brother, Stan, crowed.

"Yeah, I thought Micah was cool," her other brother, Justin, muttered. Caitlyn knew he was excited to be a freshman this year, and part of that was because he looked up to Micah. Their family had watched the football games last year, and everyone knew Micah long before Caitlyn actually became friends with him.

"He's not crazy," Caitlyn stated firmly. "None of you guys understand what's really going on."

"That's enough," her mom cut in. "I won't be having you tell your brothers about all *that*. He may think what he is doing is meant to be, but I don't want you to have anything to do with it."

Caitlyn frowned.

"I still can't believe I let you go on that trip," her mom continued. "Feels like your friends are all part of some religious cult if you ask me."

"Are you serious, Mom? My friends aren't part of a cult! And what Micah is doing *is* important."

"Caitlyn, just stop," her mom said sharply. "You're not allowed to see

them anymore, and that's my final word."

* * *

"I guess I only have you left to talk to after all," Caitlyn whispered later that night in her bedroom. Lying on her back, staring at her ceiling in the dark, she blinked back the sting of tears. For half a second, she wondered if it would be worth talking to her dad about it. Maybe he would be more understanding. She shook her head. *Mom would go ballistic if I did. She thinks Dad can't handle anything anymore.*

"Alaina, I don't know if you're there or not, but I'm feeling pretty lonely right now. I told my mom about Micah and the others, and she doesn't believe me. Well, more like she thinks it's evil." Caitlyn's throat constricted. She swallowed and continued. "So, not only do I have that *other* problem I wanted to talk to you about, now I have no friends at all. At least, that's what my mom wants, but I know Micah needs me for his mission."

Caitlyn lay there for a minute, waiting for something. Anything. It wasn't that she wanted Alaina to appear; she just wanted to feel like this was all still real. Since they'd gotten home, she hadn't seen anyone. It had started out on purpose. She felt she needed a few days to sort out what had happened. She still felt all too responsible for Andrew and Eden's break up. She just didn't know how to tell him. She didn't trust herself. What if she said or wished something again that wasn't meant to be and it happened, because of her gift?

"Telling my mom was a mistake. I know Micah said we should, but my folks aren't like his or Eden's. They're superstitious. They don't trust things or people. There's a reason we never went to church. My mom thinks they are set up to brainwash people and take their money," she whispered to her bedroom.

"So now what do I do? Deliberately disobey them? I don't even know if they'll let me out of the house." She groaned. "This is going to be a long summer."

The worst part for Caitlyn was the fact that she felt her gift should help with her own mother's faith. *I'm failing. I'm terrible at this. If I have the gift of faith, shouldn't I be able to help others believe? Maybe it's just as well I'm grounded. At this rate, I'm probably not much help to Micah anyway.*

Chapter Seven

Eden could hardly contain herself. She knew he'd be here any minute, and she found herself checking the front room window over and over again. Micah had texted they were back, and he was on his way over to see her. Her stomach twisted, her fingers felt cold, and her face warm.

When she saw his truck pull into the driveway, she commanded herself not to go running down the front steps to him. *Did he miss me as much as I did him?*

She didn't wait for him to knock, but pulled the door open as his fist rose up.

His face broke into a smile, and he swept her up into him. The way his arms kept circling her tighter and tighter, she knew he probably had.

"I can't believe it's only been a few days. How did I ever do Rome?" he asked, his lips buried in her hair, tickling her ear.

"I know," she said, still dumbfounded they were actually together. *How did I get so lucky?* They separated a bit, still standing in the doorway. She glanced up, and his eyes danced back at her.

"Want to come in?" she asked.

"Actually, I'd rather go for a drive. How about it?"

"Sure. Let me tell my mom I'm leaving."

She went to walk away, but he held on to her hand, pulling her back to him. After a quick glance around the room, he must have decided the coast was clear because his lips landed across hers. She couldn't hold back. Her body responded, her hands wrapping around his neck. She knew they stood right smack dab in the front of the house, where not only her family could see but also any passerby outside, but at the moment, all she cared about was Micah's lips.

He stopped and grinned. "Okay, now go tell her."

She inhaled deeply, trying to clear her head, nodded, and hurried to find her mom. A few minutes later, she and Micah were walking hand in hand to his truck, where he opened the door for her, and she hopped in. Once he'd started the engine and checked that the AC was on, he leaned over toward her.

"Okay, just one more," he said.

She scooted as close as she could to meet him across the center console. His lips were warm and inviting. She wanted to get lost in them, but he sat back.

"Man, I've missed you," he said quietly. Then, with that smile of his, the one that could leave a girl feeling like a helpless puddle, he threw his truck into drive and they left her driveway.

"Where we going?" she asked, smoothing her hair down.

"I thought it was high time I took you on a proper date. I mean, now that you're my girlfriend," he glanced at her and winked, "I think I should at least buy you dinner."

"Dinner? You mean we get to just sit and eat—we don't have to run for our lives or fight off demons?" Eden teased.

"Yep, no demons, just us."

Then Eden remembered the other thing that had kept them apart before. "What about Andrew? You don't think we have to wait anymore?"

"He's going to find out sooner or later about us. We got through the trip. I don't think I can wait much longer than that to be with you."

Eden grinned. "Me either."

"Besides, I have a hunch Andrew's going to get a lot of attention. I think he'll be just fine."

"What do you mean?"

"Andrew's ability is well… noticeable. It won't take long before rumors spread. The trick will be for him not to let it all go to his head."

Eden stared at Micah. "Did you see all that in visions?"

"I've seen a lot of things, about all of our friends. At least with Andrew, his gift will be popular in a good way."

Something in Micah's last words sounded sad. She searched his profile, trying to understand why.

"Is everything okay?" she asked, reaching over to take his hand. It felt natural to do it, and his fingers sliding between hers felt even better.

"Yeah. It's just strange to have people treat you different." He glanced over at her. "In Illinois, I mean. I just want to be me, but I guess my old life is really over."

"Did something happen?" she asked.

"Not really. Just don't like parents telling their kids to get away from me, like I'm dangerous."

She gasped. "They did?"

"Not in so many words, but yeah, at the grocery store." He paused. "It's fine. Just have to ignore it, I guess."

She squeezed his fingers. "Micah, you were never meant for the ordinary life. You're a natural leader; you always have been. People still want to be around you, that hasn't changed. *I* have a hunch you're going to have lots of people who absolutely love you too. Don't forget that."

He glanced over and smiled. "Like you?"

"Yes, like me," she admitted. "I'll follow you to the ends of the earth, as cliché as that sounds."

Micah didn't laugh at her joke though. Instead, he said, "Thanks, Eden, you don't know how much that means to me."

Micah handed the bill back to the waiter, leaving a generous tip. Of all the dates he'd ever been on, this was by far his favorite. Since he and Eden hadn't really connected until right before the fateful Illinois trip, he hadn't had a chance to enjoy her company all to himself. Tonight there was no Trent hovering over them, no pressing mission to complete, at least not right that second, and like Eden had said, for once, there were no demons. *And so far, no visions either.* Micah grinned. *This has been the perfect date.*

He glanced across the table; Eden was trying to dig her lip gloss out of her jeans' pocket. She was the first girl he'd known that didn't carry some kind of purse. Watching her wrangle it free and slide it on her perfect-shaped mouth, he decided it was high time they got out of there and found a place to be alone. He longed to kiss her again. *Then again, maybe we better not. Not sure I'll be able to stop.*

Micah knew he had to live a higher moral standard than most teenage boys. Sage, his guardian angel, had made that pretty clear. In order for his ability as Seer to work properly, she had informed him, he had to refrain in some areas. *In other words, no sex before marriage.* Not that he wanted to be wild in that department, but now he definitely took it more seriously.

Eden glanced over at him. *I'm so distracted by her that she probably thinks I'm having some kind of vision.*

He grinned. "You look beautiful."

Her face flushed. "Really?"

How does she not know she's gorgeous? Again, so not like any of the other girls I've dated.

He stood up. "Ready to go?"

She jumped up next to him. "Sure! Where to next?"

He pulled her hand into his, ready to answer, but in that moment, he was no longer in the restaurant. Eden was still there, but not the vibrant, beautiful girl he expected to see. Instead, she lay on the ground at his feet, curled up in a fetal position, hugging her knees. Her face pale, her lips blue, and her breathing ragged.

"Eden!" Micah yelled out in his mind, dropping down to her. He tried to roll her over, but his hands went right through her. He glanced around for Gabriel, terrified this was a vision of the future. Either way, Gabriel would be here, fighting, trying to protect her. *No Gabriel.*

Micah searched his surroundings, determined to find some details. They were in a darkened room. *It's not a house. It's some kind of. . .*

"Micah?" Eden's voice penetrated his vision from somewhere far away.

No, I can't leave yet, Micah's mind screamed. *I have to know more, so I can stop this!*

"Is everything okay?" she asked again, each word echoing in his mind.

Micah exerted all his will to finish scanning her body at his feet. He needed a clue as to what had happened. Her hair fell from a loose braid, she wore a white, lacy dress, and her feet were bare. Nothing helpful.

He was about to give up when something caught his eye. There was a small tear in her dress on the side she laid on. He leaned down close, peering through the rip at her back.

He gasped, and then groaned. "No, no, no!"

Her flesh wasn't pink, but gray and white, like the embers of a dying fire. Was that a hole in her back? Not being able to tear her dress away to see how deep or long the black injury spread, he could only shudder at what he saw. *What did this? Who did this?*

His vision gave way, and he was left to swirl back to reality like water being sucked down a drain. Everything was gone; the horrible scene tucked in the future's vault of daunting possibilities.

Micah gasped, and then fumbled to find Eden's hand.

Both of her hands reached out to steady him. "What's wrong, Micah? You just froze in place. Did you have a vision?" she asked in hushed tones.

Micah glanced around. They were still in the restaurant, with a few of the closest diners staring at them. *I have to tell her, but not here.*

He nodded. "Come on. Let's go."

Once his truck was idling, he turned and faced her. She had been quiet; he could tell she was waiting for him to say something. "Eden, I . . . did anything happen while I was away?" he asked instead.

She seemed to hesitate. "Well, actually yes. I didn't want to worry you. It's probably nothing."

"What happened? You need to tell me everything." His pulse pounded in his ears, and his adrenaline screamed for action. *I have to stop this.* The desire to beat the tar out of whatever demon had caused his vision made his heart race.

"Well, yesterday, I felt pain where Andrew had healed me, you know, from prom night. It was like I'd been stabbed all over again. Gabriel came and held me until it went away. But it scared me... and him, I think. He thinks Semjaza did something to the staff, that maybe I didn't heal all the way."

Micah clamped his jaw to keep from cursing. He didn't want to scare Eden more, but his silence seemed to have the same effect on her anyway.

"What did you see, Micah?" she asked, her eyes wide.

He wanted to say nothing, but he knew she wouldn't believe him and she deserved to know the truth. He was done keeping things from her. "I'm going to tell you, but I want you to keep in mind that not everything I see happens as I see it. Remember how I thought I wouldn't live to walk through the temple?"

He waited, and she nodded.

"Okay. So don't freak out, but I saw you hurt, and from what you just described, it sounds like it was from the Oeillet's staff. I think Gabriel's right. In fact, I'm sure of it. Semjaza won't stop trying to get you and me. But thanks to this vision, we know what we need to do."

Her face had paled at his words. "We do?"

"Yes. We need Andrew to look you over again, see if he missed anything. Maybe he can see what we need to do to heal you the rest of the way. I will talk to Sage and see what the angels know about this sort of dark magic." He glanced over and pulled her hand to his lips, kissing it softly. "And in the meantime, we need to get you to a safe place. Somewhere no Watcher, or demon, can touch you."

"Where's that?" Eden asked, her voice barely louder than a whisper.

Micah met her gaze and gave her hand a reassuring squeeze. "Enoch's temple."

Chapter Eight

"Micah, I can't just leave my family and stay in the temple," Eden protested after the initial shock of what he'd said wore off. "School starts in a few weeks and—"

"So you can stay there until then," Micah cut in.

She stared at him. What had he seen in that vision? She'd never seen him so spooked before, and they'd been through a lot of scary things together. "Micah," she coaxed, still holding his hand. "What aren't you telling me?"

He shook his head. "I'd rather not think about it."

"Tell me; I need to know."

"You don't need to worry about what I saw, Eden, because it's not going to happen. We will get you healed the rest of the way, and I'm going to take care of Semjaza."

His last statement made her rethink her question. "How? Semjaza is the leader of The Watchers, Micah. You'll be killed if you go after him!"

"No, I'll be fine. Trust me. This is something I have to do. Besides, I won't be alone, so don't worry about me." His tone was firm. He glanced her way, and she could tell all his concern was directed at her.

"You really think my parents are going to let me go live underground, in the temple?" she asked, not sure if she should make a joke or not. The whole idea seemed absurd to her.

"Yes, I do. I'll talk to them. They'll see this is the best option. The only option."

Silence fell between them. The desperation in his tone got her thinking.

"Did I die?" she asked quietly. "Is that what you saw?"

He glanced at her, and then his eyes shot back at the road ahead. He didn't say anything.

"It's okay. You can tell me. I sort of figured that's what happened with how you're acting. I can tell you're scared."

His eyes met hers, and he did something unexpected. He didn't deflect, and he didn't act brave. Instead, his voice caught as he said, "I can't lose you."

That was enough for her. "You won't. I'll go if you really think it's best." He sighed, and she added, "And if you can convince my mom and dad."

"We have to convince more than that, I'm afraid."

"What do you mean?" she asked. *Who else would be needed?*

"The safest place for you is in chamber nine. Only problem is that it's sealed shut again."

"Oh. You need Caitlyn to open it again?"

"Yeah, and I'm not sure… Well, we will just see what happens."

"What? Why do you say that?" she asked.

They had arrived back home, and Micah turned the truck off. "Don't worry. I asked everyone to come over tomorrow. It's time to get the gang back together. I'm sure Caitlyn will be there too."

Eden wasn't so sure—his tone said otherwise—but she didn't say anything. They had a very interesting, albeit unpleasant conversation awaiting them inside.

How on earth do I tell them about this? They are going to wig out. So much for assuring my mom I'm completely safe. At least this time, she wasn't alone. Micah walked alongside her as they entered the house. *Here goes nothing.*

Her mom stuttered to speak, and her dad just stared. Eden waited for either one of them to start breathing again. Micah had just told her parents her injuries hadn't healed, and that she needed to get to the temple or else.

He hadn't described her death, but he made it pretty clear that it was life or death. Eden was glad she didn't have to talk, since Micah took the lead. She fumbled with a pillow in her lap, her face feeling warm.

"But I thought Andrew healed her," her mom finally said.

"He did. At least partway. We're dealing with more than just demons here. Even healing demon attacks are hard. I wanted to tell you what I saw. I want Andrew to try again, but I really feel it's not safe for Eden to be here for the next few weeks. I understand if you don't want her to go. I know it all sounds crazy, but I don't want her to get hurt again."

Everyone heard Micah's tone change with his last few words. Her parents exchanged looks.

"What does her guardian think? Does he think she should go to the temple too?" her mom asked.

"Yes, maybe he's working on the solution," her dad agreed.

"Gabriel knows," Eden said, breaking her silence. "He said there was something familiar about this injury. He's felt Semjaza's work before. I'm sure he's working on a way to fix me too. I haven't asked him about going to the temple yet."

"Well, ask him. If he says this is the best plan, then we will take her there, Micah," her dad confirmed.

Chapter Nine

"So I know you already heard everything today," Eden whispered to her empty bedroom. As much as she loved being with Micah, she longed for the night to come so she could be alone to talk to Gabriel. She didn't know if he'd appear, but she knew he would hear her.

"Do you think Micah's right? That I have to go to the temple now? It all feels so rushed. I mean, you're always with me, keeping me safe. Why do I need to be in there?"

Warm air surrounded her, and the room brightened. She gasped and bolted upright in bed. "You're here!" She grinned. She was sort of surprised one simple question had warranted a visit. Maybe the council was loosening up a bit on the rules.

"I can't stay long because, like you said, I keep you safe," Gabriel said, his jaw set. "Eden, I think you should go to the temple. It's the perfect solution to... my problem."

"Problem? What problem? The demons being after me?"

"No," he glanced over at her, "I know I promised I'd never leave your side, but I might have to soon."

A strange feeling shot through her. A day without Gabriel there? "What? Why?"

He sighed and sat at the edge of her bed. "I had hoped I could avoid it, but things are happening faster than we'd thought."

"Are you talking about Micah going after Semjaza? Or my wounds getting worse?" she asked, hoping for a straightforward answer.

"You are perceptive. Both actually. You remember how in the temple you heard the story of how a few of the holy angels rounded up and bound The Watchers, to be buried until the day of their judgment?"

"Yes." Even if she didn't, she didn't want to stop him from talking.

"Their bindings are becoming... *looser*. The council has decided it is time to give them their choice to follow the Captain, or choose endless captivity."

"Why would any choose captivity if given a choice?"

"You'd be surprised," Gabriel muttered. "Each of the fallen ones will be unearthed and stand before two of the Holies to make their decision."

"So that's why you have to go? You are one of the Holies?"

He nodded. "I have been tormented on how to best protect you. My original plan to leave you in the custody of my finest Cherubim doesn't seem enough now, not with how many we are facing."

It seemed strange to think her guardian tirelessly defended her, literally fighting off clawed, fanged demons, while she went about her day, brushing her teeth, eating her meals, even taking a nap. It seemed so unfair to Gabriel. When did he get to rest?

"I think this plan of Micah's might be the best fit. You will be safe for the next few weeks while we complete our first mission." He glanced over at her. "And then we will return, and I will be back at your side."

Eden cocked her head to the side; she supposed it did all make sense. "Micah has to go with you then, to see what they decide?"

"Yes. Nothing will harm Micah. You don't need to worry about him."

"So it won't be like the well again, with him trying to trick them out of the ground, using himself as bait?"

"No. Nothing like that. They will be glad to come up. And they will still be bound while they decide their fate. Once they've made their choice, they'll be sent to the appropriate place."

It sounded pretty risk free. So why did she feel so uneasy? *Because these are fallen angels.* Even with not knowing all their names, or what their power had been before they'd forsaken their glory to be with mortal women, her experience with Semjaza sent dread trickling down her spine. *If he's so bound, how does he keep getting to me?*

Like Gabriel read her mind, he said, "We will wait on Semjaza. There are others… less threatening that we can start with."

Great, even Gabriel's worried about facing him.

"Were you the one to put them in the ground in the first place?" she asked, trying to remember what she had learned in the temple. It seemed so long ago, not just last week. At the time, they'd all just survived a huge demon battle. She hadn't realized the Watchers would play a part in their immediate lives. *Other than Semjaza's desires to have Micah and me.*

"No, that was Raphael and Michael's task. Mine was to destroy their offspring—the giants."

"Oh, yeah." She considered him a moment, wanting to know more, but decided to ask instead, "So will one of the Holies be with you on this?"

She thought it was an easy enough answer, but Gabriel hesitated, and then said, "Two did the burying, and two will do the unearthing." She opened her mouth, but he said, "I need to go. It's much easier to protect you in my sphere." He was gone before she could say another word.

Chapter Ten

The doorbell sent Trent jumping off the couch and to his feet. "Time to get this show on the road."

Micah watched Trent half-walk, half-shuffle to the door, while making beat-boxing sounds in his mouth. *He's sure in a good mood.* Knowing how Trent had gone out with Jessie, Eden's friend, last night, Micah grinned. *I've got to thank that redhead. She's made Trent so much more bearable.*

Then again, Trent hadn't been so bad since they'd gotten through the battle in the cornfields. *Can't blame him for dreading that crud*, Micah decided.

Willow entered the living room followed by Trent; she was the first to arrive. Micah was surprised it wasn't Eden. He pushed aside thoughts that she might be in danger. *It's barely eleven. I'm sure she'll be here any minute. Her text said she was on her way.*

"Hiya, Micah." Willow beamed at him. She always was an attractive girl, but now that she didn't overuse makeup, and her hair wasn't perfectly done up, she was beautiful in a new way. *Not that I'm checking her out*, Micah thought, feeling slightly guilty to even have such thoughts. *It's just cool to see her changing.*

"Hey Willow, glad you could come over. How are things at home?" he asked, wanting to know if her presence here today meant her family was okay with all this.

"My parents are awesome," she said and hesitated, "oblivious, and couldn't care less. But don't worry; I'm good. I have my passport and everything. They've always let me travel during school breaks."

Micah just stared at her. "How did you...?"

"Know? It's so written all over your face right now." She laughed, her blue eyes lighting up. "Want to know a little secret?"

Micah couldn't help but lean in. "Sure."

"Heck yeah," Trent added.

She glanced at Trent, and then back at Micah. "I've been practicing my gift, and I've gotten pretty good at it."

"Really?" Micah leaned back, suddenly wondering how 'good' she was. "So you can discern..."

"Thoughts? Yes. For the most part. It helps when the person is easy to read," she admitted, tilting her head to the side. "Like you are."

"Oh, great." Micah couldn't help but wonder if his earlier thoughts about her looks had been plastered on his face as well.

"Whoa, that's trippy," Trent said, grinning. "What am I thinking right now?"

"That you don't believe I can do it."

"Well, that's not very convincing," Trent grumbled.

"It's what you thought, though," she countered. Then to Micah, she added, "Don't take it the wrong way. It's a good thing, Micah. It means you're pure. You have less deceit within you. And don't worry," she added with a wink, "I won't tell Eden you think I'm hot."

"Say *what*?" Trent exploded.

Micah threw his hands up. "*Seriously?* That's not what I meant by that." He wanted to shout, *Get out of my head. Are you reading this, Willow? Cut it out!*

Willow threw her head back, laughing. "Relax, Micah. I'm just messing with you! I know you just noticed I'm different now. And I am. I love the new me!"

She waltzed away, leaving the boys staring after her.

Trent rubbed his chin. "Better watch ourselves with that one. She's trouble."

Micah nodded, hoping Trent knew better than to bring *any* of this up around Eden. "Tell me about it."

Micah glanced around the room—Trent, Damon, Andrew, and Willow. *No Caitlyn. And no Eden.* He didn't know whose absence he was more stressed about.

He glanced at his phone again. Eden hadn't responded to his last few text messages or phone calls. *Where the heck is she?* He grabbed his keys, heading for the front door, not bothering to tell anyone he was leaving. *Trent can explain things.*

The doorbell chimed, and his heart stopped. *Please be Eden. Please be Eden.* He threw the door open. "Eden," he gasped, relieved beyond measure it was her. She smiled back at him. *She looks tired... no, drained.* He closed the gap between them, taking her arm. "What happened?"

She appeared fine, at first, but then he noticed her body was trembling.

"I'm sorry. I didn't mean to keep you waiting. I..." she began.

He pulled her closer. "Did the pain come back again?"

She nodded, her eyes drifting to the floor. Scanning her body, he reached around to touch her back. He stared at her shirt, his hand fumbling to make sure there was no gaping hole there.

"Are you okay?" he asked, pulling her into his arms and embracing her. He didn't care if Andrew could see them in the entryway. They had bigger problems than his feelings right now.

"Yes. It's gone now. Gabriel came again. I'm sorry I couldn't answer my phone."

"I knew I should've come over. I knew something wasn't right," he muttered, mad at himself.

"It's okay. It's over now." Her voice didn't sound confident. In fact, even her arms felt limp in his.

He pulled back and looked her over again. "It hurts still, doesn't it?"

"No."

"Eden."

"A little. But I'm fine, really, Micah. It's much better now."

Micah sickened. *This is happening too fast! I need more time!* "Let's get you sitting down." He ushered her toward the living room, not missing the small wince that escaped her lips. *Curses. I should've gone over.* "Were your parents home?"

"No, they'd gone shopping with Brendon. He needs some new stuff for soccer this fall." She glanced over at him. "I'm glad too. It would've scared them."

It's terrifying me. But Micah didn't tell her that. Instead, he tried to act confident, like he had the solution to this problem. "Almost everyone's here so let's get to fixing you," he said, forcing a smile as they entered the room.

Gazes shifted their way, and within seconds, Willow bounded toward them. "Oh my gosh, Micah! What's happening to her?"

Eden's eyes widened, and Micah cringed. *Great, Willow, way to panic her.* He glanced over at Eden. She dropped her gaze to the floor. He could only hope it was because she was embarrassed by Willow's statement and not because she was in actual pain.

"Well, there's no hiding the fact," he said to Willow. "Eden's hurt."

Immediately, Andrew rose to his feet, and Micah felt Eden stiffen under his arm. He gave her shoulder a squeeze. "It's going to be alright. We'll get you healed."

Eden knew her face flamed red. *Everyone's staring at me.* She tried to remind herself it was because they all cared for her, but she still felt like a puppet on display. When Andrew stepped closer, she was surprised when Micah released his grip on her and gently pushed her closer to him.

"It's from the staff wound, Andrew," Micah explained. "It didn't heal all the way."

Andrew's emerald eyes widened. "Really?"

Micah nodded, and Andrew's gaze fixated on her again. There was uncertainty flashing through his face as his hand rose. "May I?" he asked.

She nodded, and his hand landed across her heart. *Oh my*... She knew it was all medical, but it was still a bit uncomfortable. She tried to keep her breathing even, but her heart galloped in her chest. Micah cleared his throat; she was too mortified to look anywhere but at the carpet.

Andrew withdrew his hand, her chest warm from either his touch or from all the blood racing through her at the moment. He gingerly touched her back next. This time, the warmth in his touch felt good. She closed her eyes, and a sigh escaped her lips. His fingers seeped something soothing inside her, like honey poured down a raw throat. She never wanted it to end. She opened her eyes and found herself gazing directly into Andrew's. He glanced away quickly, and then moved, taking his healing touch with him.

"It feels like some kind of poison. I've never felt anything like it before. I can sense her injury, feel it, but I can't... *grip* it." Andrew met her gaze briefly, his expression clouding over. "I don't know if I can heal it."

There was a rumble in the room, everyone talking at once.

"It's okay, Andrew," Micah said, and everyone quieted down. "I didn't think you could, at least not alone. You're right on the poison. We're pretty sure Semjaza did something to that staff. He changed it, used his powers somehow. It's going to take some work to undo his enchantments."

Willow was still at Eden's side, even sitting down next to her when Micah insisted on her taking a seat. Eden didn't like being the center of attention, but she had to admit, her knees felt wobbly.

Willow placed a hand on Eden's shoulder. "Undo his enchantments? Mm... how do we do that?" And then, like Willow was having a conversation with herself, she responded, "Ah... yes, the temple. Good idea, Micah. We start with that."

Andrew glanced around. "Okay, am I the only one who has no idea what she's talking about?"

Trent shook his head. "It's a little freaky how you do that, Willow." Trent glanced at Andrew. "She's gotten pretty good at discernment. Better watch out, man. I'm just saying."

Andrew's brow line lowered. "Huh?"

At the same time, Damon shifted his gaze to the floor. *Bet he doesn't want her reading his mind.* Then seeing how Willow unabashedly grinned in his direction, Eden thought, *Too late. She already did.*

Willow glanced around. "Am I the only one who practiced their ability in the last few days? It's not my fault if I'm getting good at it. Besides, no one here needs to worry."

"I practiced, but it's not helping much with Eden," Andrew muttered. "So what's this about the temple? Will getting Eden back there heal her?"

Eden had to speak up. She felt like everyone was carrying on like she was an invalid. "Micah thinks the safest place for me is in the final chamber, but the temple itself won't heal me. Semjaza has to be destroyed."

"Destroyed?" Trent sputtered. "Hey, Micah, that's not what you told me. I thought this deal of yours was simply to see what the Watchers decided. What's this about destroying fallen angels?"

Damon spoke and, because of the rarity, everyone quieted down. "Micah isn't the one destroying them, Trent. I am."

Everyone stared at Damon; Willow grinned.

Chapter Eleven

"Alright, alright. I know I need to fill in a few gaps," Micah said, holding his hand out. "I haven't had a chance to get you all together and do it. And it looks like we're still missing Caitlyn."

Eden didn't miss the strain in Micah's last words. *We need her...wonder why she didn't come?* She was happy the attention shifted to Micah, away from her. Willow still kept her arm wrapped across Eden's shoulder, holding her like she was afraid she might fall apart if she let go. Eden appreciated it, but she wanted to tell her she was okay. It made her feel like she was two steps to her deathbed, if she was honest.

Glancing around at her friends, Eden realized it wasn't just Caitlyn missing. *Jessie should be here. She's had my back since day one moving here. I need to tell her everything. She deserves to know what's happening.* Thinking of her friend, Eden wondered what her gift might be, if she had one. She'd never felt the need to awaken her, but sitting here now, she felt something stirring within. She decided after this was over, she was driving over to Jessie's. *Time to find out.*

"Yeah, what's up with Caitlyn?" Andrew asked, bringing Eden back to the present situation. "I've been calling her for days, and she's totally ignoring me."

That got her attention. "Really? I've texted her a few times. She's just said she's been busy with family," Eden admitted.

Micah sighed. "There may be more truth in that than you know. I know I asked you all to talk to your family. The reason is, I need them to support you and understand why you need to travel in these next few weeks, before school starts."

"Travel?" Andrew asked. "Where we going?"

"Europe," Trent answered, grinning.

Willow's face lit up. "Oh, nice. Like I told you, Micah, I'm all set. My parents don't mind." Eden didn't know much about Willow's home life, but she knew her parents were loaded, and from the few offhanded comments she'd made in the past, Willow's parents didn't seem to care where or how their daughter spent her generous allowance. It had created a spoiled monster before, but Willow wasn't the same person.

"Hey, what about the rest of us, who aren't as rich and free as Willow?" Andrew asked. "I mean, I'm going to tell my parents, but that still doesn't mean they're buying my plane ticket."

That's true, Eden realized. She wondered about Damon's circumstances. She didn't think he came from a lot of money either.

Micah shook his head. "Don't worry about money. We are all set there."

"Your parents aren't paying for all this, are they?" Eden asked. "I'm sure my family could help out."

"No need, Eden. Nobody's family has to pay for any of it. Do you guys remember the jewels and stones we saw in the temple?"

Willow gasped. "You're stealing from the temple?"

"Heck no," Trent said. "What do you think we are—crazy? Micah was told to take it. How do you think we're building that city? Enoch knew we'd need money. He left it all for us."

Willow considered his words, and then nodded. Damon stirred and his very movement had everyone glancing his way, waiting for him to speak.

"Micah and I went down to retrieve the gems. The room told me it was meant for our use, but Micah is to be the steward over it. No one else," Damon's eyes shifted through the room, and Eden wondered if he didn't trust them. *Maybe he thinks we'll get greedy.* "After we left, chamber nine sealed."

The implications of his last words caused a momentary silence to fill the room.

"So how do we get Eden back in there?" Andrew asked, glancing her way. Their eyes met, and she saw it there for a split second. *He's worried about me.* Her heart ached to tell him she'd be just fine.

Micah cut in, "We need Caitlyn. Unfortunately, her family is dead set against her having anything to do with us."

"Really? How do you know?" Willow asked. "Oh, yes, your visions."

"It was a short one, but it was enough for me to see that Caitlyn's mom thinks we're devil worshippers," Micah answered. "Not sure how her dad feels about it. He didn't say much. I'm not sure he's well, actually."

"Oh," Eden gasped. "Poor Caitlyn. You're right about her dad; he had a stroke years ago. Caitlyn doesn't say much about her home life, but I think her mom calls the shots."

"Well that explains why she's ignoring me," Andrew muttered, more to himself. "I think I might be able to change Caitlyn's mom's mind."

Micah seemed to consider him, and then nodded. "Worth a try."

Andrew gazed back at Eden, his expression hard to read. "So what are the rest of us doing in Europe while Eden's in the temple? Are we helping Damon destroy that Watcher or something?"

Eden was glad Andrew always asked the questions everyone was thinking. Although, glancing around the room, she had a hunch Trent, Damon, and even Willow already knew. *So we're the clueless ones*, she wanted to say to him.

"You guys won't be going after Watchers," Micah answered. "I need you to use your unique gifts in a different way. As you know, we just got back from Vern's farm. The city has been started, and for now, we can leave that to Vern and those he's hired to help. But Vern's isn't the only city we have to get started. I've seen four. There will be one in the north, the east, the south, and the west. So when the Captain comes and gathers His people, He can call them from the four corners of the world. I don't know how familiar you are with your Bible, but Isaiah, Daniel, and John in Revelations all talk about the four corners. What we've started in Illinois is the western city. We are going to Europe like Trent said to start the northern city. We don't have to physically build each one ourselves, but we need to call those who the Captain has prepared to do it. Like Vern, being the head architect. So, I need you," he paused, glanced at Willow, and said, "to find those who are ready. And call them to the work."

Willow nodded. "So you want me to discern each city's architect? You haven't seen them all in visions?"

"Nope, and even if I had, I won't always be with you. Caitlyn will be there to help you." Micah glanced at Andrew. "And you too, Andrew. We'll start in Rome. I've had visions about my host family, the Genaros. I figured we'd take the first trip together, do it as a team. Make sure everyone is comfortable with what's asked of them. And then we'll separate."

Eden half hoped she could go too. She'd always longed to go to Rome. Hadn't Micah promised he'd take her there?

"So while we are recruiting, you and Damon will be destroying Semjaza and the Watchers?" Andrew asked.

Eden felt her stomach twist within her. *I guess going to Rome with Micah isn't really an option anyway.* The thought of Micah having a face-off with these evil angels terrified her.

"Yeah, well, we aren't exactly destroying all of them," Micah said, and then his face brightened. "In fact, there's a small chance we won't have to destroy any. I've known for a while the day would come for the fallen ones to make their choice on whose side they're on for the final battle. I hoped we'd have more time, but with what's happening to Eden, I think time's running out. Semjaza won't be our first stop. There's another one I want to see first. And if it all goes as planned, we might not have to face Semjaza."

"I like the sound of that," Trent muttered.

Micah glanced at Damon. "At least, not right away."

Chapter Twelve

aitlyn turned her music up, stuffing her earbuds farther into her ears, trying to drown out her anger with the loud lyrics. *I can't believe she took my phone away.* She stared up at her ceiling and groaned. *Shouldn't have checked my messages after dinner.* Her mom had gotten suspicious, grabbed the cell, and seeing the missed calls from not only Andrew, but also Micah, that was that.

I'm sixteen and grounded for life. She knew she shouldn't feel sorry for herself, but self-pity wrapped around her like it was her only friend left. *At least summer is almost over. Maybe once school starts, Mom will calm down. Plus, she won't know who I talk to there.* She wished she could have at least explained things to everyone. Let them know why she wasn't responding. *Maybe I can talk Mom into letting me call Eden.*

She decided it was worth a shot and jumped off her bed, determined to try. *Is it bad if I try to use my ability to change her mind? It's not like I'm brainwashing her, right? Or is it?* Then doubt shot through her. *It probably wouldn't work even if I tried.*

Her mom hadn't always hated religious stuff, but when her dad had a stroke six years ago, she had taken double shifts at the hospital, to make ends meet and to repay hospital bills. Somewhere in those years of working herself to the death for their family, Caitlyn's mom changed. *She doesn't laugh anymore. She hardly even smiles.*

Caitlyn landed at the base of the stairs, squaring her shoulders. *Time to plead my cause.* As she stepped toward the kitchen, where her mom was finishing the dinner dishes, the doorbell chimed. Making a rash decision, she opted for the door rather than face her mom.

She couldn't stop the gasp that flew from her mouth. "Andrew!" She tried to recover by stepping out on the porch, hoping her mom hadn't heard her outburst. "What are you doing here?" she asked quietly.

Andrew went to speak, but they both heard, "Caitlyn!" from behind. Too late. *Crud.* Her mom stood right behind her, with lips set in a firm line.

"Hi, Mrs. Berkley." Clearly, he hadn't picked up on how *unwelcome* he was at the moment. Her mom pushed past her, filling the doorway. Caitlyn gnawed on her bottom lip. *This isn't going to be pretty.*

"Andrew, I'm sorry, but Caitlyn's no longer allowed to see you, or any of your other friends, especially Micah."

Wow, Mom. Can you make this anymore humiliating?

"Oh. I'm sorry to hear that, but I'm actually not here to see Caitlyn. I'd like to talk to Mr. Berkley. Is he home?" Andrew responded.

Caitlyn's head popped up, and her mom stammered, "Uh… yes, but I don't think he—"

"Mom, Dad hardly ever gets visitors," Caitlyn cut in, deciding this was her one chance to be bold. "Andrew volunteers at the hospital, all the time. He likes to do this sort of stuff. Besides, it might be good for Dad."

Her mom sighed. "Oh, alright. But you only get to see Bill, you understand? Don't get any funny ideas."

"Mom," Caitlyn protested. She wanted to say, *whether you believe me or not, you're being really rude.*

Like she'd read her mind, her mom exhaled, her shoulders falling. "You're right, Caitlyn. Bill doesn't get many visitors. And it is very nice of you to offer, Andrew. Come on in."

As soon as the door opened up, Andrew bounded in, his tan skin and tousled blond hair reminding her once again how much he resembled a surfer or beach bum. He caught eyes with her long enough to wink as he followed her mom. She ached to tell him how much it meant to her that he was here. He was one of her best friends; he understood her. That was why ignoring him had been so painful. She hurried to catch up, not daring to speak a word for fear her mom would whisk him away.

Her mom called out, "Bill, you have a visitor."

Andrew glanced over at Caitlyn again, this time his eyebrows upturned. She wanted to tell him a thousand things in that moment, but she couldn't. He mouthed the words, "It's going to be okay. Trust me."

She silently mouthed back. "Thank you." She knew what he was about to do; it was something she'd secretly desired since the day she realized he could heal, but there had been so little time and things had happened so fast. When she'd told her mom, Caitlyn had hoped for a better reception. *I wanted Mom to realize this could help Dad, but she hadn't let me get that far, not even close. She shut me down as soon as I told her Micah was a Seer, Eden an Awakener, and I. . . Well, she didn't wait for me to tell her that.*

When Andrew grinned and shot her another wink, she realized he was doing his best to comfort her. *He must have known somehow about my mom grounding me.*

Being around him now, it was impossible to deny her feelings; they bubbled up within her, ready to erupt or explode. Either way, it would be messy and painful. *Andrew will realize how I betrayed him. How it's all my fault that Eden broke up with him. He can't know how I feel. He just can't.*

They entered her dad's study, where he'd spent most of the last six years. When her young, healthy dad had a massive stroke which left him completely paralyzed on one half of his body, with a drooping face and slurred speech, the doctors tried to reassure her family that with enough physical, occupational, and speech therapy, he could regain *some* of his motor skills.

There had been no reassuring her mom. They'd made the best of it; he usually sat day after day, in this room, reading. The therapists didn't come as often as they used to; it was like everyone had accepted that this was it. After a year of working hard, Caitlyn watched her once-social dad withdraw from everything and everyone. The doctors said depression was a common thing, tried to prescribe antidepressants, but her dad refused them.

Now his eyes lit up when they entered the room. *Oh good. He wants visitors today.* Her dad's gaze landed on Andrew, and he murmured something.

"What was that, Bill?" her mom asked.

He grabbed the keyboard that was always near him and typed. Immediately, the words flashed across the monitor screen next to him. Everyone just stared at the words written across the screen. Her mom made some kind of noise in the back of her throat. Even Andrew seemed to jump a bit.

Caitlyn read the words. *Finally, he's come.*

How could her dad have been expecting Andrew? He knew so little of him. Then, in that moment, Caitlyn remembered something. The night Andrew had come to tell her Eden had broken up with him, and they'd sat outside her home in the drizzly rain. *Andrew had healed my leg, and we realized what I might be able to do with my mind.*

Caitlyn's eyes met her dad's. His were wide with excitement, half of his face pulling into a smile.

"You remember that night, don't you, Dad? When I came to talk to you, and I told you about... Andrew." She drew closer to her father.

His eyes danced back at her, and he typed. *Yes.*

Andrew glanced over at her. "You did?" He seemed surprised. "What did you tell him? Does he know I can—?"

"No," Caitlyn said quickly, not wanting Andrew to say anything else. Her mom would make him leave before he even had the chance to touch her dad. "I just told him about your break up, and how I felt bad because you are... my good friend."

Her dad made a grunting sound. Then the words, *I wanted to meet you, Andrew. I can tell you mean a lot to Caitlyn,* came across the screen.

Caitlyn flushed, and Andrew grinned. "I'm happy to meet you too, Mr. Berkley."

Andrew held out his hand to her dad, who struggled to lift an arm. His words slurred, "This is good one."

Andrew took the offered hand into both of his. "Mr. Berkley, I don't know if Caitlyn told you about how some of us have gifts and *abilities?*" Caitlyn's mom sucked in air. It was clear this was not what she had bargained for. Andrew ignored her. "Well, my ability lets me heal people. And I, for one, think it's about time you have two good hands to shake with and two good legs to walk on. How's that sound?"

Her dad's eyes widened as he stared back at Andrew. Caitlyn's mom stepped forward. "Now see here, this is exactly what I didn't..." Her words faded.

Right before them all, the muscles that had hung like dead weight on her dad's face began twitching.

Her mom gasped. "Bill... your face! It's *moving!*"

Her dad's posture changed; he sat up straighter. The grin that for so many years had only hitched up half of his face, now spread from ear to ear. Wrinkles crinkled his eyes, lined his forehead, and dimpled his cheeks. *Funny, I've missed seeing my dad's wrinkles.* Each line brought expression back to his face.

"You *actually* did it. I can't believe it. It worked!" No longer slurred or stuttering, it was the voice Caitlyn had longed to hear for years. The voice that told her stories, soothed her fears, and used to joke and tease her; it was her dad's voice.

Her mom pushed past everyone, her hands fumbling to grab hold of her dad. "Bill? Is this really happening? Can you feel again?"

Her dad didn't answer. Instead, he let go of Andrew's hands and reached for her mom. Both of his arms wrapped around her, and in that moment, Caitlyn stared in awe as her mom collapsed in tears, weeping into her dad's shoulder. No one spoke as her parents embraced. No longer a sideways hug, which had disappeared over the years too, they were actually holding each other.

"It's real, Laura." He pulled her mom's face back with his hands, leaning down to kiss her lips. As the stroke had left half of his mouth numb and useless, Caitlyn knew her parents hadn't kissed in a very long time. She looked away, not wanting to pry, and caught eyes with Andrew. She reached over and took his hand.

"Come on," she said, leading him from the room. She heard no protests from behind.

Chapter Thirteen

Once they were out of the den area, Caitlyn faced Andrew. She could barely get the words out. "Thank you."

Andrew's smile was genuine. "I would have done it a long time ago, if I'd known about his condition. Why didn't you tell me?"

"I wanted to, but everything happened so fast. And then when I tried to tell my mom about... well, us... she totally freaked out."

Andrew reached over, and Caitlyn resisted the urge to duck away. His hand brushed hairs from her face, his eyes softening.

"I couldn't understand why you were ignoring me," he said. She cringed. She'd hoped to avoid *this* conversation, at least for a bit longer.

"Then Micah told us about how your mom felt about us all," Andrew continued. "That's when Eden told me about your dad."

"I can never repay you for what you just did," she whispered. *Maybe I don't have to tell him, not yet anyway.*

"Repay? Caitlyn, you're like my best friend. I'd do anything for you. You know that."

She shifted under his gaze, her face feeling hot. "I still feel like I owe you."

He grinned. "Well, if you really want to do something, come to Rome with me."

"What? Rome?"

"Yep. Micah called us all together to tell us he needs our help again. And by the looks of it, you, Willow, and I are a team." He chuckled. "Trust me, I know it sounds weird, I'm still wigging out myself, but we have to find people to build more of those cities."

"Oh. I doubt I'd be much help there."

"What are you talking about? You can do anything you put your mind to." Andrew grinned. "I'm sure convincing a few strangers of what they need to do will be easy for you."

She stared at him. "I couldn't even convince my mom. I think you have way too much faith in me."

Andrew cocked his head to the side. "And you have too little. What happened? Why are you doubting yourself?"

She didn't want to admit that since they'd come home, she'd bottled herself up, stopped thinking or wishing anything if she could help it. She was so afraid of her own wants getting in the way and altering the future for her own selfish desires.

She swallowed and said, "Nothing happened. I'll try, if I'm allowed to go."

"Don't think that'll be a problem now. Let's ask. Probably a good time to go back," Andrew said, and to her surprise, his hand reached for her. "But first, I need to tell you something."

Her skin burned where he touched her. She wondered if he was actually healing some unknown hurt or if it was truly just from her own feelings running rampant.

"There's another thing you have to do, and only you can do it," Andrew said softly.

She waited, her eyes seeking his. She couldn't help but get lost in their emerald color.

"Eden's hurt, like real bad," he said. His words caused her to rock back.

"*What?* How? What happened?" she sputtered, the moment she'd been feeling shattered by the seriousness of Andrew's words and the guilt that crept in whenever she thought of his feelings for Eden.

"It's a long story, but basically, remember prom night, when she was stabbed? That injury has come back again. We think she was poisoned."

"Oh my gosh! Can you heal her again?"

Andrew sighed. "No, I can't." She didn't miss the ache behind his words. "It's like nothing I've felt before. So while Micah tries to find the cure, he thinks the safest place for her is inside Enoch's temple."

Caitlyn nodded, and then asked, "So what can I do to help?" She hadn't forgotten prom night. That was the first time she'd seen Andrew heal someone. *And I suppose I played a part in it. At least, that's what Andrew thinks, but I really don't see what I did.*

"Chamber nine has been sealed shut, Caitlyn, and you're the only one who can open it."

Doubts shot through her like pointy shards. "What if I can't do it again?" she gasped.

His eyebrows rose. "You did it before, I'm sure you can…"

"But what if I can't!"

Andrew stared at her, and then took her by the shoulders. "I know you can. Caitlyn, remember what your gift is. You got this."

She could only gaze back at him. They were interrupted by her parents walking out of the den. Her dad's arm was wrapped around her mom's shoulder. Her mom was… smiling. Like really smiling.

At the sight of her dad on his feet, moving with ease, Caitlyn rushed over to him and threw her arms around his waist. "Dad!" she said, squeezing him tightly. She was thrilled to feel him return the hug, his arms strong again.

"Yep, it's finally me again, Cat."

She grinned at hearing her childhood nickname. It was as if time had been erased. Like the stroke had never come and sucked the life out of her dad. When Caitlyn stepped back from her dad, she was shocked to see her mom frown back at her. *Oh, no, now what?*

"Caitlyn, I need to apologize. I should've believed you. I should've at least listened," her mom admitted, her frown giving way to tears.

Caitlyn could only stare, dumbfounded. She couldn't remember the last time her mom had said she was sorry. "It's okay, Mom, really."

Her mom glanced over at her dad. "I'd given up on miracles."

He smiled back at her. "It wasn't easy on any of us. Don't beat yourself up too bad, hon. You weren't the only one who'd given up."

In that moment, Caitlyn realized what had been missing in their home for all these years—her dad's optimism. He'd always been the more lighthearted of the two, the one who could make a joke out of any bad situation. *When he lost hope, we all sort of did.*

"Sometimes the hardest part is just believing," Andrew said, and then he glanced at Caitlyn. "If you believe, anything is possible."

Andrew stayed for another hour, explaining things to her parents. Caitlyn appreciated it. It was obvious her parents adored him now; her dad wouldn't stop thanking him for what he had done, and her mom kept plying him with food.

As soon as Andrew told them none of this would have been possible without Eden, Caitlyn's heart ached. No matter how unsure she felt about using her gift properly, she had to try for her friend. *I have to open chamber nine; I just have to.*

She glanced over at Andrew, who was polishing off the ice cream sundae her mom had insisted on him having. *Hard to believe that this morning, everything felt like it was stacked against me.* She wished she could have a minute alone with him, to tell him how much this meant to her. He changed everything. Her parents not only believed her, but they also believed *in* her. *More than one miracle happened today.*

Andrew caught her gaze and grinned. Her heart pinched, and her face heated. *Too bad I can never tell him how I really feel about him.*

Chapter Fourteen

Eden tried calling Jessie on the way back home, but she got voicemail. Feeling impulsive, she headed up the turnpike. *Just hope she's home.* Since getting back from Illinois, she'd seen little of her friend. She wasn't sure how much of that was because they were both crazy busy, or because Jessie felt left out. They'd talked on the phone a few times, chatting mostly about Trent.

Thankfully, Trent had made good on his promises so far; he seemed to genuinely care for Jessie. Micah had confided to Eden that he'd never seen his cousin so whipped over a girl. Thinking of Trent with his ever-flirtatious smile, Eden grunted. *Never in my life would I have put those two together. But I'm so glad it worked.*

Seeing Jessie's car parked in front of her townhome, Eden grinned. She shut her car off and, pushing the feeling of apprehension aside, jogged up to the front door. She didn't even get to knock because Jessie's younger brother came running out the front door just as she arrived.

"Hi Eden!" Derek hollered, his freckled face splitting into a grin.

Eden smiled back at him. Jessie liked to tease her eleven-year-old brother about having a crush on her. "Hi Derek. Jessie around?"

"Yep, she's in the house. I don't know where, but she and mom keep yelling at each other, so just follow that."

Eden laughed. "Okay, thanks." She stepped inside. "Jessie?"

She heard nothing at first, then the upstairs creaked, and she heard Jessie call down, "Eden? That you?"

"Yeah," she called up.

Jessie appeared at the top of the stairs. "Hey, come on up. I'm getting ready to go out."

"Really? With who... Trent?" Eden bounded up the stairs, grinning.

Jessie's face split into a wide grin. "Maybe, what's it to you?"

"Nothing, I'm just glad Trent's being a gentleman and treating you right. You deserve it."

Jessie made a face. "I never said he's a gentleman, but he's not too bad," she added with a wink.

Eden had never seen Jessie happier. Did she dare spoil it? What if Jessie didn't like what she was about to hear? She decided either way, it was time she knew what was really happening.

"Hey Jessie, can we talk for a second?" Eden asked, sitting at the foot of Jessie's bed.

Jessie stopped rummaging through her closet and poked her head out, her eyebrows rising. "Sure. Sounds serious. Everything okay?"

"Yeah, everything's great." *Okay, maybe not everything.* She didn't want to tell her about her new health development. "I need to tell you some things, and I want you to hear me out, because frankly, you're going to think it's crazy."

Jessie's lips twisted to the side before she grinned. "Do I finally get to know what's really going on? I know you, Trent, and Micah are into something, and I feel like the only one who doesn't know. I mean, even Caitlyn and Willow seem to know about it. And these 'trips'?" She threw up quotations. "I saw Micah on the news too, you know. What the heck are they building that city for anyway?"

Wow. Eden sat back. *Poor girl has bottled up a thousand questions!*

"You're right. We're into something big. And it is more than time that you know about it. I've kept things from you up 'till now because I didn't want to scare you."

Her eyes widened. "What do you mean?"

Eden began at the beginning; she told her about her gift, how she awakened Micah, Trent, Andrew, Caitlyn, and even Willow and Damon. She told her about how each of them had new 'powers' and responsibilities. She described the demon attacks, the fights, the angels, and she even told her about her guardian angel, Gabriel.

Jessie's eyes grew wider and her mouth dropped open more with every new development. When Eden reached the part about Trent translating in Illinois, Jessie finally sputtered a few words, "So he really is translating ancient writings? He's helping build this city?"

"Yeah, Trent is Micah's translator."

"That's why he's going to Rome then?" she asked, her tone strained.

"Yes, why else would he? Oh... you thought maybe he was going to Rome to meet girls?"

"Well, yeah, sort of. He just told me last night they were going on a trip to Rome, and he wouldn't tell me much about it. I got suspicious. Figured maybe he wanted to see some old girlfriend there or something." Jessie sighed. "I'm so glad I know now."

"From what Micah told me, I don't think Trent thinks about any other girl but you. He really likes you, Jess."

Jessie's face flushed. "Well good, because I've never felt like this before." She met Eden's gaze. "I'm sorry I gave you such a hard time about Micah, when you broke up with Andrew and stuff. I had no idea how insane love makes you. I'm glad it worked out for you and him."

Eden decided this was the moment she'd been waiting for. She stepped forward and even with Jessie not being a 'huggie' person, she reached out to her friend. "Jessie, you're the best, you know that right?" she said, hoping the hug wasn't too obvious.

Jessie sort of patted her back before rocking back on her heels. "Whoa, wait a minute. Did you just awaken me or something?"

Eden grinned. "I don't know. Do you feel any different?"

"I don't know. What should I feel like?"

Eden shrugged. "Everyone has been different. I guess we will just wait and see."

"Should I be worried? I mean, you only awaken those who are supposed to be, right? I'm not going to get some bad ability, am I?"

Her words tugged at Eden, making her temporarily forget where she was. *I only hugged one person I wasn't sure of. And so far, nothing seemed to come of hugging Chase. . .*

She met Jessie's gaze. "Nope, only those who are supposed to get the gifts, and don't worry, they're always good."

Chapter Fifteen

When Andrew called four nights ago to let Micah know everything was fine now with Caitlyn, Micah felt a weight lift. He'd hoped her parents would feel differently after a healing, and they had. He glanced down at the plane tickets. *Hard to believe this all fell together so easily.* Everyone had passports, tickets bought, cars rented, and places to stay all lined up. Micah wanted to believe the angels had a hand in it and that it meant everything would go without a hitch, but the unease in his gut told him otherwise.

Trent was in his room packing up, instead of doing it last night like Micah. He'd stayed out late last night with Jessie. Micah didn't mind. Hanging out with Jessie for the last few days had improved his cousin's mood.

Glancing at his suitcase sprawled across his bed, Micah half hoped to see Eden appear in his doorway, like last time. He'd never forget that night or their first kiss. Even the thought of it now got his blood pumping. Like she'd read his mind, his phone chimed. He had a text message from her.

Hey, I'm all packed up. Want me to come over?

He grinned and typed. *Yes!*

He was about to text more, but Trent waltzed in. Micah peered over his phone. "What's up?"

"Why don't you ask Eden?"

With one glance at him, Micah knew something was brooding behind his furrowed brow line. "What do you mean?"

"Last night, Jessie told me Eden *hugged* her."

"Oh." *Mm . . . wonder what that means?*

"You know, I'm okay Eden told Jessie everything. It was something I needed to do anyway. It saved me the hassle. Although, I had plans to really wow her, you know? But what's up with the hug? Jessie says she feels the same, like nothing changed. Have any visions about her yet?"

Micah rubbed his chin. "No, I haven't. This is first I've heard of it. You seem upset about it. Don't you want your girlfriend to have some superhuman power? I thought you'd be down with that."

"Yeah, well, that part, yes. All I know is the moment *your* girlfriend started hugging people, demons entered our lives," he grumbled. "What if Jessie ends up gifted? The demons will come after her too."

Micah cocked an eyebrow at him. "Wow. I've never seen you like this. Looks like Jessie's the first to tame the wild stallion."

"Just because I don't want her to get torn limb from limb by the spawn of Satan, I hardly think that makes me a softie."

"Uh, yeah. It does actually."

"Oh, just shut up and have a vision already, will you? Ask Sage if her guardian's a tough mother."

Micah chuckled, and then noticed how Trent kept on staring at him. "Oh, you mean right now?"

"Micah, we leave tomorrow, and she's going to be all alone."

If anyone understood the torture of worrying over the girl you cared about, Micah did. He decided to stop teasing. "Okay, I'll try, Trent. But just know I don't always get Sage to appear."

Trent nodded. "Sure, sure, I know."

"Alright." Micah rubbed his hands together. "Sage, I know you probably overheard all this. Can you let Trent know Jessie will be—" His words faded when the room suddenly brightened. His guardian stood close enough that her black hair brushed Micah's arm. He glanced over, mesmerized by her onyx eyes. Still wearing the red dress, there was something different about her. Micah just couldn't pinpoint what it was.

"Perfectly safe," she said, finishing his sentence for him. Her soft voice was rich and full at the same time. She glanced over at Trent. Her red lips twitched into a smile. "Glad to see you have finally found your redhead. Brutus feared he disappointed you."

Trent guffawed. "Yeah, well, sorry to break it to you, but I don't dig dudes."

Sage laughed, the whimsical sound almost making Micah forget all his worries. Now that he had Sage here, he knew he had a few questions of his own.

Sage's attention was on Trent. "Don't be concerned over Jessie's awakening. Eden did well. It was right on time. She sensed the need; it did not have to be forced. She's progressing. Jessie's gift will not be needed yet, but in the meantime, her guardian will keep her safe. Don't fret, my friend."

By Trent's expression, Micah knew he was about to launch into a barrage of questions, so he cut in, "Sage, about Eden. It's not just her ability that's progressing. She's getting worse. And we know Andrew can't stop the poison, for whatever reason. Can Caitlyn help him again, like last time with me?"

Sage frowned. "I wish it were that simple. Truth is, Semjaza was entrusted with heavenly knowledge before his fall. That makes his power that much stronger than mere demons. In general, angels' powers outrank demons', unless you get high enough. So you can see how a fallen angel is that much worse than a demon."

"What do you mean if you get high enough?" Micah asked.

"There are a few close to Lucifer, Son of the Morning, who none but the Captain and His Holies can stop."

"Okay, that is just plain freaky," Trent muttered.

Sage nodded. "Yes, but there are some battles you are not expected to win alone. The Captain is readying His army. Don't let today's fears consume you; they will cripple your tomorrow."

"You're right," Micah agreed. "And that's what I want to focus on now, what we can fix today. I have to stop Semjaza. I have to save Eden. If what you say is true, to fight a Watcher, I need a Watcher."

Sage cocked her head to the side. "Interesting proposal. What do you have in mind, Micah?"

"I've been reading about the fallen angels' abilities. Under Semjaza, it says he's known for his enchantments and root cutting. Now I don't know what the heck root cutting means, whether he literally cuts roots, mixes them up, and enchants them to kill someone, like Eden, but I do know there is one other Watcher listed whose power might help us. In Enoch's writing, it says Armaros can *resolve* enchantments. Makes me wonder if he can break Semjaza's curse."

Sage nodded. "You are correct on Armaros. He can undo enchantments. You think you can convince him to break his oath to Semjaza to help you?"

"It's all we have at this point. I can't imagine the Captain wants His Awakener to die." Micah could hardly stomach saying the words. "I wish there were an easier way, but there was one thing I learned facing Astaroth at the well. The path we've got to take is usually the hardest and scariest one imaginable, but the Captain won't let us fail. And I, for one, can't sit around, watching Eden suffer in the hope that somehow Andrew can suddenly heal her. I'm moving forward with this plan. We'll travel to Rome as a group. I hope being there will help Damon, but just in case, we will bring Eden with us just long enough for him to find out who he really is."

Trent's head popped up. "What do you mean? Last I checked, Damon was a mean machine with his gift."

Micah met Trent's gaze. "Trust me; we haven't even begun to see what Damon can do."

Chapter Sixteen

The doorbell ringing ended their conversation with Sage; Micah was disappointed. He wanted to hear if she thought their plan was sound. He tried to sound confident, but it still wouldn't hurt to get the thumbs-up from upstairs on it all. Micah knew Trent wanted to ask more about Damon, but when Eden entered the room, he must have remembered the other bone to pick.

Trent threw his hands up at Eden. "So, you had to hug her, didn't you? Just had to change her, make her vulnerable. Make her *demon* bait."

Eden's face blanched and Micah jumped to her rescue, moving to her side and shoving Trent out of the way. "Oh, don't worry, Trent's just teasing you. Aren't you, Trent?" He reached over and jabbed his cousin in the ribs with his last words.

Trent grinned. "Yeah, I'm totally stoked. She's like an egg waiting to hatch. Who knows what her power will be. Maybe she'll be a mad ninja fighter, or turn invisible, or maybe she can see through walls."

"Hate to burst your bubble, but I'm pretty sure that last I checked, no one in the Bible saw through walls," Micah said.

"It's in the Old Testament, scouts honor," Trent said with a wink.

Eden giggled, and Micah rolled his eyes. "Why don't you get out of here? Go spend time with your precious egg and wait for her to hatch."

Trent grinned. "Good idea, I think I will. Later, losers."

With that, Trent left, and Micah had Eden all to himself. He figured sitting down on the couch was innocent enough, but with her so close to him, all he could think about was how soft her hand felt secured in his, how good her body felt next to him, and when he leaned over to kiss her mouth, how tempting her lips were. Being with her felt like he could escape reality, even if it was only for a minute. He wanted to stay there, lost in her magic. No other girl had made him feel this way; there was something so different about Eden's touch. It filled him with comfort and yearning at the same time.

She was the one who pulled back and grinned over at him.

"Sorry," he admitted. "I'll let you breathe now."

"I'm fine. I could kiss you all day—that's the problem."

"I know, me too." He gave her lips a quick peck. "You look good. Feeling better?"

"Yes, I haven't had any pains since the last time. I'm totally ready to go tomorrow," she said, her grin spreading wider. When Micah had told Eden he wanted her in Rome too, she'd seemed surprised. *I guess she's dreading the day she's locked up in the temple. If everything goes as planned, it won't have to be for long, at least I hope.*

Micah was about to reassure her, but the doorbell rang. He wasn't too surprised to see Damon at his doorstep. *Had a hunch he'd show up sooner or later.*

"This a bad time?" he asked, glancing at Eden.

"Nope, come on in," Micah said and stood back to let him pass.

"Hi Damon, how are you?" Eden asked, tucking a strand of hair behind her ear. Micah thought it was cute how she got flustered around Damon. *He makes her nervous.* He glanced over at Damon. *Wonder if she can sense it too?*

"Uh, I'm good." Damon shoved his hands into his pockets. He didn't make eye contact while asking, "Have any more pains, Eden?"

She shook her head. "Nope. I'm doing much better, actually."

"That's good," Damon said, still staring at the floor. *Huh, Damon's just as uncomfortable around her.* Micah didn't know if he should feel jealous or amused.

"Are you hungry, Damon? I was thinking of getting some food," Micah said, breaking the awkwardness. He knew Damon wanted to speak privately, but Eden had just gotten here and he wasn't about to send her home yet.

"No, I'm good. I won't stay long. I just had a quick question for you." Damon paused and glanced quickly at Eden.

She perked up. "I can go, if you guys need to talk…"

"No, wait," Micah cut in, "Don't go. Just give us a minute, k?"

She nodded and Micah left her in the living room, leading Damon into his dad's study. He had a feeling he knew what was on his friend's mind. It'd been on his mind too, and in his dreams.

Once the door shut, Micah asked, "Everything okay? Still comfortable with the trip and all?"

"Yes, that's not it. I… just… I've been having these feelings lately. Like I should be remembering something I'm not. Even the elements are whispering it to me. I know it's important to this mission, and I know I need it for facing the Watchers, but I just don't remember."

"When do you feel different?" Micah asked. "What do the elements tell you?"

"That I'm more than I think… that I need to remember who I really am. And that the Watchers haven't forgotten who I am." Damon ran his hands through his black hair. "I'm about to just ask Willow. Pretty sure she's figured it all out."

Micah chuckled. "Yeah, she's a sharp one. Be careful. She might see more than you want her to."

"What do you mean?" Damon's brow furrowed.

"Ah… nothing." Micah wasn't about to tell Damon it was clear he had feelings for Willow. None of that really mattered now. "Tell you what, let's go on this trip. And if you still feel unsure, I'll do what I can to help."

"So you know what it all means?"

"I think so. It's a feeling for me too. I've had no definite confirmation, just a few dreams. I wish I could just tell you, honestly, but it won't help. For it to mean anything, you have to figure it out for yourself."

Damon's shoulders squared. "That's enough for me. Thanks, Micah."

He nodded. "Anytime." He clapped his hand on Damon's shoulder as they walked out. "See you tomorrow, bright and early, for another wicked adventure."

Damon chuckled. "I'm looking forward to it."

Chapter Seventeen

Eden's seatbelt clicked in with a snap. The *fasten seat belt* light flashed overhead, while the air vents blew muggy air into her face, and flight attendants in a navy-blue suits hustled up and down the aisle, making sure everyone was ready for take-off. Since this was her first flight, Micah had sandwiched himself between her and Trent, giving her the window seat. Caitlyn and Willow were directly behind with a stranger getting their window seat, and Andrew and Damon were a few seats behind them. At least they all had someone they knew to sit by, but it was going to be a long day.

Micah grabbed her hand, pulling her arm over to rest their fingers on his leg. She shot him a questioning glance. He shrugged.

"I don't think he can see through seats," he said. "Which reminds me, are you going to tell him or should I? Because I'm not promising I won't hold your hand in Rome."

"I know." The thought of being in Rome with Micah made her want to grin like a schoolgirl, but instead, her lips turned down. "I should do it, but I don't know what to say. I feel awful, like he'll think I picked you over him."

He stared at her. "Well, didn't you?"

"Yes, but it still feels funny telling Andrew that."

"I'll do it then," he offered.

"No, it should be me," she decided. *Just what I wanted to do when I got off this plane.*

Trent leaned over. "What are you two monkeys whispering about over there?"

Micah glanced over at him. "Eden just told me Jessie thinks your kissing could use some work."

"Whatever, dude." Trent's eyebrows shot up and down. "I've got mad skills." With that, he sat back and snatched one of the plane's magazines. Eden smiled, noticing how quickly he flipped through the pages before shoving it back in the pocket in front of him. As he ran both his hands through his spiky hair, she wondered if his agitation was really over what Micah had said.

She was about to tell him it wasn't true, when Trent mumbled, "Sage better be right. That's all I'm saying."

Sage? What does she have to do with Trent's kissing? "Be right about what?" she asked, instead.

Micah glanced over at Trent. "She'll be fine." To Eden, he added, "Trent's worried about Jessie's safety, since she's been awakened."

"Oh," she said, realizing with a stab of guilt she should be a bit more worried about her friend too. She'd just been happy to share this part of her life with her; she hadn't thought the whole demon bit through. "She has to have a guardian angel too, right?" she asked, trying to push down the rising panic.

Micah nodded. "Sage said she does, and she'll be safe."

"Oh, good. Wish we could've just taken her with us. I mean, everyone else came." She felt bad that once again, her best friend was the one being left out.

Trent slapped his hand on his knee, making her jump. "See, even Eden thinks it was a good idea!"

"Trent, it's not that I don't want her here. We just don't need her. Why put her in more danger when Sage said her gift isn't needed yet?" Micah answered.

"It's not?" Eden asked, ignoring Trent's stammering. "That's interesting. Wonder what hers is."

"*I* need her," Trent said, pointing at his chest. "Maybe her gift's to keep the Interpreter from going mad, huh? Ever consider that? I mean, I can't always be the strong one around here. With keeping you from insanity, a guy might need a break sometimes. I have needs too, and my needs are met oh so well by—"

"Yeah, yeah, we know. Red hair and red lips," Micah cut in.

Trent sighed, and then grumbled. "I still don't see why you get to bring the love of your life."

"The love of my life? Now who's acting like the teenage girl?" Micah asked.

Eden giggled as Trent struggled to respond. The plane lurched forward and with it, her laugh died. The plane left the terminal, rolling forward slowly. Her grip on Micah's hand tightened. Her stomach felt funny. Her ears were ringing. The overhead intercom binged loudly, and then a feminine voice announced they were approaching the runway and would be taking off shortly. She glanced over, meeting Micah's blue eyes.

"You okay?" he asked.

"Yeah, just nervous. I've never flown before."

"I'm pretty sure Gabriel has taken you for a ride or two. Doesn't that count?" he teased. She knew he was trying to reassure her by reminding her Gabriel was always near to keep her safe, but that was the problem. Her heart squeezed, her breath caught. *Gabriel's leaving me.* The thought of being in the temple without him terrified her. *He's never left me... what if I need him?* She didn't want to tell Micah her true feelings though. She felt like she was being selfish. Gabriel was so much more than her personal babysitter. *How can I expect him to sit around in the temple with me when there are more important things for him to be doing?*

"I think I trust Gabriel's flying more than this," she managed to say.

Micah opened his mouth, but the plane jetted forward, the propulsion making them both sink back into their seats.

"Here we go. Don't worry, it's sort of fun," Micah said, giving her hand a squeeze.

She tried to nod back at him, but her eyes were glued to her window. She licked her lips, unsure if the adrenaline was just from excitement or nerves. Even with all that had happened in the past few months, she couldn't help but feel that she'd just left a chapter of her life behind. She couldn't decide if being in the temple would simply be a new adventure or was a scary, impending doom. Inhaling deeply, she tried to focus on her small, rectangular window. The scenery below had changed rapidly, with large buildings turning into geometric shapes from above and cars and trucks resembling matchbox cars. With this new perspective, the city below felt almost fake, like a large board game. She knew whose hands moved the pieces in the 'game,' and yet, it overwhelmed her to see just how small and insignificant she was.

The warm hand clutching hers brought her back to reality, stilling her racing heart a bit. She glanced over and tried to smile.

"See, told you it'd be fun." Micah cocked his head to the side. "Are you sure it's really the flying you are worried about?"

She sighed. "I guess there's no point in ever keeping secrets from you."

She was surprised Trent leaned in, over Micah, filling the space. "Nope, no point at all. The dude sees all."

Micah shoved him back. "Apparently, the Interpreter hears all too. Even private conversations."

"It's okay; I don't mind." Eden was glad to see Trent was back in a good mood. He made her laugh, which was something she needed right now.

"See Eden, I knew we had something special, you and I," Trent said, giving her a crooked grin before falling back into his seat.

She smiled. "I'm just glad you're not mad at me anymore for hugging Jessie."

Trent unlatched the lock in front of him, letting the tray fall into his lap. "No way, other than the demon thing, I think it's gnarly."

"Gnarly?" Micah repeated.

"Yep. Now where's my soda and peanuts?" Trent asked, peering around the plane.

Apparently, Trent had caught eyes with Caitlyn behind him because he turned in the aisle to face her, saying, "Caitlyn, work some of your mojo and get us some food."

Caitlyn's voice barely carried over the roar of the plane. "I think you'd have better luck with Damon. Maybe he can tell the peanuts to march down the aisle to you, Trent."

"Yo! Damon!" Trent hollered loudly, catching the eyes of several passengers nearby.

"Trent," Caitlyn said from behind. "He can't hear you. He's too far back."

Trent turned back around to face Micah. "Huh. Guess I'll have to learn tree talk or something, because the dude can hear an ant a mile away, but he can't hear me."

"I think everyone in the plane just heard you, Trent, including Damon," Micah answered.

Trent gasped in mock horror. "After all we've been through, he's pretending he doesn't know me?"

"I'm about to pretend I don't know you. Now sit down and be quiet," Micah muttered.

Eden didn't care how loud and obnoxious Trent was to everyone else on the plane. She needed his humor like a drug. She hadn't noticed how out of control her laugh had become until she realized both Micah and Trent were gazing at her. Micah seemed amused, but Trent looked a bit confused.

"You okay over there, partner?" Trent asked, cocking an eyebrow at her.

She tried to stop, but she honestly couldn't think of the last time she'd giggled this hard.

Micah squeezed her hand and bumped her shoulder with his. "I love seeing you laugh. All the color comes back into your face when you do."

His words brought her bliss to a halt. "What do you mean—the color in my face?"

He flinched. "Nothing."

"Micah, tell me."

Ironically, it was Trent who answered, with a glance towards Micah. "You've been looking kind of pale lately, Eden."

"I have?" she asked, her hand instinctively clutching her shirt above her chest.

Micah's eyes swept her face, the sadness in them all to clear. "Don't worry; we're going to get you better."

Eden nodded before blurting out. "I don't want to go to the temple." She regretted her words instantly.

Micah sat back a bit. "Is that what's bothering you?"

"Yeah." She didn't say more. She feared she'd gush about missing Gabriel.

Micah wrapped an arm around her shoulder, pulling her closer. "Honestly, I don't want you in there either. I'm going to miss you so much, but I really think it's the safest place for you."

"What about Rome? You're taking me there, not that I'm complaining. You must think it's sort of safe there, right? Maybe I can just stay?"

Micah glanced down, breaking eye contact. She felt his hesitation like a sledgehammer. "Rome is a bit *safer,* but not off limits. Trent and I were still attacked by demons there, remember?"

"Yes, I know, so why are you letting me come along?" She hoped he didn't take it the wrong way; she was thrilled to go. She knew there was something he wasn't telling her.

His lips turned down. "I need your help in Rome."

"I don't mind helping. Why do you act like it's a bad thing?"

"Because you're so… weak that I shouldn't be asking anything of you right now. The first thing should be to get you somewhere safe and find your cure." Micah's shoulders slumped. She sensed this had been weighing heavily on him. *He feels guilty about bringing me.*

She reached up and touched his cheek. "Micah, don't feel bad. This is my gift. This is what I'm supposed to do. You're so good at being the Seer; let me do my job too. What do you need me to do?"

Micah's voice was low, almost a whisper. "I need you to awaken someone. As soon as you do, I'm getting you to that temple. I know you don't want to go, but I can't lose you. I'm sorry you don't want to be in there. I wish I could change that. Trust me; I've racked my brain for a better plan."

She leaned her head against his shoulder. "I know and you're right. The temple is the safest place for me without Gabriel." She ignored the squeezing pain she felt over being away from her guardian.

Micah kissed the top of her head. "You're amazing, you know that?"

She smiled up at him. "And so are you."

Trent shifted in his seat, giving Micah more room. For all his bantering, he seemed to know this was a private moment.

"So Willow will find the person I need to touch?" she asked.

"Yes. I'm pretty sure it's someone the Genaros know. I keep seeing them in vision. For all I know, it's Fredo himself. But I want Willow to confirm."

"You must really trust her."

"I do. I trust all of you." He bumped his forehead against hers. "You most of all."

Chapter Eighteen

Funny how an eight-hour flight can feel so short, Eden mused as they gathered their belongings from the overhead compartments. Their first flight to Boston had taken a little less than two hours, and after a two-hour layover, they'd boarded their second plane, which would take them all the way to Rome. This time, they'd been even more spread out, and Eden had been happy Micah still managed to sit next to her. All the comfort he'd been to her for the past hours seeped away, knowing now that they'd landed, she needed to talk to Andrew privately.

It was heaven knows what hour, or what day for that matter. Even her bones felt like they were begging her to find a soft bed to lie down in. Micah pulled her backpack out from overhead, and she reached over for it.

He shook his head. "I got it." He swept it easily onto his broad shoulder, along with his own. If she hadn't been feeling so dizzy, she probably would have protested more. The plane felt stuffy, like the AC had been set to lukewarm. She found it harder and harder to get adequate air in. Standing in the aisle, waiting to unload, she leaned into the closest seat. Her stomach squeezed, nausea making her ears ring.

I'm going to puke!

She fumbled forward to grab Micah's arm, her fingers barely grazing his shirt as her knees buckled. The pain seizing her felt as real and tangible as the arms grabbing her.

"Eden!" Micah cried, his arms securing her waist, keeping her from collapsing completely.

No words could form, no air came in. She could only stare at his eyes, which were darting back and forth between hers.

"Is it the pain?" He pulled her closer, his hand cradling the spot on her back.

It felt like actual flames coursed up her back, wrapping around her torso, and gouging her lungs like daggers. The flames threatened to tear her from Micah's arms.

Gabriel! Help! her mind screamed, as gray dots hit her vision like mud on a windshield.

Micah clutched Eden's body, terrified his vision was about to come true, as her body threatened to fall to the ground. *I'm not letting that happen!* He held her up, trying to keep from screaming out her name. For everyone else on the plane, it appeared a girl had merely passed out. It caused alarm; passengers cleared the aisle, a flight attendant rushed over, but no one suspected the real danger of the situation.

Only Micah and his friends knew. Andrew was there instantly, his hands reaching out to touch Eden.

"Can you help her?" Micah asked in a whisper.

"I don't know. I can try," Andrew responded, his hands wrapping around her.

"Everything okay here? Did she pass out?" The flight attendant asked, concern on her face.

"Our friend faints sometimes when it's too hot, and the plane is really stuffy," Willow answered immediately. "Can we get her off? Get her somewhere cool to lie down?"

"Of course, let's get her to the first aid."

Good idea, Willow! Micah knew there was nothing the first aid could do, but he knew they had to get off the plane and get her somewhere Andrew could try something. *Anything!*

They had just entered the long jet bridge when Micah felt something wasn't right with Eden. He glanced down at her, so still in his arms. *Her chest isn't moving!*

"Andrew," he hissed through clenched teeth, trying not to alarm the flight attendants who were ushering them out, "She's not breathing!"

Andrew blanched. "Give her to me."

Micah hesitated, only because he wasn't sure if Andrew would be able to touch her wounds while holding her body in his arms.

"I have an idea," Andrew said. Micah passed her along, with Trent right there to make sure she didn't drop.

Micah scanned her body, desperate to see any sign of life. Andrew pulled her near, practically crushing her against his chest. Micah heard her inhale.

"What did you do?" he asked.

"I don't know really, I just thought maybe if it was more than my hands touching her, it would help," Andrew replied.

"Well, keep doing it! It's working; she's breathing again," Micah said.

They had entered the unloading area. Many of the other passengers had cleared the terminal, but the chairs and benches were filled up by those waiting to load the next flight out.

Willow touched the attendant's shoulder. "Is there a quiet place nearby where we can lay her down? A little more private?"

Perhaps the attendant was uncomfortable by a teenager passing out on her watch. She nodded quickly and said, "Yes, right over here."

They followed the woman in the navy suit out of the terminal and down a small hallway. "This leads to some of the janitorial areas. There's a bench right there, on that wall. I'll be right back. I'm going to get some help."

"Perfect, thank you," Micah said, glad the woman was leaving. They needed to be alone. Andrew went to lay Eden down, but Micah stopped him. "Wait, will she be able to breathe if you let go?"

Andrew stopped. "I don't know."

"We can't risk it. Can you sit down still holding her? I can help..."

Andrew didn't wait for Micah to help him, but sat down, clutching Eden to his chest. Micah had to swallow back his emotions. He had to stay focused on what they could do, not how terrifying it was at the moment.

"What can we do?" Caitlyn asked, stepping closer to Andrew and Eden. Micah noticed how Caitlyn's hands were fidgeting at her sides. *Her gift! Maybe she can help!*

His thoughts were interrupted by a warm blast of air hitting him, and suddenly Gabriel's huge frame appeared. He rushed forward, kneeling down by Eden, placing his hands on her head and then her heart.

"You got her breathing again. Good," Gabriel said to Andrew. "We need to get her out of here. Micah, I'm taking her to the Genaros' house. Meet us there."

"Gabriel, Andrew has to go with you. His touch is what's keeping her breathing. Semjaza's hold is strong this time," Micah said, stepping forward as Gabriel began scooping Eden up into his arms.

Gabriel seemed to consider his words before saying, "Daniel, come."

Immediately, another angel appeared—Andrew's guardian, Daniel. Still wearing leather straps, swords, and a bow and arrow, Daniel took two seconds to scan his surroundings and then nodded at Gabriel.

Gabriel had not removed his hands from Eden, but he said to Andrew, "Stand up. You're about to fly again."

Andrew stood and asked, "Won't people see us? We're in an airport."

"Not the way you're going today," Gabriel said, readying Eden between him and Andrew. "Hang on to her, no matter what. Daniel will hold your shoulder. You should be fine."

Andrew seemed a bit nervous.

Caitlyn jumped forward, touching his shoulder. "You'll be fine, Andrew. I flew like this once with my guardian Alaina. So we could get to Micah faster. Remember? Just close your eyes."

"And don't let go of Eden," Micah said firmly.

Andrew nodded. The angels stepped closer, placing their hands on Andrew's shoulder, and then they were all gone.

Micah didn't wait around. "Come on; let's get that rental car. We've got a twenty-minute drive to the Genaros'."

"Why couldn't we just fly with them and our guardians?" Willow asked, following him.

Damon broke his silence and said, "Flying like that is only done in emergencies. It takes a lot out of an angel."

Micah was sort of surprised Damon had known that.

"It does?" Caitlyn asked.

"Yeah," Micah answered. "So the rest of us can travel the old-fashioned way. Eden has who she needs right now." Then he stopped and peered at Caitlyn. "Unless you feel you can help, Caitlyn. You did help before."

"No, no, there's nothing I can do. I'll travel with you guys," she answered, ducking her head down.

Micah wanted to protest, but he didn't want to take the time. All he could think about was getting back to Eden. An hour later, after grabbing their luggage and haggling with the rental car company, he finally did. He felt bad not even saying hello to the Genaros, the couple who had housed him, taught him, and groomed him to be the Seer. Caterina ushered Micah straight back to his old room, her apron was on, and Micah heard the kettle whistling.

"I'm brewing some herbs," she answered. "We have to try everything, and The Watchers aren't the only ones who know about the natural medicines God gave us in the earth, you know."

Micah squeezed her shoulder. "Thank you, Caterina. How is she?"

"Still unconscious, but she's breathing. Go see for yourself."

Micah felt the group follow him, Trent on his heels, but Caterina held her hand out to them. "Give him a minute alone. Gabriel wishes to speak with him privately."

Trent raised an eyebrow. "Sounds like he needs his interpreter. Angels can be confusing, you know, with their cryptic riddles."

Caterina tried to protest, but Micah said, "Trent can come. Willow, Caitlyn, just give us a minute."

The girls agreed, and Trent followed after. With his heart galloping, Micah entered the bedroom. He wasn't sure what he'd expected to see. No, that wasn't true. He knew exactly what he'd feared to see; Eden's skin blue, her body lifeless, and her ripped dress revealing a black hole in her back.

He sighed in relief to see she still wore jeans. Andrew cradled her in his arms, sitting on the bed. Her eyes were shut, but he could see the rise and fall of her chest. She appeared to be sleeping.

Like Caterina had said, Gabriel was there, pacing the floor next to the bed. *Bet that shocked Caterina. Two angels appearing holding teenagers.*

"Gabriel, what do we do?" Micah asked, knowing there was no time to waste. Eden was breathing, she was alive, but she was far from okay. He shuddered to think she could be in pain right now.

The room brightened a bit and warmed. Sage appeared next to Micah. She reached over and touched his shoulder. "It's going to be okay, Micah. Gabriel has been to see the council."

"You have? What did they say?"

"I have taken this all the way to the top, Micah. Your plan is still sound. They feel you should proceed."

"But how can I? Look at her! *I* brought her here!" Micah said, hitting his chest. "I trusted the council that she would be fine for this awakening. She should never have come!"

He hated to question the angels, but all he could see was Eden's labored breathing before him. *The northern city could have waited. One awakening isn't worth the Awakener's life.*

"Micah," Gabriel said evenly, "Andrew's ability is holding the poison at bay. I can feel Semjaza's power waning, at least this round. When this passes, get her to the temple. The council thinks Semjaza's attacks can be slowed, almost stopped, as long as she is protected by the temple walls."

Micah nodded. "I understand that part. I just don't see why she came. What if she doesn't survive this round of attack? This was too big of a risk!"

Gabriel glanced at Eden, his jaw bulging as he silently appraised her condition. "I understand the risks as well as you, Micah. However, you aren't seeing the bigger picture. What you have suspected is truly the case. That is the real reason she came here. She had to come. It was the only way to truly save her life."

Trent lifted his hands up in the air. "See. What did I tell you? Angels and their riddles."

Andrew nodded. "Yeah, I'm as lost as you are."

Micah ran his hand across his mouth, noting for the first time, the sweat shining on Andrew's face. *How long can he hold back the poison? Time to get moving.*

To Trent, Micah said, "Take Willow and find the one Eden needs to touch. You know Rome's streets and Willow can guide you with her gift. Hurry back. When Eden's up, we'll have her awaken him."

"Okay, will do. And then we'll get her out of here?" Trent asked.

"Yes, but first Damon and I need to have a little talk."

Trent glanced at Micah, and then he wordlessly left the room. Eden moaned, and Gabriel and Micah jumped nearer. Gabriel's hand pressed on her forehead. Micah reached forward as well, knowing his touch could do little to help her. He fumbled to find her hand. He knew Andrew saw him do it.

"She's burning up," Micah said, feeling her hot skin in his.

"Yeah, she's been burning for a while," Andrew said.

Now the sweat on Andrew made sense. Eden's body was literally like fire in his arms. Micah surveyed his friend, grateful for his selfless love for Eden. He knew it must pain Andrew to be so near the girl who no longer wanted to be with him.

With a wave of guilt, Micah offered, "Do you need more pillows? Want to lean back more?"

Andrew shook his head. "I'm fine."

Gabriel grunted. "Your arms are going to get tired like that. Lay back against the headboard. Here." Gabriel shoved some pillows around Andrew's arms, to support Eden's weight. Micah helped, swallowing back his emotions.

It wasn't that he was jealous of Andrew—far from it. He couldn't help but wonder if Eden would forever need Andrew's touch to be okay. What if they failed against Armaros? What if he wouldn't help them break Semjaza's enchantments? They'd have no choice but to face Semjaza, and even with his show of confidence to the others, Micah's gut told him his chances of survival were minimal. Maybe his vision of seeing Eden marry Andrew had to do more with the fact that she literally could not live without his touch? *Or the fact that I die trying to save her.*

He stepped back from the bed, unsure of so many of his decisions lately. Even knowing Damon probably needed Eden's touch, he wondered if they should've at least tried it in Virginia first. Maybe it would have worked. He sighed inwardly. *We thought being in the northern lands would help Damon. The plan was to get her here, touch those who needed it, and get her out. I guess we all thought we had more time.*

Caterina met him in the doorway. She seemed surprised to see Micah leaving, but then she held out a bowl towards him. "Here, take this in. I've put together as many healing herbs as I could find. I cooled the tea to make a compress. Take it and wipe her face with it. It might cool her fever."

Micah nodded woodenly and walked back toward Eden and Andrew. To his surprise, Gabriel had disappeared already. Andrew's eyes were shut, but Micah didn't think he was sleeping. *Probably just exhausted.*

Sage remained in the room. She set her fiery gaze on Micah, almost causing him to take a step backward. He'd seen that look before, and it was when she was about to ignite herself.

"You are doubting yourself, aren't you?" she said more than asked. "Don't. Don't let Semjaza win, Micah. He revels in doubt and discouragement."

Micah struggled to respond.

"Don't let him have any more footholds on Eden," Sage continued, her words firm. "Chase your thoughts far from you, because with thoughts come power. This is especially true for those who have been entrusted with gifts. There is much doubt in your ranks. Strengthen your friends. They look to you. Your seeds of doubt will weaken their resolve."

Sage took a step closer, touching Micah's arm. "Gabriel has gone to ready things. He is near, with Eden, but your next mission must be successful."

With that, she was gone.

Andrew opened his eyes a crack. "She sure doesn't mince words, does she?"

Micah ran his hand along his jaw and shook his head. "No, she doesn't, but she's right. Eden needs my faith. You need my faith. My doubting my every decision does little to help us now." Micah spun on his heel, ready to leave.

"Where are you going?" Andrew asked.

"I'm going to get Caitlyn to help with these herbs. There's something else I need to do right now."

"Alright. Do what you have to. And Micah, for what it's worth, I know I haven't always agreed with how you've handled things, but I know you're doing the best you can. Honestly, I don't envy you at all."

Micah didn't miss the swift glance at Eden Andrew made. *He may not envy my responsibilities, but if he knows about Eden and me, I bet he envies that.*

"Thanks, man," Micah said, his heart heavy as he left the room. *If none of this works, you may get the girl you love back after all, Andrew.*

Chapter Nineteen

"Eden, can you hear me?" a masculine voice asked. She felt pressure on her stomach, like someone was resting against her. *That voice... it's not Micah*. She knew it, but her mind refused to place it. She tried to stir, but her eyelids still wouldn't budge. A moan escaped her, but it sounded foreign.

"Eden! Are you okay? Is the pain gone?" This voice was definitely Micah, and it came from her other side. The pressure against her stomach was becoming more recognizable. It felt more and more like hands holding her. *Hands. Andrew?*

She forced her lids to open up and through her lashes, she made out Andrew, lying alongside her in bed, holding her. She sucked in air, confused by his proximity. Movement in her peripheral caught her attention. Micah stepped closer to the bed, on the opposite side of Andrew. She didn't recognize the bedroom.

"Where am I?" she croaked, her throat raw. "What's going on?" *Why on earth am I in Andrew's arms like this?*

She half expected Andrew to bolt, like he usually did, but he didn't. Instead, he moved slowly, deliberately, removing one hand, watching her face intently as he did. She stared back at him. *He's been healing me.*

When he cocked his head to the side, as if trying to decide if he could take his other hand back too, she said, "I'm okay, really. The pain's gone."

He removed his other hand and sat up. She watched him rub his wrists and then stretch his arms above his head. His back popped loudly.

"We're at the Genaros', Eden," Micah answered instead of Andrew, who still didn't hop up from the bed and run from the room. In fact, she was shocked when he reached over to touch her again.

She inhaled, and his face flushed. "Sorry, I just wanted to check on you. Make sure you're okay."

"Oh. Yeah, no, go ahead." She knew her face burned. Having Micah right next to her as her ex-boyfriend gently prodded along her stomach and back with his fingers was not exactly comfortable. Then she noticed how it really felt, his touch. Everywhere he pushed, a coolness seeped into her burning skin. He began to pull back, but she grabbed his hand, not letting him move it.

"No, wait, it helps." She sighed. She inhaled deeply, feeling like she hadn't had a proper breath in days. Her lungs felt hungry for it.

"You passed out on the plane," Micah continued. *He's either pretending he doesn't mind Andrew so near, or I'm in worse shape than I thought.* Even with the strain in his voice, she couldn't decide which way he was feeling. "We couldn't revive you, but as long as Andrew held onto you, you kept breathing. We got you here and—"

"I wasn't breathing?" she whispered.

Andrew shook his head and Micah looked away, refusing to meet her gaze. *He thinks bringing me here was a mistake. He's mad at himself.* She'd have to find a quiet moment to tell him it wasn't his fault.

"Thank you," she said instead to Andrew. "How long have I been out? You seem pretty stiff."

Andrew rubbed one hand against his forehead. She felt bad she still clutched his other hand to her. Did healing wipe him out? Was she putting a strain on him right now?

She wanted to ask him, but Micah abruptly left the room, and her eyes automatically followed him out. *Darn. I need to tell Micah I'm okay now. He shouldn't feel bad about all this.*

She tore her gaze away from the now-empty doorway and caught Andrew gazing down at her. Since he sat close enough to touch her, she felt she had no choice but to glance up and meet his gaze.

"Gabriel and Daniel brought us to the Genaros' last night. It was pretty late. With the time difference, I really have no clue what time it is. Caterina said dinner's almost ready if that helps."

She stared at him. "I've been unconscious since last night? A whole day?"

"Technically half a day, so don't feel too bad," he said, giving her a smile.

"That's never happened before. I... but you stopped the pain! Your touch helped me this time!" She didn't want to acknowledge the fact she was getting worse.

"Eden, I can only slow it a bit. This attack you had was intense. It took everything I had to just get you breathing again."

"Oh." She felt at a loss for words. What must that have been like for all her friends to see? *For Micah to see?* "You said attack. Do you think Semjaza is attacking me with the pain?"

"Yeah, that's how it feels to me."

She nodded. "Me too. Almost like Semjaza is literally there, pulling me apart with his power. I think you chased him off." Eden couldn't help herself. She pulled him down closer and wrapped her arms around him. "Thank you, Andrew."

He leaned down to hug her back. "I'll do anything for you, Eden. You know that." His tone sounded raw.

Oh gosh! What am I doing? She felt terrible inside. He pulled back quickly, his face switching to a blank mask immediately.

"Sorry, I shouldn't have done that. I just really appreciate what you've done for me. You've saved my life, *again*."

"You, of all people, don't have to apologize for hugging someone. Who knows, maybe you just amped up my ability to heal."

His grin was contagious, and she beamed back at him. "You never know."

He glanced away, staring across the room at nothing. "Eden, I know about you and Micah." He met her gaze. "I know you're stressing yourself right now, trying to figure out how to say it to me, so I'll just say it. You don't need to worry about telling me. You need to focus on getting better. And I'm really fine with you and Micah being together. Really, I am."

"Oh... did Micah tell you? While I was unconscious?"

"No, he didn't. I just knew. I guess I've known for a while. I suspected when Micah almost died at the well. The way you acted and looked at him."

"Andrew, I'm so sorry. I should've just been honest with you from the beginning. I wasn't trying to hide it... I just..."

"Didn't want to hurt me? Eden, there will probably always be a part of my heart that... well... cares for you. But I want you to believe me when I tell you I'm over us. I'm good. I want you to be happy."

"Really?" she asked, not sure if she believed him.

"Really. You just concentrate on getting better. Micah's a good guy; I know he'll take care of you. I guess, if I'm going to be replaced by someone, at least you picked a good one."

"Andrew," she began, but Willow's voice cut her off.

"Eden! You're okay!"

The room rapidly filled with people. Everyone except Micah. She needed him. Where was he? She began to sit up and everyone protested, including Andrew. He pushed her back down.

"Just rest, you're still not a hundred percent, remember?" He glanced at his hand still pressed against her stomach. "You can't hide it from me."

"Or me," Willow said firmly, plopping down on the bed next to her. "I can't tell you what a relief it is to see your color back."

There's that color thing again. What do I do—turn chalk white?

Caitlyn had come near too, standing next to Willow. "Eden, you scared us all half to death. How are you feeling?"

"I'm good, guys. Really I am. Sorry I passed out."

"Oh, you more than passed out. You had a near-death experience, my dear," Willow stated matter-of-factly.

"Willow," Micah said as he entered the room. "Don't scare her to death."

Eden knew her friends loved her but seeing the pain in Micah's expression, she wanted desperately to have a moment alone with him. To tell him to stop blaming himself.

"Sorry, I wasn't trying to," Willow replied. "Andrew has been holding you non-stop. Caitlyn has been applying medicine Caterina put together. She did that almost the entire night. That's when your fever broke."

"Thank you," Eden said. "Thank you, everyone. I feel much better now."

Caitlyn flushed. "Nothing I did. Caterina made the medicine."

Eden didn't miss the way Micah stared at Caitlyn. Everyone knew her ability was faith. *Maybe she willed my fever to break.* Either way, Eden was happy to be alive and pain free. In fact, she felt wonderful.

She glanced at Andrew. "I really want to sit up now, may I?"

Andrew hitched his lips to the side, and then sighed. "Oh, okay, might be good for you. You do look a lot better."

Micah and Andrew reached over to help her up at the same time. They awkwardly gestured for the other to do it, so she grabbed both of their hands, forcing them to focus on her and not each other.

"Aw. That's better," she said, smiling at everyone now that she was upright.

Micah still stood near. He gazed down at her, giving her a reassuring smile. "Eden, do you think you feel up to using your gift?"

She nodded. "Yes, of course. Did Willow already find the one?"

Damon left the room as Willow beamed with pride. "Yep. Trent and I went yesterday. It was so much fun, wasn't it, Trent?"

Trent began grumbling something under his breath. Eden caught a few phrases like, "Crazy girl... almost got us killed."

Eden wanted to ask what had happened, but Damon had re-entered the room followed by a stranger. Though older in years, the man was tall with surprisingly good posture. He strode in, his white hair and wrinkled face the only indicators of age. His frame seemed agile and quick. The older couple who shuffled in after him contrasted sharply in both height and build. *That must be Fredo and Caterina.* She'd wanted to meet them for so long. She supposed now wasn't the time for proper introductions. This was obviously the man Micah had brought her to see.

Time to hug.

Chapter Twenty

Damon watched Armando approach Eden while she moved to get up.
Micah told her not to worry about it, to which she shook her head.
"Micah, I'm fine really."

She seemed intent on standing, so Micah helped her to her feet.

She smiled. "See, I feel great." To Armando, she said, "Hi, I'm Eden."

"It's a pleasure, truly. I'm Armando."

Her smile deepened. "What a lovely name."

"It means of high rank, or ranking," Trent said off-handedly.

Damon considered what Trent said for moment. His mom had always
told him names had meaning. She'd even gone as far to say she picked his
name with that in mind. *Constant.* For years he'd thought, *great, it means
I'm constantly in trouble, I'm constantly late, or I'm constantly the last
chosen… Perhaps constant means something more now.* Only question
was—what? He thought his amazing gift was enough. What more did the
earth want of him?

Eden stepping over to Armando caught his attention. The embrace was
quick, with everyone quietly watching. Damon scratched his sideburn and
glanced away, meeting Willow's gaze. Something about the way she peered
back at him completely unhinged him. He fought the temptation to stare at
the floor, the walls, the ceiling, anywhere but those bright blue eyes framed
in black lashes. He didn't waver; their eyes locked. He let her rake through
him, knowing her sharp senses took in everything. *She sees me—the real me.*

I have to know who I am, he thought.

Willow nodded back at him, and then mouthed, "Yes, you do."

Tell me then. You know. I know you do.

She glanced at Micah, and then Eden. A smile curled on her lips. Silently she mouthed, "Come with me."

Damon stepped forward, but his way was blocked by Eden. Her big, blue eyes squinted up at him as one of her hands slowly reached out. Micah stood next to her, his arm wrapped around her side.

Damon figured he was merely in her way and moved over. "Sorry."

"Damon?" she said softly, her brows scrunched.

"Yeah?" he asked, confused why she was staring at him like that. Then she fell forward, her arms wrapping around him. He grabbed on to her, convinced she had lost her balance. At her touch, a feeling shot through him, a rush of power coursing through his veins, speeding his heart and making his ears buzz. He didn't let go, but he did step back a bit. His eyes met Eden's.

"What... what was that?" he asked, breathless.

Eden stepped back too, her face flushed.

"That, my friend, was you—the real you," Micah replied.

"I don't understand," Damon said, still reeling from what he'd felt. His spine tingled, goose bumps shooting across his arms. A hand landed on his arm, and he glanced over.

"Come with me," Willow repeated.

He didn't argue, just followed her from the room, her black hair bouncing down her back with her steps. He didn't say anything; he didn't want to. Everything had shifted. The world had shifted. What had Eden done? He could still hear the voices, the constant thrum of nature and the elements speaking to him. *So I didn't lose my gift... but I'm what now? I feel different.*

Willow insisted on going for a drive. She even convinced Fredo she was a safe driver before leaving. As he handed her the keys, Trent grunted behind them. Damon wasn't worried; he could handle Willow's driving. As the city gave way to country and fences began lining the roads instead of bustling cafes, Damon exhaled.

"You need to let go, stop holding on so tight to your reality. See it... I know you do."

Damon glanced over at Willow, ready to argue, but then he stopped. He wasn't seeing Willow, at least not the girl in jeans and ponytail. It was Willow, but she was different. She was in a white dress. *Her hair is the same. And those eyes… I know her eyes.* His chest stirred. A deep yearning filling him. Like nothing he'd felt before.

He reached over and stroked her cheek. She inhaled sharply. "Do you remember?"

His hand jerked back. "Sorry, no… I don't think so… Did we know each other… like before?"

She smiled at him, her eyes lingering a bit too long on him, not noticing how she had drifted into the oncoming traffic lane. *And there's a car coming!* "Willow, the road," he blurted. *Maybe I'll have to call down my powers to keep us safe after all.*

That thought stopped him. *My powers? I don't have power. I speak the languages the Captain allows me to.* His fingers tingled in his lap. He stared at his hands.

"You feel it, don't you?" Willow said. She pulled off the main highway. The car now bumped along a country dirt road. She let the car roll to a stop on the side, pulling into some grass.

"Let's go for a walk," she said, shutting off the car.

Good idea. Less chance for crashing. He hopped out. Besides, fresh air would do him good. The field in front of them looked inviting. The grass swayed, long and unkempt.

Willow fell in beside him. Her gait was familiar in a déjà vu way. He peered around. An old-looking cottage dotted a hill, fences, a few small barns, and a long, green meadow. *I've never been here before.*

It wasn't the place; it was Willow. He stopped walking and turned to face her. Her long ponytail stirred in the breeze, and her face was bathed in a warm, orange light. The sun was setting, making the scenery gold and magical.

The breeze whispered, "Remember, remember your true name."

His vision blurred, the white dress flashing before his mind's eye. Willow's eyes were bright, her hair covering her shoulders.

What am I—Micah now? Having visions? He shook his head.

"No, they aren't visions. They're memories," Willow said.

She held her hand out to him. He hesitated, and she wrapped her fingers into his. The power shot through him again, like it had with Eden.

He gasped and stared at Willow. "What did Eden do to me?"

Willow grinned. "She did what she does best. She awakened you."

"I don't understand; she already did that before."

"You needed a little more prodding. Micah hoped it would come on your own, but with how bad Eden is, he couldn't afford to wait anymore. He was going to ask her to try it, hug you one more time, but apparently, she sensed the need and did it all on her own."

"Great, I feel like an idiot now, because I still don't know who I am," Damon grumbled. "And I need to; we can't wait to face the Watchers on my account. I can't let Micah or Eden down."

Willow's fingers tightened around his. "Don't worry; you won't. I knew there was something different about you, even in the beginning when I could hardly use my gift. You walked out on to Micah's deck, and you just shined."

He cocked an eyebrow at her. "Shined?"

She slapped his arm. "Stop! I know it sounds silly, but it's true! Everyone looked beautiful to me at this point—Micah, Eden, Trent—but then you came and I was in awe. I knew you were special, not just gifted."

Damon decided to continue walking as Willow spoke. Suddenly, it felt natural to have her hand in his. The hill was gradual and the slope easy to stroll down.

"More than just gifted?" he repeated. "You obviously know who I am. When did you figure it all out?" Maybe her response would give a clue.

She grinned. With her free hand, she gripped his arm. "The first time I saw Gabriel, he shined in the same way. There was something about you two. I didn't understand what it was until we were inside the temple. Then it became all too clear."

She pulled him to a stop, her eyes peering up into his.

She's waiting for me to be like aha... Too bad I'm going to disappoint her. Still, her earnestness made him pause and think. *I'm like Gabriel somehow? Can't imagine what I have in common with a Holy.*

The power surged through his core, shot through his chest, and down his arms. His hands burned with a fire he didn't recognize. It wasn't the earth speaking. It wasn't a language. It was power. Raw power.

Power the Captain gave me.

Flashes of images shot through his mind, causing him to almost stumble as they walked. He stopped moving, his eyes taking it all in.

Two men... no, they were more than men—they were angels—standing near Damon. Each one orchestrated something with their hands. Colored lights blasted through the darkness shrouding them. Both angels stood with feet apart, shoulders erect, like soldiers ready for battle.

"The Arc has been prepared. Noah is ready," Damon heard himself say to the other two. Only his voice was familiar to himself. He glanced down to see he wore the same strange robes these angels wore. He was seeing himself in another time, maybe even another dimension.

One of the angels turned to face him. His black hair and hazel eyes were somehow familiar. "We move forward then," he said in a rich voice. Then he turned to the other angel, whose brown-black hair and bright blue eyes filled Damon with the same feeling of familiarity.

"Raphael," the hazel-eyed angel said, "bind Azazel hand and foot, as the Captain instructed. Cast him in the darkness of the desert, where jagged rocks will forever block his way and power. I will go to their leader, Semjaza, and the other fallen ones, and bind them for seventy generations in the deepest valleys of the earth, until their day of judgment."

Then those hazel eyes turned back to Damon. "Instruct Enoch in all these things. He must be prepared for what is to come. The Great Flood.

And the destroying of the Watchers' posterity—the giants who roam the earth, filling it with blood and unrighteousness."

Damon felt himself nod. "Yes, Michael," he heard himself say. Damon's mind reeled. This angel with the hazel eyes was Michael, the archangel! His memory continued with him saying, "Feels strange that Gabriel is not here with us now. He did not know me, as I know him, when I instructed him."

Michael and Raphael murmured their agreement, and then Michael said, "We all take our turn walking this earth as mortals. Mine is finished, Gabriel's is now, yours, my dear friend, is yet to come."

"Damon," Willow called, but it sounded worlds away.

Damon's heart raced, the tingling spreading over his entire body. The vision, the memory, was fading, but he'd seen enough. *I was there.*

He opened his eyes, meeting Willow's wide eyes. Had she just seen all that too? Was her gift that good?

Damon reeled at what he'd seen. From what he'd learned from studying with Micah, God left four Holies in charge of the four cardinal points—the north, the east, the south, and the west. They stood as sentinels, holding back the four winds, which would come forth from the four corners of the earth when the sixth seal was broken.

Gabriel. Michael. Raphael. *And Uriel.*

"I hold back the Northern wind," Damon said at last, the words shaking his frame. "I know now who I am. Who I've always been. I'm Uriel."

Chapter Twenty-one

Willow's grip tightened on his arm. "You finally see!" she gushed. Her bright eyes drew closer as she leaned into him. "Micah hoped your being in the Northern lands, about to start the Northern City, would help you."

If it weren't for the fact that his sense of his entire existence just shifted once again, he'd be more concerned about how near she was, how she didn't seem to mind invading his personal space.

"I don't remember everything, but I saw enough. Micah told me two Holies did the binding, and two Holies would do the un-binding. I just never dreamed I was one of them. Now it all makes sense. Gabriel and I are the two Holies."

Everything around him rejoiced, the earth, the air, the flowing grass. He glanced around, overwhelmed by the welcome he was getting. *"Finally, finally, he knows!"*

With one arm trapped by Willow's embrace, he rubbed his free hand across his forehead. He had so many questions since the slice of history he'd just witnessed opened up a whole new can of worms for him. Gabriel wasn't with them as a Holy angel; he'd been a man at that time. *Wonder what he was doing? Didn't he say his job had been to destroy the giants? Weird Gabriel didn't know he was once a Holy angel. Wonder if Michael did when he walked the earth. Didn't he say he'd already lived his mortal life? And what about Raphael? Has he lived his life already?* Thinking of Raphael, his mind moved in a whole new direction. *Wonder who he was or is. I wonder who Michael and Gabriel were.*

"Wonder who we all were," Willow commented, as if he'd spoken all his thoughts aloud.

Damon jumped a bit. "Sorry. I should just say what I'm thinking. You are too good at your gift not to."

"I don't mind. Helps me practice."

"I don't think you need practice."

"Sure I do. You and Micah are the easiest by far. But lately, I'm having a hard time getting a beat on Caitlyn. So practice is good for me."

"Do you actually hear my thoughts, or just get a feel for them?" Damon asked, curious and terrified by her gift at the same time. *How much does she see? Can she see how much I care for her?*

"Like I said, you and Micah are pretty clear. I almost can sense your very words. It's like I hear them in my head. Others like Andrew, it's more a hunch that I know where his mind's directed. Not so much actual words. Caitlyn… well, I'm sort of hitting a wall there. Just left to normal perception on her."

"Wonder why."

She shrugged. "I don't know."

"Do you see the past too? Like who you were before?"

"I don't remember the war in heaven, if that's what you are asking," she said with a wink. "But I know we were all there."

"How do you know, since you don't remember?"

"I sense it. I think we're *all* more than we think we are."

Remembering the flashes he'd had of Willow wearing a flowing, white dress, he nodded. "I think you're right. I remember you, a bit, from before."

"You do?"

"Yeah." He rubbed the back of his neck and glanced down, feeling the blood rush to his face. He felt like his mind got muddled, his tongue tied, and his desire to flee almost took over whenever he got near Willow. Suddenly, he was painfully aware of how close she was to him.

She grinned up at him. "What was I doing?"

He forced himself to make eye contact.

"Tell me," she urged. "I think it's so amazing you see things now."

"I didn't see much. You were wearing a white dress."

She cocked an eyebrow at him. "White dress, huh?"

He knew his face was red. He stammered to speak.

"You know I'd say yes, if you asked me, right?" she interrupted whatever he'd been about to say.

Now his mouth fell open, speechless. He could only stare. He hadn't even asked her on a date, let alone kissed her, and she was talking marriage? She couldn't possibly mean that, could she? She only smiled back up at him, her eyes wide.

She's waiting for me to make some kind of move. Why am I fighting this? He felt the burning inside, the insane excitement Willow elicited every time he was near her. He felt like it was a dangerous fire; he was scared to death to touch.

I've never felt like this before, he wanted to say, and then knowing she sensed his thoughts, he let them flow. It was easier than speaking for him. *I've never liked a girl like you or had someone like you even remotely interested in me.* He hadn't kissed a lot of girls. In fact, there'd only been one other girl beside her, but he hardly thought it counted. It had been nothing like this. The girl had been high on drugs, grabbed Damon, and laid one on him. Completely sober and repulsed by her nasty taste, he'd shoved the girl away. After that, Damon had decided he'd rather be a true loner than associate with the druggies.

What if I disappoint you? What if I'm not what you think I am? He let his thoughts be completely honest.

Willow's bounding confidence faltered for a split second, and she let out a small, nervous laugh. His insides cringed with self-doubt. *Perhaps she is worried too.*

"Damon," she said, reaching up to touch his face with her soft fingers. "I'm the one who is worried. You can have any girl you want. I'm the lucky one here. I'm in awe of you."

"You mean what I was before—Uriel and all that."

"I mean you, Damon, the guy who'd take a bullet for Micah, who follows him with a devotion I can only admire. The one guy who has my heart," she glanced down, her eyelashes fluttering closed, and whispered, "if he wants it."

I more than want you. His hands wrapped around the base of her neck, pulling her close. His lips landed across hers. The desire he felt for her boiled within. She tasted delicious. He pressed his mouth harder on hers, wanting more. She melted into his arms. He wasn't sure where he ended and she began. She seemed to sense his every move, moving with him. Her arms wrapped around his waist, her stomach pressed against his. He lifted her off the ground, holding her up as he kissed her. He'd never felt like this before, and he felt desperate to have more of her. Nothing else mattered to him but her; it was the strangest surrender he'd ever felt.

I'd do anything for you. I'd pull heaven down if you asked me. There was nothing he could hide from her now.

Something tugged at him—whispering voices. He ignored them. He didn't care what the insects were doing; he didn't want to know what words drifted in the breeze. The voices grew persistent. The whispers turned to chanting. *"They are coming! They are coming! Get away!"*

He rocked back, pulling away from Willow abruptly. She stumbled forward with a look of surprise. Then her eyes darted around, honing on to something to their left.

"Damon, something's coming... fast!"

He grabbed Willow's hand. "I know, come on!"

They sprinted through the grass, back up the small hill they'd come down. The car wasn't far away, but it didn't matter, what approached was far too fast to outrun. They heard the howl from behind, like a pack of wolves was on their heels.

Damon whirled around to face their enemy, expecting to see black demons. Willow screamed as a gigantic, wolf-like creature collided right into them, slamming them to the ground with its enormous paws. Gasping in shock, Damon shouted out a stream of commands as his arms fumbled to secure Willow's hand or arm. As soon as his fingers got a grip on her, he pulled her to him, and shoved her body beneath his own, cradling her protectively on the ground.

The creature tore at Damon's back with its razor-sharp claws only once before his previous commands took effect. With little to work with, the grass became hard, pointy missiles, covering the beast's hide in deathly jabs.

The creature yelped. Something hit the beast at full speed, the impact pushing the weight of the animal down hard on them temporarily, and then it rolled off to the side. Damon pushed it off them all the way; the fence post he'd shot at it was sticking up through its rib cage like a large spear. Damon didn't wait around to see if there were more coming. He knew there were. The earth cried for them to move, and he obeyed. He hoisted Willow into his arms like she weighed nothing and bolted back up the hill. He wasn't sure if it was merely adrenaline, or his power, giving him the extra strength and speed.

The boisterous howling from behind sent dread trickling through him. They wouldn't make it to the car in time. There were too many coming, and they couldn't outrun them. Even with the grass and fence, he wasn't sure he'd kill them all fast enough. The thought of anything happening to Willow was unacceptable.

Think, think….

He stopped running and turned to face the monsters head on. Sweat dripped into his eyes. There were probably thirty of them.

The earth hissed, *"Bury them."*

Damon understood immediately. His words rushed out, telling the earth to do just as it wished. Immediately, the ground before them collapsed, a sinkhole forming. The demonic wolf pack tumbled, falling into the sudden chasm. Some creatures tried to stop in time to keep from falling. Damon commanded the earth to sink deeper. The howling, shrieking beasts were a tangle of fur, fangs, and claws as each one fell off the cliff.

Then, in a flash, the earth came together, swallowing up the evil beasts. Silence greeted them. The only evidence of what had been there was the patch of dirt breaking up the green meadow, like a ragged scar from sudden surgery. Damon surveyed the land, satisfied they'd gotten them all. He refused to put Willow down until she was inside the car.

Her body was shaking as he fastened her seatbelt. He shut her door and climbed in next to her.

She glanced over, her face pale. "What were those things?"

"I don't know. Whatever they were, they were made from the devil himself. Are you okay?"

"I'm fine... but you're bleeding. Your poor back!" Willow fumbled with the glove box and retrieved some napkins.

"Nothing Andrew can't fix," he said, appreciating her best efforts to cover his back with the tissue. Even if he could be healed, that didn't change the fact they didn't want to get blood on Fredo and Caterina's car. He navigated the roads, trying to remember the way Willow had taken them. "We need to get back and warn the others. They could be in danger."

"Damon," Willow said softly as she sat back into her seat, "I don't think that was a random attack."

"What do you mean?"

She bit her lip. "You'd just proclaimed out loud who you really are, one of the four holy angels. I'm pretty sure you're right. Those monsters weren't from the Watchers. They *were* fashioned by the devil himself."

Chapter Twenty-two

"Just like Legion, you know the demon that was cast out and begged to be in the pigs?" Trent exclaimed, his eyes about ready to explode in his head. "The pigs ran off the cliff, because demons are dumb."

Micah nodded, eyeing Damon, wondering if his little getaway with Willow for the past hour had helped him remember or if they'd simply been attacked by demon-wolves. That was all they told everyone when they had shown up five minutes ago. Trent had immediately spouted off that the Italian Gray wolves never got that large, which led him to the conclusion the devil had made them, just like the pigs in the New Testament. Andrew had jumped up to heal Damon.

"You get way too excited about this stuff, Trent," Andrew muttered. "Demonic wolves don't put a smile on my face." Andrew lifted his hands off Damon's bare back and said, "There, that ought to do it."

Damon threw a new shirt on. "Thanks, Andrew."

"Sure, don't mention it," Andrew replied. "Figure I'll always want you on my side in a fight."

"I just don't think it's a coincidence that you decided to bury them in the earth and throw them down a cliff, just like the pigs," Trent continued, the goofy smile Andrew had alluded to still plastered on his face.

"You know," Micah said, "I think I agree with Andrew. You seem almost jealous that you missed out on this one, Trent."

"Well, maybe I am," Trent countered. "I mean, any fight with Damon is pretty sweet to watch. As long as I'm just watching, you know, like from the car or something."

"We're about to face fallen angels. You're welcome to join us," Damon said with a laugh that completely shocked Micah. Even Willow glanced over at him with a look of surprise.

"Nah, not interested in the Watchers. I don't trust them," Trent said.

"And you trust *demons*?" Caitlyn asked incredulously.

"Not so much trust them, but like I said, they're dumb. Predictable. All fangs and claws. The Watchers are wicked smart and conniving."

Thinking of the fallen ones, Micah's mood sobered. Eden had fallen victim to the very trickery Trent alluded to.

"You're right about that, Trent, and it's time we get moving." Micah glanced at Damon. "You ready?"

Damon nodded his head. "Yeah, I know now."

Somehow hearing Damon say that made the truth of it sink in for Micah. Quiet and unassuming Damon was Uriel. The passage he'd first read here in Rome, in this very apartment, had been about Uriel and the fire. *Incredible*.

"Good," Micah said. "Eden, are you feeling up for some traveling? It's time to get you back to Illinois. Caitlyn will go with you and open the last chamber." Micah paused only long enough to see Eden nod. He needed to give the instructions, or he feared he'd weaken in his resolve if he didn't get it all out now. "Then Caitlyn, you will come back and rendezvous with Willow and Andrew. They'll be tracking down where the Northern city will be built. Armando is ready to be the architect, but Willow feels the city isn't in Rome. Or maybe even Italy, right Willow?"

Willow shook her head. "No, it's not to be here. I'm still figuring out where, Micah. So Andrew and I might be driving for a bit."

"How will I know where to meet you?" Caitlyn asked.

"You're traveling by angel," Micah replied. "Makes it a bit easier than booking flights."

"Oh, okay," Caitlyn said. Was it his imagination, or did she pale? Something nagged at Micah about Caitlyn, but everything was happening too fast for him to stop and ask what it was. All he could focus on was getting

Eden to safety. He feared another attack from Semjaza might prove fatal. He pushed the feeling away. Caitlyn wasn't in danger right now, Eden was.

Besides, she'll be with Willow soon, and I'm sure she will sense it and help her out. I'm lousy at that sort of thing anyway.

"Trent will continue to instruct Armando here about the city plans, and then he will go back to the temple with you, Eden. So you won't be alone for long. Damon, Gabriel, and I will be visiting Armaros."

Micah didn't miss the way Eden's eyes widened with his last statement. She didn't say anything; she didn't need to. He knew she was worried. Not because she feared they'd fail at convincing Armaros to help them, and her life would still hang in the balance, but because she didn't want anything to happen to Micah or Damon in the process. *That's my girl, always worried about everyone else but herself.*

Micah moved to stand closer to her. "Everyone feel good about the plan?"

Several nods and murmured agreements. "Alright," Micah said loudly. "Gabriel and Alaina, are you ready?"

Both angels appeared. Gabriel stood right next to Eden, his brows furrowed as he looked her over. He scooped her up in his arms. "Close your eyes and rest, Eden. It won't take long to get there."

She smiled at Gabriel, and then her eyes sought out Micah's. "Promise you'll be careful." Her words were strained, her eyes wet.

"I've got Damon with me. He doesn't lose in fights, remember?" He reached over and brushed her hair back with his fingers. "I'll see you real soon. Promise."

She nodded, her eyes not leaving him, and then they disappeared from view.

"You don't have to carry me do you?" Caitlyn asked Alaina.

She placed her hand on Caitlyn's shoulder. "This is enough if you are comfortable."

Andrew stepped over and squeezed her other shoulder. "Caitlyn, you've got this."

Caitlyn met Andrew's gaze, and then nodded to Alaina. "Okay, I'm good."

They too disappeared, leaving Micah feeling strangely hollow. *Eden's going to be fine,* he tried to reassure himself.

Willow slapped Andrew's arm playfully. "Ready to hit the road, Drewster?"

Andrew jumped, staring at her. "I guess. From what I hear, you're a terrible driver though, so I get the keys."

"Ahh, I don't think so. I know the way, remember?" she countered.

"You can just tell me where to turn," Andrew said, not backing down.

Damon stepped forward, and Micah almost laughed to see how Andrew cowed. *Like he's worried Damon's going to take Willow's side.*

Instead, Damon smiled at Willow. "I think you should let Andrew drive. When you are using your gift, you sort of block out everything, including oncoming traffic."

Trent chuckled. "I tried to warn you, man. She's a nut ball behind the wheel."

"Hey, I resent that, Trent," Willow said with a grin, then her smile turned mischievous as she glanced at Damon, "Besides, even you, Damon, get distracted by *other* things too."

The way Damon flushed, Micah had a hunch being chased by wolves hadn't been their only excitement today.

Chapter Twenty-three

E den gazed over the cornfields as they flew. Gabriel had already told her they wouldn't be stopping to visit with Vern. He wanted to get her inside the temple right away. When they'd arrived at the farm, Gabriel had broken through whatever barrier lay between the world of angels and the world of men. Whether it was an actual physical divide that separated the world of spirits from view, Eden didn't know, but she had seen enough of the other side to never doubt in the reality of it. She loved being near Gabriel. She treasured every moment he held her in his arms. *Especially since I know he's leaving.*

The ache that filled her stole her breath, squeezing her chest. She didn't want him to go. She understood why he needed to. He wasn't just any angel. He was a Holy. One of the chosen four.

But he's my guardian... my best friend. Her heart didn't care that he was one of the most powerful angels next to the Captain. All she knew was she could hardly go a day without knowing he was right there next to her. The real terror about being in the temple was not the stone walls, or being underground. *It's being there without Gabriel.*

She felt too selfish to voice this though as he landed on the ground, still cradling her in his arms. He peered down at her.

"How are you feeling?" he asked, his eyes clouded with worry.

"I'm completely pain free. No more attacks," she said, releasing his neck and making moves to get down.

He shook his head. "No, I'm carrying you down."

She cocked her head to the side. "What happened to the 'come on, Eden, you're slowing everyone down'?" She hoped her referring to the last time they'd been down here would lighten the mood a bit. Climbing down the slippery well then, she'd wanted nothing more than for Gabriel to carry her. He had basically told her to be careful and hurry up.

He grunted. "We're not going down the well this time, now that it's full. We'll go through that back way. The entrance isn't far." He glanced down at her as he walked. "I can't risk you tripping and falling. You're way too fragile these days."

She wasn't sure if he was joking or not, but she chose to smile. "You have so little faith in me," she said, slapping his arm. "Last I checked, I could still walk. Then again, nobody has let me try since getting to Rome, now that I think about it."

Gabriel chuckled. "You can still walk. I don't know why you are giving me a hard time. Last time, you cried for me to carry you. This time, you're begging for me to let you down. Mortals are so fickle."

Even with his teasing, her heart squeezed again. *I can't do this without you,* she wanted to say. She leaned her head against his shoulder. "You're right, Gabriel. I'll stop fighting you."

Clearly, he hadn't expected her reaction because she felt him glance down at her, and then he remained quiet as he trudged through the field. They were almost to the entrance, a large, rock-like boulder leaning against a sloping hill. Eden recognized where they were, although now the grass grew long and green. This was where they'd come up out of the ground carrying the stone tablets.

Caitlyn and Alaina appeared right as they reached it.

"Is this what I have to open?" Caitlyn asked.

Eden expected him to set her down now, but he didn't. Instead, he flicked his hand at the boulder.

"No," he said, his voice rich and full against Eden's body. The boulder rolled easily to the side. "The sealed entrance is within."

Without another word, he climbed into the hole, carting her along with him. It felt surreal to be back in the long, brick-lined tunnel. Last time she'd been carrying the ancient stones with Enoch's blueprints on them. Her arms had ached, sweat had clung to every inch of her, and Gabriel had been near enough to help shoulder her burden. This time, with each step echoing down the chamber, she felt his grip on her body tighten. She couldn't help but wonder if he dreaded the moment they parted ways as much as she did.

The path didn't take as long this time. *Probably because I want it to last forever.* They reached the backside of the now-sealed-up sun motif.

Remembering how Damon had opened it up with his words, she asked, "Couldn't Damon just reopen this again?"

"The entire chamber has been sealed shut. Only one with true faith can open it," Gabriel answered, gazing intently at Caitlyn.

Caitlyn looked at the sun motif and traced her hand along its edges. She continued to stare at the marking, her back toward them.

"What if I can't do it?" Caitlyn murmured finally.

Eden felt Gabriel stiffen. She tapped his shoulder and said quietly, "Can you put me down?"

He hesitated before gently setting her down. In some ways, her feet hitting the ground was a welcome relief. It felt wonderful to stretch her muscles. To feel alive and normal again.

She stepped closer to Caitlyn. "What's wrong—does it feel different this time?" She hoped her friend would open up to her. Eden couldn't shake the feeling there was something unsaid between the two of them. It made no sense. Nothing had happened that she could think of, but Caitlyn seemed to tense up around her now. It saddened and confused her.

"No, it's... it's not that," Caitlyn said.

"Are you worried you can't do it? I know, last time, it took a minute... and Andrew." Eden stopped. *He'd helped her believe in herself. Crud, maybe we need Andrew here too. Funny thing, since Andrew sometimes needs Caitlyn around to heal too.*

She was about to voice her discovery, but Caitlyn's expression made her hold back. Caitlyn's eyes darted between hers, wide and... terrified.

"What is it? What's wrong?" Eden asked, feeling desperate to understand what her friend was going through.

"Caitlyn," Alaina said, her voice soothing. Caitlyn shifted her gaze, landing on her guardian.

Eden realized that since they'd appeared, Alaina had seemed a bit winded from the journey. Now Alaina's presence was bright, her light warm and glowing within.

"Remember your father," Alaina urged.

"But Andrew did that. How does that help me now?" Caitlyn asked.

"Why do you think your mom allowed Andrew in your home in the first place? Because you believed and had faith. It was your faith that allowed the miracle to happen that day. Don't forget that. Just think of your father."

Caitlyn seemed to consider Alaina's words and then turned to the sun motif again. Pressing both of her palms against the stone wall, Caitlyn shut her eyes.

Eden was near enough to hear her whisper, "This one's for you, Dad."

The effect was immediate. The stone jolted forward, splitting at the seams, and then collapsed inwardly, like an ancient hole punch. Air wafted out, the smell old, but not unpleasant. It was cool and earthy.

Eden smiled at Caitlyn. "I knew you could do it. Thank you."

She met her gaze and to Eden's surprise, said, "I'm sorry, I wish I was better at using my gift. Maybe if I was, you'd be fine and not need to come here."

"Caitlyn, how can you think any of this is your fault? We're up against evil, fallen angels. None of us feel capable of stopping them. Not even Andrew, who can heal, or Micah, who can see the future. We're all scared. No one expects you to be able to use your gift perfectly right this second." Eden hugged her friend. What she had sensed before she felt now. Something wasn't right with Caitlyn. Eden stepped back and searched her eyes. "The trick is to not stop trying. Promise you won't, okay?"

Caitlyn nodded, averting her eyes. "I promise." Then she glanced back. "Be careful, Eden. Promise you'll stay put until Micah gets this figured out."

Gabriel answered for her, "She's not going anywhere until it's safe."

Caitlyn didn't stay much longer. They hugged again, said their good-byes, and then Alaina whisked her away, into the angel realm to travel back to Italy... or wherever Willow felt the Northern City should be.

That left her and Gabriel. They stepped inside, memories flooding in. It felt strange to be here without her friends. She glanced at Gabriel; his eyes roamed the room as well. *At least he's with me... for now...*

"Gabriel." Her voice shook. She cleared her throat and tried again. "What do I do down here? Can Vern come see me? Do I have to stay in this very chamber the whole time or can I go up to other rooms? When do you think my parents can come?"

Gabriel met her gaze, and his eyebrows lifted. "Did Micah not explain anything to you?"

"I think he did. I mean, he may have wanted to tell me more, but I sort of blacked out and all. Why? What do you mean? Explain what?"

"Oh." This seemed to trouble Gabriel. His face was conflicted, like he was considering how to answer her.

"Okay, just go ahead and spill it. I can tell you're stressing right now."

"Eden..." He took a step closer, his hand reaching out to her, and then he stopped. "The reason you were brought here is because no one, not even me, can enter without Caitlyn's gift. The doors will seal again when I leave."

"Wait, what? Micah didn't say I'd be sealed shut in here. What about my parents... and Trent? Micah said Trent's coming. Does Caitlyn have to let them all in too? And what about food?" She glanced around, panic completely taking over. "I didn't think I was going to be literally locked in the chamber! I don't see a kitchen in here... or a bathroom!"

Gabriel closed the gap between them and took both of her arms in his. "Slow down. It's going to be okay. You're only going to be here a short while. We're going to Armaros now. We will make him comply, he will break his oath to Semjaza, and he will undo this enchantment. This chamber is much like the widow woman's barrel of meal and cruse of oil."

Eden stared at him. "I don't understand. What do you mean?"

"When Elijah came to the widow and asked for some bread, she'd been about to feed her starving son their last meal before they died, but because she chose to feed the prophet Elijah instead, her barrel of meal never emptied. She never wanted for food again. This chamber will provide for you, Eden. Just like the jewels Micah needed to fund the cities. Enoch has blessed this chamber to always provide for those within its walls."

She glanced around the room, and then met his piercing blue eyes.

"You won't be alone here, either." Gabriel's voice deepened. "Even though I'm not with you. You won't be alone."

She could only nod, the lump in her throat feeling like the size of Texas. She threw herself into his arms, half expecting the usual awkward pat on the back. He surprised her, embracing her with the same tenacity she felt.

Neither one of them spoke, he just held her. *I'm not going to be the one who lets go first. I can't.* Letting go of Gabriel wasn't the same as saying good-bye to Micah or her parents. It felt like half of her heart was being torn from her. She couldn't release him. He'd have to be the strong one today.

He finally moved back, his eyes wet. "I'll be back soon. You just rest. Get strong and healthy. Once we rid you of Semjaza's poison, you will be free to go back to high school. This is only temporary."

She wondered if he was telling himself the same message. Like everything would return to normal soon. *And I'll be your guardian angel again.*

"Not everyone gets to spend time in this hallowed room," he said, gesturing around with his hand. "You might want to look around while you're here. Enoch crafted this chamber himself. You may be surprised what you find. He was a very wise man."

"Sounds like you knew him personally." Swiping the tears from her eyes, she tried to be strong. She remembered how Gabriel had alluded to spending time in the temple as a kid, the last time they'd been in here.

"Yes, I did." He met her gaze. "Enoch was my great-grandfather."

Chapter Twenty-four

"Traveling by angel, as Micah put it, is sort of exhausting, isn't it?" Caitlyn asked after Alaina let go of her shoulder and they found themselves standing inside a bedroom, at what Caitlyn could only guess was some kind of inn or lodge. She would've thought motel-hotel, but it didn't exactly fit the mold. With two skinny beds, right next to each other, covered in simple blue blankets, the room was pretty bare. She peeked into the bathroom, relieved to see a shower, sink, mirror, and a normal toilet.

Alaina smiled, her usually bright light dimmer somehow. Micah had said angel-travel taxed the angel.

"It does take a bit out of me, but I'll be fine in a moment. Don't worry," Alaina answered.

Caitlyn nodded and sat on one of the beds. "Wonder where Willow and Andrew are. This is where we're supposed to meet, right?"

"This is the right place. I'm sure they will be here soon." Alaina flipped her long braid back over her shoulder. It seemed like such a normal, teenage thing to do, not angelic. "Caitlyn, I want you to know I heard you that day."

"What?"

"That day you were in your room and wanted to tell me something. You spoke to me, aloud. I was there, listening. I just thought you should know. You can talk to me anytime. I am probably more aware of what you are struggling with right now than you think." She smiled, her cheeks dimpling. "And I never judge."

"How do you know? I mean, I've never really said the words out loud to anyone."

Alaina's smile deepened. "You don't have to. I lived once like you, not that long ago either. I remember what love feels like. Well, enough anyway. Those memories are fading," her voice softened, "too quickly, but I see how you feel about—"

"No, wait. Don't say it," Caitlyn cut in. "I'm not supposed to feel this way."

Alaina's beautiful face twisted in confusion. "But why not? Love's a good thing. You should have love in your life. Why deny your feelings for him?"

"Because I think I used my gift to change fate for my own selfish desires." The words came out and with each syllable, Caitlyn felt both relief and dread. It was a burden she hadn't shared with anyone. Now she wanted it all off her chest. "I didn't know how I felt about him, I really didn't. We were just friends, and then I told Eden to break up with him, before I knew what my gift could do."

"So why is that a problem?"

"Because when Andrew and I were in the motel room right before the whole battle by the well and temple, Andrew had been trying to cheer me up because Dave broke up with me, and he started tickling me. We fell on the ground and there was this moment, when he just held me and we stared at each other... and I couldn't help but wish that he'd love me like he did Eden." She met Alaina's gaze. "That's when I knew I'd messed up. That I'd changed how things were supposed to go. I'd done it before I'd realized my true feelings or known what I could do with my thoughts. Subconsciously, I must have wished for the break up. I made it all happen with my gift. How can I trust myself now? Micah almost died because of me. Eden's injury... well, I just know it's my fault somehow."

Alaina held her hand up. "Caitlyn, you don't understand how these gifts work. That's not—"

The door banged open, and Andrew filled the doorway. "You're here!" he exclaimed, cutting off Alaina's words. He glanced over at the angel. "You're both here. Awesome!"

Willow came in after him. "Perfect timing, Caitlyn. We just paid for the rooms and we're going to order some food downstairs. Hungry?"

Caitlyn felt her face flame. She could only hope that her discussion with Alaina had not been overheard by Andrew. *Pretty sure there's no way I can hide it from Willow, though.*

Caitlyn was sad to see Alaina wordlessly disappear from view. She'd enjoyed opening up to her angel. It had soothed her inner turmoil, giving her a few minutes of peace. With her gone, the anxiety crept back in, settling over her heart.

"Yeah, I'm pretty hungry. Where are we anyway?" she asked.

"Prague. Don't ask," Andrew said, holding up his hand. "It's been the longest thirteen hours of my life. Willow's directions are—"

"Oh, stop complaining, Andrew. It's not like I'm a GPS. I can't help it if the feelings come suddenly. I told you I should drive."

"We would have ended up hitting a few fences if you had. You can't just turn whenever you want. It helps if there's a road to drive on," he said, plopping down next to Caitlyn. She wished she didn't crave his closeness so much. She had to resist the temptation of reaching over to touch him, even if it was just his arm.

"Ha, you almost put us in a pond, too, you know," Willow countered. "Anyway, we aren't actually in Prague anymore. We're south of there now, in Moravia. It's such a beautiful place, Caitlyn. Vineyards as far as the eye can see!"

"So we are in Czech Republic?" Caitlyn asked, hoping her geography was correct.

Andrew grinned in her direction. "Yep. I'm glad you're back."

Her heart fluttered. "Me too."

"So," he added, "you got Eden into the temple? She's safe now?"

Caitlyn swallowed. *Oh. That's why he's happy. I can report Eden's well-being. Just as well, if he were crazy for me, I'd feel terrible because I forced it.* "She's totally safe."

Caitlyn tried to take everything in; the restaurant downstairs felt as foreign and fascinating as if she'd stepped into JR Tolkien's Middle Earth. A long bar with wooden stools, several tables, and booths lined the walls. Everything screamed she'd just entered the Prancing Pony and Gandalf might show at any minute.

They got a booth in the corner. A small band, made up of two guitars and one accordion, played a lively tune. There was a pleasant hum of conversations filling the space.

Caitlyn sliced another piece of rye bread, stacked three different cheeses on top, and shoved it into her mouth. Even with all the cured meat, brown rice, and vegetables she'd eaten, she couldn't stop picking at the cheese selection sitting before them. She realized her error in calculating how much her mouth could hold, however, when a young woman approached their table. Trying to chew and swallow, Caitlyn noticed how the girl's eyes immediately fell on Andrew and didn't leave. It was hard to judge her age, with two long braids, a small apron that barely covered her short-shorts and tank top, and hardly any makeup, she could pass for twelve, if it weren't for the fact her body curved in just the right places. Caitlyn felt a twinge of jealousy to see how quickly Andrew's attention turned to the girl.

"Everything tasting fine? My name is Brita," she said, her words rich with an accent. "Do you like the cheeses?" Her eyes flicked in Caitlyn's direction, long enough for Caitlyn to finally swallow down her bite.

"Yes," Andrew replied. "Everything's great." He glanced around. "What happened to our waiter... what's his name... Vlad?"

"Yes, Vlad, he had a family emergency. I will take care of you rest of evening. More drinks? Are you having the house wine tonight?"

"No, thank you, Brita. Water's fine," Willow said as Andrew opened his mouth to speak. Brita nodded and left, probably to get more water. Willow faced Andrew. "Need I remind you that we are all underage?"

Caitlyn stared at Andrew. *Andrew doesn't drink. What's gotten into him?*

"I wasn't going to get any, geez, Willow. I can't help it if I thought it would be fun, though."

Willow frowned at him. Caitlyn wasn't sure why her heart felt so funny. Brita came back with water before she could place it. Was it just Andrew joking about drinking?

"Brita, you said Vlad had a family emergency? Is everything okay?" he asked.

Brita filled the glasses with more water. "Oh yes, don't worry. His mom fell ill a few days ago, and she was getting better, but tonight, the sickness returned." She stopped filling the glasses and smiled at Andrew. "You are very kind to be so concerned."

The way Andrew grinned back at the girl made Caitlyn want to puke. Brita stayed at their table too long for Caitlyn's liking, talking and laughing with Andrew. After about five minutes of them straight-up flirting, Caitlyn left. She didn't care if it was rude. She couldn't be around Andrew right now. She knew it wasn't fair to him. Logically, they were just friends, and he was free to flirt with whomever he wanted, but it still made her heart feel like a twisted-up pretzel.

I'm probably just tired. She went back to their room and changed into her pajamas, grateful that Willow had the foresight to bring her belongings along with them when they drove. With how fast she'd left to help Eden back into the temple, she hadn't even thought about her suitcase.

Caitlyn climbed into the narrow bed, not caring Willow would be sleeping right next to her, since the place mashed the two twins alongside one another. *Just glad Andrew has his own room.* Whether or not it was justified, she fell asleep furious with him.

Chapter Twenty-five

"Caitlyn, you up yet?" Willow asked.

Caitlyn stretched and yawned. "Yes, I think so. What time is it? Feels like three in the morning."

Willow stood next to the small bathroom, completely dressed and ready for the day. She smiled at Caitlyn. "It's not three. I think you still have angel jetlag."

"I think you're right," she agreed, sitting up. She didn't want to stand up just yet.

"Want to grab some breakfast with me? And then I was thinking we could go for a walk."

"Sure, just give me a sec to get dressed." Caitlyn stood, and then noticed Willow was still gazing in her direction. "What is it?" She knew better with Willow. Might as well ask what she was thinking.

Willow shrugged. "Nothing. Is everything okay with you?"

"I'm great," she replied, too fast to be believable. "Besides, don't you see all my thoughts and innards anyway?"

Willow chuckled. "Innards? You're not a turkey, Caitlyn."

Caitlyn cocked her head at her. "You don't know what I'm thinking? Like you do Micah, Andrew, and everyone else?"

"Interestingly enough, you're much harder to read right now. Not that that's a bad thing," she added quickly.

Caitlyn wasn't so sure it was a good thing either. "Oh. I'm fine, really. Don't worry about me."

"Caitlyn, I may not be able to discern your thoughts, but I can tell you're not fine. What's going on? You seemed pretty upset last night."

"I'd rather not talk about it, Willow. Can we just get going on finding where this city should be?"

Willow's lips twitched to the side. "Okay, just know you can tell me anything, anytime."

"Thanks," she said, and then her tone softened. "I appreciate it." If it weren't for the fact they had things to get done, she might have spilled her guts right then. Might be nice to confide in someone other than her guardian. It didn't take her long to get ready. They went to the room next door and knocked. There was no answer.

"He's probably still sleeping," Caitlyn offered, hoping that didn't mean he'd stayed out all night with Brita. She shook her head and walked toward the stairs, which led to the restaurant. She didn't want to think about that scenario.

The noise from below surprised her as she descended. It was more lively and loud than last night. *Guess Czech's are morning people.*

She heard Willow's small gasp as they entered the room. It was packed with people. Not all sitting at tables either. They seemed to be facing one direction, the opposite far end of the room. *Wonder what they're watching?* Willow and Caitlyn tried to navigate through a bit.

To the lady on her left, Caitlyn asked, "What's going on?"

The woman's eyes danced as she spoke, "*Léčitel je tady.*"

Several others around chanted the same word, "*Léčitel.*"

"What are they saying? What does that mean?" Caitlyn asked Willow.

"I don't know, but I have a hunch I know who they're talking about. Look over there." Willow pointed to the back, and Caitlyn strained to see what she gestured to.

The tall man in front of her shifted his position, and she got a peek. There, at a table, surrounded by many people, sat Andrew. He was holding a small baby in his arms, rocking the babe back and forth. Then he smiled up at who appeared to be the baby's mom.

Caitlyn could hardly hear Andrew's words, but it sounded like, "There, all better."

"Andrew's healing people," Willow said, confirming what Caitlyn had just witnessed.

"Wow, look at all them, lined up for their turn," Caitlyn said, taking in the whole room. Her gaze returned to Andrew. When he stared back at her, his grin widened. He motioned for them to come over.

Nobody in front of them budged. Andrew leaned over and said something to the girl next to him. Brita.

Brita stood up. "Each will have a turn. Please allow Andrew's friends to come here." And then she switched languages, probably repeating the same message, "*Každý bude mít řadu. Prosím dovolte Ondřeje přátelé přijít sem.*"

People turned and noticed Willow and Caitlyn for the first time, making a way for them to get through the crowded restaurant. Caitlyn noticed how Brita sat back down next to Andrew. *Did she just put her hand on his knee?*

She swallowed back the acid taste in her mouth. Either Andrew didn't notice Brita's advance, or they'd done more than that. *He probably kissed her last night*, Caitlyn decided.

"Isn't this incredible?" he asked, somewhat breathless, when they finally got to him.

"Yes, it's amazing," Willow said, smiling. "Have you been healing all night?"

Caitlyn noticed then Andrew still wore the same clothes as last night. His T-shirt looked a bit more rumpled, and his hair messy. *It always looks good messy.*

"Yeah, well, I asked Brita to tell Vlad to bring his family here, after the restaurant had closed."

Brita glanced over at Andrew, lowered her eyelashes, and smiled.

Oh my gosh, she's blushing. Just what did they do after closing time?

Andrew continued, "Vlad came with his mom and when I healed her, Brita went out and told more people to come and see what I'd done. And well... you see the room now. It's been filling up all night. Brita said people are showing up from hours away now. Guess word travels fast."

"Andrew, I'm so glad you're using your gift for good," Willow gushed, making Caitlyn cringe.

I'm a horrible person. Here I am getting ticked that he made out with Brita and the truth is that he's been healing others all night. Guilt-ridden, she couldn't bear to look in Andrew's direction. In her peripheral though, she sensed his gaze on her.

She forced herself to meet his emerald eyes. Her words of praise were drowned out by Brita, who had exclaimed, "They are calling him *Léčital;* it means the healer!"

Andrew must not have heard Caitlyn because his attention turned to Brita, and his face flushed. "I'm just happy I can help."

Brita flashed a smile and winked at him, right in front of them all. *I have a feeling Brita isn't only interested in the healing show.*

"Andrew, you look busy, and this restaurant is too full to order food. I think Caitlyn and I are going to go for a walk."

Andrew moved to stand up. Brita appeared quite alarmed. "Want me to come too?" he asked.

Caitlyn wanted to say, 'yes, come with us and leave this girl with her roaming hands!' but she knew it was purely selfish. Andrew was doing a lot of good here. People had traveled to see him, to be healed.

"Willow and I got this. Why don't you stay and keep healing? We'll be back soon," Caitlyn said instead.

Andrew's eyes sought hers. Was that hesitation she saw in them?

Then Brita's arm was snaking around Andrew's. "Come, there are many waiting, *Léčital.*"

"Okay," Andrew said, still holding Caitlyn's gaze. "But be careful. Don't go too far away."

Caitlyn grinned. "We'll be fine. We're walking. Not driving."

"Hey, I *am* right here, you know," Willow cut in. "Besides, I think we need to tell *you* to be careful more."

Caitlyn knew Willow was teasing Andrew. There was a pretty girl tugging on his arm after all, but Caitlyn couldn't stand the surprise in Andrew's expression, nor the way his face flamed. *Ugh... I'm out of here.*

She tore from the room without another word.

Willow was on her heels. "Whoa, Caitlyn, wait up."

Chapter Twenty-six

Micah glanced over at Damon as they got out of the car. "Are we ready for this?" he asked.

Damon stretched his arms out, a few joints popping as he did. "Guess we'll find out."

They had spent most of the day driving straight north. When Micah had learned the Watchers had been buried in the valleys of the earth, he really had no idea what that meant. After everyone had left, and Gabriel had returned last night after leaving Eden in the temple, they'd gone to the maps. Since Damon, or Uriel, and Gabriel weren't the Holies to bury The Watchers, they didn't have direct memories of where that was. Even if they had, the earth had changed a lot since the days of the Great Flood. Gabriel had consulted with Michael before returning to Micah to find out exactly where the Watchers were buried.

"I know where to find Armaros," Gabriel had announced the night before.

Micah had felt a twinge of disappointment. Not that he didn't want to get going right away, but if he was honest, he wouldn't have minded being in on the counsel with Michael. Micah was in awe of Gabriel, and frankly, Damon too, but the very thought of meeting Michael, the angel said to have thrown Lucifer out of Heaven in the Great War, gave him chills.

Still, he was relieved to see Gabriel was in no mood to waste time. *He's as anxious as I am.* Micah didn't like the idea of Eden being in danger, but he hated the idea of her being locked away in the temple too. He felt guilty he didn't explain the living conditions in chamber nine. He hoped she'd forgive him for omitting certain details. *Like she'll be sealed in... alone and underground.* He hoped Trent could join her soon. When he'd mentioned to Trent he should skip out on seeing Armaros and go be with Eden in the temple, Trent had balked. Micah had reminded him last night of all the scrolls just lying there... unread... untouched. That was all he needed. Now Trent was chomping at the bit to finish instructing Armando and to hook up with Caitlyn to get his 'ticket' inside.

Gabriel had pulled out a map of Italy and told them they were in luck. As fate would have it, Armaros was buried close. In one of the great valleys of the earth, Po Valley, Italy. They'd decided they would set off first thing in the morning.

Now, Damon and Micah stared at the valley before them. Micah tried to push thoughts of Eden aside. He needed to focus all his thoughts and energy on what lay ahead of them. *Or, really, beneath us.*

"Where to, Gabriel? Should we just start walking?" Micah asked, happy to see Sage suddenly appear. He felt like he hadn't seen her in a long time. Her presence comforted him. She drew near, her black eyes roaming what lay before them.

The valley before them was like a green carpet, with a river snaking through and the Alps surrounding it. *Hard to imagine such an alive, beautiful place housing a monster.*

Gabriel glanced over at Sage; she nodded back at him. Micah wasn't sure if they were actually communicating something or just acknowledging one another.

Then Gabriel pointed ahead, saying, "See that space between those two large peaks just ahead? We follow a straight course to there. We will come upon the burial site soon."

Damon looked to Micah, who shrugged and said, "Sounds good to me."

Damon nodded and wordlessly marched forward into the long grass. Micah wasn't surprised to see Seth, Damon's guardian, appear alongside him. Damon wasn't short by any means, but Seth towered over him. With his arms swinging double-sided battle-axes and his ice-blue eyes sweeping the land around them, Seth's physical form was intimidating.

Micah glanced around. Something about the land sent a shiver through him. Even with the sunlight bathing the grass in bright light, each step forward made Micah's insides twist. He had no idea how this all worked. Was calling up a Watcher the same as calling up a demon? He felt like a fish out of water when it came to the fallen ones.

He glanced over at Damon, whose brisk strides forward showed no sign of turning back or slowing down. *Hope his silence means confidence. I think this time, I'm counting on Damon to get us through this more than ever.*

Damon's blood roared in his ears, almost drowning out the incessant whispers and groans from the land. *Almost.* The rage mounting within him was tangible, like the color red flooding his vision, making him almost forget who was around him. The land cried for vengeance. It was weary from housing Armaros. It warned Damon there were secrets seeping through the soil, trickling down the river, and filling the deepest crevices of the earth.

"There is no hiding from the Watcher's touch," the land kept crying. "Give us peace, oh Holy Ones."

Damon glanced over at Gabriel. "You direct the Cherubim. The soldiers for the Captain, they each carry a sword of fire. Right?"

Gabriel gave a swift glance at Micah, and then nodded. "Yes, I can call them down, if it comes to that. How much do your remember of your former life, Damon?"

"You mean about being Uriel?" The words still filled him with a strange detachment. He'd seen himself as Uriel in a vision, but he still couldn't absorb the truth.

"Yes, about being Uriel," Gabriel said as they continued their march.

In all their haste, this was the first time Damon had really thought about what he knew of himself. "Well, when we were in Enoch's temple, on one of the pillars, it said Uriel was over the earth and Tartarus," Damon said slowly. "I guess I can see the earth part. I mean, I can speak to it. I feel pretty attached now."

"You're dang good at commanding it too," Micah commented, and then he asked, "What about Tartarus? That's the lowest level of Hell, right? What does that mean?"

Gabriel stared at Damon, and then stopped walking. "Do you know, Damon?"

He shook his head. "I have no idea. If I'm over the lowest level of hell, how did those wolf-demons attack Willow and me?"

"That's probably exactly why they attacked you, Damon. Demons hate you, more than anything. They despise you," Gabriel said. "The Captain made you the ruler over them."

"How was that my first run-in with them then? You'd think with how Eden and Micah have been personally attacked, I would've too, long before any of this."

Gabriel slapped Seth's shoulder. "You have this guy to thank for that. He's one of the best guardians you could have. Before the Awakening, none of you teens were in serious danger, other than mild things. I mean, demons don't sleep or stop to eat. They are always trying to find ways to make mortals miserable like they are."

Damon considered Gabriel's words. *Makes sense. Before Eden touched me, I was a loner. I didn't belong anywhere. I never fit. I always felt off.* That was why his gift had been exactly that—a gift. It had given him purpose.

They continued pushing ahead. Damon could feel the tension in the ground beneath his feet. They were getting close. On the outside, it appeared to be no more than a green field of grass rising up to the mountains framing it. But underneath, the evil seeped out. The ground literally felt hotter to him with each step he took.

He finally stopped and held his hand up. "This has got to be it."

Micah stopped and stared at the ground below them. "Right here? There's no real marking or anything. Not that I expected there to be." Micah rubbed the side of his face with his hand, and then used it to shield his eyes as he looked around.

By the way he kept fidgeting, Damon could tell Micah was nervous. It felt off to see him so unsettled. *Usually Micah's the sure one. Maybe it's because he's not the one doing it this time. I should be nervous.* Damon searched his heart. *But I'm not.*

The elements' pleading filled him with too much rage to be nervous. He was furious—ready to explode with commands.

Gabriel held up his hand too. He closed his eyes, and then opened them to stare directly at Damon. "You're right. This is it. Now, remember, we have to offer Armaros his chance at redemption. His choice. Hopefully, he'll take it and end Semjaza's curse on Eden. We *can't* destroy Armaros until he chooses, no matter how he infuriates us."

Damon stared at Gabriel. *Does he feel the same rage I do? Or is he warning me?*

Micah's brows gathered. "Gabriel's right. No matter what, we've got to get Armaros to agree to help us."

"I'll do what I can. I'm not really sure what that is just yet," Damon said to both of them.

Micah grinned and nodded him on.

This was it. Damon clenched his jaw, his body felt tight, ready. The words flew from his mouth. The language wasn't one he immediately recognized, but he instantly remembered. This was his native tongue, the tongue of angels.

Gabriel joined in and, together, they chanted a stream of commands. The earth not only heard them, but it also groaned audibly. Micah gasped, and Sage pulled him back a few paces. It was clear by her protective stance in front of him that Sage wanted no harm to come to her Seer.

At first, Damon felt like he was merely uttering syllables, but after a moment, the language itself took on its own form. The power from the language whirled around them, like a wind he'd never felt before. The thrumming from the elements grew silent. The earth was waiting; the moment it had wanted since Michael had first thrown this Watcher into his prison had come.

The ground split before them; a chasm reminded Damon of the one he'd formed to save Willow from the wolves. Only this hole didn't grow in diameter, staying only five or six feet wide. Its depth didn't seem to end.

A voice sang out to Damon, "*We have fulfilled our promise to the Captain. We release Armaros into the Holies' hands.*"

Since Damon had seen a prince of demons emerge from the well, he sort of expected the Watcher to do the same thing. Pop up. Be mean, menacing, and ugly. Instead, he was shocked to see what appeared to be an average-sized man, dressed in a brown tunic, with long, unkempt hair and a beard, rise through the hole. Armaros' face stayed downcast, shielding his eyes from view. His hands hung before him in manacles. He made no move to even glance up. The very lack of emotion on the fallen one's part made the moment precarious.

Gabriel moved closer to Damon, murmuring, "Wait."

Damon wasn't sure what he could be referring to, but the dread tingling down Damon's spine made his fingers curl into fists.

Gabriel took a step forward. "Armaros."

The fallen angel didn't move.

"We come to fulfill your probation," Gabriel continued in a loud voice. "We are the Holies of the Captain. We summon you forth, out of the earth, giving you your one last chance to leave your oath to Semjaza behind and side with The Captain. This will be your final call. Choose wisely."

Still, the Watcher's head remained pitched forward, his long hair shielding his face from view. It was impossible to tell if it was remorse or fury that kept him from acknowledging them or the fact he was no longer buried.

Micah stepped forward, his expression set hard, his eyes narrowing as he took in Armaros. Something about Micah rang familiar, like a distant memory from another time, but Damon didn't have time to wonder as Sage tried to usher Micah back.

This isn't your fight, he wanted to shout at Micah. *Stay back*. He felt protective of his new group of friends, but there were two people he wouldn't think twice about laying down his life for—Micah and Willow.

"What do you say, Armaros?" Gabriel called again. To Damon, Gabriel muttered again, "Wait. Not yet."

Damon felt something surge through his frame. A tingling of power that left him dizzy. *What's he so afraid I'll do too soon?*

Armaros' head still did not lift.

Gabriel muttered something under his breath, and then declared, "The choice is before you. Denounce your oath to Semjaza and save the Awakener. He has cursed her to die. Only you can undo Semjaza's enchantments. Share your knowledge with us, tell us what to do, and mercy will be granted. Your days of shame and reprobation will end. I will call Cherubim down to escort you from your prison. Or side with death and destruction, to be carried down to the deepest hell. What is your choice?"

It seemed strange that given such a 'choice,' that anyone in their right mind would choose the latter. It was clear what the consequences would be for Armaros if he refused to comply. *Why on earth wouldn't he?*

Damon felt something arouse within, the tingling power he'd come to feel since Eden hugged him for the second time and awakened him to his true identity. Somehow, he sensed what Armaros answer would be. *He's not going to help.* A sound filled the space between them—laughter. A low, rumbling laughter coming from under the mop of tangled hair. *How dare he laugh at us!*

Damon felt the energy in his gut stirring, mixing with his anger.

The hair flew back as Armaros' neck snapped up. His face was pale, unremarkable. No scars, no nasty, yellow teeth. He appeared to be nothing more than a man with dark eyes and pale lips. His gaze landed on Gabriel, then darted to Damon, and finally to Micah. His eyes narrowed and then shot back to Damon.

"Come to collect my damned soul have you, *Uriel?*" Armaros asked finally. His voice was calm, level, like this was a simple business transaction. "Yes, I recognize you, but I do not fear you."

"I don't have to collect your soul," Damon said. *Not exactly sure how to do it anyway, but man, do I want to.* "You don't have to be damned. Help us cure Eden."

Armaros glared at them, his shifting dark eyes taking in each one of them. "I am clearly outnumbered. Outranked. I will not fight my fate."

"Does that mean you'll help us?" Micah asked, as Sage tried to tug him back.

Armaros' gaze landed on Micah. His lips sneered only momentarily before he was a blank mask again. Damon had the feeling Armaros was a simmering tempest behind the calm façade. *Just like me.*

"Help *you*?" Armaros repeated. "You who threw me into the endless night? The pit that has swallowed me in the earth for thousands of years? Why would I forsake my true leader for you?"

Damon bristled. The calmness in the Watcher's face caused sirens to go off in his head. Almost like he was watching a puppet move, Damon's hands rose before him. The temptation to destroy the smug Watcher's face made his ears ring.

"You threw yourself into that pit the day you signed your secret pact with Semjaza," Gabriel roared. "The day you left your holy home to defile yourself. You sealed your fate. The Captain in His great mercy gives you this one last chance. Tell us how to undo Semjaza's enchantment!"

Armaros didn't hide his sneer this time. "There is nothing you, the Holies of the Captain, can say or do to make me forsake my true leader. Semjaza's praise and glory be mine!" Armaros lifted his bound hands above his head and stared at the sky. "Let it be recorded in the heavens and by these angels, I will not help you! Your Awakener will die, for nothing you can do will undo Semjaza's power!"

Damon's body reacted before he could second-guess himself. Both of his hands rose above his head and came down with such force that the earth shook. Somewhere, he heard someone yell, "No!" but he couldn't stop once he'd started.

Instantly, thunderheads rolled in, blocking out the sun. Winds howled, pulling at their bodies with such force that it was hard to stay upright. Lightning tore through the sky. Thunder bellowed above them, reverberating off the mountains, filling the valley. The air filled with an eerie hum; lightning came down all around them, striking at the very ground they stood on, at the exact same time there was a crack as thunder erupted, rolling across the sky, leaving an angry wake behind.

Damon shook from the power coursing through his body. With hands outstretched to his sides, he met Armaros' jeering smile. His voice sounded strange to himself. "You have made your choice, Armaros. We, the angels of the Holy One, have recorded it. Your fate is sealed. I, Uriel, send your soul to *Tartarus!*"

A bolt of pure light struck Armaros in the skull, his frame exploding with blinding, white light, and with the final clap of thunder, the Watcher was gone. *Carried to Tartarus. Gone forever.* Damon turned, the silence more alarming than the passing storm.

Meeting Gabriel's gaze, he realized what he'd just done. *That's why he kept saying to wait... He knew what I'd want to do... what I'd be compelled to do. Send Armaros to Tartarus. But he made his choice,* Damon wanted to argue, *there was nothing they could have done to change it.*

When Micah fell to his knees, the crush of defeat written all over his face, the horror of the situation finally hit Damon. More than one person's fate was sealed today. Damon felt sick. *I let Micah down. I failed when failure wasn't an option.*

Chapter Twenty-seven

*C*aitlyn's feet hurt. Bad. They'd been walking for hours. Willow would get a feeling, plod forward one way for a bit, and then on second thought, double back to walk another twenty minutes in the opposite direction.

She apologized to Caitlyn over and over, saying this was new and not an exact science. It was harder to pick a location. At first, Caitlyn hadn't minded. She needed to put as much space between Andrew and her as possible. What had started out as simple guilt over the fact she might have influenced him with her gift unknowingly had turned into frustration that he didn't return her feelings. This led her to the conclusion that if Andrew didn't love her, it meant she was even worse at her gift than she thought. It should be a relief. That would mean she hadn't interfered with fate, right? So why didn't she feel relieved?

She'd hoped as they passed shop after shop, walking through the downtown life of Moravia, that she could chase the growing pressure in her chest away. It was like a panic attack waiting to happen. The scary part was, she didn't know how to stop it. Now they were far from town, strolling past vineyards and fields. All of which were gorgeous, but the sun was hot and the air humid. Caitlyn inhaled deeply, taking in the earthy smell around them.

Willow's lips puckered as she scanned the countryside. She grinned and pointed. "I really think I got it this time. It's over there."

Caitlyn wiped the sweat off her forehead. "Okay. Let's go that way, then."

Willow glanced over. "Thank you for believing in me. You don't know how much your faith means to me."

Caitlyn about jumped in her skin. *My faith? If only you knew how little faith I have in myself right now, Willow. Maybe this would be the right time to tell her. Bare my soul. Get this weight off my chest once and for all.*

But Willow was off, determined once again to find where the city should be. She'd begun singing, which was something she had done on and off for the past few hours. Caitlyn thought nothing of it as she scoured the ground, debating whether it looked friendly enough to take her shoes off. When venturing off this morning, she should have thought better of the sandals she'd grabbed. The small, wedged heel left something to be desired in support, and her baby toe was rubbed raw by one of the straps.

Then Willow surprised her by giggling. "Caitlyn, can I tell you a secret?"

Caitlyn stooped down, deciding her baby toe could take no more abuse. She slid her shoes off and sighed in relief. "Sure," she said, catching up to Willow.

Willow's eyes danced. "Damon kissed me."

"Oh my gosh, really? When?"

"Right before that wolf thing attacked us yesterday. Oh… it was so wonderful! He'd just realized who… he was." Willow's tone went funny.

"What do you mean? Who he was?"

"Um, well, I guess I can tell you. I don't think that's a secret too. Damon's Uriel."

"Uriel?" Caitlyn knew the name sounded familiar, but they'd learned so much about angels, demons, and Watchers in the last few weeks that it was all starting to blur together for her.

"Uriel is one of the Holy angels, like Gabriel," Willow explained.

"*What?* Damon's an angel?"

"Well, not technically right this second. I mean, we were all angels of sorts before we came here. We all played our part in the war in heaven. Getting the devil out with all his followers and all that. Damon was called Uriel then. Uriel was the one who told Noah how to build the Ark. Anyway, now that he's on earth, we know him as Damon."

Caitlyn had stopped walking. "Wow… that's crazy!"

"I know, right? You were someone special before too. That's why the Captain entrusted you with something so rare. I'd say you and Damon got the Captain's most powerful gifts. Makes me wonder who you were before," Willow said with her happy smile. She said it so carefree, like this was the most natural thing to discuss with someone.

Caitlyn shifted under Willow's gaze. *I don't feel very special. I feel like a mess.*

"I think you're the gifted one here, Willow. You're so good at this. I mean, look at us, out here finding where the city should be, with nothing but you guiding us."

Willow cocked an eyebrow at her. "Yeah, well, you've got blisters all over your feet. I'm not as good as you say."

Caitlyn laughed. It felt refreshing. She needed something fun to think about, so she said, "No, really, I'm serious. Now why don't you tell me about that kiss? I mean, it's not every day a girl gets kissed by an angel."

Willow sighed, a smile on her lips. "Well, when you put it like that, you're right. And Damon did *not* disappoint. It was pretty incredible, right up until the wolf knocked us over." Her voice was singsong, even referring to the demon that had attacked them.

Caitlyn smiled and strolled along, happy to listen to Willow talk about Damon. She couldn't help but wonder what it would feel like to kiss Andrew. Her heart squeezed painfully, reminding her that would never happen. The pain was almost unbearable. Was this what Eden felt when she pined for Micah? *Is this what Andrew feels when he thinks about Eden?*

She decided to focus on Willow's talking, when she realized she had stopped and was staring across the road from them. In all their meandering, they'd cruised through quite a few small villages. Most homes were simple, yards were clean, with small shops and farmer's stands dotting the road. This time, right across from them, sat a bar. Since beer was everywhere here and they'd already passed some pubs, Caitlyn thought nothing of it.

Willow grabbed Caitlyn's arm. "Look," she urged.

Caitlyn glanced across again. All she saw were motorcycles lining the entire front of it. A few bikers lounged on the bikes, talking to one another. Most were inside, considering there were about twenty motorcycles out front and only five or so riders sitting outside.

"Come on," Willow said, striding across the street.

Really? Here? The Northern City is going to be where this bar sits? She had no choice but to follow. Willow didn't go into the bar, though, which was even worse. At least inside they could get some water. Willow had her eyes on one of the bikers.

Caitlyn cringed. *Maybe she's just getting directions to some place.*

The biker Willow beelined for was fiddling with his handlebars and hadn't see them approaching. Caitlyn would guess he was probably in his late thirties, early forties. He was slender with brown hair pulled back into a short ponytail and suntanned skin. Wearing a brown leather jacket, he pulled some riding gloves out of a compartment on his bike. Turning around to slide them on, he noticed Willow coming over.

He smiled, his teeth a brilliant white against his dark skin. "Hello there." His voice was rich with an accent.

"Ah wonderful, you speak English then. I realized we might be in trouble if you only spoke Czech," Willow said.

I didn't even think of that, Caitlyn realized as she stepped closer to be next to Willow. She didn't miss the way the guy sized them both up as he finished putting his gloves on. *Oh, crap, Willow. I think this guy is getting the wrong idea about us.*

"Yes, I speak English. I can tell you are American. Tourist, eh?" he asked. He glanced around. "Foreign-exchange students, perhaps?"

Get your directions and let's get the heck out of here, Willow.

"We're tourists, of sorts. I'm Willow." She offered him her hand.

He shook it. "Pleasure, Willow. I'm Marek Tomas."

When Marek's eyes landed on Caitlyn, she stuck a hand out too. "Caitlyn."

His gloved hand lingered a bit too long on Caitlyn's. She pulled back and glanced over at Willow. Couldn't she sense this couldn't be right?

"Marek, I'm wondering if you could help us find someone. Do you live around here by chance?" Willow asked.

Marek nodded. "Yes, I know pretty much everyone and everything around here. Give me a try; let me see if I can help."

"Wonderful. You see, we're searching for someone who owns vineyards nearby."

Marek nodded. "Sure, there are many vineyards around here. What is the man's name?"

"Well, that's just it. I don't know his name... At least, I'm not sure if I do."

Caitlyn saw the confusion on Marek's face. *Pretty sure I'm mimicking him. I thought we were looking for land. Oh, maybe she's trying to find the owner of the vineyard.*

"Okay, go on. Do you know where the vineyard is exactly? Maybe I can take you to it?"

Willow's gaze went out of focus for a split second as she gazed at Marek. "I think he owns many acres. It would be a very large vineyard. It's been in his family for centuries, passed down to the sons, to carry the family name on."

Marek shifted in his weight. "Go on."

"The man I'm looking for is unsure of things right now, though. He doesn't want to leave the family business, but he's been feeling restless. Like there might be something bigger out there for him."

Marek's brows gathered, and he folded his arms.

I'm not sure he's liking the mind reading, Caitlyn thought desperately. *Wish Willow could read my mind right now.*

"Sound like anyone you know, Marek?" Willow asked.

"Aw, no. Sorry that I cannot help you," Marek said, turning away from them abruptly and climbing on his bike.

"Is that an Ecosse Titanium?" Willow asked.

Marek stopped and stared. "What?"

"Your bike. Is it an Ecosse?"

Marek's face relaxed, and he smiled. "Wow, I am impressed. You know your bikes."

"My dad is sort of a bike connoisseur. I recognized it by the titanium pipes with the ceramic finish. There's only thirteen ever made, right? I wish my dad could see this."

Marek hesitated before climbing off. "You have a camera? I can get a picture of you next to it for him."

Willow beamed. "Cell phone work? Here, just press right there…" She handed him her cell and grabbed Caitlyn.

They positioned themselves in front of it, Caitlyn careful not to touch the bike. Knowing there were only thirteen of these ever made let her know one thing; it was worth a lot of money.

Marek snapped a few shots, and then handed Willow her phone back. He considered them for a moment and said, "May I ask why you seek this gentleman? You seem to know an awful lot about him, without knowing his name."

Willow met his gaze. "I seek him because he's troubled. And no amount of beer will chase away the dreams he's been having."

The man jumped a bit, visibly startled. "My dreams… but how do you know so much? I don't understand. Who are you two?"

Caitlyn felt like the mute partner, watching Willow's fascinating show. She was horrified to see Willow turn to her instead of answering. *What? Does she want me to answer him? I don't know what to say…*

Caitlyn cleared her throat. "We have gifts, Marek. Some of us see things… sense things. I know it sounds strange, but I promise we aren't scam artists. What Willow said is what she sees in you. You *are* the man we're looking for." The words started coming easier, more natural off her lips. "We have the answers you're seeking. We've come to help you."

Marek scratched his jaw, sighing. "I have been searching for guidance, I guess you could say. I never would have thought it would come from a pair of American teenagers." He chuckled. "I was just heading across town. Word is spreading that there's some American kid healing everyone around. Thought I would go see the miracle for myself. I was hoping he could heal my troubled soul, give me rest from my nightmares."

"Oh, that's Andrew," Willow said. "He's our friend. We probably should get back to him… not even sure which way we came, actually. We sort of took the scenic route."

Marek was on his way to Andrew. We could have just stayed at the lodge. Oh well, it was good to get out. Walk some.

"Can we give you both a lift?" Marek said. "Then maybe we can discuss how you think you can help me," he added.

Caitlyn wasn't sure how to take his comment and wondered who the 'we' was he referred to. The thought of climbing on a motorcycle terrified her enough, but holding on to some strange biker sounded even worse. *Let's just walk, Willow*, she wanted to say.

"Oh, would you? That would be awesome!" Willow replied, and Caitlyn cringed.

A young man waltzed out of the pub, laughing a bit, and Marek hollered, "Lucas, come down here."

The guy, Lucas, glanced over at them, looking like Marek but twenty years younger. He shared the same thick, brown hair, suntanned skin, and white smile. *One guess who he belongs to.*

Lucas glanced at Willow, and then his gaze landed on Caitlyn. He jumped over the railing and down to where the bikes sat. "Who are your friends, Dad?" he asked, while his brown eyes remained on Caitlyn. She felt the blood race to her cheeks.

"These are Americans. They are friends with the healer we were hearing about. I know you weren't interested in going to see him, but maybe you can help me give them a ride back."

"Sure thing." He smiled at Caitlyn. "You want to ride with me?"

Willow grinned encouragingly at Caitlyn, and then she glanced at Marek's bike. "Do I really get to ride on *this*?"

Marek grinned. "I never mind giving a ride to someone who appreciates fine art."

Lucas rolled his eyes at his dad before saying to Caitlyn, "My dad gripes at me for not appreciating my bike. Thinks I don't understand art. I tell him I am into a different form of art." His eyes twinkled.

Caitlyn's heart banged against her rib cage. *Does he mean me?*

He hopped on and smiled at her. "Come on. This will be fun."

She swung her leg over the bike and scooted on behind him. She wasn't sure what to do with her arms, her hands. It felt like such an intimate thing with such a complete stranger.

"You need to hold on, because I do not drive like my dad," he said over his shoulder to her.

She wanted to say, "Smooth one," but she knew he was right. Wrapping her arms around his torso, she tried to ignore the anxiety. She wasn't sure which scared her more—falling off the back of this thing or holding on to the warm body in front of her.

Chapter Twenty-eight

Caitlyn wasn't sure what she expected to find when they got back to the lodge, but the size of the line out the door shocked her. They had to muscle their way through, trying to explain they were friends of the *Léčital*. Finally, they found someone who spoke English, and Willow hastily said they weren't in line to be healed but needed to speak to their friend, Andrew.

Five minutes later, they were making their way back to the table Andrew sat at. Only he wasn't there. He'd moved to the long bar, sitting on the last stool. One glance at Andrew and alarms went off in Caitlyn's head. His complexion was pale, his brow furrowed, and his shirt hung too loosely on his frame. *He's about to fall off that bar stool!*

Caitlyn pushed through the remaining people, determined to get to him. All the earlier frustration she'd felt toward him vanished in that moment. *He needs to rest. Enough of this healing business.*

Willow must have sensed it too because she gasped. "Oh, Andrew."

Marek, who had followed closely after them, asked, "Is that the healer?"

"Yes, but he's done for the day," Caitlyn said firmly.

Andrew had been so absorbed with healing the child in front of him that he hadn't seen them coming until Caitlyn was right next to him. She ignored the fact that Brita sat on the stool next to him. *How can she let him go on like this? It's obvious he's exhausted!*

Andrew's face brightened. "Caitlyn, you're back and you guys are fine. What a relief."

He was worried about us? "Hey, I think you're the one we need to be worrying about right now. You look wiped out, Andrew. Have you been doing this all day? Have you even stopped to eat?" Caitlyn asked.

Andrew smiled over at Brita. "Oh, I've had lots of good food, thanks to Brita. She gave me this thing called svíčková. It's roast meat with dumplings and lots of gravy. So good, you got to try it. You guys hungry?"

Honestly, Caitlyn was starved, but all she cared about was getting Andrew out of here. He needed a break. The woman next in line after the child moved to the front and began speaking in Czech to Brita. Brita laid a hand on Andrew's shoulder. He leaned in to hear what she was saying, and then he smiled.

"Sure, I can help with that," he said.

Brita translated back to the woman, and Caitlyn reached over to Andrew. She wasn't sure what she wanted to accomplish, but she touched his arm. He glanced over at her. Sitting on a high bar stool made them eye level. She saw something in those emerald eyes; she just wasn't sure what.

"Andrew, tell them to come back later or tomorrow. You need to take a break," she urged.

"Caitlyn, I'm totally good. These people are in pain. A lot of them drove all day to see me." He reached up and covered her hand with his. Initially, she felt the thrill of his touch, but then the warmth seeping into her was different. Warm, comforting, inviting. She hoped her face wasn't flaming red.

"You look tired," he said, "and hungry. Why don't you and Willow get some food? Brita can get you a table."

"Good idea," Willow cut in. "I'm sure Marek and his son want to eat too, and we still need to talk to him."

When she mentioned Marek, Andrew's eyes sought out the guys behind them. "You found who you were looking for, Willow?" he asked.

"Yes, Marek, I'd like to introduce you to our friend Andrew," Willow said.

Andrew reached out and shook Marek's hand. Then, almost like an afterthought, Andrew placed both of his hands over Marek's.

"Nice to meet you, man. I'm Andrew." He hesitated, and then said, "There, that should help you, I think."

Marek's eyes widened. "What did you do?"

"Healed you. No worries, no extra charge. I just ask that you listen to these two fine ladies. They have some important things for you to do."

Marek nodded, seeming a bit dumbfounded, and followed Willow, who was making her way to a table.

Lucas, Caitlyn noted, stood right next to her, waiting.

Andrew noticed too. "And you are?" he asked.

"Lucas, Marek's son. And I am good, thank you." He waved his hand off with a smile. "I do not need healing. I'm just waiting for this lady to join me for dinner."

Andrew's eyes widened, and Caitlyn stammered, "Oh, um. I'm coming." She turned and followed Willow, positive she could feel Andrew's stare on her back the entire way.

The dinner Andrew recommended turned out to be delicious, and Caitlyn hated to admit the company wasn't all that bad either. Chatting with Lucas, she discovered she had more in common with the eighteen-year-old than she'd thought. When she wasn't learning about Lucas's hobbies, she and Willow took turns explaining the cities to be built and what they were for to Marek. They told them about the coming fire, how those within the city would be safe from the flames. Marek listened the entire time, quiet and thoughtful. Then he shocked them by saying that this was the very thing in his dreams. He kept seeing an enormous building on his land. He hadn't understood it and frankly, it came frequent enough that it had become disturbing. He'd gone to clergymen, priests, even a few gypsies, trying to search its meaning. He told them he was anxious to meet Micah and to see the city that was already under construction in Illinois.

Everything was going great. Willow and Caitlyn had completed their first 'mission'. They'd found the land and the man who owned it. Andrew had healed almost all of Moravia. Now, hopefully, people would be more accepting of what was to be built here.

To top it all off, I even got to go to dinner with a pretty hot guy. Caitlyn knew Lucas was probably just a nice distraction for her; she couldn't help glancing over at Andrew. It was more than jealousy over Brita, she felt genuinely worried about him. She was convinced at any moment he would just slide off that stool and land on the ground with a thump. Yet, seeing him now, laughing with a little girl on his lap, he did seem alive in a different way.

Andrew's gaze shifted over and their eyes met; Caitlyn swallowed and glanced away. Willow excused herself for the ladies' room and even though Caitlyn could use a break too, Lucas was in the middle of telling her the funniest story, so she decided she should stay. A few minutes later, Willow returned with an expression that made Caitlyn's stomach turn sour.

She sat back down, her eyes downcast.

"Willow, what's wrong? What's going on?" Caitlyn asked.

She glanced up. "I decided I would let Micah and Damon know we've found Marek. To see where he'd like us to meet up."

"Oh, how did you do that? I thought our cell phones didn't work that great here."

"I, um, decided to use a different network," she said and her voice dropped a few notches, "sort of like the special travel arrangements you had getting here."

Oh. You mean you told your guardian angel, Esther. Caitlyn nodded that she understood. "So, did you get word back, then?"

Willow nodded slowly. "Yes, their mission didn't go as well as ours." Her voice caught. "Armaros refused to help."

Caitlyn sucked in air. "Oh no! Eden! What's going to happen to her?"

Marek cut in. "I'm sorry, but is everything alright? Is one of your friends in trouble?"

"Remember the girl we told you about, the one who gave us our gifts?" Caitlyn asked.

Marek nodded. Lucas said, "Yes?"

"She's sort of sick right now, and we're trying to find a cure," Caitlyn explained.

"What about Andrew?" Lucas asked. "Can't he heal her?"

Shaking her head, she glanced over at Andrew. She caught him staring in Lucas's direction before he looked away.

"No, he tried," Willow answered. "This one is beyond even the *Léčital*. Micah said we should meet up with Trent in Rome and then head back home. You need to make a detour and let Trent into the temple first." Willow cocked her head to the side, her eyes studying Caitlyn's face. Caitlyn wanted to blurt, *what is it? Can you read my mind now?*

Her lips to puckered to the side, and then she smiled. "Yes, you and Trent go to the temple. Micah said other than that, there's nothing we can really do with school starting in a few days."

Caitlyn listened but had a hard time processing it all. *School? Who cares about school? Eden's going to die! How can this happen? How can the angels let this happen?* Her heart raged with a new dark, thought. *How can the Captain let this happen?*

Chapter Twenty-nine

"Micah, I'm sorry," Damon mumbled.

Micah shook his head at him. "Damon, stop blaming yourself. Armaros made his decision. He asked the angels themselves to record it, for crying out loud. There was nothing we could do." His last statement came out more like a question, and Micah couldn't help that his eyes sought out Gabriel's. He wanted to ask, *was there? Did we just throw away our one shot?*

Instead, he said to Gabriel. "I want to try again. Let's travel fast. Try at least a couple of more. Then, if they won't side with us, take me to Semjaza."

Gabriel sighed heavily. "You know none of them have the same knowledge as Armaros did. These other Watchers know the secrets of the earth, the sun, the stars… I'm not sure they can heal her."

"I know," Micah said firmly, noticing how Damon's head hung low. "But they all knew Semjaza. Maybe they can tell us his weaknesses, give us some kind of way to get under his skin."

Gabriel nodded. "That might work, actually. We know how to defeat him. Uriel, or Damon, can call down the lightning of Tartarus and he'll be no more."

Damon flinched. "I shouldn't have done it so fast. Maybe you could have tortured Armaros with the Cherubim to make him comply."

"Uriel," Gabriel said, his voice deep. "No amount of torture would have made that worthless piece of garbage talk. He swore by the heavens his allegiance to Semjaza. Micah's right; we need to think ahead now. We don't want to destroy Semjaza right away. We need to find a soft spot. Something to use as leverage against him. Then, maybe he'll relent on his pursuit of Eden."

Damon lifted his head and nodded. "Tell me what I can do to help and I'll do it. I'll do anything."

Micah slapped Damon's shoulder softly. "I know you will, and between the three of us, hopefully we can find something."

The way Gabriel kept fingering his sword's hilt, Micah knew he was anxious. "Gabriel, who are the closest Watchers? Is there anyone you recommend we start with?" Micah asked.

Gabriel stared out over the land. "There's one who might help. Ezeqeel."

"Great, where do we find him?" Micah asked, stepping closer to Sage, who had remained quietly standing next to him for the past hour after they'd failed with Armaros. Her presence itself calmed Micah, made it so he could think clearly and move forward. He hadn't forgotten her warning to him, that he shouldn't lose faith. *I can't lose faith. That's all I have right now.*

Gabriel scratched his sideburn. "He's in Lötschental Valley. It's in Switzerland, just on the other side of these Alps."

"Let's go then. On second thought," he added, "anything we should know about him first?"

Gabriel's lips twitched to the side. "He has the knowledge of the clouds. Other than causing quite a few storms, I think he's pretty harmless."

Damon perked up. "What do you mean, cause storms? I thought they were buried, without their powers."

Gabriel glanced over at Sage, and she answered, "The bindings over the Watchers are ancient. They still hold true, but as we've seen with Semjaza, some of their powers are managing to leak through. Remember the hurricane that left most of the southeast coastline destroyed a few years ago? And the ones that hit the islands of Asia? Or even that tornado that raged across the Midwest?"

"You think Ezeqeel caused those?" Damon asked.

"We don't know for certain, but the storms and tempests raging on the earth are not like any we have seen before," Sage answered. "And Gabriel and I have been on the earth, for many, many years. I think the earth had grown weary of housing these Watchers."

"You're right about the earth, Sage," Damon said. "And speaking of that, when I saw myself as Uriel, in that vision, I learned you, Gabriel, were on the earth at the time of the Watchers."

"Really?" Micah said. "You lived through the reign of the Watchers? And the flood?" Micah cocked his head to the side. "Just *who* were you?"

Gabriel shifted his weight, and then folded his arms. "Does it matter now?"

"It might," Micah said. "If you were alive then, you must have known the Watchers. Maybe you know Semjaza's weakness better than anyone."

"I did know the Watchers and Semjaza. Not like Uriel, Michael, or Raphael did." His gaze landed on Micah. "I didn't know I was Gabriel at the time."

"Wonder why I get to know then?" Damon asked, interrupting. "Not that I mind, but it makes me wonder about Michael and Raphael. Did they know who they really were too?"

"It depended on what was needed. That knowledge wasn't important for me, during my life. Michael didn't know right away, but he was like you, Damon, he learned his true identity with time. Raphael, well, he's more like me. He didn't need to know."

"I wish Trent was here right now. He'd gobble this stuff up, and then make some off-color joke," Micah said, realizing how much he missed his cousin's commentary.

Gabriel grunted. "Yes, Trent would enjoy this history lesson, but when he joins Eden in the temple, I'm sure he'll figure it all out anyway."

Having just heard from Willow's guardian, Esther, that the Czech trip went great, and everything was underway with the Northern City, Micah had relayed a message to the guardians that he wanted Trent inside the temple as soon as possible. Not knowing when he'd be able to rejoin Eden, it relieved Micah to know Trent would at least be there with her.

"Or Eden will tell him," Gabriel said casually. "I told her Enoch was my great-grandfather."

Micah gasped. "Wait? That would make you *Noah?*"

Damon nodded. "Ah, that makes sense. In what I saw, I'd just given Noah instructions on how to build the Ark."

Micah finally put all the pieces together. "It does make sense. Perfect sense! The four Holies each were given specific tasks to perform. Michael and Raphael got the job of rounding up and burying the Watchers. Uriel, or Damon here, the task of instructing Noah, or you Gabriel, on how to build the Ark, and Gabriel... you had to kill the Watcher's offspring. What better way to rid the earth of unnatural monsters than a flood?"

"You and I, Micah, are more similar than you think," Gabriel said.

"What do you mean?" Micah asked.

"We were both given the assignment or mission, to build something which could save mankind. I built the Ark. Uriel instructed me how to do it. You have to construct these cities, using the blueprints from the very city my great-grandfather Enoch built. Now, Uriel and I are here to help you see it done. Although, there is one major difference between us."

"Yeah, the part about you being a holy angel and me being just a regular guy," Micah said with a laugh.

"No." Gabriel's voice was deep. "Your 'arks' will save thousands, maybe even millions, while mine only saved eight." There was no mistaking the sadness in Gabriel's tone. "You asked me if I knew the Watchers, if I knew Semjaza. I did. Their influence over the people made it so no one would listen to me. No one believed what was coming. They all imagined themselves as gods, better than gods. They listened to the Watchers, saw their powers, and learned the art of war from Semjaza's right hand, Azazel, who craves blood and lives off the pain and destruction of humanity."

Gabriel's gaze turned to stone as he glanced over at Micah. "And under no circumstances will you be with us when we face Azazel."

Taken back by the sudden intensity, Micah nodded. "Fine by me. Semjaza's the one I want. He's the one killing Eden."

Anger flashed through Gabriel's eyes. "Semjaza has one weakness that

I know of. It's one he has always had, and always will have. He craves the women he cannot have." The way the words were said, Micah couldn't help but wonder if Gabriel had firsthand experience with Semjaza's cravings. It felt like it was personal.

Damon shook his head. "That's what got us into this whole mess in the first place. Semjaza was forbidden to be with mortal women, but he did it anyway."

Micah gasped. "You mean, he may not just want to kill Eden? He may crave her? Oh, I think I'm going to be sick." He rubbed his forehead, and then said, "But that can't be right. He had her stabbed with poison. If he wanted to be with her, why would he be trying to kill her? If she dies, she'll go back to the Captain."

"Yeah," Damon agreed. "Doesn't seem like Semjaza thought this one through all the way."

"That's what troubles me." Gabriel sighed. "I know Semjaza. He thinks *everything* through. There's more to this than we're seeing."

Chapter Thirty

*E*den wrapped herself up in the blanket. *Just fall asleep.* It wasn't that the bed was uncomfortable. The long pad, which had appeared last night, was surprisingly comfortable. The food that appeared for her had been delicious as well. Gabriel had been right. *This chamber has provided everything I've needed... physically.*

"Just not you, Gabriel," she whispered. She hugged the blanket, trying to squeeze the pain from her chest. Every thought, every word she'd said for the last two days, she'd said and thought only to herself. *Gabriel's not here.*

She'd never felt so alone in her life. She had tried to entertain herself by perusing the shelves of scrolls, but without Trent here to translate, it lost its appeal after a few hours. The large, golden delta had captivated her most of the next day. Even without understanding all the markings on the tall gold, triangle, its beauty called to her. It was something she could gaze at. It calmed her.

The one thing that had thoroughly fascinated her about chamber nine was the small room she now lay in. After Gabriel had left her yesterday, she'd spent most of the time in the large chamber. It was about the time she realized her stomach was about to eat itself that she noticed the wooden door in the corner. Positive it hadn't been there before, she'd flung it open to see a small room made entirely of wood planks. Floors, walls, and ceilings, sort of like a log cabin, except for the fact it was round in shape. There had been a table with two chairs sitting in the middle of an otherwise plain room. The table had nuts, berries, chicken, cooked potatoes, and some kind of warm flatbread all spread out on platters for her.

She'd gasped, remembering how Gabriel had said the chamber was like the widow's barrel. She hadn't thought he'd meant literally. She had stepped into the room gingerly, almost afraid it was all an illusion, but hunger had won out. She sat down and feasted. The food had been delicious, so much so, that after she'd finished and left the room, she'd decided to re-enter to nibble some more. To her shock, the room had changed. The table was gone, replaced with a pillow and blanket, a washing basin, and a wooden partition in it. She had glanced behind the divider and found the other thing she'd worried about—a toilet.

She'd tried not to think about how the plumbing worked in this place, and had been grateful that this room seemed to sense all of her needs before she even did. Now, lying on the pad, holding the blanket more for comfort than warmth, she realized the one thing this chamber had not given her. Companionship. No Mom, no Dad, not even her brother Brendan to bug her. No friends. *No Micah.* She shut her eyes. Not even the one person who was always there for her.

I miss you, Gabriel. The loneliness she felt was tangible, like it could squeeze the very air from her lungs. She tried not to sob. She tried to be strong.

I always talk to you at times like this, but no one's here with me.

A scraping noise echoed through the room. She bolted upright, unsure where it'd come from. The room wasn't dark. That was something she was extremely grateful for; the candescent lighting throughout the chamber never turned off. Last time, most of the temple had been lit by the angels themselves. Being by herself now, she would be in darkness.

She waited, listening. Nothing. She decided to settle back into bed when she heard a low groan, like a large stone moving across a hard floor.

She hopped up from her bed, hoping Trent had finally arrived. Rushing from the room, her eyes sought out the sun motif. *Nope, still sealed shut. No one's here.* Feeling disappointed and slightly uneasy, she hustled back. *I'm shutting the door behind me. These noises are freaking me out.*

"Help me," a voice whispered from behind.

She gasped and whirled around, scanning the empty room. "Who's there?" she called out, heart thudding in her chest. "Caitlyn? Trent? Is that you?"

"Help me," the voice urged, not a whisper, but clear and sounding female. Eden felt frozen by terror, while part of her was sure the voice sounded familiar.

"Eden, help me!" the voice called out again.

"Caitlyn?" Eden forced herself to scan the room. "Is that you?"

This time, there was no mistaking the pain in the cry. "Yes, Eden! I need help! *Please hurry!*"

"I'm trying! Where are you?" She dashed around, searching everywhere— under tables, around corners, even between large shelves.

"Over here." Her voice sounded muffled, like it might be behind the sun motif.

She sprinted over, but the entrance was sealed shut. "Caitlyn, I'm here," Eden called through the stone.

"Help me!"

"Oh my gosh! Is something attacking you? I can't open this! Caitlyn, you have to open it. You're the one with true faith," Eden yelled back through the stone, panicked she couldn't get to her friend.

"Put your hands on the s-stone," Caitlyn urged, her words slurring together. "We'll d-do it t-together."

She's in so much pain! She had to get this entrance open. She pressed her hands against the sun motif.

"Okay, I'm touching the wall. Now what?" she asked, pressing her face against the wall.

There was a large crack and then the stone started moving forward, taking Eden's body with it.

"Caitlyn! We did it," she called, climbing through and entering the tunnel. "Caitlyn... " The words echoed up the empty tunnel.

"Eden, hurry!" Caitlyn urged from above.

She ran straight up the tunnel. She wasn't sure why Caitlyn's voice affected her so; was it from the profound silence she'd been in for the past two days or the fact that this didn't make sense. *Where is she? How can I hear her everywhere? What's happening to her?*

"Help-p m-me," Caitlyn voice rang out just ahead of her. Eden reached the end of the tunnel out, sweat dripping down her back from running straight up hill.

"I'm coming! Where are you? I can't see..." Eden's words failed as she found herself suddenly standing under the night sky. Stars dotted the blackness, the night breeze stirring the cornfields around her.

Fresh air. If she hadn't been on an urgent mission to find her friend, she probably would have sat down and just gulped in the cool, night air. She could feel autumn kissing her skin.

"Eden!" Caitlyn begged.

Eden spun around, trying to decide which way to go. All she saw was cornfields. Caitlyn's sudden, horrifying screech pushed her into action. She dashed forward, plunging between the dark stalks, throwing her arms in front of her, trying to navigate through.

"Caitlyn! I'm coming! Where are you?"

"Over here, you're getting close. Hurry, Eden!"

Eden pushed harder, tripping and falling a few times over the dead stalks on the ground. She wished Andrew were here. *Caitlyn's hurt. Where's Trent? Wasn't he coming with her? Did something happen to him? Were they ambushed or something?*

So many questions ran through her mind as she continued running toward the voice urging her on.

"Come on already, Caitlyn," Trent called from the other side of the door. "We don't have all day. Brutus is here and one thing I've learned is you never keep a guy in flannel waiting. Plus, he's got his axe. Need I say more?"

Caitlyn opened the bathroom door up. "Trent, don't you know it's bad to fly by angel when you got to go?" She finished dabbing her wet hair with her towel before tossing it at him.

He snatched it, and then pointed it back at her. "Really? A shower? Now?"

"I just think we all could use a minute," Caitlyn replied. Having just arrived by angel, with one look at Alaina, Caitlyn knew her guardian needed a breather before taking off again. So, she purposely went into the bathroom and took a long shower. She needed one anyway. A full day of hiking through Moravia had left her feeling sticky.

Andrew rubbed his neck a little, his eyes landing on Caitlyn. "Yeah, I think I could use one of those too. Flying by angel is definitely an experience. I think I want to lie down."

"Wimp," Trent snickered. "Can't be that bad."

Caitlyn wondered if it was really just the flight exhausting Andrew. *He healed too many. He still looks pale to me.*

Perhaps Willow sensed her own angel's fatigue because she said, "I think all of our angels need a minute." Willow glanced at Alaina and gave her a slight nod, which Caitlyn found odd.

To Trent, Willow said, "Don't worry, we'll leave soon, promise."

Trent sighed, and then grumbled to Brutus, who was by far the brightest angel in the room, having not just carted a mortal along, "Sorry, chap, looks like we have to wait."

Brutus didn't really react or say anything. He just stood there like a lumberjack, waiting to swing his axe. It was more than a little unnerving the way his eyes kept darting in Caitlyn's direction. She purposely sat on the edge of the bed, putting her back to Trent's guardian. Alaina moved to be nearer.

Caitlyn smiled up at her. "You're looking better." For some reason when they arrived, Alaina was by far the dimmest of them all. Was it just because she was younger? Which really made no sense because how old were any of these angels anyway?"

"Yes, thank you. I should be ready to go soon," Alaina replied. "How are you feeling?"

"Oh, I'm fine. Don't worry about me." But some reason, Caitlyn couldn't shake the feeling that that was exactly what Alaina was. *Worried about me. But why?*

Caitlyn glanced around, taking in the angels still with them. If anyone just happened to pop in, they would get the surprise of their life. *Although, Marek and Lucas handled the angels' company fairly well when we said good-bye.*

Andrew walked over, stealing her attention, pushing thoughts of Lucas aside. He glanced over at her, grinned, and then sprawled across the bed behind where she sat.

Alaina noticed and shot Caitlyn a look, lifting one eyebrow. *Andrew and I are friends,* Caitlyn wanted to say. *He does this sort of stuff all the time. It doesn't mean anything, Alaina.*

Only problem was, it meant the world to Caitlyn. She had to resist the temptation to snuggle down next to him. She wanted to wrap herself up in his arms. Thinking of the last girl wrapped up in Andrew's arms, Caitlyn grimaced. Brita and Andrew had shared an extra-long embrace when saying goodbye earlier. At least they hadn't kissed, not in front of her anyway.

Little did I know Lucas would be the forward one. Caitlyn's face flamed at the memory. He had swept her up in a tight hug and then, to her complete horror, kissed her firmly right on the mouth before releasing her. His dad, Marek, had laughed, saying something about it being the Czech way. Caitlyn had mumbled her good-byes, while Lucas had promised he wouldn't forget her. The only consolation in the whole ordeal was the way Andrew had glared at Lucas.

The memory thrilled her even now. *Maybe, just maybe, Andrew cares for me as more than a friend. No... can't go there. Stop it, Caitlyn.*

Caitlyn curled her fingers, unaware of the fists she'd made until her nails bit into her palms. *Those thoughts are forbidden. Not allowed. If he loves you, it's only because you forced him to with your gift.* Her mind taunted her, throwing her worse fears right before her.

As she pushed away her feelings for the guy sleeping behind her far from her heart, the anxiety crept back in. Even with his body next to her, she felt worlds apart. Separated by something becoming more real and tangible by the minute. *Is this how it feels for everyone? I've never felt so desperate before. So depressed... so scared....*

Caitlyn met Alaina's gaze, hoping to find some solace in her angel's bright eyes. Instead, Alaina's eyes were squinting back at her, studying her face.

I feel like I'm trapped within myself, she wanted to say to her guardian. *Can you help me? Can you lift this... thing... off my heart? It's like a heavy weight that won't let up. Feels like something has a hold of me. I don't know what it is, but it's winning. I can feel it. I'm losing myself to it.*

Willow's hand landed on her shoulder, startling her. "Caitlyn, something's not right."

Caitlyn swallowed. "What's wrong?"

"You're wrong," Willow blurted, at which Andrew sat up promptly.

"Gee, thanks," Caitlyn said, trying to make light of it. *Of all the times for Willow to take notice of my inner turmoil, does it have to be now, in front of everyone? In front of Andrew?*

"No, that's not what I mean, something *sinister* surrounds you. I feel it. That's why I haven't been able to read you. I've been trying to place it. It's a strange feeling. Like every time I see you, I feel doubt and hopelessness."

"Um," Caitlyn cut in. "Okay, can we go talk somewhere, private?" She stood up, ready to bolt.

Trent moved closer. Andrew climbed off the bed. Everyone was staring at her, including all the angels. She felt the blood pounding in her face. *Willow just broadcasted my feelings for everyone to see. Thanks a lot, Willow.* Tears stung in Caitlyn's eyes. She hardly ever cried, Andrew stared at her face, and then stepped forward.

"Caitlyn, come here," he urged.

She backed up a step. "No, I'm fine. Really, everyone. Let's just get going, okay?"

Alaina reached over and placed a hand on her arm. "It's okay, Caitlyn.

We're here to help you through this. Let Andrew touch you. It might help."

"I don't *want* his help!" she yelled, pulling her arm free and shocking herself. The panic she felt inside had risen to a fever pitch. She felt desperate to flee the situation.

"You *need* him to touch you," Willow urged. "Andrew, do it now."

"Has everyone gone crazy?" she heard herself scream. "I'm fine! Totally fine! Leave me alone!" *Crap. What am I doing? This isn't me. None of this is!*

Andrew moved forward, the horror in his expression just making her shrink away more. *He's upset. He sees what an ugly person I really am!* Her heart squeezed painfully. *How could he ever love me! I'm selfish… I'm faithless…. my gift. I can't even use my gift right!*

The doubts shot at her from all angles, like pointy arrows, every single one hitting its mark, making the weight on her chest grow heavier.

Alaina moved swiftly and grabbed hold of both of Caitlyn's arms, pinning her from behind. "Andrew, try now! I've been trying to fight this off, but she's let them in. She's been letting them in for a while."

"What are you talking about?" Caitlyn shouted back at Alaina. The anger she felt inside raged. It felt almost foreign. "Let me go!"

"Andrew, be careful," Willow warned.

Daniel moved alongside Andrew. Drawing his sword, he stared down Caitlyn.

What the heck is going on? Why are they acting like I'm the enemy here?

She got her answer when Andrew reached for her. He aimed for her face, her cheek, with his kind, wonderful, healing hand. She longed for his touch— for him to soothe the pressure in her chest. Instead, as he inched closer, her neck snapped sideways… and her teeth sank into his flesh, drawing blood.

Chapter Thirty-one

Everything went white, then gray, and then black. She felt herself soaring forward, slamming into someone's body, pulling them both to the ground. The grunt she heard made her think it was Andrew. *What am I doing! Attacking him?*

She didn't have time to process it, because someone else grabbed her from behind, tore her body off Andrew, and threw her on her back. Knees landed on her arms, and dead weight rested on her chest. She glanced up to see Daniel had pinned her down, sitting on her body, with his sword aimed at her face.

"*Wait,*" Andrew gasped. He sounded like he was in pain. Real pain. Caitlyn turned just as she realized something warm and metallic filled her mouth. *Blood! Andrew's blood!*

"Andrew!" she cried, but her voice sounded gravelly. She wanted to say, *I'm so sorry*, but the words wouldn't form. Instead, she began hissing and growling.

Andrew was on his knees next to her. He cradled his bloody hand against his body. "Don't worry, Caitlyn. I'm fine. This will heal." He spoke to Daniel. "Don't hurt her."

She struggled to speak, but words wouldn't form. *What's happening to me! Why am I acting like… an animal? I bit Andrew! I'm the worse person ever! I'm not gifted or chosen! How could the Captain have picked me? He made a mistake…*

The last thought shot a wave a terror through her, and her body began thrashing against the angel hovering over her. Something held on to her legs. In a moment of throwing her head back and forth, she saw it was Brutus. Trent and Willow were on her left, Andrew on her right. *Willow is chanting something… what is she saying?*

Caitlyn tried to focus. It felt so difficult. Her mind wouldn't obey her wishes. *My mind is not my own.*

"I think Caitlyn is like those wolves and those pigs," Trent muttered. "Brutus, get word to Micah, fast. I think we're in over our heads here, unless one of you have the gift of expelling demons."

Demons? She felt her eyes bulge. Her stomach clenched, and she fought against those holding her down. *I have a demon in me!*

"I knew something was off," Willow said, Caitlyn hearing her clearly this time. "The whole time we were in Czech Republic, I couldn't see her thoughts. Something kept blocking me, keeping me out. Alaina saw it too, told me to watch her closely. Stay nearby."

"Why didn't you tell me?" Andrew blurted. "Maybe I could have helped her before it got to *this*."

Caitlyn shuddered. At least, she thought it was her doing the shuddering. *I'm in a freaking horror film, and I'm the possessed star!* She feared any second her head would start making three-sixties, and she'd be helpless to stop it. They all spoke like she wasn't even there. *I'm here still,* she wanted to scream. *Help me! Someone help me, please!*

"Sorry, Andrew. I didn't want you to worry," Willow said, "I don't think this is something you can heal out of her."

"Well, let me at least try," Andrew spat back. *He's so angry. Why's he so angry?* Her mind couldn't connect what was happening with reality. Everything felt more and more remote. The smell of the room, the taste of blood in her mouth, the sound of her friends' voices… all growing dimmer. All fading away.

Searing hot pain laced across her forehead. She convulsed, her entire body feeling like it was being ripped from her soul. It took her second to realize it was Andrew's hand on her causing the pain. She screeched, "Get it off! Get it off!"

Andrew flinched but kept it there. *Does it hurt him?* one very small part of her mind wondered. The stabbing agony shot down her spinal column, every fiber feeling like it was being torn in half.

"Stop! Please stop!" she sobbed.

His eyes sought hers, sweat dripping from his forehead. "Caitlyn, are you in there still? Caitlyn, fight this! You can fight it!"

She kicked her legs, thrashing her arms. One of her feet slipped from whoever hold them down and connected with something. She heard Trent swear, and then hands pinned her down again.

"I can't... I can't," she moaned to Andrew. *"Help me!"*

Andrew covered her heart with his hands. "Come on, Caitlyn. You got this. Come on! You can do this!"

"I can't," she wailed, and then she growled, her entire frame shaking like the worst case of the chills. Her teeth chattered, her jaw muscles almost locking in place.

Andrew fell back, taking his warm hands with him. "I can't get it out!" He ran his fingers through his hair, rocking back on his heels. Swear words fell from his lips. "Why can't I heal those I care about? First Eden, now Caitlyn! My gift is worthless!"

"Stop that right now," Willow commanded. "It was those very thoughts that got Caitlyn into this mess in the first place. She let doubt creep in. She wouldn't tell anyone either. I sensed it at the beginning. Her doubts have put walls up. Andrew, don't you *dare* do the same thing now. None of us can do this; we need to find someone who can."

Can that be true? I let the demons in by doubting myself? Chills rocked her body. *Funny how at first it felt like fire consuming me... now it's just cold. Really cold.*

Sage set her hand on Micah's shoulder. They were about to leave. This was it. Off to get answers from Ezeqeel. At least, Micah hoped.

Sage glanced over, her brows knit. "Brutus is here. Something's not right."

Micah gazed in the same direction to see the red-bearded angel had indeed appeared. Heart pounding, Micah raced over. "Brutus, what happened?" he asked, not wanting to hear the dreaded news—that they took too long and Eden was in bad shape… or worse… dead.

"Trent sent me," Brutus said.

"Is Trent okay?" Micah asked, fearing for his cousin's safety.

"He's fine. It's Caitlyn. She's possessed," Brutus said.

"*What?*" Micah gasped.

Damon asked, "How did that happen?"

"Alaina thinks she's been letting the demon come into her bit by bit by doubting herself and her appointed mission by the Captain. She went crazy when we rendezvoused in Rome. She bit Andrew and is being held down."

"She let the demon in?" Micah asked. "How did we not know about it? Didn't Willow see it if it came in slowly?"

"She knew something wasn't right," Brutus answered, "but the demon put walls around Caitlyn's heart, making it hard for Willow to see in. Alaina was afraid that it might be happening."

"Why couldn't Alaina stop it? Fight it off?" Micah asked, rubbing his face with his hands. He'd been so worried about Eden's safety that he realized he'd neglected the rest of his friends. He'd even had feelings about Caitlyn… *that I needed to talk to her. I should have done it. I took for granted that she'd be fine. Safe. That talking to Willow would help.*

"As guardians, we can fight off many demons to keep you safe from harm in many incidences, but as mortals, you still have your choice," Sage said evenly. "We can't force you to choose wisely. We can only try to influence you, remind you of who you really are. You're still free to listen to the Deceiver's messengers, who never rest from whispering doubt, fears, and discouragement into your heart. Alaina must have seen Caitlyn succumbing to the fears."

"Seems a bit severe though, I mean, everyone has fears and doubts. Doesn't mean they are possessed, right?" Damon asked.

"No, it doesn't. Nothing is as it should be," Gabriel muttered. "I'm sure we can thank Semjaza for this. The demon shouldn't have been able to get in at all. None of this is Caitlyn's fault."

"But Trent sent Brutus because they need help," Damon stated. "Caitlyn might hurt the others, or herself." He glanced over at Micah. "What do you want us to do?"

Micah wished everyone's eyes didn't shift over to him, waiting for direction. He needed more time, but he did agree with Damon. Caitlyn was a danger to herself and the rest of them. This took precedence over Ezeqeel. *She needs our help now.*

"Watchers will have to wait. Sounds like Andrew can't heal it out of her, right?" Micah asked Gabriel.

"No, casting out a demon takes a different gift. I can do it."

"You can?" Micah asked.

"Well, I'm not the greatest at it. That always fell under Raphael's department." Gabriel glanced over at Sage and then Micah. "But I can make do."

Micah's words, "Okay, let's go," faded away as, suddenly, he wasn't seeing Gabriel, Sage, Damon, and the others. He just saw a little girl with bright red hair and freckles. *That face... I've seen her before. But where?*

Then she was smiling, saying with confidence, "I told you one day I'd go to your beautiful city, Micah. I can help you now. Let me do it. Let me help Caitlyn."

"Olivia!" Micah blurted, bringing him back to the present. Everyone glanced his way as the girl disappeared from view.

"Olivia?" Damon asked.

"It's a girl who lives near the new city. I met her once. She can cast the demon out. Brutus, go back. Take Trent and everyone back to the temple. Find Olivia. She can help Caitlyn."

Brutus apparently didn't need more instructions. He nodded and was gone.

"Wait, we aren't going now?" Damon asked.

Micah shook his head, and Gabriel asked, "You sure about this Olivia?"

"I'm not sure of anything anymore," Micah said honestly, but then he glanced at Sage, "but I'm not going to lose faith now. Especially in others. Sage warned me the faith of my friends was being tested." He sighed heavily. "I felt there was something about Caitlyn, but I've been so worried about Eden that I didn't do anything."

"You can't blame yourself for that," Sage said. "Remember, Caitlyn made her choice not to believe in herself. And somewhere along the line, she must have stopped believing in the Captain too. I think that's how the demon got in all the way."

"That's a scary thought," Micah said soberly. "Well, all I know is, Olivia just told me she could do it. I'm going to have faith that's how the Captain wants it done. Semjaza might have created this diversion just so we'd give up our quest with the Watchers. I say we trust in those the Captain chose, and go find how to stop Semjaza."

Chapter Thirty-Two

Eden felt desperate to find Caitlyn. Her pleas for help filled her with dread. Every time she'd fear she'd lost her way, the voice would call out again. "Help...me..." The words echoed across the cornfields.

She had lost track of how long she'd been running and had no idea which direction she headed. After a while though, new fears closed in. *I'm out of the temple, out in the open, an easy target for Semjaza. I promised Micah and Caitlyn I'd stay put, stay safe. The last thing Micah needs is to worry about me more!*

She slowed her pace, doubts of what was even happening causing her to stop and catch her breath. Everything about this scenario seemed wrong. If Caitlyn needed help so badly, just where was she? After her manic run, she now glanced around. The night air clung to her, drying her sweat, leaving her feeling cold.

It was deathly quiet. The cornfields swayed around her.

"Help me," the voice whispered behind her.

That... doesn't sound like Caitlyn. She turned around slowly; no one was there.

"Help me," it said again a little louder from behind.

Eden didn't turn. The voice had taunted her, led her to where it wanted.

"Help me, help me, help me," it sang out, from every angle.

She couldn't help but spin, searching the stalks around her for the voice's owner. There was a rustling crash, like stalks being broken under foot. She didn't wait to see what was coming; she bolted in the opposite direction.

Even knowing Gabriel couldn't help, she still screamed his name as her feet carried her through the maze of corn. She heard it, the growling hiss she knew all too well. It was prom night all over again, only this time, there was no Gabriel to save her. Sharp claws threw her to the ground, knocking the air out of her. She could feel the demon's cold flesh through her clothes. She wiggled under its weight, trying to crawl away. It growled, and then suddenly, the weight lifted. The night sky lit up in all different directions, the corn reflecting crazy shadows. Multiple shadows. She bolted upright and saw that Cherubim surrounded her, slicing into the blackness, cutting down demons with their swords of fire. One with dark hair she recognized. Aaron, the one Gabriel had entrusted her with before.

Aaron glanced over. "Why are you outside the temple walls? Why are you running *straight* to the demons?" He sounded angry. Probably with good reason. Eden could see the dark shadows emerging all around. The swords of fire lit them up, their red eyes glowing in the darkness.

"I thought Caitlyn was hurt," Eden cried back. "Or I'd never have left."

"Caitlyn?" Aaron reached over and shoved her behind his back. Three more angels crowded around her, forming a shield. "Caitlyn's not here. How did you get out?"

"I don't know," she said, realizing she really didn't. "I thought Caitlyn did it. I ran out here to save her."

"Save her?" Aaron grimaced. "With what?"

She knew the angel wasn't trying to be rude, but at the moment, Eden didn't care. "I had to do something," she yelled back at him. "She's my friend, and she was begging me to help her! I didn't know it wasn't really her. I didn't think demons could open chamber nine."

Aaron glanced over his shoulder, making eye contact. He grunted, and then faced her. "Alright, here." He shoved a flaming sword in Eden's direction. "Take one of these. You need something to defend yourself with, when they break through the line."

"*When?*" she asked, scared to touch the fiery thing being offered to her.

"We are limited in number and without Gabriel here to call down more…" He left the rest unsaid. There was no time for words anyway. The demons were everywhere, snaking through the corn like black lizards.

He shoved the blade into her palm. "Don't worry, the flame won't hurt you." Then, like a second thought, he added, "But hold it away from you, just in case."

Oh, that's comforting. She had no choice. She gripped the handle, surprised by how light it felt. Then feeling its heat seep through her, warming her within, she was glad to have it. *Now, I can defend myself.* She didn't feel quite so helpless. Never mind the fact that she'd never swung a sword before in her life. She hardly thought the wrapping paper tubes her and Micah used as kids counted.

It didn't take long for her to be given the opportunity to prove herself. Within seconds of being handed the sword, demons converged upon them. They crawled in from all angles, throwing their bodies at the Cherubim. Aaron and the others fought hard, moving fast, their aim accurate, but one snarling demon broke through their line, lunging at Eden's body.

Without enough time to pull the sword back and swing, she thrust it forward, puncturing the demon's chest. It burst into ash before her.

Oh my gosh! I did it! I actually killed a demon! If Micah could see me now, she thought, thrilled for once she wasn't the damsel in distress. *See, I told you I could slay the dragon…* Her last thought was stopped by the new 'dragon' upon her. Only it wasn't one, it was three. *Oh boy.*

She braced herself against expected pain, but instead, she found herself raising the sword and bringing it down as she twisted at her waist. Shocked, she watched all three demons burst into ash before her. *Did I really just do that?*

Glancing up to see Aaron's wide eyes and half-opened mouth, she knew he was stunned too. More demons crashed in on them, and she prayed the same trick would work again. She swung out, but this time, she rotated her wrists as she slashed out. One, two, three more demons fell to ashes before her. *No way. I can't believe I'm really doing this.* It was strangely empowering not to be at the mercy of others. Not that she didn't need the angels' protection, she was just glad she could actually do something to help.

"Eden," Aaron called to her, "we've got to get you back inside the temple. Since I am not your guardian, I cannot transport you by angel flight. We must make a run for it."

She nodded, and Aaron pointed his sword. "Go that way. I'll protect you from behind. Joshua and Jarem," he called out. Two blond angels appeared. "Take the lead! Let's go!"

Joshua and Jarem leapt forth, each carrying two swords, clearing a path with their blaze of swirling fire. Eden scrambled to keep up. She felt Aaron behind her; he didn't leave much space between them. Demons were everywhere, their progress halted quickly by the sheer number of the onslaught.

"I don't understand!" she yelled to Aaron, striking another demon with her blade. "I thought this land was purged! Where are they all coming from?"

Aaron pushed his back against hers. They could no longer run or move. There were just too many demons. She felt his body move, fighting off the hordes. Joshua and Jarem were still near, swirling their swords of fires around in circles. The effect in the night's blackness was mesmerizing.

"The Temple and the city are purged. Demons can come in the outskirts. Gabriel left." Aaron grunted, and she felt his body slam into her back. She whirled around with her sword, stabbing at the demons surrounding them, connecting with one. Hearing Gabriel's name, Eden thought, *if only he could see me now too.*

Aaron continued speaking, as if they weren't in the middle of a battle. "He left us here to protect the city limits, and of course, to guard the Tree of Life. We have been keeping the demons on the outside of the stone wall. That's why I could not understand you marching straight into their realm, out of the protected area."

On second thought, maybe I'm glad Gabriel can't see me. I'm such an idiot.

"I didn't mean to," she shouted, to be heard over the wailing and screeching demons surrounding them. "I thought—"

"I know. Caitlyn. I understand, Eden," Aaron said. "Still doesn't change the fact you are here. And Gabriel… will not be understanding if I fail him again in keeping you safe."

"Oh." She felt even worse. *None of this was Aaron's fault. It's mine. Time to fix it.*

Eden saw a gap in the demons and shouted, "I'm going for it."

She dashed through, Aaron following after, killing demons who got in the way. Joshua and Jarem quickly caught up to them and took the lead again. She had no idea what happened to the rest of the Cherubim, and with everything happening so fast, all she could focus on was killing every red-eyed thing before her. She wondered if she should be feeling some kind of remorse. She'd never killed anything before, and she even felt guilty if she stepped on a large ant hole.

But these demons aren't animals; they aren't even bugs. As she sliced through two more black-bony demons, she felt only satisfaction. *Even Trent would be impressed.* Hope that they might actually succeed in getting back to the temple filled her, and then everything went wrong.

Joshua and Jarem suddenly disappeared and with the loss of their swords' light, blackness engulfed her vision. The sound of horrible wailing greeted them. *What was that?* She turned to ask Aaron, but she was horrified to see he, too, was gone. Darkness encompassed her, only her sword giving light.

"Help me," a voice taunted.

Eden whirled around. Even the black demons were, for the moment, gone. *What's going on?* She realized her mistake in turning so much; she was completely disoriented. *Crap. Which way's the temple now?*

Her hand shook as she held the sword out. "Who's there? Show yourself?"

"Can you help me?" the voice said again, this time sounding so small. *Young.* Not the same one she'd heard before. It came from behind.

Eden took a deep breath, readying herself. *On the count of three, I'm turning and slicing down whatever's there. One… two…*

"Please, can you help me? I'm scared," the voice whimpered.

Three!

Eden turned, sword raised, a scream dying on her lips. Her hand remained frozen in the air. A small, redheaded girl stared up at her. Her arms lifted, with upturned palms, her eyes wide.

"Please! Don't kill me!" A sob escaped the girl's lips.

Is this a trick? Some kind of new demon? Eden hesitated, and then shook her head. *No way. She looks too human...*

"Who are you? What are you doing here?" Eden asked, lowering the sword slowly.

"I just came to see the city. I only wanted to see the city," the girl wailed. "I snuck out. My mom doesn't know. I only wanted to see the city, honest! Please don't hurt me."

Eden eyed the girl warily. Nothing had made sense tonight, starting with the odd voice that had chanted to her in the temple. Her nerves felt frazzled, her mind unable to process what stood before her. *Micah said there was a girl he'd met who wanted to go in the city. Can this really be her?*

"It's okay," Eden said, deciding she'd have to trust her instincts on this one. She dropped to one knee and reached out to the girl. "I'm not going to hurt you, promise."

The girl didn't budge, just sobbed some more.

"What's your name, honey?" Eden stepped closer to the girl, while scanning the area. *No demons, but no angels either.*

The girl sniffed. "I'm Olivia." The bright green eyes lit up for a moment. "I just wanted to see Micah's city. Can I go home now?"

Eden smiled, glad to hear Micah's name. "Olivia, I'm Micah's friend, Eden. I want to help get you home because it's not safe out here..."

A low growl rumbled around them. They both heard it. Olivia whimpered but did not scream. Eden held her sword out, pulling the girl close to her body, trying to shield her from what was coming.

Olivia glanced up at her and whispered, "If we're quiet, they won't touch us. Just be real quiet."

Eden glanced down at her. "What?"

"I just get real quiet, and they go away. They're monsters. Black monsters."

Eden whispered, "Okay, I'll be really quiet, but we need to get you out of here." She didn't want to scare the girl, but she knew at any moment, the 'black monsters' would descend upon them.

"Hold still too. They'll go away. Just hold still," Olivia urged, closing her eyes.

"Olivia, how long have you been out here? The black monsters never touched you?"

"I don't know. I got lost trying to find the big, golden city, and then the monsters came. Hold still, be quiet, and they don't hurt you, you'll see. They don't touch me. They leave me alone."

Eden wished she could believe the girl, but she knew better. She couldn't comprehend demons showing mercy to anyone, but if what Olivia said was true, for whatever reason, they'd left her unscathed.

Which means, the longer I'm around, the more danger she's in. I've got to leave, draw the demons away from her. Aaron's got to show up, and surely, Olivia has a guardian, right? Eden knew she was trying to reassure herself that leaving a kid in the middle of a demon-infested cornfield was the right thing to do.

"Olivia, listen to me," she said firmly. Olivia peered up at her. "The black monsters want me, not you, and they won't go away if I'm just quiet. They've been attacking me. See, I've got this sword to fight them even."

Olivia's gaze took the sword in.

"I need to leave you here, for just a little bit. I will take the black monsters with me and get help. Can you stay right here? Don't move until I, or someone like me, comes back to help you?" On second thought, she added, "There aren't just monsters out there tonight, there are angels too."

"Really? Real live angels?"

"Yes," Eden said and tried to smile at the girl, "real angels. Some of them carry fire swords like me. They can help you."

"So what are the black monsters?"

Eden hesitated. "I don't want to scare you, Olivia."

"I want to know. I've seen them. That's scary enough."

"Okay, you're right. The black monsters are demons."

A small gasp escaped the girl's lips. "Demons?" she whispered.

"Don't worry; they won't hurt you. They want me."

"Why?"

"It's a long story. I promise I'll explain one day, but for now, here," Eden held the sword out. "Take this, just in case the demons come near you while I'm gone."

"But you need it more, Eden! You said they'll chase you," Olivia argued.

"I don't care. I can't leave you defenseless."

"No, I won't take it. I can't. It's made of fire."

"It won't burn you. I've been holding it all night." Eden took the girl's hand and tried to place the hilt in her palm

Olivia yelped in pain and drew her hand back. "See! I told you! It burned me, real bad."

Terrified, Eden withdrew the sword. "I'm so sorry, Olivia! Are you okay? Let me see your hand."

Olivia cried out, but not from her burn. "Watch out behind you!"

Eden whirled around to see a demon emerging from the cornstalks, walking upright. Olivia gasped. Its beady, red eyes glanced from Eden to Olivia. It stopped and dropped to its hands and knees, clawing at the dirt with its nasty nails.

"Get behind me, Olivia." Eden held the sword out to the demon. "Get away," she commanded the demon. "I've got a Cherubim sword. I *will* kill you."

The demon roared, spit dripping down its chin and neck.

"Olivia," Eden whispered over her shoulder, "on the count of three, I'm making a run for it." *Leaving you with nothing to defend yourself with*, Eden thought desperately. Knowing Olivia couldn't even hold the sword of fire without hurting herself, that weapon wasn't an option anymore. She scoured their surroundings, hoping to find something, even a stick the girl could use.

The beast clawed at the ground, chanting something under its breath.

It took Eden a minute to realize what it was saying. Then it became all too clear, the wet voice slurring the words, "Awakener. Awakener. Awakener."

That's it! It was the *only* thing she could do.

Eden turned quickly and hugged the girl, whispering, "May the new gift I give you protect you, so that no demon can ever touch you again!" She felt the rush of warm energy leave her body. With each awakening she did, the power of the feeling grew.

Olivia's eyes were wide when Eden tore from their embrace and whirled around to face the black demon. It took only one lunge, and the demon burst into ash around her blade. She didn't stop there, but dove into the field, slashing at whatever came near. All she cared about was getting far from Olivia and protecting the child from the hell surrounding her.

Eden didn't get far before black claws descended all over her body, pulling her to the ground. One demon used its body to pry her sword from her hand, half its arm bursting into ash before the sword fell to the earth, lighting up the ground. Eden tried to get near it, the dancing flames her only hope.

"Aaron!" she screamed. More claws—securing her hands, her arms, her legs, pinning her torso to the ground, grabbing her neck, twisting her face around, and then red, beady eyes appeared directly above her.

The demon spoke, "Semjaza's praise and glory be mine!" and the night erupted in the howl of demonic laughter.

Semjaza. He tricked me with Caitlyn's voice to leave the temple. Eden realized something as the demon hoisted her up and threw her over its cold, hard shoulder. They hadn't actually hurt her. *Semjaza's been trying to kill me with his curse. Why not order the demons to kill me right now?*

She didn't fight the demon horde that carried her along, into the blackness of the night, through the cornfields. All the demons surged in the same direction. She knew who they were taking her to. She didn't want to waste time struggling against the enemy that had won the battle. *It's time to win the war. If Semjaza wants me alive for even a few minutes, maybe I can figure a way out of this.* Because the night had shown her two things.

The demons couldn't have broken the temple's seal. If Caitlyn hadn't been there, then that leaves only one other person who could have done it. Me. And if Olivia can't even touch the Cherubim sword without getting burned, and I can, then maybe I can do more than I thought.

Chapter Thirty-three

Micah didn't care about how beautiful the valley was, or how magnificent the Swiss Alps were framing it, all his thoughts were on the evil Watcher buried within. Ezeqeel. They needed to get information out of him and get out of here. It wasn't just Eden's life hanging in the balance anymore. Micah would never forgive himself if Caitlyn didn't pull through this. Demon possession was something he knew very little about, other than what he'd seen in bad horror movies and several TV series. Now his plan to let a nine-year-old cast out the demon sounded like a pretty bad one.

He glanced over at Damon, who must have misunderstood Micah's frown, because he said, "Don't worry. I won't send him to Tartarus, at least not right away."

"Good, man," Micah replied, deciding to keep his thoughts to himself. It wouldn't help any of them focus now if he admitted he was terrified he'd made a mistake leaving Caitlyn alone.

Micah squared his shoulders. *Just get this done.* "Gabriel, ready?"

Gabriel's arms dropped, and a line of Cherubim appeared. "Just in case."

Everyone was ready. No one wanted it to go wrong.

Micah nodded, and Damon and Gabriel once again spoke the strange language that would summon the Watcher from his muddy grave. As the words filled the valley, Micah felt a part of himself getting pulled into its intonations. The language felt familiar in some way. He'd had the same feeling before when they'd summoned Armaros.

Micah shrugged it off and focused on the earth opening up before them, anticipating Ezeqeel's appearance. He held his breath and shifted his weight as a man with brown hair and the same brown tunic emerged. His hands were chained before him, with handcuffs like the ones Armaros had worn. The only major difference was this fallen angel's hair was much shorter, making it easy to see his features. He looked like a man maybe in his thirties, with dark hair and dark eyes. *If he had a suit, he could pass as businessman.*

Micah gazed into the dark eyes. Ezeqeel didn't flinch, just stared right back. Micah hoped the eagerness he saw there might mean he would cooperate. Where Armaros showed no interest in being above ground, Ezeqeel's eyes scanned the sky and the ground with a grimace-like smile spreading on his pale lips.

"Ezeqeel, we, the Holy Angels of the Captain, summon you for the day of your judgment," Gabriel called out. "We offer you your choice. To side with the Captain and fight for His cause, or choose to remain bound by your oath to Semjaza, who serves the Deceitful one, and who will lose the final battle."

Ezeqeel's eyes narrowed as he took in each of them, lastly Micah.

"The choice is yours, choose wisely," Gabriel finished.

"And if I choose the Captain? What will He do for me?" Ezeqeel asked.

"He will pardon you, end your probation, and with time, allow you to regain some of your former glory. You can rise above this," Gabriel said, gesturing to the angel's shackles.

Ezeqeel cocked his head to the side. "And what, remain nothing more than an angel? Semjaza gave me life, *real* life! I had offspring—posterity. I shared my knowledge with man, didn't hoard it away for my own selfish use. The *Captain* would strip me of my knowledge and return me to His courts to be nothing more than a subservient *angel.*"

Uh-oh. Micah felt the anger seething off Sage. She'd been so quiet through it all, but at Ezeqeel's last statement, heat poured off her.

"You know nothing of the Captain's courts!" she roared, catching them all by surprise. "You speak of things you are not *worthy* to *utter.*" Flames erupted, covering her body. Micah took a step away to keep from being burned.

"Sage," Gabriel blurted, "not your flames. We *need* him."

"I will purge you from the earth." Her voice rang out, like she hadn't heard Gabriel at all. "I will not stand by while you defile my Captain with your worthless tongue. I will be flames to that tongue, purging your words from within, like live coal."

"Sage, wait!" Micah yelled. Of all the things he'd been worried about facing Ezeqeel, the last thing he'd thought would be an issue was his own guardian angel, Sage, but suddenly, he understood her wrath. Ezeqeel mocked the very thing Sage was—a Seraph angel appointed to the highest court to sing praises to the Captain. Like she said, Ezeqeel knew nothing about that. No one did. Micah sure didn't. He didn't blame Sage for being upset… but the transformation of his usually well-mannered angel caused him to reflect on the power she held when it came to her flames. He hadn't forgotten the times she'd cleared leagues of demons within seconds, with them.

Sage wasn't listening to Micah, though. She marched forward, arms outstretched. Her flames grew in intensity, spanning the area around her. Even Damon took a few steps back.

Gabriel rushed forward. "Sage, though he spoke blasphemy, he still must make his final choice. It must be recorded. This is the way the Captain would have it be."

Sage's trance broke. At least, she stopped long enough to glance Gabriel's way. "So be it. But his final decision will be the last words he utters with his evil tongue if he chooses unwisely."

"Fine by me," Gabriel agreed, closing the gap between him and Ezeqeel. He drew his flaming sword and pressed it against the fallen angel's chest.

"You think you are so fierce, Gabriel, now that you are surrounded by angels of fire. But I seem to recall the scared mortal you were, hiding in that vessel, running from the Watchers' reign and glory," Ezeqeel muttered.

"You mean the Watchers' funerals," Damon said, his hands outstretched. Clouds gathered overhead. "Gabriel saved mankind while *your* offspring drowned."

Ezeqeel glanced up at the brewing storm. "And what is this? A summer storm, perhaps?"

Damon's hands curled, and the thunder cracked at the same time lightning scratched across the darkening sky. Ezeqeel's eyes narrowed in on Damon.

"You fancy yourself the master of the skies now, Uriel," he sneered in Damon's direction. "You know nothing of the cloud's true majesty and power."

"Clearly you have forgotten what Uriel can do then," Gabriel retorted.

Ezeqeel grimaced as lightning struck down all around, just barely missing him. The ground rumbled underfoot.

Gabriel leaned into Ezeqeel, pressing his sword down harder. "Tell us of Semjaza's plan."

"Or what? You'll destroy me?" He glanced over at Damon. "Send me to Tartarus, Uriel?" He threw his head back and laughed. "Go ahead. Send me. I welcome it. For my master will reclaim me from its hold. In the day he triumphs, he will free us all."

Gabriel's sword slid up toward Ezeqeel's throat. "The Deceiver does not reward those who serve him. He abandons them. Why would you think he would listen to Semjaza and free his precious Watchers?"

"Aw, but you are wrong, he will listen, because Semjaza has made a deal with him."

"The devil only makes deals he breaks," Gabriel hissed back, the sword's flame leaving angry, red burn marks on Ezeqeel's face.

"It is an unbreakable oath, fashioned by Semjaza himself," the fallen angel sneered. "So you see, in the end, all, even the great Deceiver, and your precious Captain, will bow down and serve Semjaza. I choose and forever will choose to serve and honor my true master, Semjaza. Send me to Tartarus, *Uriel.*"

Ezeqeel's smug face enraged everyone. Without even a weapon, Micah raced forward at the same time Uriel's lightning came slicing down again. Gabriel pulled his sword back and then swung forward with multiple blows to the angel's neck and torso at the same time Sage tore Ezeqeel's tongue out with a mere flick of her wrist. Flames burst out from the Watcher's mouth as he screamed in agony.

"Purged from within," Sage commanded. Her flames burst from his eye sockets, ears, nose, and throat.

Thunder cracked and Uriel's lightning found its mark; the fallen angel was no more.

Micah just stared at the space left behind. Sage's flames were gone, leaving smoke curling around her red dress.

"Ripped his tongue out, huh?" Gabriel asked.

"Oops," she said, her black eyes smoldering.

Gabriel muttered something, and then rubbed the back of his neck. "I think Uriel here sent chunks to Tartarus this time."

"Yes," Sage purred. "Let's see how kind and merciful his master is to him now."

Damon nodded. "Does anyone else get the feeling none of the Watchers are about to break their oath to Semjaza?"

Micah sighed. "You're right, Damon. I doubt any will."

Gabriel glanced over. "These missions are for them to each proclaim their final choice. We can't change their minds; we can't influence them one way or the other. They were stubborn and evil in my days, and they are just as set in their ways now."

"But what about Eden? What do we do if Semjaza's oath seems to trump everything else?" Damon asked, forming the question Micah didn't have the heart to say. All his hopes that the Watchers would somehow help him defeat Semjaza, or at least stop the disease spreading in Eden's body, were going up with the flames the angels had just used. All it left was dark, black smoke. The only thing left to try was to face Semjaza. With how it had gone with the last two, he feared Semjaza would happily welcome Uriel sending him to Tartarus, though.

Gabriel scowled. "Semjaza's pride will be his downfall."

"That's it!" Micah exclaimed, "Perhaps these missions weren't so pointless after all."

"What do you mean?" Damon asked.

"Didn't you find it odd that Armaros and Ezeqeel almost welcomed the thought of going to Tartarus? I mean, I thought it was the lowest level of Hell? Not only will Semjaza stop at nothing to get what he wants, in this case, Eden, but he also fears no one, not even the devil. He made some kind of deal. I think we found another weakness."

"How is making a deal with the devil a weakness?" Damon asked.

"Because, we all know that in the final battle, it will be the Captain and the devil. Not the devil and Semjaza. Or Semjaza and the Captain. Semjaza loses somewhere along the way. He's not going to win this. Not if we believe in all the prophecies. Gabriel's right. The devil can and *will* break his oath to Semjaza and all the Watchers will remain trapped in Tartarus."

Gabriel and Sage both nodded.

"We need to figure out what the deal was they made with each other, and maybe we can use that somehow to free Eden," Micah said. He glanced around. "I don't think we will learn more here. Let's go back. I need to make sure Caitlyn's okay, that Olivia actually got rid of that demon."

He left unsaid he felt something didn't feel right. He couldn't shake the pit in his stomach. Was it his own guilt for neglecting Caitlyn? Or was it because Semjaza had used Eden's injury to toy with them all? Either way, both thoughts sickened him.

He tried to focus on Caitlyn, wanting to check in on her. He saw nothing. He shifted his thoughts to Eden, trying to picture her in the temple. Nothing. Frustrated, he decided to just think of Eden. The curve of her lips when she smiled at him. Instead, he saw her blonde hair whipping across her face, covering those soft lips.

She was moving fast, running, and most definitely was not in the temple. Cornstalks surrounded her. Demons were everywhere! The only light he could make out was from a flaming sword *she* was wielding! Shocked at what he was seeing, Micah cried aloud when demons knocked her to the ground, ripping the sword from her hands. Within seconds, she was whisked into the blackness.

He didn't wait to see more, but shook his head, desperate to pull himself out of the vision. He'd seen enough; he needed to tell the others. *Demons have Eden!* He struggled against the vision, trying to backpedal out of what he saw. Since they usually ended on their own, he found himself lying on the ground when he came to. Sage knelt over him.

"Micah, what is it?" she asked, shaking his shoulder.

He tried to bolt to his feet, but he ended up falling over. "Eden's not in the temple!" he yelled, stumbling to his feet again. "Demons have her!"

Without a word, Gabriel disappeared from sight.

Chapter Thirty-four

aitlyn screamed until her voice was hoarse and then gone. The arms carrying her tightened, every place her body touched his shot agonizing pain through her. She could feel Andrew trembling. She wondered if it pained him too, carrying a possessed person around. As soon as they had landed, Alaina had handed her off to him. Caitlyn wanted to check on her angel, make sure she was all right, but Alaina was gone from view. Andrew had cradled her, pushing her head against his chest, where she'd longed to be for so long, close to his beating heart. Now the heat from his skin burned her. A fire so hot that it felt cold.

"How do we find Olivia?" Trent barked, "We're here, but we can't even get inside the temple without Caitlyn. I sort of doubt she's feeling very *faithful* right now."

Caitlyn heard a deep grumbling, and then realized it came from her own body. *I'm a monster,* she groaned inwardly.

"Release me!" she managed to whisper into his chest, but Andrew's arms only held her tighter.

"No way. I'm not letting you go, I'm not giving up on you," he said firmly. "Willow, how do we find Olivia?"

Caitlyn heard collective gasps. Then Willow said, "I think we just did."

She wanted to see what was happening, but Andrew's grip was like iron, holding her to him.

"I'm Olivia," a small voice said. "Are you Eden's friends? She said she'd send someone to help me."

"Ye-s… er, wait," Trent said. "Eden? Where did you see her? In the temple?"

"Temple? I was only trying to see the city you and Micah are building. What's the temple?"

"Never mind that, where did you see Eden?" Willow repeated in a soft tone, probably trying not to scare the girl.

"Out here in the corn. She tried to protect me from all the demons. She ran off, took the demons with her to save me. I thought she'd sent you."

Andrew gasped. "Eden's running from demons?"

"Crap, crap, crap," Trent muttered. "What in the *cavelo* is she doing out of the temple? Micah's going to go ballistic. We've got to find her. Come on, Andrew. Let's go."

Caitlyn felt the grip on her loosen. Her body slid down until her feet landed on the ground. *He made his choice. See. He will run to rescue Eden now, and leave you here… to die. He doesn't care about you,* the voice in her head taunted her.

"Shut up! Just shut up!" Caitlyn wailed, falling to the ground, practically tearing her hair from her head.

"Caitlyn." Andrew dropped down next to her and pulled her into his lap. "I'm here. Willow, go with Trent, find Eden. I'm not leaving Caitlyn until she's healed."

"Smart choice, Andrew," Willow stated matter-of-factly. Then, to Olivia, she said, "Did Eden by chance hug you before she left?"

"Yes."

"Perfect," Willow replied. "You see, Eden's hugs are very special. They make it so people can do extraordinary things. My friend, Caitlyn here, needs help. Maybe you and Andrew can help her while Trent and I go find Eden. Sound good?"

Caitlyn managed to glance up and saw Olivia nod. Something about the redheaded girl made her uneasy. She curled up against Andrew.

Trent clapped his hands together and said, "Perfect. Open up those spidey senses of yours, Willow, because we are going to need them tonight.

Brutus and Esther, are you with us? Let's go!"

The four of them bolted into the cornfields as Caitlyn eyed the child warily.

Olivia squinted back at her. "What's wrong with her? She looks sort of crazy."

Andrew chuckled. "Yeah, I suppose she sort of does right now. But Caitlyn isn't usually like this. She has this... er... dark thing in her right now making her act this way."

"You mean, like the black monsters? Eden told me they're demons. Is there one of those inside her?"

Caitlyn heard herself snarl. She didn't like the child getting closer. She didn't like the way the child looked at her. "Keep her away!" she shouted when Olivia got too close.

"You're a pretty brave kid," Andrew said, his grip on Caitlyn tightening. "You said you were in a field tonight? Trying to see the city?"

"Yes, I keep seeing it in my dreams. My mom thinks I'm crazy. I snuck out tonight. Rode my bike. I saw this place on the news, and I know Vern's farm. We only live a few miles away. But when I got in the cornfields, I got lost... and then there were demons everywhere! So I held real still and nothing hurt me. I tried to tell Eden that. They go away if you close your eyes, like a bad dream. Only I guess with dreams, you open your eyes to make the monsters go away."

"The demons left you alone?" Andrew cut in. "They don't usually do that. They must have sensed something about you even before you were awakened."

"What's that mean? Awakened?"

"When Eden hugged you, she gave you a gift, like a... superpower."

"Cool!" Olivia said loudly.

Caitlyn growled and grimaced within.

Andrew continued speaking as if Caitlyn hadn't just acted like a wild animal. "You seem to repel demons, Olivia. That's a pretty good superpower to have if you ask me. Do think you could help me with my friend here?

Maybe if we do it together, we can make the bad thing inside her go away."

"The demon, you mean?" Olivia stated.

"Yes. Maybe if we both put our hands on her, we can push that demon out."

"Okay." The voice sounded so confident. *So trusting.*

Caitlyn hated that part of her pitied the girl, wished she wasn't in such a dangerous situation, and the other shied away, terrified of the young child. The terrified side won out.

"Keep away!" Caitlyn shrieked as Olivia inched nearer. "Don't touch me!"

Andrew cradled Caitlyn tighter against him, once again pressing her face to his chest, blocking her vision. "Okay, we'll do it together," his voice rumbled in her ear.

Hands landed on Caitlyn's back, only they didn't feel like hands, they felt like meat cleavers tearing through her flesh. Her body convulsed and rocked in Andrew's hold. The agony was too much, her vision exploding in white spots. An acrid taste filled her mouth, then everything went black and silent.

"Wait!" Damon shouted, seeing the scene before him; Andrew holding Caitlyn's thrashing body down as a redheaded girl pressed her hands against Caitlyn's back.

Damon bolted over, dropping to his knees next to Andrew. Gabriel and Micah had gone to find Eden, but demon distraction was more Damon's department.

Andrew glanced over. "We don't know exactly how this works, but Olivia's touch seems to be pulling the thing out. It's fighting it, and Caitlyn... well, I'm not sure if she's even aware of what's going on now."

Damon glanced over at the girl. *She's just a kid.* "Are you okay? This doesn't hurt you, does it?"

"No, it doesn't hurt. Just feels like I'm pulling on a very hard rope. Like when I play tug of war with my dog."

Damon smiled. "Perfect. Just picture that and give that thing a hard yank. I'll take care of it when it comes out."

At least, Damon hoped he could. Traveling back, he'd devised a plan on how he might seize the demon's spirit when it left Caitlyn's body. He worried he'd miss the moment.

Olivia nodded and closed her eyes. She grunted before plopping down on her backside. Caitlyn's body immediately fell limp in Andrew's arms as a black shadow emerged. Damon stretched his hands out, commanding the elements around to block its passage, the air molecules forming a shield around it, keeping the spirit from escaping or worse, implanting itself into another living thing nearby.

"Stop," Damon commanded, holding the evil spirit still. It wasn't the same as the bony demons they usually faced. "Before I send you to Tartarus, where you belong, you will tell us how you took hold of Caitlyn's body."

The black shadow made some kind of whimpering sound.

"You recognize me, don't you? Then you know I can demand you to answer my question."

The shadow cried out, "Yes, *master*."

Damon found it odd how this mere demon apparition feared him; Watchers seemed to sneer at his power. He could feel the shadow creature shaking where he held it. *Good, maybe I can get something useful out of this thing.*

"I was sent by Leviathan," the shadow-demon wailed. "I failed. Leviathan will not be pleased. He will punish me."

"Don't worry about your demon prince. Who are you? Why did Leviathan send you?"

"I am Doubt, one of many," the shadow said in a deep voice. "Formed and sent to possess this child to keep her from realizing the power of her gift. Leviathan, prince of heresy, tempts people to give into me. I can seep into anyone who allows passage, anyone who will listen and deny their faith."

"But why Caitlyn? There are many gifted ones now. Why single her out?"

"I take my orders from Leviathan, who serves our Master."

"I am your master now, answer me," Damon said firmly. "Why is Leviathan after Caitlyn?"

"Yes, my master. Leviathan was instructed to thwart the powerful one. To keep the powerful one bound by her own limits. To never realize the potential within. For all things run on Faith. Faith is power. Power the Great Deceiver despises and fears. Leviathan is third in line to the throne, binding the one who possesses the true gift of faith would have moved him in demon hierarchy."

"So it's all a big battle for position among the demon princes then? It had nothing to do with Semjaza and his plans?"

"The Watchers and the Deceiver work as one, for now," the shadow hissed.

"But that won't always be the case, I take it," Damon concluded. "So Leviathan eliminates the one with faith, cripples her gift by you possessing her body. I find it hard to believe this just happens to coincide with Semjaza being after the Awakener."

The shadow pushed against Damon's hold, and he immediately seized the demon with more binding.

"Why do you fight me?" Damon asked. "Am I getting too close to the truth? Does your old master not want me to know why these two are under direct attack more than the rest?"

The shadow screeched and fought the bindings.

"Answer me, Doubt. You have lost. I command Tartarus. I am the only master you need to worry about now."

"Semjaza desires the Awakener. The Deceiver allows him the use of his minions to do his bidding. Even now, the demon spawn have proven victorious and carry her to him."

"To Semjaza?"

"Yes. To where only Semjaza can reach her."

Damon heard Andrew gasp. "Where's that?" Damon asked.

"You will have to face Semjaza to save her."

Damon nodded; he had thought as much. "And Caitlyn? Semjaza wants her too?"

"He does not *desire* her. It was a trade."

"Trade?"

"Semjaza's enchantment allowed me full passage into this human vessel. Allowed me to penetrate her soul."

"That's how you could possess Caitlyn like you did?"

"Yes, without his power, I would have been left to little more than thoughts in her mind."

"So Semjaza gets the Awakener with the devil's help, and what, the devil gets Caitlyn with Semjaza's help?"

The shadow wailed out, "Yes."

Damon noticed Caitlyn had begun stirring, lying on the ground in Andrew's arms. Olivia was curled up next to Andrew, wide-eyed and watching.

"Was this the deal made between Satan and Semjaza?" Damon asked, turning his attention back on the shadow-demon.

"Yes."

"Was that all there was to their oath? Or was there more?"

"I do not know more of their dealings. That is all I know."

Damon debated whether to test the shadow more, to see if he were lying, but sensed it spoke true. High-ranking demons wouldn't entrust demon spawn with all their plans.

Damon wished Micah and Gabriel were here. He tried to think of anything else he could ask the thing before sending it away. If he felt a bit more comfortable with the art of holding it captive, he would have kept it longer, but as it was the first demon he'd ever held and interrogated, he decided it was time to get rid of it.

A few words and the storm rolled in. Like it'd become second nature, Damon sent the demon down to Tartarus with one bolt of lightning and a resounding crack of thunder.

Chapter Thirty-five

Eden could see little. All she could do was feel was the cold blackness surrounding her. She kept telling herself over and over not to panic. The mad race through the cornfields, the demons pulling her through the earth, through passages she didn't think were humanly possible to cross, were now memories. At some point, she'd passed out; at least, she thought she had. When she'd come to, she found herself sitting in the dark. Alone.

Better alone then with demons all over me. She tried to formulate a plan. She'd long discovered she sat in some sort of prison cell. The ceiling was probably only five feet; she couldn't stand up without stooping over at the waist. She could only go a few feet without bumping into a wall. It was a tiny, stone prison. Semjaza's holding cell.

She curled in on herself, her back pressed against one wall and her arms providing a ghost of a barrier against the cold. Hugging her knees tightly, she rocked herself, trying to keep from panicking. All she could do was pray and beg that Gabriel would find her somehow. *Micah will see me . . . He'll have a vision.*

As much as she wanted to just close her eyes and wish her friends could save her, she feared she might be out of even Gabriel's reach this time. *I need to save myself. But how? I have nothing. This room has no way out. No window, no door that I can feel. It's completely sealed in.*

She squeezed her knees harder. She couldn't think about how small her prison was; claustrophobia would engulf her if she did.

The blackness was stifling, suffocating in its own nothingness. Like she'd entered a strange void. The only tangible thing keeping her nailed to reality were the hard walls surrounding her body. She ran her fingers along it—smooth. She kept inching her fingers, not really sure what she was searching for. There had to be something, a crack, a break, even a bump. Nothing.

Discouraged, she let her hand fall.

Although there were no angels here, she thought of one person who might hear her. With that hope, she cleared her throat and whispered, "I know Gabriel isn't here, but you are. I know you can hear me. At least, I hope you can. I... need help. I'm buried somewhere, taken by demons to be Semjaza's prize. Can you help me?"

There was a loud bang above her head. She yelped and then pleaded over and over, "Please, help me! Please!"

The entire ceiling to her prison lifted up, and an eerie blue light filled her cell. She ducked down, shielding her eyes. The loud grating sound continued, until the entire top of her cell was gone. *I was in some kind of stone container*, she realized.

"Even He can't hear you here," a deep, masculine voice called down to her

She couldn't see who the voice belonged to. She wasn't sure she wanted to. She'd seen too many demons and princes of demons. She knew whatever awaited her would be ugly and evil.

She crouched down, curling tighter into a ball, and squeezing her eyes shut, continued to chant her prayer. "Help me! Please, help me!"

There was a rich roll of laughter; not the hysterical hackling of demons she'd grown used to, but a human-sounding laugh. "I already told you He cannot hear you. Why not be a good girl and come out, let me see my prize, since you just named yourself such."

She sickened, knowing who waited for her, but she didn't budge. "I won't come out, and I'm not your prize."

"I merely repeated what you just said," he said with a chuckle. "I knew I'd picked the right one. Your spirit is strong. Your ability quite astounding."

The blue light was everywhere. Eden tried to study her stone box to see where she was, but she could make out nothing.

"So why kill such a strong spirit?" she asked, trying to keep him talking. In books, that was what the heroine always did, right? They got the enemy blabbering while they formulated their escape.

"Kill you? I think you have the wrong idea. I have no desire to kill you."

She tried to keep from gasping. "You're lying. You've been sending demons after me, in my bedroom, and on prom night. What about Oeillet's staff wound? You cursed it, didn't you?"

"Yes, all you say is true." His voice echoed down to her. "But never to kill you, only to bring you to me. I needed a ruse, something to scare your guardian into actually leaving you. I still can't believe how beautifully it worked. Your precious Seer played right into, assuring Gabriel the temple was the safest place for you while they searched for a cure."

She kept to herself the fact that Gabriel would have left her anyway, if what Micah had said were true. Micah needed him to unbury the Watchers. Maybe Semjaza didn't know that.

"You must really fear Gabriel."

"Ah… I don't fear Gabriel, but as I am confined. I had to use demons to reach you. They cower and snivel around angels, especially him. They are worthless most of the time. I'm afraid using them has given you the wrong impression of me. Demons aren't… how should I put it… gentle as us mortals are. I'm afraid they are a bit rougher in the handling of such precious cargo."

"Mortal? You're not mortal," Eden said, not sure if it was brilliance or insanity making her so bold. "You are a fallen angel."

"As are you, Eden."

"What?"

"You and I aren't so different. You are, in essence, a fallen angel while you walk the earth as a mortal. You were there before, an angel to the Captain. Now you are here, allowed to love whom you choose. Allowed to have families. Isn't that what you want, Eden? To be with your precious Micah?"

She didn't miss the malice behind his voice while he spoke of Micah.

"I simply desire the same thing. To live, to have the mortal experiences, to feel pain and joy like humans do. Why should I be punished for having the same thing the sons of Adam did?"

She stammered to speak, "Because you weren't peaceful like you're saying. You didn't want happiness or love. You destroyed humans. Your families were monsters."

"You were not there, so you do not know of what you speak. I came to earth and brought many with me who desired the same things as I did. We lived lives. We had wives, children, and happiness. It wasn't my fault the Captain cursed my offspring, making them giants with unquenchable appetites." His voice echoed down to her.

"You were forbidden from coming down; you disobeyed. And you taught men to do evil. To kill, to hurt each other. Now you are defending yourself like what you did was right." She swallowed. "If you're so noble, why not free me? Why do I sit in this prison?"

"Oh, but I have freed you. You can come out whenever you desire. Come and meet me, see that I am not the beast you think I am."

Eden stared at the blue space above her; it was like a blue, iridescent fog. Did she dare climb out? Was this all a trap?

"I think I'll stay in here," she said firmly.

"You choose to remain in your prison. So be it." The voice didn't sound angry; it was calm. "I will not rush you. You will see how kind and considerate I can be. Come out when you are ready, my prize."

Eden sank back down into her corner and hugged her knees tightly. *I'm never coming out then. I'd rather die of thirst and starvation than meet you, Semjaza.*

Chapter Thirty-six

Gone, how can she be gone? Micah shoved his hand through his hair, which was sweaty from running through the cornfields for the past few hours. They had found Trent and Willow. Willow had been tracking the demons' path. Gabriel quickly joined her, and the group of them had hoofed it through the fields until suddenly the scent or marker they had been using was gone.

They all stood now, staring at the ground Willow pointed to.

"I don't know how they did it, but they took her underground somehow," she said.

"That's impossible," Gabriel muttered. "At least, it should be."

Sage nodded. "Yes, as a mortal, she shouldn't be able to descend into that realm."

"Does that mean she's not mortal anymore?" Micah asked, the panic making his voice raise.

Gabriel peered around, inhaling. "No, she's alive. If they'd killed her, she'd be with the Captain. Semjaza must keep her alive in order to claim her as his own."

"Claim her as his own?" Micah repeated, not liking what it sounded like.

"Semjaza wants Eden physically," Sage said quietly. "Like Gabriel said before, Semjaza's one weakness is he craves the women he cannot have. He is never satisfied. It consumes him. He has set his eye on Eden; there is no way he'd let her die now."

"I don't know if I should be comforted or horrified," Micah muttered.

Trent slapped Micah's back. "Dude, you have some serious competition."

He glanced over, debating whether to punch Trent in the nose for joking at a time like this or to be grateful for his sense of humor. I guess the last thing I need now is to despair. He left Trent's nose alone.

Gabriel dropped down to the ground and began tracing the earth with his finger. As he did so, the dirt gave way, sinking into cracks and grooves. Within seconds, a silver symbol emerged, drawn into the ground. Micah shuddered at it—a large, upside-down triangle with an 'X' running through it. The point of the triangle ended with a swirly 'V' pattern.

"What is it?" Micah asked, as both he and Trent stared down at their feet.

"That thing gives me the heebie-jeebies," Trent said, "And my heebie-jeebies are never wrong. That's ancient and evil. Don't touch it, Micah."

Gabriel glanced up. "Trent's right. It's a demon portal. That's how they got her through the divide; this symbol acts as a passageway between worlds." He rubbed his forehead. "I don't understand why Lucifer is allowing Semjaza the use of his dominion. I know they made an oath, but I can't imagine what it could be."

"I think I can answer that," Damon said, startling all of them as he walked toward them, his guardian Seth following him. "I just got done interrogating the demon in Caitlyn."

"How is she? Is she okay?" Willow asked, rushing over to him.

Damon glanced at her, and took her hand in his. "She'll be fine. Andrew's with her, and the demon is definitely out." He shifted his gaze to Micah. "I questioned it before sending it to Tartarus."

"Why do I miss all the cool stuff?" Trent complained. "Seriously, Damon, just wait till I get there next time, okay?"

Damon snorted. "I promise I'll put the next one in a shoebox for you. Just make sure you poke holes in the top."

Trent rubbed his hands together. "Sweet, I've always wanted a pet demon."

"Okay, you two, knock it off," Micah cut in. "I'm just glad Caitlyn's okay." Inwardly, he breathed a sigh of relief. Now we just have to save Eden. "What did you learn, Damon?"

"That part of the deal Semjaza and Lucifer made was a trade. Semjaza gets Eden and well, the devil gets Caitlyn."

"What?" Willow gasped. "I mean, I know he wants us all, but that's just plain horrifying!"

Gabriel nodded. "That's why Semjaza gets free use of the demons. Even the Deceiver's sign."

"Well, deal or not, looks like the devil just got gypped on his end of the bargain," Trent said. "Wonder how the big guy will take that news."

"Not well," Gabriel said, and then he grinned. "Best news I've heard all day."

"How's that?" Micah asked. He couldn't imagine how there was anything good in any of this. Caitlyn might be safe, but Eden was not.

"Because their deal, with all its facets, isn't working exactly as planned. This oath Semjaza made with the Deceitful One won't last long. We might not have to be the ones to stop Semjaza in the end. His own arrogance will bring him down on himself."

"Fight the enemy with the enemy," Micah mumbled. "Only problem is, until that time, Eden is with the enemy. Wherever that may be. For all we know, she isn't even by Semjaza."

"No, she is someplace near him. The demon said we'd have to go through Semjaza to ever find her," Damon added.

"Okay. Well, that's where we go then," Micah said, trying to sound confident. "Semjaza is still buried. He can't hide or go anywhere. We just have to go summon him up, that's all. And find out where he's hiding Eden." Even as he said it, he already saw the huge snag in his plan.

Damon said it for him, "Only problem is, he will happily let me send him to Tartarus, thinking he'll be free one day by his deal with the devil."

"And if you send him there, we'll never find where he hid her," Micah finished. He glanced around, discouragement taking hold. "So what can we do? Gabriel? Sage? I'm open to suggestions."

Gabriel and Sage glanced at one another, and then she answered,

"Micah, we wish we could tell you exactly what to do, but part of this human existence is to figure things out on your own. Honestly, at this point, neither one of us has been given further instructions other than to let you lead the way. You are the Seer. Use your gift."

That's it! Of course. He nodded and spun on his heel, striding away from the group.

"Hey, where are you going?" Trent called after him.

He turned around for a moment. "Give me a few minutes alone. I need to find someplace quiet," Micah said, "Sage is right; it's time for me to start acting like the Seer."

Chapter Thirty-seven

Caitlyn's eyelids were too heavy to open. She could feel someone's arms wrapped around her, their warmness seeping through her veins, soothing her. Somewhere in her consciousness, she was aware of something else lulling her. Humming. Was he actually humming? It felt so out of place considering the last thing she remembered was screaming at a little girl to get away. *Why was I so afraid of a child?* Bits of memories floated around her mind. Flying by angel, Alaina straining to hold her through the spectrums they'd passed through. Andrew promising to stay with her until she was better. *Andrew. . . I bit Andrew.*

She groaned. The humming stopped.

"Caitlyn? Can you hear me?" he asked. His grip around her shoulders tightened.

"Yes," she slurred at the same time she forced her eyes open. Emerald eyes gazed down at her. Andrew cradled her in his lap, sitting on the ground.

"What happened?" she asked, glancing around. "Where's Olivia? Is she okay?"

"Yes, she's fine. Vern has her. He's showing her the city real quick before getting her home safe to her mom. She's been out here all night."

Caitlyn realized the sun was shining. "What time is it?"

"I don't know, maybe six or so. I didn't dare move you after the thing left. You've been unconscious. How do you feel now?"

She gazed up into his eyes. "Much better. I feel like I can breathe again. Like a weight's been lifted off my chest."

"Good." His eyes lingered on her face.

There's something he's not saying. "Where's everyone else? What happened to Eden? Did they find her?"

"I don't know. Damon left to join Trent and Willow. No one's come back."

"That's not good. We should go after them. Someone might need healing," she said, moving to get out of his arms.

"Caitlyn, wait," he said, not really releasing his hold. "I think we should... talk... before we go."

"Talk? Andrew, don't worry. I'm good now. We should go. What if the others need you?"

"And what if they need you?" he asked.

She stared at him.

"You have a gift too. More amazing than mine. When did you stop believing in yourself, Cat?"

It warmed her heart to hear him use her dad's nickname for her. She sighed and climbed out of his lap. This time, he didn't stop her. She sat next to him and shrugged. "I don't know; it just sort of happened." *Do I really have to tell him the truth?*

He frowned. "Something happened, didn't it?"

She didn't say anything, and he said, "All I know is something changed between us. One minute, we're best friends and then the next, I feel like you can't get away fast enough. Did I do something?"

"No, Andrew. You didn't do anything wrong. In fact, you do everything just perfectly," she said. *Oh boy. I guess I have to.* She braced herself for his hurt when he found out she'd cost him the girl he loved more than anything. *Better to be honest, just get it all off my chest now. Holding it all in got me in this mess in the first place. And I can't be letting more demons in!*

"Then what is it? I feel like ever since we got back from Illinois, before I mean, you've been pushing me away."

She glanced over at him. "You're right; I have been. But not for the reason you're thinking," she added, seeing the hurt flash through his expression. "I didn't want you to know what I'd done."

"What do you mean?"

"Before I knew what my gift could do, I think I might have wished some things to be… that may have changed things for you."

"I have no idea what you're talking about. Come on, Caitlyn, just tell me."

"I think I influenced Eden to break up with you."

"We've been through this already, just because you told her to do what her heart thought was best doesn't mean you caused the break up," he said, plucking some stray grass strands off the ground. "That's what you're beating yourself up over?"

Caitlyn squeezed her eyes shut and blurted, "That day in the motel, I wished you cared about me like you did Eden."

Andrew glanced over, and his mouth dropped. "Wait, what?"

She rushed on, "I realized then that I'd used my gift of faith to wish something for myself. You asked when I stopped believing in myself. It was the day I realized I'd hurt the one person that means more to me than anyone. I'd been selfish, wanting you to like me. And so Eden broke up with you… because of me."

She couldn't bear his shocked expression any longer, so she glanced away. "I'm so sorry, Andrew. I understand if you hate me now."

"You stopped believing in yourself because of me?" he asked softly. "You stopped having faith because you like me?"

Her face felt hot. She stammered, "I guess I was afraid if you liked me back that meant I'd done it all with my gift. That it wasn't real, but then you didn't like me more than a friend, so then I doubted I was even gifted."

His face seemed surprisingly calm. I guess he's not too mad about the whole Eden thing.

"Caitlyn, you're wrong about two things," he said at last, nudging her shoulder with his.

"Oh really, just two things? I thought my list was much longer these days."

He grinned. "No, just two things… at least for now."

"Okay, fine," she said, glad he was teasing her. It made the awkwardness over the fact she'd just spilled her heart out to him a little more bearable. "Tell me the two things."

"First of all, you really have no idea how your gift works, or what it even is. You're looking at it all wrong. I know you aren't seeing all the things that have happened because of your faith. You make everything run smoother... easier. You're like," he snapped his finger, "like the oil in this crazy group's engine. Eden would be like the ignition, gets it all started, but we all have to have you to work right. I need you. Willow needs you."

She shook her head, wanting to protest his car analogy.

"Stop that," he said, grabbing her face with his hands, squeezing her cheeks playfully between his fingers. She giggled, but he didn't remove his hands. His grip loosened, his fingers caressing her cheek, sending goose bumps across her skin.

"Willow needed you with her to find Marek. I've needed you to heal Eden and Micah. And don't forget about your dad. Your mom wasn't going to let me in, but you did it. You made it happen with your gift."

She stared back into his eyes, his words filling her with a new sensation. Maybe I have done some good. She swallowed, his closeness making her pulse rage.

"So if that's the first thing I'm wrong about, what's the other then?"

"You're wrong about how I feel about you." He closed the gap between them, his lips landing on hers. Fire plummeted through her stomach, reaching her toes, filling her whole body with a strange new ache. She tried to push him away, half scared of what she'd just felt.

"No, wait. Andrew, see this is what I was afraid of. You don't really like me. I misused my—"

He pulled her to him, grinning. "You think you're forcing me to kiss you?"

"Well, yeah." She bit her lip. Pretty sure I can't say no to him again, even if I brainwashed him.

"I thought I just covered all that? Now, why won't you let me heal you? All the way, like I want to."

He didn't let her respond, but pressed his mouth against hers. This time, she didn't resist. She kissed him back, climbing into his lap, wrapping her arms around his shoulders, her fingers getting lost in his hair. His healing hands pulled her closer, thrilling her with his warm touch. She didn't know if they were merely kissing or if he truly was healing her 'all the way'. She felt free. The heavy sadness in her heart was gone. Andrew kissed her harder, his tongue finding hers, his hands securing her around the waist, locking her body close to him. Something about how frantic he'd become thrilled her even more. Her blood pounded through her, her body aching for him.

Then he stopped and his eyes met hers. She wasn't sure how to take his almost stunned expression. He grinned, and she relaxed.

"What?" she asked. "Why are you looking at me like that?"

He pulled her into a bear hug. "Oh, Caitlyn. You... you are exactly what I need. I feel so selfish."

"What?" she asked, laughing and sitting back so she could see his face. "How is needing me selfish?"

"Because I thought I was the one doing the healing today, but turns out, you just healed me."

Staring at him, she wondered if he were joking. She knew how much he'd hurt after Eden had broken up with him. She hoped she wasn't merely a rebound. Caitlyn was unsure how Andrew felt about Eden. Did he still want to be with her, even now?

She ran her hand through his hair, not really smoothing down its mess. She liked it this way. "You're wrong. You're still the *Léčital.*" She grinned. "Maybe we can get that printed on your spandex outfit," she teased.

He laughed. "Hey, I'm game. I'm dying to see you in yours, remember?" Then his expression sobered. "Caitlyn? Can I be honest with you?"

"Yeah." Dread trickled in—would he say regretted the kiss? That this was a fluke thing? Better to know now.

"I've never felt this way for anyone else," he said instead, taking her by surprise.

"You don't have to say that. I know you probably still care for Eden, and

I'm okay with it, really."

He shook his head. "What I had with her... was different. It was never like this."

"Is that a good thing?" she asked.

"Yes, a very good thing."

"What about Brita?"

"Brita?" He sat back a bit and chuckled. "You're worried about her?"

"You two flirted like crazy with each other!"

"If I'd known how you felt about me then, Caitlyn, I'd never have flirted with her. But you acted like you could hardly stand to be around me anymore."

"Okay, sorry. I should've been honest. I was just so afraid you'd be mad at me."

"You didn't cause the break up, Caitlyn. That was meant to be, and I'm okay with that now."

She squinted at him. "You sure?"

"Yes. Besides, I think you're forgetting about Lucas. You kissed him right in front of me for crying out loud. I about socked his pretty boy face."

She wasn't sure if he merely wanted to get the subject off Eden, or if he truly was bothered by Lucas. "Hey, for the record, he kissed me... and I don't care about Lucas. I only want you."

He met her gaze. "I like the sound of that."

She felt embarrassed by her own honesty and glanced down.

He tucked his hands around the base of her neck and dropped his head down, trying to make her look at him again.

She hesitated, and then met his piercing gaze.

"I'm sorry," he said, "that it took a demon for me to realize I can't live without you. I'll do anything to keep you safe. To keep you... well, you. That demon scared me."

"Trust me; it scared me more."

He laughed. "I bet."

"Sorry I bit you."

He grinned. "Nothing I couldn't handle, but it was a little freaky. You should have seen yourself."

"Um, I think I'll pass, but I am sorry I hurt you."

"I can heal just about anything but a broken heart." He kissed her lips softly, and then he added, "Just promise me you won't break mine and we're all good."

"I was possessed by a demon because I fought liking you. I don't think you have to worry."

"That's a comforting thought." He pulled her closer and kissed her forehead. "We should have done this a long time ago."

"What? And miss out on being possessed?" she teased, but then she frowned. "I've been so dumb. I wonder what other things happened because I doubted, because I'd lost my faith. Maybe Micah could've convinced the Watchers to help. Maybe Eden would still be in the temple safe."

"Oops, there you go again. Looks like my healing didn't take," he cut in. "Guess I better try again."

He kissed her, his lips warm and soft against her mouth. She knew with all his joking, he was right. No more second-guessing. *Time to be me and let my gift work for once, the way it's supposed to. Eden's going to be okay because we're going to get her back.*

Chapter Thirty-eight

Micah had seen Semjaza once before. It'd been on prom night, the night Eden had been attacked by Oeillet's staff. He'd had a vision of Semjaza's dark pit. He could still remember the white teeth, the blood-red gums. And the horrible feeling I had when he spoke about wanting Eden. At that time, Micah had only thought Semjaza desired to kill her, like he wanted to kill Micah.

I had no idea he craved her, had set his sick mind on making her his. Micah groaned. And now he has her.

He shook his head. He had to think clearly. He needed a vision of what to do. Everything up to this point had failed or gone backwards. Was it because he hadn't relied enough on his visions, his gift? Was he trying to 'think' of the solutions all on his own too much?

Micah knelt down. He'd found a place off by himself. He knew Sage was near, even if she wasn't visible. She was always close by, watching over. "Sage, guide me now," he said quietly to the space around him. "Captain, if you can hear me, it's your Seer." He cleared his throat. "It's me, Micah."

A breeze lifted the leaves around him, the field bathed in sunlight.

"It's been a while since I've come to you like this. Sage is always telling me that we are here to learn. To solve problems and try to do it ourselves. But that's the thing—I've tried everything I can think of and I failed. I'm not here to complain. I'm here because I don't know where else to go. Eden's gone… and I don't know how to get her back."

He swallowed down the lump in his throat, his eyes blurring. He blinked, clearing his eyes. "Sage reminded me just now that I'm the Seer. She told me to use my gift. So that's what I'm going to do. My Captain, please hear me now. I'm your Seer. I see what you allow me to see. Help me see what to do now."

The breeze grew in strength, and the field around him rustled.

"Micah," a rich voice called back to him. "I hear you, and I am here."

He knew the voice; he'd heard it once before in Rome.

"Fear not, my Seer, for I have not forsaken you. You have served me well, and I am pleased. For what you see as failure, I see as progress. I see all, the beginning and the end. All things will come together. You have shown your faith and allegiance to me, even when all hope felt lost. You have sought my council, and I am here."

Micah listened, desperate to absorb His words. The voice filled him with such hope.

"Tell me, Captain, how do I convince Semjaza to let her go? He fears nothing. He will gladly go to Tartarus. I'll trade anything—do anything—to get her back." A new thought came to him. "I would gladly take her place, if that's what it takes."

The voice was silent long enough for Micah to realize that thought might not have come from himself.

"Is that it then? See if Semjaza will take me instead?" Micah asked.

"Would you do it? Would you lay down your life for your friend?" the Captain's voice asked.

"Yes." Micah stared up into the sky. "No doubt in my mind, yes."

"Micah, your courage pleases me. Now listen to my counsel. Semjaza desires one person more than even the Awakener."

"Okay, I'll do it," Micah said, squaring his shoulders. "He can have me. I just want to get Eden out of there."

"It is not you, my friend. At least, not directly."

"If not me, who then?"

"Azazel. The fallen angel of war."

Micah gasped. "That's it, isn't it? The deal between Semjaza and Lucifer.

The devil wants Azazel. That's the one thing Semjaza can offer him."

"Yes. Azazel knows the art of war. Lucifer wants him to fight the final battle for him," the Captain said. "The Watchers have been bound, but their influence has corrupted much of the earth and mankind. That is why I have instructed you and the other Holy angels to release them and give them their final choice."

"They're all choosing Tartarus, Captain. At least, so far. So what do I do? Tell Semjaza we'll go to Azazel, give him his choice? That's enough for him to let Eden go?"

"Semjaza does not know what you have been doing. He has no knowledge of the Watcher's final choice. He will see this as an opportunity for Azazel to escape, the very hope of which will be enough for him to let Eden go. It is the one thing you can offer him. The only thing he will take."

Micah stood up. "Then that's what we'll do." Somewhere in his mind, Micah remembered Gabriel's insistence of him not being there when they faced Azazel. Although he did not understand why, Micah knew Gabriel would have to relent. This was their one chance.

"Thank you, my Captain. We will do as you have instructed us."

"Micah," the voice called one more time.

"Yes?"

"Remember, you can always come to me for counsel. I have seen your heart and know that it is pure."

Micah nodded. "I won't forget. And I promise, I will act more like the Seer from now on."

Micah marched back to Trent, who had waited not far away.

Trent gave him an appraising look.

"What?" Micah asked.

"Nothing, just looking for those white hairs, Moses," Trent said with a shrug.

"You sound like Eden," Micah replied, his heart twisting at her name. He reminded himself that they had a plan now. Something that would work, after his two other foiled attempts.

"Third times a charm," Micah mumbled.

"Sweet, you had a vision," Trent exclaimed.

"Not exactly," he said, but he stopped walking and grabbed Trent's shoulder, "but I heard the Captain's voice."

Trent grinned. "Even better. What did He say?"

"He told me how to get Eden back."

"Really?"

"Yeah, but let's gather everybody and I'll tell you all at once. And I know just where to do it too."

Trent glanced over. "The temple? Please say yes."

Micah grinned. "Yes. Besides, I made you a promise you'd get to go back, so I better make good, or I'll never hear the end of it."

Trent slugged his shoulder. "Darn straight. About time you start thinking about me. Let's go find our sweet, possessed, hand-biting Caitlyn."

Micah chuckled. "That bad, huh?"

"Dude, it was like the exorcist. You have no idea. She kicked me in the head."

Micah made a face at him.

"No, with like demon-strength. Felt like a friggin' sledgehammer."

Micah grinned. "Well, that explains your big head... oh, wait."

"Whatever, man," he grumbled, and then he glanced over. "So I take it we finally got some good news."

Micah's grin widened. "We got some great news, Trent."

Micah found everyone together, joined up with Caitlyn and Andrew. He was relieved to see her smiling and talking with Willow. He scanned the area, hoping to see Olivia nearby.

As if he sensed who he was looking for, Damon walked over to him and said, "Vern took Olivia home. We're lucky her mom isn't filing a kidnapping report. Vern said she blames you for her running off the way she did. Said it's your fault she wanted to see the city. Think you made yourself an enemy there, Micah."

Micah frowned. "That's one brave little kid. Wish I could've thanked her before she left." He sighed. "I'm afraid we'll be making more enemies than just Olivia's mom."

"I'm no stranger to people avoiding me, I don't care what they think," Damon muttered.

Micah nodded, thoughtful. "Yeah, I suppose you're right. Sorry, Damon. I honestly didn't know you back at school. Thinking back now, I didn't notice a lot of people. I only cared about playing football and having a good time."

He wasn't sure why he was getting sentimental, now of all times, but he wanted Damon to know he'd do things differently now.

Damon squinted back at him, shaking his head, but Trent blurted, "Aw, Micah, I'm touched, but can we move on from the mushy stuff? Let's hear the news." He rubbed his hands together, "Oh, Caitlyn," he called. Micah knew Trent was anxious to get back inside the last chamber, and Caitlyn was the only way in.

Micah grinned. "Alright, Mr. Impatient. Let's get to it."

Damon stopped Micah as he walked by, however. "None of us are the same anymore, Micah. I, for one, am never looking back to who I was before. You shouldn't either."

Micah just stared after him as he passed. Wow, he's changed.

His friends were gathered together, everyone's gazes shifting in his direction. Micah sped up and joined them.

"Caitlyn, how are you feeling?" he asked, eyeing her. She seemed fine on the outside, but looks could be deceiving he'd learned.

She grinned, the smile reaching her eyes. "Better and I'm ready to help. Trent said you need me to open the chamber again."

"Yes, though we could use a minute to regroup before I take off again. There are things I need to tell you all, and I've been running too fast and hard to stop." Micah paused. "I felt I should've talked with you before, Caitlyn, and I didn't do it. I'm sorry. I want you to know that what happened to you is my fault."

She shook her head. "Micah, no it wasn't. Don't say that."

"No, I should say it. You're all my friends. I was so preoccupied with Eden that I overlooked the rest of you. I shouldn't have left you on your own, Caitlyn, to fight a battle you couldn't possibly win." He glanced at all the faces around him. "I won't abandon any of you from now on. You have my word."

Again, with the sentiments, his mind screamed. Must be from talking to the Captain.

He caught Trent staring at him and grinned. "Yeah, I know, Trent. I'll stop the gushy stuff. Let's get inside."

Chapter Thirty-nine

*E*den lost track of time, sitting in her corner, the eerie blue light surrounding her. Her body felt different; she wasn't sure if it were shock or fear paralyzing her. She waited to feel hunger, to even feel the need to use the restroom. Anything that would let her know she was still alive… still human.

She felt nothing, a strange absence of sensation terrifying her almost more than the fact she had no idea where she was. Didn't Micah say the Watchers were buried in the earth? Did that mean she was trapped underground in Semjaza's prison with him? She gazed up at the drifting blue fog surrounding her. Even in her little stone holding cell, she sensed the room was larger. *How can I be underground?*

As tempted as she was to stretch, stand up, and peer around, she resisted. One thing did terrify her—Semjaza waiting for her. *He doesn't want to kill me so what does he want?*

She swallowed, not liking where her thoughts went. She shut her eyes. Last time she'd called out to the Captain, Semjaza had mocked her. This time, she kept her thoughts private, hoping He could sense them.

Gabriel always seemed to hear me, so here goes nothing. Captain, if you're there, I need you. I'm so scared. Please, can you help me? Is there anything I can do to get out of here? Should I even try to escape? Or should I just wait and hope that Gabriel or Micah can find me?

A loud bang stopped her short. She glanced around. She didn't see anything in the blue light. She waited, her breathing speeding up. Was it help? Her rescuers? Did the Captain hear her?

His deep masculine voice echoed down to her. "I see that you are quite stubborn, but I will not pressure you."

She pulled her body in tight, wrapping her arms around herself. Semjaza.

She heard something before she saw it and gasped. A black demon had climbed down into the box with her. *I thought you said no pressure!*

She held her tongue and watched the black body slithering nearer. It wasn't snarling or making horrible hissing sounds but instead, it held something in its bony, black hands. She squinted to see better, and then the demon thrust it out to her.

A chunk of bread and some kind of crude, metal cup.

Seeing the offered meal, she shook her head. "I don't want it."

The demon snarled, and Semjaza snapped. "Don't."

When the demon bowed and dropped its head, she realized he was speaking to the black creature, not her. Perhaps she'd offended the demon by refusing its offering.

Semjaza commanded, "Leave the food and water. She will change her mind with time, once the thirst settles in."

The demon bent low and set the food down, then with one last sneer in her direction, it slunk away, climbing up the wall and disappearing.

"Eden, you have to understand something. I am a very patient man. Yes, I know you do not consider me a man, and I suppose by your standards, you are probably right. I've existed far too long. A cruel punishment. To be left in the dark, alone, for thousands of years. That in itself is truly damnation. Nothing happening. Nothing making even the slightest noise. Just a void. Leaving me to question who I even am. What I am."

There was a pause, and Eden stared at the food before her. Funny how the moment he mentioned thirst taking over, she realized how dried out her tongue and throat were. Now staring at the cup, she felt human again. She wasn't sure if the new craving relieved her or upset her. She didn't want to give in to Semjaza, in any way, but the night before had been physically exhausting. The natural desire to quench her thirst was suddenly over whelming.

No, I need to show him I'm not weak. That I won't take what he gives me.

"I have realized something over the past centuries of time. I do not desire revenge. I only want what I no longer have. I may have made mistakes in the past. My mortal life was so brief, and so long ago."

Eden hated that she had to listen to him. There was nothing she could do to block him out though. The absence of anything terrified her. Much like he just described, being trapped underground with nothing. Nothing.

She shivered, and her eyes landed on the water once more.

"I once had love. Real love. Human love. I had children. Do you think I am not capable of feeling? That was why I left, you know. I wanted to feel. To experience the human condition firsthand. The Captain forbade it, but how could that possibly be fair? Wasn't I an angel, one of the highest? Was I to bow down to man? To these mortals who fumble about making messes of their short, meaningless lives? They didn't even appreciate what they had. Did they know what passion was? Did they know what they were capable of feeling? Of being? No." He groaned. "They only saw one day at a time. They got lost on trivial matters. They did not deserve what they were given."

She couldn't take his words anymore. "For someone so condescending of man, you gave up a lot to become just like them, you know."

"I do not see why I should be required to give up anything in the first place. How is it fair some of the hosts of heaven were given their time on earth and some were not?"

Eden wasn't sure she knew the answer to his question, it was something she'd never really thought about, but she wasn't about to let his words get to her. He lies. Everything about him screamed deception. I can ask Gabriel this stuff later.

"So you think because you didn't get your turn, your actions are justified?" she said instead. "The family you created were giants. They hunted down humans, drank their blood even! You didn't try to stop them. The angels had to, before they killed everyone."

Semjaza chuckled. "Again, you speak of things you know so little about. My offspring weren't the ones who did that. If I showed you what your precious Gabriel did back then, you would be horrified. He not only slaughtered my offspring without mercy when he built that ark, he murdered every living thing."

Eden stared at the space before her. When Gabriel had told her his great-grandfather was Enoch, she had been a bit lost at first, trying to remember who had whom. Then she had finally settled on he had to be Noah. It'd been a strange revelation, one she'd had while staring at the large delta. At the time, the thought had filled her with wonder and awe.

Now, Semjaza was painting such a negative image of her guardian, making it sound like he had happily slaughtered everyone.

"Stop!" she blurted. "Now you talk about things you know nothing about. Gabriel didn't bring the flood, and he did everything he could to save who would listen. He hardly speaks of his life before which makes me wonder who he lost to your lies. You took someone from him, someone he loved deeply. Who was it?"

There was silence. "I have waited so long for someone like you, Eden. You see things as they are, and yet, you stay strong. Amazing."

"So I'm right then?" she asked. "You did hurt Gabriel directly."

"Yes," the voice purred back. "And the beautiful thing is, I shall do it again now with you."

"No, you won't. Because I'm not listening to your lies. I don't believe you. You are selfish and evil. No matter how you try to twist it, you will always be a fallen angel." She waited, positive he would swoop down and end her. Surely, her words would elicit some kind of reaction. She heard nothing, saw nothing. Her heart hammered in her chest.

Then, slowly, she heard soft laughter. "I am so pleased with my decision. Your strength while stripped of every security and comfort is truly commendable. It is a trait I desire."

Then come and kill me for it, she thought angrily. She had no idea where her courage was coming from, and then it hit her. It came from her love of Gabriel. How dare he slander Gabriel's name? I'm not letting Semjaza hurt him again.

"I will leave you now; I see that I have upset you. Please eat, drink, and rest. Because like I said, I'm a very patient man."

"I'm not upset. You just reminded me of what I have to live for," she retorted.

She heard the small gasp. Her remark must have surprised him. Maybe he thought he'd won this round, or whatever this was. *Why doesn't he just come grab me? If he's waited so long, what's he waiting for now?*

Silence filled the space and this time, Eden welcomed it. Shutting her eyes, she pretended Gabriel was there, holding her, keeping her safe. She had no idea how long she stayed like that before her mind drifted into a welcome sleep. *The Captain knows I'm here... He'll protect me.*

Chapter Forty

Micah figured Gabriel would resist his plan, but he was a little shocked on how agitated the angel became after he'd explained to everyone what the Captain had told him. While everyone else readily saw the solution as the one that made the most sense and the only thing left they could try, Gabriel crossed his arms and marched away. Micah wasn't too surprised to see Sage follow after him and since everyone was taking advantage of the small slice of time to explore vault nine, with Trent planting himself in front of the shelves with hundreds, possibly thousands of scrolls, Micah had a minute to himself. Even Damon was distracted at the moment, as Willow pointed to something on the large delta where they stood.

Micah inhaled deeply, trying to understand why Gabriel had been adamant about him not coming along. It seemed harmless enough. They would go to Semjaza, tell him of their plans to face Azazel. Hopefully, that would be enough for Semjaza to release Eden. Then all we have to do is give Azazel half a second to make his choice and then bam, Damon sends him straight to Tartarus.

Micah scratched at his chin, noticing for the first time how rough it felt. It'd been a while since he'd had a shave or a haircut. He had hardly slept, hardly ate, since the moment he realized Eden's life was in danger. None of that mattered anymore. Micah sighed and stepped over to Gabriel.

"I know you don't want me there, I guess you fear Azazel can hurt me more than the others, but the Captain advised me, Gabriel," Micah said firmly. Both angels glanced over at him. "He's the one who said it's the only way to get Eden back. I get the feeling things might not end well for me, but I don't care. I'll do whatever it takes."

Sage placed her hand on Micah's arm. "We're not going to let it come to that. Gabriel and I will protect you."

"I'll pull down my whole Cherubim army if I have to," Gabriel said quietly. "Micah, there are things you should understand before we go."

Micah nodded. "Okay, so tell me, and then we leave. Everyone else can stay if they want or head home, but I can't wait any longer."

"Neither can I," Gabriel muttered. "She's calling for me, I can feel it."

Micah's insides twisted. He realized the panic he felt probably paled to what Gabriel was experiencing. The bond between mortals and their guardians felt like a forged link, made with fire, and completely unbreakable. Micah had come to understand it with Sage. In some ways, she was his other half, always there, always ready to fight.

"That's why I have to do it, Gabriel," Micah said softly. "I would rather die than see him touch her."

Gabriel grimaced. "Come with me, then. There's something you need to read."

He led them to a door in the corner of the room, one Micah had not noticed last time he'd been here. But my mind was only on finding Enoch's blueprints; I probably just missed it. Gabriel pushed the door in, and as they stepped inside, Micah gasped. The room was round, the walls, floor, and ceiling made up entirely of wooden planks. There was one wooden table in the middle of the room, and then shelves with scrolls lining all the walls.

"I feel like I'm in some kind of hobbit hole," Trent said from behind, startling Micah. Then again, anything with ancient writings was bound to attract his cousin. The rest of his friends filed in after Trent.

"Where did all this come from?" Willow asked. "It wasn't here last time." Her eyes were wide as she glanced around the room. "This room is special, isn't it?"

"Always perceptive, Willow," Gabriel said. "The room is very special. It took care of Eden while she was here."

"Doesn't look very comfortable," Andrew said. Micah had to agree with him. There wasn't a bed. He glanced around. Not even a chair.

"While she was here, it met her needs," Gabriel said. "Enoch left this to always take care of those who enter."

Micah stared at all the scrolls. *Well, I guess Gabriel said I needed to read something. Sure hope it's not all those.*

"There's a feeling in here," Willow commented. "I can't quite put my finger on it."

Damon nodded. "I know what you mean, Willow. The room's speaking to me."

"What's it saying?" Micah asked, hoping the room would tell them how Eden ended up being chased by demons.

"It says it took good care of Eden. Fed her, gave her rest. Then the evil thing came, taunted her, called to her." Damon paused, as if he were listening and then translating. "She was tricked by the evil one's game. She followed the voices and opened the chamber."

"Wait, she opened the chamber?" Micah asked.

"I thought only Caitlyn could do that," Andrew said.

"She opened it," Damon repeated. "She is the Awakener. Her gift is like the tongue of many. Her languages extend far beyond what she knows."

Gabriel shifted, his hand on his sword, as he gazed around the room. "She left because she was tricked? But what of the Cherubim? I've been searching for my elite guard. For Aaron, for Joshua, and Jershon. The tree is still guarded, but my fighters are gone."

Damon was still for a moment. "They were overwhelmed. The numbers were too great. They were taken."

Gabriel let out a stream of words, none of which Micah understood. Then, all too clearly, he murmured, "Semjaza will pay for this."

"Gabriel, we will get Eden back. And Aaron. We'll get them all back," Sage said quickly.

Micah hadn't ever considered how Gabriel felt about the Cherubim he commanded. He knew now Gabriel didn't see them as nameless angels. They were like family to him.

Damon closed his eyes, still listening to the room. "It spoke to her with Caitlyn's voice. When Doubt took hold of Caitlyn's form, it was able to use her inner thoughts to call to Eden."

"Wait, what?" Caitlyn blurted. "I called to her?"

Micah saw the way Andrew grabbed her hand, pulled her close, and whispered, "It's okay; it's not your fault."

If things weren't so crazy, Micah would have been more excited to see Andrew might have finally moved on from Eden, but as it were, Micah could only tuck that away for something he would tell Eden. Because I'm going to get her back.

"Caitlyn, you were taken over," Micah said. "The demon must have streamed all your inner cries for help and shouted them out to Eden. It wasn't you."

"How's that even possible?" Caitlyn asked. "Can they do it again?"

"With fallen angels and the devil working together, all sorts of mayhem is possible, but now that you're free of the demon, I think you're fine," Gabriel confirmed.

Caitlyn frowned. "So Eden left trying to save me?"

Andrew wrapped his arm around Caitlyn's shoulders. "It wasn't you, Cat."

She was quiet.

"Andrew's right; don't feel bad, Caitlyn," Micah said. "Now listen up, everyone. We're up against the devil. The real live devil here. Yeah, we're fighting Semjaza and his Watchers, but let's not forget, it's the first Fallen One who's orchestrating this whole thing. Semjaza thinks he's going to beat out Satan because he has that much pride."

"And he's that stupid," Trent quipped. "Old Pitchfork breaks every deal he makes. And he's going to double-cross Semjaza too."

"Yeah, so no matter what's happened, or will happen, remember we're on the winning team. We're with the Captain," Micah said firmly.

Everyone was quiet, and then Damon said, "We need to give Micah a minute alone in here. There's a message in here for you, Micah."

"From who?" Micah asked, hoping somehow it was from Eden.

"Enoch," Damon and Gabriel said together.

Micah's eyes widened. Oh yeah, the thing I need to read. His stomach clenched with nerves. He wasn't sure if he dreaded or longed to hear his personal message from a prophet who lived five thousand years ago. Excitement won out; even if it was horrible news, he wanted to hear what Enoch had to say to him.

"Now by alone, you mean with his Interpreter, right? Because I'm telling you right now, those scrolls aren't in English," Trent said, hands on hips.

Damon went to argue, but Micah waved his hand. "It's okay. Trent can stay. I need to know everything; I don't want to mess this up."

Slowly, one by one, everyone left, leaving just Trent, Micah, Sage, and Gabriel.

They waited as Gabriel scanned the shelves. Then, after a moment, Gabriel hefted a long, skinny parchment wrapped up in some kind of twine.

"This is the one." He unrolled it slowly on the table, the parchment making soft crackling sounds. Hope it doesn't break.

As soon as he saw it was filled with strange markings, he knew he was right to have Trent here by his side. Another mistake I keep making, trying to understand all my visions on my own. I need to rely on Trent's gift more.

Trent was practically bouncing on his toes with anticipation. "Now let's see what we have here," he said, rubbing his hands together. His eyes scanned the parchment, his mood growing quieter by the passing second.

Poor guy. I don't think he likes what he's reading.

Damon waited just outside the door, itching to be inside. When the widow's barrel had whispered to him Micah should be alone to receive his message, he'd wanted argue. From the moment Damon had stepped inside the wooden space, he'd known it was a blessed place, still enchanted by Elijah's words long ago. How this barrel became a room in Enoch's underground temple, Damon had no idea. Enoch built the temple long before Elijah's time.

"It felt so strange in there, like nothing I've felt before," Willow commented next to him.

He jumped a bit, realizing since he'd left Micah and Trent, he'd been lost in his own thoughts. Glancing over at her, he smiled.

"You didn't by chance sense what the message for Micah is, did you?" he asked, knowing the answer was probably no.

She shook her head. "Just like the room didn't tell you either, I guess."

Damon sighed. "Just as well, that's probably why I got the boot."

"What do you mean?"

"Means I'm not going to like the message he's getting. Micah only keeps me in the dark when he's going to get hurt. He knows I'll interfere and stop it."

Willow smiled up at him. "Yes, you would." She slipped her hand into his. "Let's just hope that's not why this time. So why are you thinking about the prophet Elijah?"

"Still amazes me how much you can see," he said, wondering if his thoughts were played across his forehead like a sentence for her to read. "I'm just confused how that room came to be. Enoch lived around 3000 BC, and Elijah wasn't around until 850 BC."

Willow cocked her head to the side, her dark brown hair falling over one shoulder.

"What do those dates have to do with it?"

"Yeah, I don't understand either," Andrew said, coming over to them, Caitlyn following him.

"The little space in there's somehow the widow's barrel, blessed by Elijah," Damon said. "The widow fed Elijah her family's last meal. In return, Elijah promised her the barrel of meal shouldn't waste. At least, that's what the room told me. So I was wondering how Enoch got it in his temple since it was built over two thousand years before Elijah."

"And how it became a room, not a little barrel. It is shaped like the inside of a barrel. Maybe we shrink as we go inside," Caitlyn offered with a grin.

"You might be right," Willow said in all seriousness. Caitlyn and Andrew glanced at each other, and then laughed a little.

"I wasn't serious, Willow," Caitlyn said.

Willow shook her head. "No, I mean it. It feels so different in there. I can tell it's almost. . . magical."

"I don't know about us shrinking," Damon said, "but the room is blessed, enchanted, whatever you want to call it. It gave Eden what she needed when she was in there, and now it's giving Micah what he needs."

"Which is?" Andrew asked.

"I wish I knew," Damon said truthfully. "But I can assume it'll help him when facing Semjaza."

Andrew seemed thoughtful. "Maybe the barrel wasn't in the temple when Enoch originally built it. Maybe Elijah put it in there during his time. I mean, I'm sure other prophets knew about this place, right?"

"Yeah, you could be right. There seems like there's some kind of link between those two prophets since neither one of them ever died," Damon said, recalling some of the facts he'd learned studying with Micah. "And according to Revelations, they're both prophesied to come back again one day."

"Wait, they never died?" Caitlyn asked.

"No, it says in Genesis that Enoch was lifted up to heaven, never to see death, and we know his city was taken up, saved from the flood." Damon rubbed his chin with his fingers.

Willow nodded along and added, "And Elijah was taken up in a whirlwind to heaven riding a chariot of fire. Says so in second Kings."

Damon smiled. "You've been reading too."

"I can't get enough of this stuff. I find it fascinating! Especially since my boyfriend," she paused, giving him a shy grin, "is the one who gave Enoch the blueprints in the first place for his city, and he instructed Noah how to build the Ark."

Everyone's eyes turned on Damon.

"Am I the only one lost here?" Andrew asked. "Who are you talking about?"

"Damon, of course," Willow said.

Caitlyn's eyes widened. "Oh yeah," she said. "Willow told me you're Uriel."

"Say what?" Andrew asked, his eyes shooting to Damon.

"It's not a big deal," Damon countered.

"Whoa," Andrew gasped. "That's freaking awesome! You're like Gabriel? But living your life now?" Andrew ran his hands through his hair. "I can't comprehend this stuff."

Caitlyn glanced around the room. "Me either. You know, Eden noticed Enoch's symbol last time we were here. The oval. It's everywhere in here. I guess we just figured out another way things keep coming back around again. Damon, you helped Enoch build his indestructible city, you helped Noah with his waterproof Ark, and now you're helping Micah build the fireproof city."

Damon didn't like all the attention. He shifted under everyone's gawking. "Hey, it's still just me here. I don't remember all the heavenly stuff."

"None of us remember what we did before," Willow said, "but that doesn't mean it's not true and part of who we are. Even your gift links you; you share the same gift as Enoch. You both speak the pure language of Adam. Not many have had that."

Damon turned to her, ready to change the subject. "Not many have had your gift either, Willow. In fact, I know of only one other who had discernment like you."

Willow's eyebrows rose. "Really? Who?"

"Solomon. He asked the Lord for an understanding heart, so he could discern between good and bad. And everyone knows King Solomon was known for his wisdom and discernment."

"I didn't know that," Andrew said under his breath.

Damon chuckled. "Yeah, actually, I didn't know it either until I started reading with Micah. He researched all of your gifts. Found them in the Bible, read about those who had them before us."

"In all your reading, did he teach you about the stars too?" Caitlyn asked, glancing up at the ceiling, "Because I would love to know what all this means. I feel like this painting of the galaxies and that huge sun over there, above the delta, means something."

Damon nodded. "You're right, it all does. Just wish I could read it."

"Read what, the stars?" Andrew asked.

"One time when I went over to Micah's, back when he was helping me understand how to use my gift, he had maps with the constellations on them out, all over his dad's desk. I'd asked him about it, and he'd said, 'It's all written in the stars, Damon. Trick is to know how to read it.'"

Damon glanced up, the swirling patterns meaning little to him. "I wish I understood it better, but if you study Einstein's theory of Relativity, there's something about space and time. How the stars might be more like a record of what's been, and what will be."

"You mean the whole if you travel at the speed of light, time goes slower," Andrew said, "Like they do in the movies. A guy goes in space and comes back the same age, maybe days older, and everyone he knew on earth is like eighty."

"Exactly," Damon said. "Micah told me a lot of the prophets of old, like Moses, Abraham, and Enoch, were shown the mysteries of the earth and heavens, by seeing the stars. I think it's sort of a language. Once you can read it, you can see everything through space and time."

All of them were staring at the ceiling now. Willow kept arching her back further, craning her neck to see more, until she lost her balance and stumbled backwards. Damon quickly caught her and kept her upright.

"Be careful, you could get lost up there," Damon said, squeezing her hand. He'd been joking, but her expression turned thoughtful.

"You don't know how right you are, Damon," she said, just as the door to the widow's barrel opened up.

Trent was the first one to come out.

"Hey, Trent, think you can translate what's written on the ceiling?" Andrew called out, grinning.

Trent, however, did not return the smile. Instead, he brushed past them all, muttering, "I think I've translated enough today."

Damon's eyes followed him, his stomach sinking. *There's only one thing that gets Trent ornery… Well, maybe not just one thing, but Micah getting hurt is at the top of the list. He's keeping me from knowing, just like he did at the well.*

Micah entered the room and met his stare. Damon had never seen such resolve in those blue eyes.

"Ready?" he asked Damon.

Damon gave Willow's fingers one last squeeze before letting her hand go. "Yeah, let's go get Eden back."

And you better not think you're going to sacrifice yourself to do it.

Chapter Forty-one

When Eden's eyes opened, she had no idea if she'd slept for ten minutes or ten hours. The small room she sat in still remained open, with the iridescent blue light filtering in. She glanced around, the food and water laying before her, untouched. She swallowed; her tongue felt thick, her throat dry. The water mocked her, assuming it was water. Then it dawned on her. *Micah and Gabriel are out there searching for me, I know it, and they won't give up, so why am I? I need to be strong. What good is it if I pass out now from thirst?*

She reached for the cup, peering in at its contents. In the dim lighting, it was hard to tell what it was. She bit her lip, said a silent prayer, and downed the beverage. Relief flooded her when it tasted like nothing. Water.

Like the cup had been booby trapped, the moment she'd drunk it, he chuckled.

"So glad you've finally come to your senses."

She rubbed her hands on her thighs, glancing around. *I don't know about that,* she wanted to say, *but I can't sit like this anymore.* She closed her eyes and inhaled, trying to dig up the courage. Then before she could second-guess herself, she forced her body to stand up. Her knees felt stiff, and her muscles sore. This time, with the roof or top off, she could see out. She did a one-eighty, seeing nothing but blue fog surrounding her.

No Semjaza and no demons.

"I don't see you. Where are you?" she asked, trying to keep her voice even. "Where am I?"

"So many questions, my dear one. Why don't you climb out and see for yourself? I am very near."

Climb out? And what, walk right to you? She needed some kind of plan that didn't involve complete surrender.

She stalled, pacing the box she'd been in. "I know you're buried in some valley of the earth, Semjaza, and I know you're bound. So I'm beginning to wonder if you can even get to me. I mean, you've had your demons do everything for you. I sort of think you might not be so near. Just like Caitlyn's voice in the temple, she wasn't really there. I don't think you're really here either."

Not sure what I'm hoping to accomplish here, she thought as she studied the box's walls. How do I climb out of this anyway?

"Oh, I assure you, I am close by, but you are correct. I am bound in a valley. It has been my prison. I may be bound physically now, but freedom will soon be mine. As I said, I have waited a very long time for this moment."

"Then what are you waiting for now? Why must I come to you? Why don't you just come and get me?" she asked, wondering why in the world she taunted him. It seemed like the worse plan possible, and yet, that was all she could come up with.

"Are you ready to meet me? To meet the one who will make you glorious, who can take your gifts and expound them? You will be more powerful than the waves of the sea."

"Such promises from a bound man," she mumbled, her heart racing. I'm in over my head here. "I don't think I can get out of this even if I wanted to," she admitted.

There was silence and then, "Really?"

She couldn't help the manic laugh that escaped her. He apparently expected more out of me physically. "No, I can't scale walls. I don't see a ladder or steps…"

There was a rumble and then she heard him mutter something, whether it was directed at her, she couldn't tell.

"I see," he said. "Well, we can't have that, can we? I shall deliver you from your prison, because I am merciful. I don't like things to be trapped."

Oh yes, you do, she thought, while noticing how hard her knees were shaking now. Adrenaline made her feel disoriented and giddy. What do I do when he comes in here? her mind shouted.

She saw something descend in the corner. She held her breath, and then let it whoosh out in relief, when red eyes peered back at her. Never thought I'd be relieved to see a demon. But the very fact that Semjaza didn't come down to get her himself made her wonder if perhaps he couldn't. Maybe that's my hope.

The black creature moved closer. She eyed it, unsure if she should let it pick her up or not. If only I knew what was out there. If it is even possible to free myself. Am I deep in the earth?

Questions would have to wait because two more demons joined it, and the three of them circled around her. None were bearing their teeth or snapping. They must be under orders to get me to him in one piece. The closest one stepped in front of her, reaching to grab her body.

She didn't know if it was her, or somehow Gabriel's idea to do it, but she threw her arms around the cold, black creature, releasing herself into its touch. The demon jolted in her embrace, falling to the ground, taking her with it. It began hissing into her ear, but she felt no claws, no stabbing pain anywhere.

The other two demons, however, wailed and began gnashing their teeth down at her and the fallen one she held onto. She had no idea what she'd done to the demon; she had hugged it out of desperation. Hoping beyond hope that maybe her gift could deliver her.

Now on the ground, she heard Semjaza command, "What is happening down there? Just bring her to me!"

The two demons standing over her reached down, snatching her arms and hefting her up to her feet. The demon she'd hugged remained motionless below her. Did I kill it? The other demons didn't wait to see; they dragged her to the side. One hoisted her up, and she stared over its shoulder at the motionless demon she'd awakened. Can I kill them with my gift?

Her answer came when the demon suddenly rose up, jumping to its feet, its red eyes peering back at her. Cocking its head to the side, it let out a screech, and then hurled itself toward them.

Eden screamed, with no idea what was happening, as her body was torn from the demon's shoulder. The 'awakened' demon threw her to the ground behind it, and standing over her, bore its teeth to its comrades. She gaped as the demons crouched down and began circling one another. The one standing over her howled and clawed at its own chest. She gasped in horror, seeing what little flesh it had over bones tear away and hang from its ribs.

The other two demons followed suit. I wonder if it's some kind of showdown to establish dominance. Whatever their actions meant, one thing was clear, the demon she'd touched was now defending her.

"What is happening?" Semjaza bellowed down at them.

One of the other demons howled, and then spat, "It touched us. Confused us."

"What? Oh." Semjaza was quiet for a moment. "Kill the confused one, then."

Eden never thought she'd have empathy for a demon, but watching the other two come down on her 'protector,' she did. As they literally pulled at its body, trying to tear it in half, she bolted to her feet and threw herself on one of them, doing her best to get her arms around it. It fought her back, and then like it realized this was what Semjaza wanted, it left her awakened demon alone and jumped up on the side of the wall, taking Eden with it. She closed her eyes. Please work. Just one more time!

She released her gift again. The demon scaling the wall stopped, and like the other, its body jerked and went rigid in her arms. They both tumbled to the ground. Though the air had been knocked out of her, and she gasped for breath, she knew what she needed to do. She left the one to its transformation, or whatever it was, and ran straight at the last untouched demon. It screeched at her, backing away.

"Confused us! Confused us!" the demon screeched.

"Enough of this," Semjaza muttered. "You can't touch every demon, my dear one, though I commend you for trying."

Eden approached the last demon. "I'll be Micah's dear one, or even Gabriel's dear one, but never yours, Semjaza," she shouted back at him as she threw her arms around the wailing demon.

Semjaza growled, and it terrified her that her words might have finally pushed him to anger. She couldn't think about that. She focused on releasing her gift into the demon she held, tumbling to the ground as it went stiff in her arms. After the initial shock of once again slamming to the floor wore off, she sucked in air, seeing what Semjaza's frustration had summoned.

Black bodies dropping into the box, too many to hug individually. Too many to fight. Though her three touched demons rose up and formed a cocoon around her, hissing, snarling, and ripping at their own flesh while they did it, she knew she'd lost. There were too many demons. Just like there were in the cornfields when they'd overrun the angels.

If only I had Olivia here, she'd ward them off. They don't like her for some reason, she thought desperately. *But I'd never wish a child here.*

Despite the number of demons smashed in the small space she crouched in, none of them advanced for some reason. The three hovering over her began speaking a language she didn't understand. With deep voices, they chanted sounds over and over, like the rhythm of a drum. Eden watched as the three began to bob their heads with the language's syllables almost like a down beat. Then, to her delight, the demons smashed in with them began doing the same thing.

Their words are hypnotic. Whatever they are saying or doing, it's stopping them all. The demons are following orders from these three.

There was a growl from above. *Semjaza doesn't like it, but I do!* Eden stood up; the three surrounding her gave her space to do it. Their red eyes peered up from bowed heads, their necks turning slightly to the side.

"Command us," they said in unison.

"Stop this instant!" Semjaza roared down to them. "I command you! I am your master!"

Some of the demons hesitated, their eyes darting up and then back at

Eden. She had no idea how well the ones not touched by her would follow orders now.

She didn't waste more time and made a decision. "You know the way out," she whispered, hoping Semjaza wouldn't overhear. It was a foolish hope; the Watcher seemed to see and hear all somehow. "You brought me here. Now get me back out!"

The three nodded in unison. "Yes," they purred.

One scooped her up and the other two flanked its sides. Within seconds, they were up and over the wall. Blue fog was everywhere. Eden tried to see through it, but it felt like they were running through a dank haunted house. It was too misty to make out anything definite. With limited vision, her hearing amped up.

"Kill the confused ones and bring her to me! I order you with the authority given me by Leviathan, Prince of the Seraphim!"

The words echoed through the space like rumbling thunder; demons wailed and yowled. The trance had been broken; they were coming. She could hear them. There would be no escaping this time.

Within seconds, their progress halted. Claws sunk into her flesh as her body was torn from her protector. The ambush didn't stop. Thrown over another cold, bony shoulder, she closed her eyes. She couldn't bear to see the demons still trying to fight for her while their limbs were torn from their bodies. It was too much. Demon or not, it was cruel. It felt wrong.

Semjaza's roar transformed into the rumble of laughter, deep and throaty. "Much better. Finally. Now come to me, my sweet Eden. You have a fighting spirit, the courage of a warrior. You please me greatly."

She kept her eyes shut; she didn't want to see where the demon carried her. Her failed escape smothered her hope. *I can't hug every demon here; there are too many.* She tried to come up with some other option. Then it hit her. *What happens if I hug Semjaza?*

It seemed a crazy notion, insane. Maybe insane enough to work? She clung to that hope. Slowly, she forced herself to glance around, still nothing but blue fog. *I was right. Semjaza isn't here. They have to carry me to him, to* where he is bound.

Eden didn't close her eyes; she wanted to take every detail in now. The demons surrounding her ran, their pace urgent. At first, she couldn't make out much, then slowly, the blue fog began lifting and she could see muddy-looking walls. We must be in some kind of underground tunnel. The space grew narrower. Soon, they were sprinting single file through the labyrinth, turning down different holes, speeding through ever-smaller openings. The claustrophobia overwhelmed her, and then her demon ran straight into a dead end. Demons continued to follow him, smashing them up against the earth. She could barely make anything out, the blackness growing.

She heard the demon hiss out strange sounds, followed by the groan of the earth. The ground shifted; there was an audible cry from the walls surrounding them. She didn't understand what was happening until she felt herself swallowed up by the walls themselves. She screamed and shut her eyes. Her body pulled through the earth, riding on the demon's shoulder.

She managed to get her arms around her head, trying to protect herself from the terrain sliding across her body. It smashed her, squishing the air from her lungs, and filled her mouth and nose with dirt. I'm suffocating! I'm going to die!

Then like it'd never happened, the earth gave way and the pressure was gone. She gasped for air, rubbing her hands over her face, trying to clear the dirt away to see clearly.

The demon had stopped running, and stood still. From her vantage, she could only see walls surrounding them, like a vast chamber. She glanced around. Like a cave. She strained her neck to look upwards. There was no ceiling that she could see, only inky blackness.

"Welcome, Eden, to my home," she heard from behind her. "Not that I mind that view, but turn her around, so I may see her."

The demon grabbed her waist and pulled her down. As soon as her feet landed, its bony hands spun her around, forcing her to face Semjaza.

She sucked in air. She'd seen too many demons, too many monsters. She'd expected him to be gory, bloody, or at least dirty. Instead, he sat on a large rock in front of her, leaning an elbow on a knee. He wore no shirt; his chest was built, stomach tight, and his arms ripped and heavily veined. He's huge! He could be a professional wrestler; the only thing that didn't fit that image was the knapsack skirt he wore, which reached his knees. She stared at his face, clean-shaven, short, dark hair, and piercing gray eyes. Though he had to be centuries older than her, his features were attractive.

The fact that he didn't appear to be a fallen angel filled her with terror. She swallowed. "Where are we?"

Semjaza grinned. "I told you, my home. Isn't it lovely? Though it has been my prison, I've taken such delight in the mortals trying to come nearer to me. Every year they come. Drawn to me, I suppose."

"What are you talking about? People come down here?" Maybe that meant Micah could get to her then! "I thought you were buried in the earth?"

"I am. I'm in the deepest part of the world possible. The deepest valley, or hole, they could find, but that doesn't stop the explorers from trying to get a bit deeper. They want to see how deep this pit goes. They want… I don't know… to touch the bottom. To break the world record. Like some kind of sport, I suppose."

"Do they get close to you?"

"Oh, no." He chuckled. "They are far away. They call it the Crow's Cave, because the entrance is marked with black crows. You'd think that'd be an ominous sign, ward off curious mortals. Instead, they seek to discover what's buried deep within. Should we tell them it's me?"

His grin spread, his eyes lighting up.

She bit her lip. "If this is some kind of cave, can't you escape? Just travel up? Since there are people cave diving down…"

"No, I'm bound, physically. But with each mortal who passes down into Crow's Cave, my influence can spread. It was a most delightful discovery. Happened when the first guy, oh what was his name? I suppose it doesn't matter now. It was around 1960. As he traversed down in, I felt this release in pressure above me." He glanced up and then over at her. He smiled and then chuckled softly. "Look at me, telling you everything. I guess I have been a bit lonely."

He stood up, and Eden shrank back.

"Don't worry, my dear. I have no desire to hurt you. Why would I?" He moved closer. The size of his frame loomed larger with each step he took. He reached over to her face, brushing her cheek with the back of his fingers. She turned away, ducking down. The demon held her from behind, keeping her in place.

"I would never hurt such a prize," he murmured. "I haven't found a woman like you in centuries. Maybe even a millennia."

"What do you want with me?" she whispered, not daring to look at his face.

"I want what I lost. I want to have restored what was stolen from me."

She waited. He removed his hand, but he didn't step back.

Guess he's waiting for me to ask. Maybe if I act cooperative, this demon will let go of me. Then... I just have to get near enough to hug him.

She braced herself and glanced up. "What did you lose? Your freedom? Your life?"

"My family," he said quietly. If she wasn't mistaken, he almost sounded remorseful even.

She stared at him. Wait... he doesn't mean...

"Your Gabriel took it from me. He killed my wives, my children. He demolished my posterity. My glory drowned in the flood. My heart, my soul, taken with it."

She shook her head. "Your family," she repeated. "Are you sure it wasn't the use of your power? I think you only glory in your power."

"You are very wrong, Eden. My greatest glory is my posterity."

She stared at him. She didn't believe him. There was no way all he craved were children.

"So you want kids? What's this all have to do with me?" she asked, not wanting to know the answer. It was becoming all too apparent the more he spoke.

"I thought it was obvious by now. I want you to bear them for me."

She groaned. She'd been right.

He smiled and continued. "I cannot think of a better woman. You are courageous and gifted. In fact, the rarity of your gift could make quite the difference in our offspring."

"Never," she shouted. "I won't do it! You'll have to kill me first!" So much for acting cooperative. She couldn't stand the thought of him touching her, let alone being intimate with her, and the horror of having monster children was even worse.

The demon's grip from behind tightened as she fought against it. Semjaza stepped away, chuckling lowly.

"Do you know how many women begged for the honor of being my wife before?" he asked, his back to her. "I could have any woman I chose. They adored me. And I did pick quite a few. I lost track of how many wives I had after a while, because that didn't matter. All that mattered were my children. They were beautiful creatures."

"You're insane. You know that? Why any woman would want or choose to be with you is beyond me," she said defiantly.

He turned around. "Do you not find me attractive, Eden?" He extended his arm out, flexing his muscles as he did it. "Am I not appealing to you?"

She shook her head.

"You're lying," he sneered.

"Fallen angels aren't my type. No matter how many muscles you have."

"Aren't you the funny one?"

"Aren't you the conceited one? How did women love you when all you think about is yourself? Your own gain? You said yourself your wives didn't matter to you. You speak of feelings and families being important to you, but you seem to miss the big picture of what love even is."

She caught the moment of hesitation before he smiled again. "You speak of love like you know what it is. You think what you and Micah have is love?"

"I know it is. What I have with Gabriel, it's love too, just a different kind. Love is selfless, not conceited."

"Aw, all this sounds so warm and fuzzy to me. But with real love, sacrifices must be made. What are you willing to do for Micah? I have made many sacrifices to get to where I am today. I have given up so much for the hope of restoring my family. So don't speak to me of love. I understand a deeper love than you ever will."

She glared at him, wanting to fight back, but choosing to remain quiet. Didn't Micah say her gift was love? It was charity, yes, but it really boiled down to love. With her gift, she could awaken in others amazing talents and abilities. She watched Semjaza's retreating frame as he returned to his rock. He sat down and folded his arms across his knees.

"I can't tell you how nice it is to converse freely with you," he said, catching her off guard with the change in topic. Two of his fingers waved at the demon. "Let her go. She can't go anywhere. There's no escaping this chamber. Believe me, I know. I've tried."

The demon released her arms, and she sagged to the ground. She hadn't realized it'd been holding her up. All the adrenaline seemed to have seeped away, leaving her exhausted and out of ideas. Except one last desperate idea—to awaken Semjaza.

Apparently, he had other plans. With a clap of his hand, two demons stepped up.

"Time to get the bride ready for her big day," he announced, grinning down at her.

She gasped. *A wedding? Here? Now? With him? Just how bound am I if this insane ceremony takes place?*

She didn't have time to think. A demon growled at her side, thrusting something white at her. She took in the lace and knew what it was.

"No, I won't go through with this, and I'm not wearing that," she said firmly, still sitting on the ground.

"You can choose to dress yourself, or have one of my fine demons do it, or even better yet, your husband to be would be happy to oblige you..."

"Fine." She reached up and snatched the dress from the demon. "I'll do it. None of you are touching me." She shuddered at the very feel of the fabric.

It felt old, cold, and scratchy. Whose was this anyway? I mean, it's not like demons can waltz into a department store, now can they?

She met Semjaza ogling eyes. "Do you mind turning around?"

He bowed his head. "Of course, my dear. I'm a gentleman."

He turned his body around and began pacing the floor away from her. She climbed to her feet and sighed. She had no choice but to undress in front of the drooling demons. Their red eyes followed her movements. She tried to ignore them and quickly stripped down, yanking the nasty lace down over her head. As the material fell down to her ankles, she shuddered at the realization of how well it fit her frame. Just how long had Semjaza been planning this day?

Chapter Forty-two

Micah wasn't too surprised Trent insisted on coming along, but even though he tried to convince the others to skip this trip, it was to no avail. Caitlyn, Andrew, and Willow were coming too and that was that. Andrew made a good point. Who knew which gifts they would need. What if Eden needed healing? What if they needed Willow's discernment? Or Caitlyn's faith?

The thought of anything else happening to any of his friends terrified Micah, but he knew Andrew was right. This might take all of them working together.

They landed in Abkhazia, a small territory of Georgia, just east of the Black Sea. Micah glanced around; all of their angels looked winded. He felt bad with how much they'd been flying by angel, but it would've taken too long to book flights to this remote part of the world. Sage seemed to handle it better than the others, which made him wonder if it was a ranking thing. The higher ranked the angel, the more abilities they had?

He shook his head, not that any of that mattered right now. He knew he was just trying to distract himself from what lay ahead. He still could hardly believe the words he'd read earlier. Shouldn't he have known? Suspected? Seen it?

Again, doesn't matter. I know what I need to do. He squared his shoulders and pointed straight ahead. "The entrance to the cave is up there, on that grassy hill," he announced.

"Semjaza's in a cave?" Andrew asked, squinting up at the mossy-looking hill before them. It was broken up by stone outcropping and a foggy mist settling down over the ground.

"Yes. Back then, they were looking for the deepest pits, or holes. Though they spoke of a valley, this one is actually a cave. It's called Krubera Cave, and it's the deepest cave on earth," Micah said, stepping forward.

Everyone fell in line with him.

"Check out all these crows," Caitlyn observed. "They're all over this place."

It was a little creepy seeing the number of black birds vying for space on the sloping hill. Micah noted how the beady, black eyes followed them as they passed. The hill became steep. He shifted his focus on climbing, ignoring the birds.

Damon, on the other hand, stopped and stooped down near one crow. Then, glancing up to Micah, said, "They're warning us to not get any closer. Evil resides deep in the ground."

"Tell us something we don't already know," Trent grumbled.

Micah knew Trent wasn't happy about this arrangement, but he saw no other option.

"Tell the crows we've come to take the evil thing away once and for all," Micah called back.

Damon said something, too quiet to hear, not that Micah would have understood anyway. Immediately, all the crows began cawing and flapping their wings. Within seconds, the ground was crow free.

"That's better," Andrew murmured. "Their eyes were wigging me out. Like they could see into my soul."

"Maybe they can," Damon said as he marched past Andrew.

"Wait, what?" Andrew asked. Damon grinned, and Andrew sputtered, "So not cool, Damon."

After that, everyone grew quiet. They were getting close to the cave's entrance; there was a definite somberness to the air. Climbing on top of the last knoll, Micah was sort of surprised to see a gaping hole before them. Black with leaves and rocks covering its walls, the cave's entrance was unmarked.

He peered down, careful to not get too close to the edge.

Andrew whistled, and Willow wrapped her arms around herself.

Caitlyn eyed the entrance. "Please don't tell me we have to climb down that... It's a total drop off. We'd need ropes, rappelling gear." She took a step back. Micah understood her reaction; the yawning blackness of what lay beyond was eerie.

"No, don't worry," he said. "We'll summon Semjaza up to us. Hopefully, if he agrees to the terms, he will tell us where Eden is." He glanced over at Gabriel and Damon. "You guys ready?"

Gabriel glanced over. "We are. Are you?"

Micah nodded, words escaping him. Trent's eyes narrowed, and he shifted to stand closer to Micah.

Damon glanced around, his eyes landing on Willow. "Maybe everyone should move back a bit. No need to have collateral damage here."

Caitlyn, Andrew, and Willow obeyed, their eyes wide. Damon began to chant, and Gabriel immediately joined in. Now their words were not only familiar, they resonated through Micah's frame.

"Oh, Eden, my dear. You do look lovely," Semjaza cooed as he turned around. "Such a beautiful bride."

"I'm not your bride." *But unless I figure out something, I just might end up being married today, like it or not.*

"You may not see your beauty, but I do," Semjaza continued, as if he hadn't heard her. He stepped closer and ran his hand through her hair, letting the strands fall between his fingertips. She held her ground, trying not to flinch at his closeness. *This is the perfect time to hug him. I should do it. Come on, just do it.* Her brain screamed at her, but her body didn't want to budge.

"You know, your hair would have been the envy of so many of my wives," he murmured. "They always kept their heads covered. As if the sight of hair was enough to make us angels fall." He chuckled mirthlessly. "I do enjoy a good head of hair, but good grief, that is a ridiculous notion, don't you think?"

Come on, Eden. Do it now! She tried to muster the courage and then she heard it; a low moan, echoing down from above. The ground beneath her feet rumbled. Semjaza shot a glance upward. Apparently, he hadn't been expecting the noise.

"What was that?" she asked, almost losing her footing, as the stone floor below her vibrated, the moaning temporarily stopping.

Semjaza squinted and then clapped his hands. "Eden, I hate to admit it, but our wedding might have to be put on hold. I do believe we have guests."

Eden stared at him; he could've been the Phantom of the Opera announcing to Christine that Raoul at last had come. She felt hope surge through her.

"I'm down here!" she screamed. "Micah! Gabriel!"

"They can't hear you; don't be ridiculous," Semjaza said, grabbing her arm and pulling her close to his chest. "What a shame, I was so looking forward to being close to you." He inhaled, his nose buried in her hair. "Why must good things always get interrupted by unwanted houseguests?"

This was her moment—her opportunity. She threw her arms around him, barely getting them around his broad chest. Holding such an evil thing, she was stunned to realize it was harder to hug him than the demons. She dug deep; she didn't have long until he'd know what she was up to. She summoned her gift, willing herself to awaken him.

She'd hoped for him to go stiff, fall over, or do something other than chuckle in her ear.

"Your embrace feels wonderful, almost magical. You know, I do love magic. Curious as to what you just changed in me. Aren't you?"

She pushed against his chest, horrified at what she might have done. He didn't seem stunned like the demons, and he was definitely not bending to her will. Her voice shook, "Let go of me!"

"Never," he purred, his lips landing in her hair, pressing against her ear. She tried to shy away, but his arms were like a steel cage. "But as it is, something is pulling me up," he continued whispering in her ear, holding her body tight against him. "I have to say I'm excited at the prospect of leaving this place, to be above earth again."

"So," he said, suddenly shoving her body away from him, causing her to stumble to the ground. "Stay here until I get back."

He stepped forward, positioning himself so nothing but blackness lay above him. "Aw, yes, I thought I sensed Gabriel... and perhaps another Holy. How wonderful! This has turned into such a day of surprises."

"Gabriel," she screamed, lying on the ground, "If you can hear me, I'm down here! Please!"

"Argh," he growled, "You know, on second thought, you are much too resourceful. And even though it's a quality I truly admire in you, I can't have you escaping, now can I?"

She gazed up at him as he stretched out his hand. Immediately, pain shot through her body. The prom injury flared up, only a million times worse.

She flailed, trying to grab hold of anything to brace herself for the pain coursing through her. Nothing but cold, hard earth surrounded her.

Her words were strangled, "You... said... you... you wouldn't... kill..."

"Kill you? Oh, I won't, but I can't have you hugging demons while I'm away."

She tried to scream, but even breathing was impossible. Semjaza shot a glance up to the black void above them, just as a bellow crashed over them.

She knew whose voice it was. Gabriel's.

"Semjaza, in the name of the Captain, we, the Holies, summon you forth!"

"Sorry, my love. That's my cue to leave, I'm afraid. Can't keep those Holies waiting. They are an impatient lot." He sneered in her direction as his body lifted off the ground. Then his head rocked back, and he closed his eyes. "At last!" he cried, disappearing into the black chasm.

Eden couldn't move; she couldn't stand. She begged for a demon to come near. None of them listened. The agony was too much; she knew she was going to pass out.

"Gabriel... save... me..."

The ground rocked below Micah's feet. He didn't have to be Damon to know how the earth felt about it getting rid of this particular Watcher. Felt like it was spewing it out.

Damon and Gabriel held their hands out in front of them. Gabriel gritted his teeth. "Hold him, Uriel. Don't let this one go."

Damon nodded, sweat beading across his forehead. Micah waited. Semjaza was coming. Everyone could hear the laughter, echoing from below. A man bound from out of the hole, hands thrust to his sides, a smile splitting his face.

"Ah," he sighed, suspended in the air. "At last, at last, at last. Smell the fresh air. What has it been? Five thousand years? Give or take a day?"

Micah stared at him. Wearing nothing but a sackcloth skirt, his chest was bare, except for a black tattoo over his heart. Micah tried to decipher the symbol and then gave up. Nothing mattered but getting Eden back.

"Semjaza," Micah said, not waiting for Gabriel to say his spiel about making a choice.

Semjaza's smile widened. "Micah. I have to say it's a pleasure to finally meet you. I've heard so much about you from Eden."

Micah stiffened. "Where is she? Where have you taken her?"

Semjaza cocked his head to the side. "She's fine. Don't worry your pretty little head over her. You see, I take good care of my wives." He grinned in Gabriel's direction.

Gabriel's sword was drawn in an instant as he flew straight at Semjaza, forgetting about the hold he and Damon had to keep.

Damon muttered, "Gabriel, don't!"

But Gabriel's sword was against Semjaza's neck. "What did you do?" he hissed.

"Honestly, Gabriel." Semjaza rolled his eyes, like the fire against his throat bored him. "I don't know what the big deal is. I always marry the girl first. Isn't that the way the Captain likes it done?"

Sage hissed, and Micah held his hand out to her. "It's okay; I don't like him talking about the Captain either." He stepped forward, placing a hand on Damon's shoulder, trying to support his friend. "He's just trying to nettle us, Gabriel. He didn't marry Eden."

Gabriel squinted down at Semjaza. "You better not have. She's not yours to have. When will you learn that, Semjaza?"

"I learn what I want, Gabriel. You unfortunately, never learn anything, old friend. Making the same mistakes as before." Semjaza clicked his tongue at him.

Gabriel punched Semjaza, sending the Watcher's head snapping backwards. "I may not be able to kill you, yet, but don't think you are getting off easy this time, old friend."

Gabriel released his hold on him and returned to Damon's side. "Sorry," he mumbled, lifting his hands and helping Damon with the task of keeping Semjaza bound in place.

"Trust me, I want to beat the snot out of him too," Damon said through tight lips.

Semjaza rubbed his jaw, his eyes taking in all of them. Slowly, he grinned. "So here we all are. Let me guess, you are here to beg me to let Eden go. To find out where I've put her. And you brought me what in exchange? All these?" He pointed at Andrew, Willow, and Caitlyn. His eyebrows rose. "I will consider your offering."

Micah shook his head. "No. We aren't offering ourselves. You will release Eden to us now in hope the Captain will have mercy on you."

"Captain's mercy?" Semjaza's eyes narrowed. "I hold something truly valuable and you expect me to trade it for something that means absolutely nothing to me? I don't know where you were schooled, young man, but by my accounts, that is a terrible exchange."

"So I take it your refuse then?" Micah asked.

Semjaza's face split into a grin. "Yes, you can mark down I refuse to comply simply on that merit, but if we speak of your friends…" His eyes raked over the others. "There might be something we could do. As much as it pains me to lose my bride-to-be."

Micah felt a smug satisfaction to hear Semjaza's slip. *He hasn't married her after all.* He saw the way Semjaza eyed Caitlyn. *Yeah, that's not going to happen.*

"I already told you, no one here is for trade," Micah said firmly. He didn't miss the way his friends huddled close together, whispering. He didn't care what plan they hatched. No one was offering themselves up for Eden. *No one but me…*

"Well, you can't possibly expect me to just roll over to your demands can you, Micah? I really expected a bit more out of all this, to be honest. A bigger show. A bit of a to-do. I have to say this has been a bit of a letdown."

Micah heard Damon's grunt at the same time he caught Semjaza's flick of his wrists. Within seconds, Micah knew they'd wasted too much time talking. With that simple movement, demons sprung out from behind rocks. His friends' guardians appeared, forming a protective stance around them.

Gabriel grumbled something under his breath, and then his arms shot up to the sky and slammed back down, the motion bringing down a whole army of Cherubim angels. Swords drawn.

"You're going to lose, Semjaza," Gabriel barked back at him. "You are wasting time. Tell us where Eden is!"

"And what, miss all the fun? No, no. This is much better." Semjaza turned to the demons. "Kill them. Kill them all."

If felt like Semjaza had opened Hell's gate; demons shot at them from every direction. Micah had sort of suspected the fallen angel would try something like this, to lure them all here in the hopes of overwhelming them with his swarms, and once the Holies fell, he'd be freed of his imprisonment. Micah had thought it'd been Semjaza's plan from the beginning; he'd never actually thought the Watcher wanted Eden for himself. He thought she'd merely been a means to an end. Learning of his intimate interest in her had changed things for Micah. *No way am I letting him touch her.*

Micah glanced at Damon and Gabriel. Semjaza's power far exceeded the other Watcher's they'd faced. They had planned on it taking both Damon and Gabriel's concentration to keep him bound. This meant they couldn't fight and keep Semjaza in place at the same time. Still, they weren't defenseless. Both of them barked orders out to their soldiers. The earth listened to Damon's commands; rocks were flying from the hillside. The hordes of Cherubim angels obeyed Gabriel, forming a protective barrier around Micah's friends.

Micah had only one thing on his mind—get Semjaza to listen. He marched forward determined to get closer, when something hit his stomach. He glanced down to see Sage's red-handled weapon, the three-pronged sai.

He looked over at her, meeting her black eyes as she said, "Here, take a few of these. You can kill the demons; just thrust them through. I'm going to clear this place out. Get to Semjaza."

Micah nodded, grabbing the offered weapons, unsure if he'd know how to thrust through anything. Of all the weapons she could have picked to use, why this one? A sword would be nice right about now.

Sage didn't wait around to see if he knew what he was doing; she ignited, flames licking her entire frame. These Watchers really tick her off. Micah could tell she itched for a reason to bathe the landscape in fire. With her flames being just as dangerous to mortals as demons, she gave Micah a wide girth.

"Go," she commanded.

He didn't wait to be told twice and ran forward, ready to make Semjaza comply. Only problem was there were demons everywhere. Time to see what these things can do.

He found out pretty quick. A demon lunged straight at him, mouth opened, snarling with sharp teeth.

Micah felt claws strike him as the black body collided into his. He shoved the three-pronged sai forward, feeling the impact of the metal sliding through the demon's rib cage. It made horrible crunching sounds as it went. When the claws fell limply from Micah, he grunted and pulled the weapon back out. The demon crumbled to ash.

He turned the sai around, staring at the pristine metal—no blood, no demon guts. Okay. Maybe these aren't so bad.

"Oh baby, give me one of those things," Trent hollered next to him.

Temporarily forgetting Trent was determined to be his shadow, Micah turned to his cousin and handed one over. "Here, the demons aren't too hard to kill."

Trent hefted it in his hand. "Oh yeah, that's what I'm talking about. Been waiting to kick some demon butt. Today's the day." He glanced around. "Too bad there's only like a thousand. Hey Semjaza, you holding back on us?"

Semjaza's attention had been steeled on Damon and Gabriel, probably waiting for the moment they fell to his demon hordes. Trent's comment brought the Watcher's gaze to them.

Perfect, Trent, Micah thought, grateful for his cousin's loud mouth for once. Time to get this show on the road.

Semjaza sneered. "Aren't you the confident one? Reminds me of myself in younger, more naïve days. What a shame you will die today."

"Nobody is dying," Micah shouted back at him, killing another demon that got in his way. He shoved the body off his weapon, the demon turning to ash as it fell. "In case you haven't noticed, you're on borrowed time with these demons."

Semjaza whooped. "That is a new one. This I have got to hear."

With Semjaza's interest piqued, Micah shot a quick glance around. Andrew, Caitlyn, and Willow were surrounded by angels and seemed relatively safe for now. Sage's roaring flames were burning through the demon masses. This is it.

"I'm sure you noticed Caitlyn's no longer possessed. You got your end of the bargain, but left the devil hanging," Micah said, inching closer to the Watcher.

"Oh, is that all?" Semjaza seemed disappointed. "I will deliver that girl to him. It's only a matter of time."

"I wonder how patient the devil is. I mean, he's no saint. I wonder if it'll drive him crazy that you get to enjoy your end of the bargain, and he doesn't. And then there is the matter of the other part still being unfulfilled. Wonder how long your limitless supply of demons will last when Lucifer doubts your abilities to actually deliver."

Semjaza's eyed Micah. "You speak of things, I'm fairly confident, that you know nothing about."

"It must drive you mad, that with all your power and influence, you can't figure out how to free him," Micah said, seeing the light flicker in Semjaza's eyes. "Got your attention now?"

"I'm listening," Semjaza said through tight lips.

"What if I offered you a trade that has some worth in your eyes?"

Semjaza licked his lips. "What kind of trade are we talking?"

"You give me Eden, safe and perfectly healthy. No more poisoned wounds. Then you have my word, I will go to Azazel, pull him up from the ground, and offer him a choice to follow the Captain or remain bound. He will get one last chance to choose."

Semjaza didn't try to hide his excitement; his whole demeanor changed. His eyes raked Micah up and down, as if seeing him for the first time.

"You go to Azazel first, and then I release Eden," he demanded.

"No, that's not the deal. If you want Azazel above ground, you will agree to my terms," Micah said firmly. "As Seer to the Captain, I've got a mission to finish. I know you don't care about the cities, none of that means anything to your plans, but they're important to me. The location of the fourth city must be found before I face Azazel. You give me Eden now, and you have my word as The Seer, I'll go to Azazel after the fourth city is formed."

Semjaza's eyes narrowed as he considered Micah's words.

"These are the only terms I will accept. Take it or leave it, Semjaza. Because honestly, I'm beginning to think Eden's down that hole, which means I shouldn't offer you anything. We can deal with you, and we can get Eden out of there." He pointed to the cave's entrance. "Ourselves."

Chapter Forty-three

"Ah, but can you heal her?" Semjaza retorted. "Nothing undoes my enchantments. That's why you need me to agree." He shook his head, breaking eye contact. "You expect me to give her away on the hope you will keep your word as the Seer?" He shot a glance back at Micah. "What do you take me as—a fool?"

"Fool, no. Desperate, yes. We both know you've got a deal to keep with Satan, and from where I stand, you couldn't even deliver a teenage girl."

Semjaza's eyes narrowed.

"Let's be clear here, I'm not agreeing to let Azazel go, but I am offering to release Azazel from his binding, something you can't do." Micah straightened his shoulders. "You will never be able to. Only the Holies can release the binding, and I think you know that."

The Watcher seemed to consider the offer. Micah held his breath, waiting. Come on, take the deal. Take it.

A smile spread across Semjaza's face. "I think I understand now," he said slowly. "Micah, Seer of the Captain, I accept the terms of your agreement, and I add only this. You must be with the other Holies the day Azazel is brought forth. Finish your precious cities. Like you said, they aren't my concern. Until the day you fulfill your promise to me, you will be marked."

Micah nodded. "Deal."

"Hold out your arm," Semjaza said.

Micah thrust it out, and Trent stiffened.

Semjaza glanced at Gabriel and Damon. "Do you mind? I won't go anywhere, but I must move a little to do this."

"You didn't have to move to summon demons," Damon countered.

"Yeah, about that, call off your dogs," Trent hollered.

Micah sort of forgot about the demons swarming around them. Between Sage's flames and Trent doing a pretty decent job of warding them off, he'd been able to focus on convincing Semjaza.

Semjaza glanced around, taking in the battle, perhaps deciding if he wanted to risk waiting to see its outcome before making his final decision. He shrugged. "Fine. Demons, leave them be."

Immediately, the black, scurrying bodies retreated. Micah glanced at his friends; they seemed relatively unharmed. Willow's eyes narrowed as she glared at Semjaza. *Wonder how well she can read his mind? Might come in handy.*

"We're fine over here," Andrew yelled over to him.

Micah nodded and caught sight of his guardian, still bathed in flames, her onyx eyes crazed. She destroyed several retreating demons before reining her fire in. With smoke shrouding her red dress, she marched over, her face determined.

"The mark you plan on giving Micah," she said and pointed at Semjaza, "will not be allowed to harm him. If you double-cross me on this, I will personally come to Tartarus to destroy you."

"Mm... even I know better than to mess with a Seraph," Semjaza said, to Micah's surprise. "You have my word, my mark will cause no harm, but if the Seer thinks he can double-cross me, by not being there the day they open Azazel's prison, my mark will ignite. And trust me, he will wish for a swift death."

"I understand. Mark me," Micah said, holding his arm out to Semjaza, palm up, exposing his forearm.

Damon and Gabriel glanced at each other, and then Gabriel said, "Semjaza, you mark him and you deliver Eden. That's it. Uriel's ready to send you to Tartarus if you get other ideas."

"Yes, I sort of gathered that's where I was heading either way by what the Seraph just said," Semjaza said, rolling his eyes.

Damon looked to Gabriel, who nodded. They lowered their arms a bit.

Semjaza stretched. "Much better. I had tired of that position. Now, let us get down to business. Micah, with this mark, you enter a binding contract with me. You will be present the day Azazel rises from the ground. In exchange, I will deliver Eden to you, unscathed."

"Okay, I agree," Micah said, feeling anxious to get this over with. He glanced over at Willow, hoping it was just his nerves unsettling him, and not more. Willow's lips pursed but she said nothing. *So far so good, I guess.*

Semjaza stretched his hand out to Micah. "So let it be written, so let it be done."

With each syllable, fire struck Micah's skin. He flinched, the marking so hot it felt cold. A blinding-white light lit up his skin, and then it was gone, leaving in its wake a black mark stretching across the inside of his forearm.

Micah stared at it—a black, elongated triangle. Nothing elaborate.

"Better give me one of those nifty tattoos too," Trent blurted, throwing his arm out before Micah could stop him.

"Trent! What are you doing?" Micah sputtered, but Semjaza didn't wait. He pointed at Trent, and the sizzling, white light landed on his cousin's arm as well.

"Hey, if you're going down, I'm right there with you. You know that," Trent said firmly, after the light was gone, and the same black triangle glared from Trent's skin.

Micah shook his head. "Aw, Trent. You don't know what you just did."

"Yes, I do. I translated the dang thing, remember? Now let's get Eden and make these tattoos worth your mom's wrath."

Micah grimaced and turned to Semjaza. "Okay, I'm marked. Now tell us where Eden is. Is she down there?" Micah asked. He still wasn't positive if Semjaza had managed to get Eden into his impenetrable prison.

Semjaza smiled. "Yes."

Gabriel leaned forward, gripping his sword's hilt. "That shouldn't be possible. She could be being held by demons anywhere. How do we know you are not lying right now?"

Micah glanced at Willow. That's how we tell.

Willow confirmed, "He's telling the truth, she's down there."

Semjaza's gaze darted to Willow, his lips twitching. "She was held by demons originally," he said finally, "Even I wasn't certain if I could get her to me, but after what she did at the temple, I had my suspicions about her abilities and what she could do if given the proper motivation. She is full of all kinds of surprises." He shot a mirthless grin at Gabriel. "Pleased I could share something special with her. What I took from her, I will treasure in Tartarus."

Gabriel came unglued. Roaring, he rushed Semjaza, striking his face with his sword. Semjaza howled, his head snapping sideways. Surprised he's not headless from that.

After a moment, Semjaza composed himself, spitting out blood. "Maiming me won't change anything, Gabriel," he muttered, turning to face them.

Micah could only stare at the cheekbone protruding through the bloody slash Gabriel had given him. The two ancient angels stared each other down, chests heaving. Gabriel drew back again, his knuckles white from his grip.

"We need to get to Eden," Micah shouted, to stop Gabriel. "Semjaza, bring her up now."

"Oh, I would be happy to oblige if you loosen my bindings. Gabriel letting go did help, but I need a bit more freedom," Semjaza taunted.

Gabriel growled, shoving his sword back into its sheath. Moving back a step, he lifted his arms. "I swear, Semjaza, when this is done, I will have my way with you."

"My, my, my. That sounds a bit dark, coming from you. I guess this one means something to you."

"They all meant something to me," Gabriel hissed.

"Oh, how sweet. I want you to know, Gabriel, they have all meant quite a lot to me too." Semjaza sneered. "Especially Eden. She is so different than the rest."

Gabriel's jaw bulged in his efforts not to kill him.

Micah jumped in. "We're not releasing you. We'll get her ourselves, but you have to heal her first and if you don't," Micah said and held up his arm to reveal his mark, "this means nothing. The deal's void, you understand?"

"Yes, yes, it's void, I get it. However, let me remind you, if you fail to be there the day Azazel rises from the ground, your marks will ignite. I give you fair warning." Semjaza closed his eyes and sighed dramatically. "There, she is whole again. Satisfied?"

Micah would much rather see her to know for certain, but with how things were playing out, he didn't have a choice. He looked to Willow for guidance.

Willow's brows gathered in concentration. She frowned. "I don't detect a lie... but I can't see clearly."

Semjaza grinned. It'd been a mistake to reveal what Willow could do before. Micah silently cursed his own stupidity. He's probably worked a way to keep her from seeing in.

"I am looking forward to Tartarus," Semjaza drawled, "It will provide a much-needed change in scenery, and I can work on healing this confounded cut Gabriel gave me."

The lack of fear or concern for the lowest level of Hell sent a chill through Micah. All the Watchers welcomed Tartarus, Semjaza included.

"Consider it my parting gift," Gabriel muttered. "Uriel, get rid of him, I'm done waiting."

Damon jumped into action, summoning the lightning storm. The thunderheads rolled in like they were on fast forward, the ground rumbling with the force of Damon's words.

The impact from the conjured lightning bolt sent everyone sprawling backwards. The only ones still standing were the angels. Micah climbed to his feet at the same time Gabriel lunged for the cave's entrance, diving in headfirst. He didn't stop to think, but dived in after him.

He knew Sage would follow, but for a split second, free falling headfirst into the blackness got him worried. Through watering eyes, the only light to be seen came from Gabriel's sword. It led their way like a beacon, a small orb of light, in the blackness they descended into.

Just as the first landing became visible, and real panic seized him, Micah felt arms wrap around him from behind. Instantly, his progression slowed.

"You could have given me a little warning," Sage reprimanded him. "You are still mortal, you know."

"Sorry."

"I know you want to get to her," she said as her hands tightened around his waist. The ground drew nearer. He expected them to land and track down the vast cave, but instead, Sage said, "Hang on."

He understood when he saw Gabriel disappear right before smacking the black ground. They wouldn't be traveling conventionally. There wasn't time. This was the world's deepest cave… and who knew how far Eden really was. Time for angel intervention.

He felt slightly guilty when they passed into the angels' realm. This would exhaust Sage, who was already worn down by battle. If she felt any fatigue from toting him through her side of the barrier, she showed no signs. If anything, she sped up.

Chapter Forty-four

Micah had no idea if they'd been in the black cave for minutes or hours; the labyrinth was daunting even in the angelic realm. It was eerie to pass straight through the ground, taking tunnels when they opened up, almost free falling through the open caverns. Traveling by angel felt like he'd been thrust in a kaleidoscope; the black cave somehow more vibrant, sounds heightened, cold air surrounding him.

Then it was over; Sage landed, stopping their seemingly endless decent. Gabriel was ahead of them, darting to something lying on the ground. Micah's mouth went dry. He caught sight of what he dreaded. A white dress. A lifeless form sprawled out on the ground. Black bodies surrounding her; one on top of her. Gabriel charged like a bull, killing demons with mighty sweeps of his sword.

Micah dashed over, eyes locked on Eden. The demon on her still form, Gabriel tore away with his hands. The demon's claws ripped the dress as it was pulled from its perch, revealing Eden's bare back. A gaping, black hole in her skin. Just like my vision...

He dropped down by her, crying out, "Eden! Can you hear me? Eden, it's me, Micah. We're here! Gabriel's here!"

He fumbled to feel a pulse in her neck. Nothing. Her skin was cold, her lips blue. Semjaza lied! He hid it from Willow! He turned her over and began chest compression, though not an expert at CPR, he wasn't about to give up now.

Gabriel finished clearing the demons away, along with Sage, and practically shoved Micah out of the way. "Let me," he said.

Micah crawled back, giving him space. "Gabriel, can you save her? Is she...?" His voice failed him.

Gabriel's hands touched her forehead and then her heart. He straightened and swept Eden into his arms as he stood. "We need to get her to Andrew. It's her only hope."

Micah jumped to his feet as Gabriel disappeared from view. "Sage," he cried out. "He lied! He didn't heal her and... there's nothing..."

He couldn't process what was happening. Sage gathered him up in her arms. "Close your eyes, Micah. We are going to travel faster this time."

Micah shut his eyes. He needed to; all he could see was Eden's lifeless form. Panic and pure rage swelled within him. Deal's off.

Caitlyn wrung her hands together. They'd been gone so long. Too long. She tried to steady her racing pulse with a few deep breaths. Willow's pacing didn't help. Caitlyn watched her friend's lips moving as she muttered under her breath. Looks like Damon's rubbing off on her.

"Willow, they'll be here any minute," Damon said, placing a hand on Willow's shoulder reassuringly.

"I know," Willow said, glancing up at him with a fleeting smile. "It's just I can't shake the bad feeling. Semjaza blocked me out... I fear he tricked Micah."

Damon frowned, and Trent jumped forward. "Tricked him how?" he asked.

She didn't have time to respond to Trent because a sudden noise captured all their attention. Gabriel had appeared, carrying Eden. Caitlyn's stomach sank to her toes. Eden's not moving. Pandemonium broke out in the realization Willow had been right. Semjaza played them all the fool; he hadn't healed Eden. He'd killed her. Andrew rushed forward, touching Eden's bare back, the black wounds glaring through her torn dress.

"You're all she's got, Andrew. She needs a healer." Gabriel grimaced.

Caitlyn saw helplessness flash through Andrew's expression as he met Gabriel's stare. "I... I'll try again."

Everyone knew he'd done his best before, but it hadn't mattered. Gabriel laid Eden gently on the ground, Andrew crouching down next to her. The moment Micah appeared with Sage, he rushed forward, kneeling by Gabriel, who was across from Andrew.

"It's different." Andrew pulled back, gasping, rubbing his hands together like they hurt. "The poison has spread. I can barely touch her."

"I'm begging, just try." Micah made no attempts to hide the tears streaming down his face.

Seeing Micah so broken stirred something deep within Caitlyn. The black tattoo on his arm was an ominous reminder of what he'd traded for Eden. Andrew nodded, placing his hands back down over the black wound. Time felt like it slowed to a crawl as they all watched. Andrew grimaced, biting his lip. It was obvious the injury caused him physical pain to heal, but he didn't remove his hands.

Blood pounded in Caitlyn's ears, her cheeks felt almost sunburned with how flushed she'd become. Every inch of her buzzed with a strange nervousness. Like adrenaline had drowned all her nerve endings. She felt compelled to move closer to Andrew. Her legs were stiff, like they weren't her own.

Andrew said I helped heal Eden on prom night and Micah at the well. He said he feels something when I touch him... Eden's going to die if I don't do something. Can't hurt to try.

She drew close, her fingers shaking, as she outstretched a hand. She caught Willow's bright blue eyes widening as she followed Caitlyn's movements. Maybe no one can tell me to do it this time. I have to believe I can do it first. That's what faith is. Walking into the darkness before the light comes. The words were so clear in her mind, Caitlyn couldn't help but wonder if Alaina had more to do with her thoughts then she'd supposed before. Either way, I'm listening.

She knelt down next to Andrew, letting her hand find its mark, landing softly on Andrew's shoulder.

"Caitlyn?" He glanced over, inhaling sharply. "Yes, perfect."

Wordlessly, she placed her other hand on top of Andrew's. She gasped, resisting the urge to pull it back. It felt like she was grabbing on to an oven rack; Andrew's skin seared her.

She met Andrew's emerald eyes. "Why don't we try together?" she said through gritted teeth. Andrew nodded, sweat beading across his forehead. A few people gasped, but Caitlyn didn't look around. She shut her eyes, focusing on what needed to be done. She didn't know if her thoughts were vocalized or not, but the words sang in her mind, over and over, growing in volume and strength each time they repeated. Eden heal, Eden heal, Eden heal. . . .

The heat coming off Andrew's hand lessoned by a degree, and Caitlyn was tempted to open her eyes. Instead, she shut them harder. Eden, you're going to be okay. Andrew can heal you. You aren't going to die. Your friends won't let you. I won't let you.

The last thought made her chest constrict. I won't let you die. You're going to heal. You're. . . Caitlyn stopped, the truth in her thoughts was almost tangible. . . You're healing right now.

Now the gasp she heard was new. Eden. Caitlyn opened her eyes to see the hole in Eden's back had closed, the skin pink again. Color brought life back to her face. Eden groaned and then coughed. There were a few cries, someone clapped. Probably Willow.

Micah gingerly pulled Eden into his lap. "You're going to be alright," he soothed, brushing her hair back, kissing her forehead. "I'm here now."

Andrew pulled his hand back, taking Caitlyn's with his. She expected him to let go, but he didn't. Instead, he gave her fingers a squeeze.

"Micah?" Eden croaked, her throat sounding raw as her eyes fluttered open. Immediately, her head darted back and forth, her eyes scanning the area, her hands clinging to Micah.

She's terrified, Caitlyn realized.

"It's okay. Semjaza's gone," Micah reassured. "No more demons. You're safe now."

Caitlyn felt bad they were all watching as Eden broke down in Micah's arms, weeping. Micah, holding her close, promised he'd never let her go again.

In the frenzy of it all, Caitlyn had sort of forgotten about Andrew's hand wrapped around hers, until she felt it tighten. She glanced over just as he leaned in. He brushed his lips against her cheek, tickling her skin as he traveled to her ear.

He whispered, "You're amazing, Caitlyn. I couldn't have done any of this without you."

She blushed, at both his compliment and his close proximity. *Now I really wish there weren't prying eyes around.*

Chapter Forty-five

E den could barely control her emotions. She felt wrapped up in Micah. After the initial shock of being alive and safe ebbed, she tried to rein in her tears. There was someone here she wanted to see, second only to Micah.

Micah seemed to sense her desire, because he let up on his grip and let her sit up all the way. Eden immediately sought him out. He stood near, his eyes meeting hers. She couldn't understand why his body seemed so tense. His back straight, arms folded, jaw set in a hard line. *He looks mad... at me.*

She swallowed and whispered, "Gabriel."

His entire stance changed, his shoulders falling, his stolid expression crumbling before her. Whatever his mood had been before, she saw nothing but kindness in his blue eyes now.

Tears stung her eyes. Hating her overactive waterworks, she decided standing up might be a better idea than trying to talk. *Maybe then, I won't cry.* Only problem was her legs felt like they were made of jelly, with not a bone in them. She struggled, using Micah's shoulder to steady herself. Micah moved to help her, but Gabriel proved faster. He jumped forward, pulling her up with a one-handed swoop.

At the warmth of his touch, she could feel the 'ugly cry' about to explode all over everything. Still, seeing the conflicted way he stared at her, she had to say something.

"I've missed you so much," she managed to get out before her throat closed up completely, and her face wrinkled up as she bawled.

She caught the flash of relief in his eyes before he wrapped her up in his arms, almost crushing her in his embrace. She wasn't going to complain. Wordlessly, he held her, his warmth seeping into every part of her, like a healing balm. The lingering chill was finally gone. The missing chunk in her soul was finally replaced. *I'm whole again.*

She didn't want it to end, the feeling of pure peace washing over her, but he pulled back a bit, retaining her arms in his hands. He cleared his throat, breaking eye contact. She wondered if he was trying to hide the tears she saw welling there.

"I had planned on reprimanding you for ever leaving the temple," he said quietly, almost to himself.

Her insides dropped. *I disappointed him.* Her head dropped in shame.

"But, I'm really the one who should apologize to you," he said, causing her head to pop up.

"Why? You have nothing to apologize for."

"I should never have left you, Eden." Gabriel made eye contact. "You have every right to be angry with me. I failed you as a guardian. You have my word; I will never leave you again."

His solemnness settled over her. He would never forgive himself for how close this had gotten.

"None of this is your fault, Gabriel. I'm the one who messed it all up. I'm the one who left the temple," she countered. "Besides, I could never be angry with you."

He gave her a small smile as Micah said from behind, "Eden's right. It's not your fault, Gabriel. It's mine. I'm the one who hatched this crazy plan, which left us running around in circles."

Eden turned around to meet Micah's gaze, Gabriel letting go of her arms as she moved. "Both of you, stop this," she reprimanded them. "You did the best you could, Micah. We all did. Maybe this was what was supposed to happen."

Micah didn't seem so sure, but he nodded anyway. Eden noted the way he rubbed his hand along one arm. He caught her staring and folded his arms against his chest.

She hated to see Micah and Gabriel blaming themselves for what had happened. It's really all my fault. I should've stayed in the dang temple while they did what they needed to.

"Not sure how much of this had to happen, but Semjaza is gone for now at least." Gabriel scratched at his sideburn and then, peering back at her, said slowly, "Eden?"

The way he shifted his weight made her nervous. "Yes, Gabriel?"

"Before Damon banished Semjaza, he said—" Gabriel began, but Eden cut him off.

"Wait, Damon did what?" She gaped at Damon.

Trent piped up, "Yep, Damon's the man." Trent slugged Damon's shoulder. "Sent old Semjaza to the lowest level of Hell with his lightning bolt. Ka-boom."

Eden could feel her eyes bulging. How much stuff had she missed while away from her friends? They hadn't been apart that long, but if felt as if the world had shifted its center in the last few days.

"We have a lot of catching up to do," Micah cut in, confirming her thoughts, "and I promise we will, but Gabriel needs to ask you something."

"Okay." She'd always viewed Damon with a healthy amount of respect... and fear... but that just quadrupled. She didn't think anyone could defeat Semjaza, let alone one of her friends.

Gabriel cleared his throat, pulling her attention back to him. "Sorry, what is it, Gabriel?" she asked.

"Eden, I need to know if Semjaza spoke the truth," Gabriel said finally. "About what?"

"When he said he," Gabriel hesitated, "took something from you."

She racked her brain. "Uh... I didn't have anything on me. What could he have taken?"

Gabriel's eyebrows lowered as he gazed back at her. "Maybe he lied."

Okay, I'm lost. She looked to Micah for help, but he had the same anxious expression as Gabriel. "What do you mean? What do you think he took?" she asked.

"Your virginity," Trent said bluntly.

"What?" Eden gasped. "What made you think… oh." Her words faded, realizing she still wore the awful lace wedding dress. "He wanted to marry me. But he didn't get to. You guys showed up before he could do anything to me… other than try to kill me."

Gabriel and Micah both sighed in relief. Then Micah asked, "So what did he mean when he said you shared something special together before we came?"

Eden flushed. She didn't want to admit her blunder, but she'd rather them know the truth than assume the worst.

"I tried to awaken him," she admitted.

Now Gabriel's eyebrows shot up, wrinkling his forehead.

"Say what?" Trent asked. "Are you supposed to do that?"

Eden sighed. "Probably not. When the demons tried to take me to Semjaza, I awakened one, sort of on accident. It fell down. I thought I killed it at first, but when it stood up, it fought off the other demons, trying to protect me."

Gabriel and Sage glanced at each other.

"I have never heard of such a thing," Sage admitted.

Gabriel frowned. "Nor I."

"I did it to a couple of more demons," she said, not enjoying retelling her story, "and they died trying to save me. I didn't know what else to do, so I decided I'd try it on Semjaza since it seemed to have worked on the demons."

"What happened when you hugged him?" Micah asked.

"He started laughing. Said it felt magical and he was excited to see what I changed in him." Eden wrapped herself up in her arms. "I just hope I didn't make him stronger somehow."

"I don't think that is possible. Your gift is pure love." Gabriel gave her a forced grin. "Maybe your awakening will do him some good."

She wasn't so sure; she felt Gabriel was just trying to make her feel better.

Micah grabbed her hand. "I don't want to think about Watchers right now. I'm just glad you're okay."

"And not pregnant with Semjaza's giant baby," Trent added.

"Trent," Micah cut in as Eden's face flamed. Everyone stared at Trent, and then at Eden, as if the reality of the situation had just hit them. Willow's gaze was the worst because she didn't hide the fact she was staring at Eden's stomach, as if sizing up the possibility still.

"What? It's true," Trent said. "Eden almost started a whole new species. Giants roaming the earth again. Can you imagine?"

"I'd rather not," Micah mumbled, shooting her a reassuring grin. "You're alive, that's all that matters."

"How am I anyway?" she asked, glancing around at all her friends. Her gaze settled on Andrew. "Was it you?"

Andrew grinned and held up the hand he held. "Nope, this one goes all to Caitlyn. I just let her think she was helping me, but I couldn't even get close to your injuries until she took over."

Caitlyn turned at Andrew, ready to argue, but Eden asked, "Are you okay now?"

The protest Caitlyn had been forming died on her lips as she gaped at Eden. "Er... what? I'm fine. I should be asking you that."

"I heard your cries for help. That's why I left the temple," Eden admitted. "Semjaza was hurting you somehow. I felt it. It was real."

Caitlyn's gaze shot downward as she frowned. *She has nothing to feel bad about. She just healed me for crying out loud,* Eden wanted to say.

"You're right," she said, staring at her feet. "He did use me to get to you. I suppose you heard my soul, or spirit, or whatever you want to call it. Semjaza forced a demon to possess me." She bit her lip. "Well, I should say, I allowed it in really."

"No," Andrew said firmly, forcing Caitlyn's chin up with his fingers. "Semjaza shoved the demon Doubt into you. You were helpless to stop it, Caitlyn."

Eden gasped. "Oh my gosh, that sounds horrible! How did you get rid of it?"

They explained everything that had happened, and Eden could only stare. *Yes, the world has definitely changed in the last few days. Caitlyn possessed by a demon, Damon able to send demons and Watchers to Hell, I barely escaped being Semjaza's bride... and being pregnant with a baby giant.*

Her head spun. Finally, she said, "Well, I guess that makes sense. In the fields, the demons wouldn't even go near Olivia. And that was before I even awakened her."

"We should keep the little ginger around," Trent said. "She wards off demons like bad-A bug spray."

"For once, I think I agree with Trent," Damon said, breaking his usual silence.

Trent grinned. "I knew there was hope for you, Damon."

Micah smiled at them, and then turned to Eden. "How about we get out of here? Catch up somewhere more comfortable. Like with a couch." *He does look pretty exhausted. Like he hasn't slept or ate in days...*

"And food," Trent added. "I've got a hunger like nobody's business."

Andrew perked up. "I know where to go for some real food. Trent, you've got to try svíčková. You're going to love it."

"Sold. I'm there," Trent said. "Let's vamoose."

Micah nodded. "Sounds good to me. Moravia is the perfect pit stop. I think I need to meet someone Willow and Caitlyn found anyway. Marek Tomas, right?"

Willow smiled and nodded. "Yes, he is anxious to meet you, Micah."

"Fine, fine, fine. Talk to Marek, but," Trent wagged a finger at him, "over food, not before."

"Hey, no argument here," Micah said, holding up his hands in mock surrender.

"Oh Brutus, where art thou, Brutus?" Trent sang out suddenly, peering around.

Chapter Forty-six

Less than an hour later, they materialized in a small side street in down town Moravia.

Willow pointed across the street. "There, that's where we stayed before. Come on."

They crossed the road; there weren't too many cars, angels disappearing from view as soon as they left the shadows of the alleyway behind.

Once inside the cozy cavern-type restaurant, Micah spied a large, empty table towards the back of the room. He gestured with his chin and Trent made a beeline for it, the rest of them following. Micah caught the stares and whispers. Seeing how, within seconds, Andrew was surrounded by people, he knew why. The healer was back. The room buzzed with a new excitement. Micah didn't mind. He needed to get word to Marek they were here, what better way than small-town gossip? Willow had informed him earlier she had sort of neglected getting Marek's phone number or address.

Trent was the first to plop down at the table. He threw his hands behind his head, sighing. "Now this is more like it."

Micah's mouth went dry. His tattoo was all too visible. He knew Eden would see it, and wonder what it was, which would lead to telling her what had happened. Something he wasn't exactly sure he knew how to do, or wanted to for that matter.

"Oh my gosh, Micah." She grabbed his arm as he pulled a chair out for her.

Dang it, she saw it. His heart sank, but when he glanced over, he saw she wasn't looking at Trent at all.

"Look at what I'm wearing!" she gasped. She twisted around, trying to hold her dress together in the back. "Everyone can see my backside in this!"

Micah stifled a grin. In all the craziness, he stopped noticing the small things like what people wore. Now he took in Eden's appearance. Her long hair tangled, her face dirt smudged, and her back exposed from the large tear in the awful dress Semjaza put her in.

Micah glanced down at his T-shirt, not exactly clean, but at least in one piece. No one wore a jacket or hoodie he could offer her. He gripped the hem, ready to slip it off for her, when Willow jumped into action.

"That won't be necessary, Micah," she said quickly. "Can't have you naked in here either." To Eden, she said, "I'm so sorry. I should've noticed. I've been a bit distracted by everything today. A lot for me to take in. Guess I stopped noticing the world around me a bit."

Willow sidled up next to Eden, wrapping her arm around her shoulders, offering a bit of cover. "Come on. There are some shops down the street. We can get you fixed up."

Caitlyn joined them as Micah moved to follow.

Willow waved him off. "We got this. You boys stay here."

He wanted to argue, determined not to let Eden out of his sight, but Caitlyn smiled at him. "Don't worry, Micah. I won't let anything happen to her."

He sighed in resignation. He knew Gabriel would be with her, and if he trusted anyone with Eden's safety now, it was Caitlyn.

Caitlyn turned to Andrew. "Mind ordering that svíčková for us while we're gone?"

"Sure," he agreed.

"Oh, and Andrew," she grinned, "this time, tell Brita to keep her hands off you."

Trent whooped, Andrew flushed, and Micah chuckled.

"Okay, Andrew. Spill it," Trent said, slapping Andrew's shoulder. "I could use some juicy details."

"Feels like old times," Willow commented.

"What do you mean?" Eden asked from behind the changing stall door. She happily stripped off the lacy nightmare she'd been forced into. That's going into the trash. She pushed it away from her with her toe, wanting it nowhere near her. For all I know, he put some kind of spell on it.

"Us, here with you, after you almost died. At least you're not covered in blood," Willow said in her usual singsong voice.

Funny how she can make anything sound like a pleasant conversation, Eden mused as she finished pulling the jeans up.

Caitlyn laughed. "Yeah, we've got to stop meeting like this."

Eden giggled, slipping a shirt over her head. "You're right, Caitlyn. No more near-death experiences for me. I think I've filled my quota."

She unlatched the door, happy the clothes had fit. She wasn't really in the mood for shopping. She longed for a hot meal and chair to sink into.

"Looks good," Willow said, grinning, and then she peered around Eden to see herself in the long dressing room mirror. "Oh my… how about we hit the bathroom and wash up? I just noticed I've got mud smeared all over my face."

Eden glanced over and laughed. Willow wasn't lying. Dried-up mud stretched from her forehead down to her jawline on one half of her face. Caitlyn started giggling too, and then noticed her own reflection in the long mirror.

"Wow," she gasped. "Check out my hair! Looks like the crows from Crow Cave took up residence in it!"

That comment pushed them all into hysterics, and for a few minutes, they were pointing out how bad they all looked, and how could the boys not have noticed, how could they not have noticed for that matter? All Eden knew was ten minutes later, they were walking back to the inn, and she had never felt better. After all the terrible things that had happened to them in the last few days, laughter seemed to have been the best medicine.

There was a light in Caitlyn's eyes again, Willow seemed more alert and happy, and Eden's heart felt light again, as the terror of being in Semjaza's presence finally left her.

Things are going to be okay, she told herself. The new city is found, I'm alive, and Semjaza is gone...

They entered the now-packed inn, barely making it through the crowd to get back to Micah and the guys. Andrew had been bombarded, no longer at the table, but on a bar stool at the bar. Maybe it made it easier for people to line up over there.

"He's so good. He will heal people until he can't physically stay upright," Caitlyn commented. "You should've seen him with you, Eden. He wouldn't give up, even though..." Caitlyn seemed to have changed her mind and stopped.

Eden turned. "What do you mean, even though... what?"

Willow answered, "It hurt Andrew to touch you."

"Oh." Eden's heart squeezed painfully with a mixture of guilt and gratitude. "I didn't know." She turned to Caitlyn, throwing her arms around her.

Caitlyn seemed surprised, hugging her back somewhat awkwardly. "Why are you hugging me?"

"Because I never thanked you, for what you did. Thank you for saving me," Eden said. "I'm so glad you're okay now."

"I'm glad you're okay now too," Caitlyn replied, still seeming surprised by Eden's affection.

Eden released her, and determined to not second-guess her actions, she marched over to Andrew, wiggling her way through the crowd. Surprisingly, they let her through.

He caught sight of her, and his eyes widened. She stepped up, close to him.

"I never said thank you, Andrew," she whispered. "I know you think it was all Caitlyn, but it wasn't. If you had given up, I..." Her throat closed up, and Andrew's expression softened.

Her heart pounded in her chest. She swallowed. "I wouldn't have lasted long enough for Caitlyn to do anything to help you." She lunged forward, draping her arms around him, before she told herself not to. She needed to hug him. She needed him to know how much she appreciated and still loved him. Maybe not in the romantic way she once had, but in a deep friendship.

His arms wrapped around her, warm and familiar.

"You're welcome, Eden," he answered into her ear. "You know, I won't ever give up on you."

He was the one to pull away first, and she realized she'd probably made her point. Their eyes met, and in that split second, she knew there would always be a small part of her heart that belonged to him. He was her first date, first kiss, and first boyfriend. He'd noticed her when no one else had—not even Micah. She wondered if that was how he felt about her too, even though they had both moved on now.

Eden tucked her hair behind her ear, feeling her face flush. "Sorry, I'll let you get back to what you were doing."

Andrew seemed to hesitate, as if debating to say something, and then he nodded. "You should go eat… with Micah. Knowing him, he hasn't slept or ate since the moment you were taken." He grinned. "He's a good guy. I'm glad you're with him, Eden."

She smiled back. "Thanks. And I'm glad you're with Caitlyn."

"How did you…?"

"Know? You two are pretty obvious. And you make a killer team. I think you're perfect together."

Andrew relaxed, seeming relieved. "Thanks, I do too."

Perhaps it was talking about their own significant others, but Andrew straightened up and motioned for the next person to come up to him. Eden knew it was high time to get back to Micah. It wasn't just his anxious glances in her direction; her own heart ached to be near him.

Chapter Forty-seven

With Trent finally satisfied by a copious amount of food, Micah had spent almost two hours discussing the Northern City with Marek, who had finally been reached by a long chain of who-knew-who until a cell phone number had been secured. Marek had shown up twenty minutes after Micah's phone call.

It still shocked Micah that a grown man, with considerable wealth and prestige in this predominant wine country, would want to meet him. An eighteen-year-old senior in high school. Marek didn't seem to see Micah that way; he immediately accepted the fact that Micah was a Seer.

After the debacle Semjaza's deal had turned out to be, Micah had to admit, it was nice to be around someone with so much faith in him. Trent had joined the conversation, talking about how cool the actual records Enoch had kept were, how ingenious the diagrams had been, and boasting about Damon's abilities in clearing away land. Marek seemed impressed by it all, and as they discussed him coming to Illinois to see the city under construction, Micah could almost convince himself that everything had worked out the way it was supposed to.

Eden, who had remained planted next to Micah the entire time listening, let her head fall against his shoulder, her body leaning closer. She's exhausted; we all are. We need sleep before traveling, Eden most of all.

"Micah?" she asked, her tone cutting through his thoughts. "What's that?"

Feeling her trace the elongated triangle on his arm with her finger, his stomach sickened. He tried to pull back, but her head popped up, her grip tightening. All night, he'd tried to keep his arm angled away from her, hoping he'd hide the fact long enough to come up with some kind of easy explanation. Talking to Marek, he must have let his guard down.

"When did you get this?" she asked, her brows knitting.

He knew she probably wouldn't care one way or another if he got a tattoo; her reaction let him know that she already sensed this wasn't a good thing.

"Don't worry," Trent answered, while Micah stalled. "They're all the rave. See, I got one too."

She glanced over at Trent, who proudly displayed his. She frowned. "You got matching tattoos?"

Micah knew he should say something, but he couldn't form the words. Any way he looked at it, the truth sounded awful. *I made a deal with Semjaza, which he double-crossed me on . . .* And even though it should be null and void, the mark unsettled him.

Willow, who sat across the table next to Damon, said evenly, "Micah and Trent were marked in order to free you, Eden."

Eden gasped. "What? Micah, what do you mean marked?" Her eyes widened as she glanced down at his tattoo. "Who did this, Semjaza?"

Perhaps Marek sensed an unpleasant conversation on its way, or maybe he knew Micah had other things to attend to, either way, he stood up.

"Micah, I will not take up more of your time tonight. Please know, the pleasure was all mine. I look forward to meeting the architect Armando in Rome, and seeing you all in America when I travel there next month."

Micah jumped to his feet, tugging his arm free from Eden's grasp. He shook Marek's hand. "Trust me, the honor was all mine, Marek. You have amazing faith; we can use someone like you. Your land is about to attract a lot of attention, but with Andrew's work here, I sense the Northern City will be well received."

Marek nodded, and then to the rest of them, he inclined his head. "Good evening to you all. Godspeed on your journey tomorrow."

They all murmured their farewells.

"I hope he's right," Trent said, folding his arms.

Micah knew Eden was waiting for him to answer her question, but he had to ask, "Who's right about what?"

"Marek said Godspeed on our journey. You know, angels can speed things along. No need for sitting on an airplane all day tomorrow."

Micah shook his head. "Sorry, friend. Not this time."

"Fine, well, at least I'll get some peanuts out of it. Can you believe that the dude in flannel doesn't even offer me a beverage?"

Micah knew Trent's teasing was trying to lighten the mood. He appreciated his cousin's efforts, but somehow, he knew jokes were not going to be enough tonight.

Eden readily agreed to the idea of taking a stroll with Micah for a few minutes, alone. Everyone else filed up to the rooms; boys in one, girls in the other. Even with many of them pairing off in couples now, Micah made it clear that it'd be best to keep separate sleeping arrangements. No one protested.

Eden grinned at Trent's parting words to them. "Don't worry, fearless leader, I will make sure there is no funny business." Then, as he retreated, he added, "Because if Trent's not getting any, ain't nobody getting any."

Micah took her hand in his as they left the inn behind. Hearing Trent complaining about his lack of companionship got Eden thinking about Jessie.

Micah glanced over. "Good to see you smile."

Her grin deepened. "I was just thinking about Trent and Jessie."

"Oh?"

"Yeah, is it weird that I can't wait for school to start? Just so I can listen to Jessie complain about how people in her drama class don't take it serious enough?"

Micah nodded. "Yeah, that is weird." She giggled and slapped his arm. He added, "No, I get it actually. It'll be nice to pretend we're just teenagers again."

She glanced over, noting how he held her hand with the arm that did not have the tattoo. They both knew he still needed to answer her questions, starting with what the marking meant, but this was the first time she'd been alone with him since parting in Rome. For a few minutes, she just wanted to drink him in.

Still, what he said got her thinking. "Is it just pretend now?" she asked quietly, already knowing the answer.

"No, actually, it's not," he said, instead turning to face her. "We're going home and you're right, we get to go back to school." He grunted. "Never thought I'd say those words, get to." He chuckled. "I hope you know I'm taking you to every school dance I can."

"I guess I better keep my dance card clear then." She grinned up at him. Even if it was only for a moment, Eden wanted to forget about the rest of the world. She wanted a minute with Micah, only Micah.

Perhaps he had the same idea, because he steered them back, into an alleyway, less traveled by the few shoppers still dotting the streets. Her face flushed as he wrapped an arm around her waist, pushing her against one of the buildings' brick walls.

The playfulness in his eyes died though, as he hesitated. "Eden, I need to tell you something."

"Wait," she said, shaking her head. "Not yet." She leaned in, pressing her lips against his.

His hands shot around her, and he kissed her back. Guess he doesn't mind waiting. He closed what little space remained between them, his lips working against hers, the warmth from his body thrilling her and somehow soothing her at the same time. She hadn't realized how chilled her soul had become until that moment; Micah lit a fire from within, chasing away the shadows. She needed him. Feeling his hands travel down her back, and then drop down below her thighs, she was surprised to feel him lift her up. Instinctively, she wrapped her legs around his waist.

Held up by the wall and Micah, she knew she'd have to be the one to stop them from going too far. By the way Micah kissed her throat, traveling to her collarbone, she knew he wasn't entirely himself at the moment. She understood; she wanted him more than she'd ever wanted anything in her life, but she knew it wasn't right for them to go too far physically. Micah told us the rules.

Even though it pained her, she urged, "Micah, wait."

He jerked back, immediately lowering her to the ground. He took a step back, breathing hard. "Eden, I'm so sorry. I . . ."

"Don't feel bad." She felt herself flush. "I liked it. But . . ." She left the rest unsaid.

He ran his hands through his hair. "I know, I know. Come on. Let's go for that walk."

They didn't talk for a while, just gazed at the shop windows lining the street. Black street lampposts came to life as the shadows lengthened. The last rays of sunset disappeared from the sky. The oranges and reds faded into a muted darkness. There was a small café open, with white tables and twinkle lights in its courtyard. Eden squeezed Micah's hand, wrapped her other hand around his arm. He leaned over and kissed her forehead.

The night felt magical, like the calm after a horrific storm.

Then Micah said, "Eden, I made a deal with Semjaza."

The magic shattered. "You did what?"

"It was the only way to get you back."

The mounting fury she felt ebbed. He did it to save her. But still!

"Micah, you can't trust anything he says or does. He's even more messed up than you know," she said, her knees feeling wobbly. They passed a small park. There were no toys, slides, or swings. Just large trees and a few random benches.

Micah pointed to one. "Want to go sit?"

She nodded, glad to. She felt a bit lightheaded. No deal with Semjaza could be a good one. What did he trade for me?

As soon as they sat down, Micah turned to her and took her hands into his. "I know you're upset. And trust me, I didn't even want to tell you, but I can't keep it from you. I don't know if I can do all this without you."

His words tugged at her heart, the desperation in his expression once again reminding her of the little boy she once knew.

"I'm sorry; I shouldn't have gotten upset with you. I know what you've been through, what I've put you through, was awful. I'm so sorry. I'll always be here for you; that will never change." She gave his lips a soft kiss. "Please tell me everything that happened."

Ten minutes later, she sat back. He'd filled her in, from when the Captain told him what to offer Semjaza in exchange for her, to when Semjaza lied about healing her.

"So you're saying the deal's void now? He won't try to ignite that?" she asked, touching the mark.

"I told him, and he agreed. So I figure I should be fine. Not that going to Azazel put me in danger really anyway," he said.

His strained tone betrayed him—going to Azazel was anything but safe. Still, if what he said is true, Semjaza backed out on his end of the bargain.

"So what happens to that, then? It just stays there?" she asked, not liking that it reminded her of a fuse, just waiting for a spark. Semjaza's spark.

"I guess so." He shrugged. "Let's not worry about it. The important thing is you're alive. We're going home. The Northern City is on its way now."

Eden nodded, wishing the nagging apprehension would go away with simply remembering all the good news.

"So there are two more cities to form, and then what? You're done with your missions?"

Micah sighed. "From what I can tell, after the fourth city is completed, the fire will be here."

She shivered, and he wrapped his arm around her shoulders.

"And only those inside the city walls will be safe?" she asked. "How can that be? There will be so many that won't even know they're supposed to go in there. And they can't possibly fit everyone in the world, can they?"

"We have to start spreading the word. Much like Gabriel had to with the flood."

"Everyone hated Gabriel when he was Noah, and no one listened to him but his own family," she insisted.

"I know, and we may not always be popular," he said, frowning, "but we still have to try."

"I never was popular anyway," she said with a crooked grin, trying to lighten the mood. What lay ahead seemed a bit daunting. "I won't be missing anything."

"Mm... I doubt that." He kissed her cheek. "You might end up being more popular than you like. Your gift's crucial, Eden. You'll awaken so many. There are so many gifted out there. Thanks to you, we won't be alone. A lot more will listen this time. Trent's still translating records from Enoch's temple. We aren't a hundred percent sure how the cities work. Whether someone merely had to have been in one or has to be in it when the fire comes, I'm not sure yet."

"What do you mean? How can just walking through it once keep people from being burned?"

"Remember the children of Israel with the lamb's blood?"

She stared at him. "Um... like Moses and all that?"

"Exactly. When Moses tried to free the children of Israel from Pharaoh, the last plague sent was called the destroyer. It killed all the firstborn in Egypt, saving only those who spread lamb's blood around their door. The destroyer passed by those homes, killing no one. Some of the records we've been studying lately seem to show some kind of mark given to those who pass through the city. I'm wondering if the mark will protect them, like the blood on the doors."

Eden tipped her head to the side, considering his words. "The Captain's mark. A mark that saves life." She couldn't help the quick glance to the black one on Micah's arm. "Maybe if you go through one of the cities, Semjaza's will go away."

Micah grinned at her. "Good idea. Worth a try." He leaned in, kissing her softly. His warm lips contrasted to the cold night air surrounding them, making her want to get lost in his arms again. Micah didn't pull back right away, but she did, because Gabriel suddenly stood behind him.

She gasped in surprise, and Micah glanced around quickly. "What's wrong? Did you see something?"

"Um, yeah," she said. "You don't see him?"

"Who?" Micah half stood, glancing around.

"Gabriel's right behind you," she said, not wanting him to worry it was something dangerous.

Micah and Gabriel both jumped a bit at the same time, startled by her statement.

Micah blurted, "Gabriel?"

As Gabriel moaned, "Oh no, not again."

Eden grinned and walked over to him. "What's wrong with me seeing you, Gabriel? Other than it making kissing very awkward," she admitted, before realizing she shouldn't have voiced her thoughts so openly. Micah blanched and Gabriel shifted his weight, glancing away.

"Was he here the whole time?" Micah asked quietly, as if Gabriel couldn't hear him.

"Uh, probably, but I didn't see him until right now," she explained, trying to reassure him. There was no way she could have made out with Gabriel standing next to them.

Gabriel sighed. "Oh, might as well cross over, make this less awkward."

Then Micah grinned. "There you are, Gabriel. Wow, Eden, how were you seeing him before?"

Gabriel answered. "The barrier between our worlds is growing thin for her. Sometimes, she sees across into my realm."

Micah's eyes widened, and he glanced over at her. "Really?"

She nodded. "I can't always do it, just sometimes." For some reason, Micah's stare was making her self-conscience.

"That's incredible," Micah said softly, easing her worry.

"Thanks. I'm not sure how I do it really."

Gabriel put his hands on his hips, one hand falling automatically to his sword's hilt. "Now that I'm here, I think it's high time you both get back into your own beds. Eden needs sleep, Micah."

Micah blanched. "Yeah, yeah, of course. Come on, let's get back."

It felt like their parents had just caught them making out behind the bleachers. She grinned to see how fast Micah moved. Guess even the Seer needs to be reminded every once in a while to be a good boy and go home. Wonder if he's just worried about me getting enough sleep, or is it Gabriel shadowing his moves now?

Eden glanced over at her guardian, who had switched back into his own realm, so as to not be seen by others. Catching Gabriel's eye, she thought, you didn't have to scare Micah half to death, you know. I think he'd rather you'd told him there were demons in the park tonight.

Gabriel's lips twitched into half a smile.

Chapter Forty-eight

Micah left Eden's house, glad to see her reunited with her family. Once everything, minus the fact he'd basically sold his soul for their daughter, had been explained to her family, he'd left her with a soft kiss, promising to see her tomorrow at school.

School. He shifted his truck into gear, backing out of the McCarthy's driveway. *How can I be expected to sit through class now? Who cares about graduating? The world is about to end...*

He wasn't too surprised to see Sage appear in the passenger seat next to him. *It wasn't just Eden's veil becoming thinner between the spiritual realms; Sage frequented his side more often as well. Although, Micah had to admit, it's on her terms. Eden seems to peek through at random times, sometimes when Gabriel would rather her not. Or me, for that matter.*

Micah's insides squirmed. *Like when we were kissing.* He was still horrified by that turn of events. He knew the angels were always watching over them, technically. But to have them actually there, staring at you, is a different story all together.

He glanced over at her. "Are you sure this is what the Captain wants? For me to waste time in class?"

"Yes, but He didn't say it in those exact terms. More like, you need to be patient. In a very short span, you have already located and begun two of the four cities. It will take time to see those through to completion. In the meantime, the best thing for you to do is be you again." She tilted her head to the side. "You have been through a lot, Micah, but so have your friends.

They need to be strengthened and renewed for what is to come. They need to be prepared."

Micah nodded. "I can see that." His thoughts shifted from Eden to Caitlyn. "I'm still amazed that Caitlyn could have saved Eden this whole time."

He left unsaid the part of why didn't they just do that in the first place? He sort of knew the why, but Sage confirmed it.

"Caitlyn could not save Eden until she came into her own. She went through her own refiner's fire. Her potential is limitless. Now you can see why Lucifer desires her."

Micah glanced over. "Yeah, because he fears her. She stopped Semjaza's enchantment; she could probably stop anything or anyone."

Sage nodded. "You have an incredible team, Micah, but do not forget, they are young, not perfect, and will all doubt themselves from time to time. I know you have been feeling some doubt. You shouldn't try to hide it from the Captain."

"But look what happened to Caitlyn. She had doubts too."

"That demon was specifically engineered, if you will, by Semjaza. Tailor-made to fit Caitlyn's specific shortcomings. Fear and doubt are part of life. Don't feel bad when they come over you, just don't give into them. Faith, hope, and charity can ward them off."

Micah cocked an eyebrow at her. "You talk like faith and hope are actual things, like that demon Doubt." He paused. "I guess, in a way, they sort of are. Caitlyn's gift is faith, Eden's charity."

Sage smiled. "If you rely on faith, hope, and charity, you won't fail, Micah."

"Even against this?" He held his arm out to her. "Can Caitlyn and Eden protect me from this fate?"

Sage's eyebrows knit. "I know you question why the mark even came to be. The Captain senses your confusion. And know this... He is not angry with you for your questions."

Micah sighed; she'd voiced the very thing building up within him. He didn't want to complain or whine to the Captain, but it was becoming more apparent to him that the mark might have been avoided, if he'd known what Caitlyn was capable of. Micah pulled into his driveway, but he left the truck idling. He wanted to hear what she had to say.

"Even I went to the Captain about it. I do not like it any more than you do. But believe it or not, it is part of the great plan, Micah. You did exactly as He instructed you. The outcome played out as it should. Each of your friends' gifts are sharpening, becoming ready for the battle yet to come. Even Eden has evolved in ways she wouldn't have if she hadn't been taken."

He nodded his head slowly. "So you're saying horrible things had to happen to us, to make us stronger?"

Sage chuckled softly. "I know it seems strange, but it is true. The horrible things are what push you to your limits, stretch you. Refines and polishes you."

"So in other words, I will face Azazel one day," Micah replied.

Sage glanced over at him, saying nothing at first. Then she asked, "You don't believe the deal is void?"

Micah scratched his sideburn and then rubbed his jawline. "No."

"Why not? Semjaza broke his oath."

"His wording was carefully crafted." He sighed heavily. "It keeps playing through my head. It's all I think about."

She waited, and he repeated, "Let me remind you, if you fail on being there the day Azazel rises from the ground, your marks will ignite. I give you fair warning."

"So?" Sage urged.

"So, he said marks. Not my mark."

"Oh." She leaned back into the seat, staring out the windshield. "He may not ignite yours if you do not show, but he will Trent's."

"Yes, and you better believe I'll be there," Micah said firmly.

They were quiet for a minute, the heater vent's hum the only sound, and then Micah's phone chimed.

He fished it out of his pocket and looked down. Sage glanced over, waiting.

It was a text from Eden. *See you at school tomorrow, Micah.* ☺

He stared at the words, and then, like she'd sensed his mood at the moment, she added.

Don't worry; everything is going to be okay!

It took some effort to type back. *You're right, Eden, it will.* ☺ *Get some sleep.* He wanted to add, *because you're going need it,* but instead typed. *See you in the morning. I love you.*

I love you too, Micah. ☺

That night, Micah traveled there again. This time, his feet plodded through the dirt and sand, not stopping, not hesitating. The desert vegetation was sparse, barely dotting the barren land around him. The only thing that stood out was the huge rock formation straight ahead. Each step, voices carried in the wind, almost like long-forgotten songs from a distant time. He knew it was only his imagination. No one was actually singing, but the way the wind howled, it almost fooled him.

His weren't the only steps; Gabriel was to his right, Damon on his left... and Trent coming up from behind.

"Sorry, I know you said to wait in the car, but I'm with you until the end on this one," Trent said, slapping his shoulder, sandwiching himself between Gabriel and him.

Gabriel grunted and made room.

Trent, you don't know how true your words are.

The dream didn't stop this time. It showed him everything, and by the morning, Micah found he barely had the strength to pull jeans on. The only thought that made it physically possible for him to climb into his truck was knowing Eden waited for him at school.

Anxious to see me. He straightened in his seat, rubbed his hands up and down his face, and cranked the radio up. *Time to start pretending I'm just a* normal teenager again.

Catching sight of Eden bouncing on her toes, scanning the crowd as he walked through the front door, eased his anxiety. She's looking for me. He grinned. Funny how the smell of new shoes, over-perfumed teens, and locker halls comforted him. I'm home.

Eden spotted him and rushed over. The light in her eyes pushed the remains of last night's vision into the recesses of his mind. As her hand slid into his, he knew there was at least one angle to being a teenage guy he didn't have to fake.

He glanced over at her and winked. "Ready for this?"

She giggled. "Funny, if you'd asked me last year, I would have probably said no. But after what we've faced, I'm pretty sure we can handle the first day of school."

Micah nodded. "You're right."

"Micah, do you realize the last time we were in these halls together was when I—"

"Awakened me?" he cut in. "Yeah, it just hit me too."

She grinned up at him. "Sort of makes me wonder what's going to happen this year."

Her optimism washed over him, and he decided not to focus on the doom and gloom. He wrapped his arms around her, right in the middle of the hallway, catching a few glances of the teens rushing by. She flushed, her eyes seeming to question what he might do next.

He dropped his lips to hers. He didn't push the kiss, he knew PDA wasn't tolerated here, and the last thing he needed was bad blood between him and the school administration. He pulled back, and her eyes fluttered open.

"Which reminds me, I'm not sure how I'll feel if you're going around hugging every guy you see here," he teased.

She twitched her lips to the side. "Hey, that's not my fault. Trust me; there have been some I'd rather not have hugged."

He glanced over at her, but he said nothing. Her words reminded him of one person he had yet to follow up with. His friend, Chase.

Eden tugged on his hand. "Come on, we don't want to be late to class. What do you have first?"

He sighed heavily. "Economics."

"Oh, come on, don't say it like that."

"Like what?"

"Like it's boring."

He eyed her. "You really do enjoy studying, don't you?"

She ducked her chin, glancing away. He squeezed her hand. "You're right. Economics can be fun and who knows, I might need it for what's coming."

She frowned, and he inwardly berated himself. *Why did I remind her of all that? She needs normal. At least for a little while. She needs to forget about Semjaza, the Watchers, and the fire.*

"Hey, sorry," he said, pulling her to the side of the locker hall they'd been walking down. "How about for today, I'm no one but your boyfriend. How's that sound?"

Her frown melted into a grin. "I like the sound of that."

"Deal, now let's get to class. Can't have you late for..."

"Calculus."

"Oh man, I'll stick with my Economics."

She laughed as they made their way down the junior locker hall, both of them pausing long enough to glance at the very spot she'd thrown her arms around him mere months ago.

Where she changed Micah—changed the world.

Acknowledgements

My heart is so full of gratitude for all of you patient readers, who didn't mind waiting this long for book two. I hope you enjoyed it! Being fairly new to the writing world, it's been a balancing act of writing, editing, marketing, and oh yes, still finding time for my wonderful family and friends.

With that said, my first thank you goes to my ever-supportive husband, Josh. Thank you for continuing to believe in my crazy stories, and for listening to me plot out loud when you'd rather be watching sports. A huge thank to my three children. Writing books takes time... and lots of it. Thank you for understanding when Mommy can't peel herself away from the computer. I love you all!

To my fabulous friend, and writing partner, Gail Wagner. Thank you for again being the first pair of eyes to read through my messy first drafts. I treasure your good eye for editing! You help me smooth out the rough patches. A thank you also to DelSheree Gladden, for all the advice on marketing, putting together all my awesome book teasers, and all the other thousand things you do to help me. I am so grateful I have you both, Gail and Sheree!

To my Clean Teen Publishing family, and I say family because I truly feel at home here with my books! Rebecca Gober, Courtney Nuckels, Marya Heiman, Cynthia Shepp, and Melanie Newton, you all rock! I couldn't be happier. I appreciate your honesty, hard work, vision, and passion for each and every book you produce. You are all amazing. Thank you!

A huge thank you to Amy Brimhall, with Dramatic Imaging. For those who don't know, The Awakener's cover had a face-lift. The original cover was replaced with a beautiful picture of Ashley Brimhall, taken by Amy. I never had the chance to say thank you in that book, so I'm doing so now! Thank you again, Marya Heiman, for the gorgeous cover designs in both books. You have all given this series new life with the beautiful covers!

There are so many of you who have encouraged me along. I wish I could thank each and every one of you who have taken the time to post, share, or tweet my book news! You don't know how much that means to us, authors, to have an online support team. Thank you all! To my Wattpad readers, I'm ever grateful to you for giving me my start. For believing in The Awakener when publishers weren't. I hope you enjoy having The Awakener back up for free now!

To my parents and siblings, thank you for thinking I've hit it big! It's one of my favorite things to hear how another niece or nephew just gobbled up one of my books. Makes me feel so special. Family is the best, and I love you all!

Lastly, a huge thank you to my God, my Captain. I would be remised if I didn't say how at times, I felt like ideas just poured into my mind. Especially with this series. Even though I have done quite a bit of research for these books, this series is a work of fiction. I feel the need to clarify because I've had readers ask me how much I've made up and how much came from the actual Book of Enoch. I did base the idea of The Watchers from the Book of Enoch. I got many of the names from that record. The Holies I speak of are listed in there, with their responsibilities and roles they played long ago.

A fun fact, when writing The Awakener, I had already decided Eden's guardian would be Gabriel. Having always wondered what the Cherubim with the Flaming Sword was in the account in Genesis, I decided Gabriel would be over the Cherubim, his weapon of choice, the flaming sword. So imagine my surprise when I later read in the Book of Enoch that Gabriel was one of the Holies and he was actually over the Cherubim, according to that record! Those are the moments when I just LOVE what I do!

About the Author

Born in Dekalb,  Illinois, Amanda Strong has called Utah, Arizona, Hawaii, Virginia, and now New Mexico home. She has loved to spin tales since childhood. It was not uncommon to find her hiding in some random corner, scribbling away in her spiral-bound notebook, with her bright pink glasses. You could say some things have not changed.

Amanda signed with Clean Teen Publishing in the fall of 2013. She is the author of two paranormal, YA series: The Watchers of Men and Monsters Among Us.

The first novel in The Watchers of Men series, The Awakener, debuted in October of 2013. It has been an Amazon number one best seller in three Young Adult categories. Book two, The Holy and The Fallen, released May 12th of 2015. She is currently working on book three, The Watcher's Mark, releasing spring of 2016.

Hidden Monster released November 4th of 2014, and it finished as a Finalist in the 2014 USA Best Book Award: Young Adult Category. It is book one of a brand-new young adult, sci-fi thriller series called Monsters Among Us.

When Amanda isn't writing, you can find her chasing her three rambunctious children around the house and spending time with her wonderful and supportive husband. On some occasions, you can still find

Amanda with her not-so-pink glasses, hiding in a corner reading her favorite young adult fantasy novels or working out only to blow her diet by eating ice cream. See more at:

www.authoramandastrong.com

http://www.cleanteenpublishing.com/authors/amanda-strong/

CPSIA information can be obtained at www.ICGtesting.com
Printed in the USA
LVOW07s0213050615

441152LV00002B/12/P

9 781634 220934